The Assassin's Touch

Also by Laura Joh Rowland

The Perfumed Sleeve
The Dragon King's Palace
The Pillow Book of Lady Wisteria
Black Lotus
The Samurai's Wife
The Concubine's Tattoo
The Way of the Traitor
Bundori
Shinjū

The Assassin's Touch

Laura Joh Rowland

ST. MARTIN'S MINOTAUR ☙ NEW YORK

www.minotaurbooks.com

Library of Congress Cataloging-in-Publication Data

Rowland, Laura Joh.
     The assassin's touch / Laura Joh Rowland.—1st ed.
          p.   cm
     ISBN 0-312-31900-2
     EAN 978-0-312-31900-7
     1. Sano Ichirō (Fictitious character)—Fiction.   2. Japan—History—
Genroku period, 1688–1704—Fiction.   3. Public officers—Crimes against—
Fiction.   4. Police—Japan—Tokyo—Fiction.   5. Assassination—Fiction.
I. Title.

     PS3568.O934A98   2005
     813'.54—dc22

                                                            2005042763

First Edition: August 2005

10   9   8   7   6   5   4   3   2   1

Edo
Genroku Period
Year 8, Month 4
(Tokyo, May 1695)

Prologue

A gunshot boomed within Edo Castle and echoed across the city that spread below the hilltop.

On the racetrack inside the castle, five horses bolted from the starting line. Samurai riders, clad in metal helmets and armor tunics, crouched low in the saddles. They flailed their galloping mounts with riding crops; their shouts demanded more speed. The horses' hooves thundered up a storm of dust.

Around the long oval track, in wooden stands built in tiers and shaded from the sun by striped canopies, officials urged on the riders. Soldiers patrolling atop the stone walls of the compound and stationed in watchtowers above it waved and cheered. The horses galloped neck and neck until they reached the first curve, then crowded together as the riders jockeyed for position along the track's inside edge. The riders struck out at their opponents' mounts and bodies; their crops smacked horseflesh and rang loud against armor. Fighting for the lead, they yelled threats and insults at one another. Horses whinnied, colliding. As they rounded the curve, a rider on a bay stallion edged ahead of the pack.

The sensations of power and speed thrilled him. His heartbeat accelerated in rhythm with his horse's pounding hooves. The din resounded in his helmet. Through its visor he saw the spectators flick by him, their waving hands, colorful robes, and avid faces a blur in the wind. He whooped as reckless daring exhilarated his spirits. This new horse was well worth the gold he'd paid for it. He would win back its price when he collected on his bets, and show everyone who the best rider in the capital was.

Hurtling along the track, he drew a length in front of the rest. When he looked over his shoulder, two riders charged up to him, one on each side. They leaned forward and lashed their whips at him. The blows glanced off his armor. One rider grabbed his reins and the other seized his tunic in an attempt to slow him down. Ruthless in his need to win, he banged his crop against their helmets. They dropped behind. The audience roared. The leader howled with glee as he veered around the curve. The pack rampaged after him, but he coaxed his horse faster. He increased his lead while racing toward the finish.

In his mind there suddenly arose an image of a horseman gaining on him, monstrous in size, black as night. Startled, he glanced backward, but saw only the familiar horses and riders laboring through the dust in his wake. He dug in his heels, flailed his whip. His horse put on a burst of speed that stretched the gap between him and the pack. Ahead, some hundred paces distant, loomed the finish line. Two samurai officials waited there, holding red flags, ready to signal the winner.

But now the monstrous horseman grew larger in his perception, storming so close that he could feel its shadow lapping at him. He felt a sharp, fierce pain behind his right eye, as though a knife had stabbed into his skull. A cry burst from him. The pain began to pulse, driving the blade deeper and deeper, harder and faster. He moaned in agony and confusion.

What was happening to him?

The sunlight brightened to an intensity that seared his eyes. The track, the men at the finish line, and the spectators dissolved into a blinding shimmer, as if the world had caught fire. His heart beat a loud, frantic counterpoint to the pulses of pain. External sounds melted into dim drones. A tingling sensation spread through his arms and legs. He couldn't feel the horse under him. His head seemed very far away from his body. Now he knew something was dreadfully wrong. He tried to call for help, but only incoherent croaks emerged from his mouth.

Yet he felt no fear. Emotion and thought fled him like leaves scattering in the wind. His hands weakened; their grip on the reins loosened. His body was a numb, dead weight that sagged in the saddle. The brilliant, shimmering light contracted to a dot as the black horseman overtook him and darkness encroached on his vision.

The dot of light winked out. The world disappeared into black silence. Consciousness died.

As he crossed the finish line, he tumbled from his mount, into the path of the oncoming horses and riders.

Above the racetrack, past forested slopes carved by stone-walled passages that encircled and ascended the hill, a compound stood isolated from the estates that housed the top officials of the Tokugawa regime. High walls topped with metal spikes protected the compound, whose tiled roofs rose amid pine trees. Samurai officials, wearing formal silk robes and the two swords, shaved crowns, and topknots of their class, queued up outside. Guards escorted them in the double gate, through the courtyard, into the mansion that rambled in a labyrinth of wings connected by covered corridors. They gathered in an anteroom, waiting to see Chamberlain Sano Ichirō, the shogun's second-in-command and chief administrator of the *bakufu,* the military government that ruled Japan. They passed the time with political gossip, their voices a constant, rising buzz. In nearby rooms whirled a storm of activity: The chamberlain's aides conferred; clerks recorded business transacted by the regime, collated and filed reports; messengers rushed about.

Closeted in his private inner office, Chamberlain Sano sat with General Isogai, supreme commander of the army, who'd come to brief him on military affairs. Around them, colored maps of Japan hung on walls made of thick wooden panels that muted the noise outside. Shelves and fireproof iron chests held ledgers. The open window gave a view of the garden, where sand raked in parallel lines around mossy boulders shone brilliant white in the afternoon sun.

"There's good news and bad news," General Isogai said. He was a bulbous man with a squat head that appeared to sprout directly from his shoulders. His eyes glinted with intelligence and joviality. He spoke in a loud voice accustomed to shouting orders. "The good news is that things have quieted down in the past six months."

Six months ago, the capital had been embroiled in political strife. "We can be thankful that order has been restored and civil war prevented," Sano said, recalling how troops from two opposing factions had clashed in a bloody battle outside Edo and 346 soldiers had died.

"We can thank the gods that Lord Matsudaira is in power, and Yanagisawa is out," General Isogai added.

Lord Matsudaira—a cousin of the shogun—and the former chamberlain Yanagisawa had vied fiercely for domination of the regime. Their power struggle had divided the *bakufu,* until Lord Matsudaira had managed to win more allies, defeat the opposition's army, and oust Yanagisawa. Now Lord Matsudaira controlled the shogun, and thus the dictatorship.

"The bad news is that the trouble's not over," General Isogai continued. "There have been more unfortunate incidents. Two of my soldiers were ambushed and murdered on the highway, and four others while patrolling in town. And yesterday, the army garrison at Hodogaya was bombed. Four soldiers were killed, eight wounded."

Sano frowned in consternation. "Have the persons responsible been caught?"

"Not yet," General Isogai said, his expression surly. "But of course we know who they are."

After Yanagisawa had been ousted, scores of soldiers from his army had managed to escape Lord Matsudaira's strenuous efforts to capture them. Edo, home to a million people and countless houses, shops, temples, and shrines, afforded many secret hiding places for the fugitive outlaws. Determined to avenge their master's defeat, they were waging war upon Lord Matsudaira in the form of covert acts of violence. Thus, Yanagisawa still cast a shadow even though he now lived in exile on Hachijo Island in the middle of the ocean.

"I've heard reports of fighting between the army and the outlaws in the provinces," Sano said. The outlaws were fomenting rebellion in areas where the Tokugawa had less military presence. "Have you figured out who's leading the attacks?"

"I've interrogated the fugitives we've captured and gotten a few names," General Isogai said. "They're all senior officers from Yanagisawa's army who've gone underground."

"Could they be taking orders from above ground?"

"From inside the *bakufu*, you mean?" General Isogai shrugged. "Perhaps. Even though Lord Matsudaira has gotten rid of most of the opposition, he can't eliminate it all."

Lord Matsudaira had purged many officials because they'd supported his rival. The banishments, demotions, and executions would probably continue for some time. But remnants of the Yanagisawa faction still populated the government. These were men too powerful and entrenched for Lord Matsudaira to dislodge. They comprised a small but growing challenge to him.

"We'll crush the rebels eventually," General Isogai said. "Let's just hope that a foreign army doesn't invade Japan while we're busy coping with them."

Their meeting finished, Sano and General Isogai rose and exchanged bows. "Keep me informed," Sano said.

The general contemplated Sano a moment. "These times have been disastrous for some people," he remarked, "but beneficial for others." His sly, knowing smile nudged Sano. "Had Yanagisawa and Lord Matsudaira never fought, a certain onetime detective would never have risen to heights far above expectation . . . isn't that right, Honorable Chamberlain?"

He emphasized the syllables of Sano's title, conferred six months ago as a result of a murder investigation that had contributed to Yanagisawa's downfall. Once the shogun's *sōsakan-sama*—Most Honorable Investigator of Events, Situations, and People—Sano had been chosen to replace Yanagisawa.

General Isogai chuckled. "I never thought I'd be reporting to a former *rōnin*." Before Sano had joined the government, he'd been a masterless samurai, living on the fringes of society, eking out a living as a tutor and martial arts instructor. "I had a bet with some of my officers that you wouldn't last a month."

"Many thanks for your vote of confidence," Sano said with a wry smile, as he recalled how he'd struggled to learn how the government operated, to keep its huge, arcane bureaucracy running smoothly, and establish good relations with subordinates who resented his promotion over them.

As soon as General Isogai had departed, the whirlwind outside Sano's office burst through the door. Aides descended upon him, clamoring for his attention: "Here are the latest reports on tax revenues!" "Here are your memoranda to be signed!" "The judicial councilors are next in line to see you!"

The aides stacked documents in a mountain on the desk. They unfurled scrolls before Sano. As he scanned the papers and stamped them with his signature seal, he gave orders. Such had been his daily routine since he'd become chamberlain. He read and listened to countless reports in an attempt to keep up with everything that was happening in the nation. He had one meeting after another. His life had become an unceasing rush. He reflected that the Tokugawa regime, which had been founded by the steel of the sword, now ran on paper and talk. He regretted the habit he'd established when he'd taken up his new post.

In his zeal to take charge, he'd wanted to meet everyone, and hear all news and problems unfiltered by people who might hide the truth from him. He'd wanted to make decisions himself, rather than trust them to the two hundred men who comprised his staff. Because he didn't want to end up ignorant and manipulated, Sano had opened his door to hordes of officials. But he'd soon realized he'd gone too far. Minor issues, and people anxious to curry his favor, consumed too much of his attention. He often felt as though he was frantically treading water, in constant danger of drowning. He'd made many mistakes and stepped on many toes.

Regardless of his difficulties, Sano took pride in his accomplishments. He'd kept the Tokugawa regime afloat despite his lack of experience. He'd attained the pinnacle of a samurai's career, the greatest honor. Yet he often felt imprisoned in his office. His warrior spirit grew restless; he didn't even have time for martial arts practice. Sitting, talking, and shuffling paper while his sword rusted was no job for a samurai. Sano couldn't help yearning for his days as a detective, the intellectual challenge of solving crimes, and the thrill of hunting criminals. He wished to use his new power to do good, yet there seemed not much chance of that.

An Edo Castle messenger hovered near Sano. "Excuse me, Honorable Chamberlain," he said, "but the shogun wants to see you in the palace right now."

On top of everything else, Sano was at the shogun's command day and night. His most important duty was keeping his lord happy. He couldn't refuse a summons, no matter how frivolous the reason usually turned out to be.

As he exited his chamber, his two retainers, Marume and Fukida, accompanied him. Both had belonged to his detective corps when he was *sōsakan-sama;* now they served him as bodyguards and assistants. They hastened through the anteroom, where the officials waiting to see Sano fretted around him, begging for a moment of his attention. Sano made his apologies and mentally tore himself away from all the work he had to do, while Marume and Fukida hustled him out the door.

Inside the palace, Sano and his escorts walked up the long audience chamber, past the guards stationed against the walls. The shogun sat on the dais at the far end. He wore the cylindrical black cap of his rank, and a luxurious silk brocade robe whose green and gold hues harmonized with the landscape mural behind him. Lord Matsudaira knelt in the position of honor, below the shogun on his right. Sano knelt in his own customary position at the shogun's left; his men knelt near him. As they bowed to their superiors, Sano thought how similar the two cousins were in appearance, yet how different.

They both had the aristocratic Tokugawa features, but while the shogun's were withered and meek, Lord Matsudaira's were fleshed out by robust health and bold spirits. They were both fifty years of age and near the same height, but the shogun seemed much older and smaller due to his huddled posture. Lord Matsudaira, who outweighed his cousin, sat proudly erect. Although he wore robes in subdued colors, he dominated the room.

"I've requested this meeting to announce some bad news," Lord Matsudaira said. He maintained a cursory charade that his cousin held the power, and pretended to defer to him, but fooled no one except the shogun. Even though he now controlled the government, he still danced attendance on his cousin because if he didn't, other men would, and he could lose his influence over the shogun to them. "Ejima Senzaemon has just died."

Sano experienced surprise and dismay. The shogun's face took on a queasy, confused expression. "Who did you say?" His voice wavered with his constant fear of seeming stupid.

"Ejima Senzaemon," repeated Lord Matsudaira.

"Ahh." The shogun wrinkled his forehead, more baffled than enlightened. "Do I know him?"

"Of course you do," Lord Matsudaira said, barely hiding his impatience at his cousin's slow wits. Sano could almost hear him thinking that he, not Tokugawa Tsunayoshi, should have been born to rule the regime.

"Ejima was chief of the *metsuke*," Sano murmured helpfully. The *metsuke* was the intelligence service that employed spies to gather information all over Japan, for the purpose of monitoring troublemakers and guarding the regime's power.

"Really?" the shogun said. "When did he take office?"

"About six months ago," Sano said. Ejima had been appointed by Lord Matsudaira, who'd purged his predecessor, an ally of Chamberlain Yanagisawa.

The shogun heaved a tired sigh. "There are so many new people in the, ahh, government these days. I can't keep them straight." Annoyance pinched his features. "It would be much easier for me if the same men would stay in the same posts. I don't know why they can't."

Nobody offered an explanation. The shogun didn't know about the war between Lord Matsudaira and Chamberlain Yanagisawa, or Lord Matsudaira's victory and the ensuing purge; no one had told him, and since he rarely left the palace, he saw little of what went on around him. He knew Yanagisawa had been exiled, but he wasn't clear as to why. Neither Lord Matsudaira nor Yanagisawa had wanted him to know that they aspired to control the regime, lest he put them to death for treason. And now Lord Matsudaira wanted the shogun kept ignorant of the fact that he'd seized power and virtually ruled Japan. No one dared disobey his orders against telling the shogun. A conspiracy of silence pervaded Edo Castle.

"How did Ejima die?" Sano asked Lord Matsudaira.

"He fell off his horse during a race at the Edo Castle track," Lord Matsudaira said.

"Dear me," the shogun said. "Horse racing is such a dangerous sport, perhaps it should be, ahh, prohibited."

"I recall hearing that Ejima was a particularly reckless rider," Sano said, "and he'd been in accidents before."

"I don't believe this was an accident," Lord Matsudaira said, his tone sharp. "I suspect foul play."

"Oh?" Sano saw his surprise mirrored on his men's faces. "Why?"

"This isn't the only recent, sudden death of a high official," Lord Matsudaira said. "First there was Ono Shinnosuke, the supervisor of court ceremony, on New Year's Day. In the spring, Sasamura Tomoya, highway commissioner, died. And just last month, Treasury Minister Moriwaki."

"But Ono and Sasamura died in their sleep, at home in bed," Sano said. "The treasury minister fell in the bathtub and hit his head. Their deaths seem unrelated to Ejima's."

"Don't you see a pattern?" Lord Matsudaira's manner was ominous with insinuation.

"They were all, ahh, new to their posts, weren't they?" the shogun piped up timidly. He had the air of a child playing a guessing game, hoping he had the right answer. "And they died soon after taking office?"

"Precisely," Lord Matsudaira said, surprised that the shogun remembered the men, let alone knew anything about them.

They were all Lord Matsudaira's trusted cronies, installed after the coup, Sano could have added, but didn't.

"These deaths may not have been as natural as they appeared," said Lord Matsudaira. "They may be part of a plot to undermine the regime by eliminating key officials."

While Lord Matsudaira's enemies inside and outside the *bakufu* were constantly plotting his downfall, Sano didn't know what to think about a conspiracy to weaken the regime within a regime that he'd established. During the past six months, Sano had watched him change from a confident leader of a major Tokugawa branch clan to a nervous, distrustful man insecure in his new position. Frequent sabotage and violent attacks against his army by Yanagisawa's outlaws fed his insecurity. Stolen power could be stolen from the thief, Sano supposed.

"A plot against the regime?" Always susceptible to warnings about danger, the shogun gasped. He looked around as though he, not Lord Matsudaira, were under attack. "You must do something!" he exclaimed to his cousin.

"Indeed I will," Lord Matsudaira said. "Chamberlain Sano, I order you to investigate the deaths." Although Sano was second-in-command to the shogun, he answered to Lord Matsudaira, as did everyone else in the government. In his haste to protect himself, Lord Matsudaira forgot to manipulate the shogun into giving the order. "Should they prove to be murders, you will identify and apprehend the killer before he can strike again."

A thrill of glad excitement coursed through Sano. Even if the deaths turned out to be natural or accidental, here was a welcome reprieve from paperwork. "As you wish, my lord."

"Not so fast," the shogun said, narrowing his eyes in displeasure because Lord Matsudaira had bypassed his authority. "I seem to recall that Sano-*san* isn't a detective anymore. Investigating crimes is no longer his job. You can't ask him to, ahh, dirty his hands investigating those deaths."

Lord Matsudaira hastened to correct his mistake: "Sano-*san* is obliged to do whatever you wish, regardless of his position. And you wish him to protect your interests, don't you?"

Obstinacy set the shogun's weak jaw. "But Chamberlain Sano is too busy."

"I don't mind the extra work, Your Excellency." Now that Sano had his opportunity for action, he wasn't going to give it up. His spiritual energy soared at the prospect of a quest for truth and justice, which were fundamental to his personal code of honor. "I'm eager to be of service."

"Many thanks," the shogun said with a peevish glare at Lord Matsudaira as well as at Sano, "but helping me run the country requires all your attention."

Now Sano remembered the million tasks that awaited him. He couldn't leave his office for long and risk losing his tenuous control over the nation's affairs. "Perhaps His Excellency is right," he reluctantly conceded. "Perhaps this investigation is a matter for the police. They are ordinarily responsible for solving cases of mysterious death."

"A good idea," the shogun said, then asked Lord Matsudaira with belligerent scorn, "Why didn't you think of the police? Call them in."

"No. I must strongly advise you against involving the police," Lord Matsudaira said hastily.

Sano wondered why. Police Commissioner Hoshina was close to Lord Matsudaira, and Sano would have expected Lord Matsudaira to give Hoshina charge of the investigation. Something must have gone wrong between them, and too recently for the news to have spread.

"Chamberlain Sano is the only man who can be trusted to get to the bottom of this matter," Lord Matsudaira declared.

It was true that during the faction war Sano had remained neutral, resisting much pressure to take sides with Yanagisawa or Lord Matsudaira. Afterward, he'd loyally served Lord Matsudaira in the interest of restoring peace. And long before the trouble started, he'd earned himself a reputation for independence of mind and pursuing the truth even to his own detriment.

"Unless the murderer is caught, the regime's officials will be killed off until there are none left," Lord Matsudaira said to the shogun. "You'll be all alone." He spoke in a menacing voice: "And you wouldn't like that, would you?"

The shogun shrank on the dais. "Oh, no, indeed." He cast a horrified glance around him, as though he envisioned his companions disappearing before his eyes.

If Lord Matsudaira allowed attacks on his regime, he would lose face as well as power, and Sano knew that was worse than death for a proud man like him. "Then you must order Chamberlain Sano to drop everything, investigate the murders, and save you," Lord Matsudaira said.

"Yes. You're right." The shogun's resistance wilted. "Sano-*san*, do whatever my cousin suggests."

"A wise decision, Your Excellency," Lord Matsudaira said. A hint of a smile touched his mouth, expressing contempt for the shogun and pride at how easily he'd brought him to heel. He told Sano, "I've sent men to secure the racetrack and guard the corpse. They have orders that no one leaves or enters until after you've examined the scene. But you'd better go at once. The crowd will be getting restless."

Sano and his men bowed in farewell. As they left the room, Sano's step was light, no matter what calamities might strike during his absence from the helm of the government. Never mind how much work would accumulate while he looked into Chief Ejima's death; he felt like a prisoner released from jail. Here was his chance to apply all the might and resources of his new position to the cause of justice.

Sentries at the Edo Castle main gate swung open the massive, ironclad portals. Out came a procession of mounted samurai, escorting a palanquin carried by husky bearers. Inside the palanquin, visible through its window, rode Lady Reiko, wife of Chamberlain Sano. Her delicate, beautiful young face shone with eager anticipation.

A message she'd received this morning from her father had read, "Please come to the Court of Justice at the hour of the sheep today. There is a trial that I would like you to see."

Reiko was glad of the prospect of something to enliven her existence. Since Sano had become chamberlain, she'd had little to do except take care of their son Masahiro. Before, when Sano had been *sōsakan-sama,* she'd helped him solve his cases, hunting clues in places he couldn't go, using her contacts in the world of women. But she couldn't help him run the government, and he was so busy she seldom saw him except when he came home exhausted at night. Reiko missed the old days, even though she was proud of her husband's important position. Facing danger and death seemed preferable to whiling away her life as did other women of her class. It didn't help that the danger of the times had kept her cooped up inside Edo Castle for most of the past six months.

Her procession moved through the Hibiya administrative district, where the regime's high officials lived and worked in stately mansions enclosed by high walls. In the streets, more soldiers than usual patrolled, on the lookout for fugitive outlaws from the Yanagisawa faction. Reiko glimpsed an estate that had burned down; only a heap of rubble remained. Arson was a favorite weapon of the outlaws.

A news-seller, hawking broadsheets, strolled amid the officials, clerks, and servants who thronged the district. "Outlaws robbed a wealthy merchant and his family who were traveling on the Eastern Sea Road yesterday!" he cried. "They killed him and violated his wife!"

The fugitives were desperate for money to support themselves and their cause, and they often brutalized citizens who had the bad luck to encounter them. Reiko wore a dagger under her sleeve, ready to defend herself if necessary.

The procession halted outside Magistrate Ueda's mansion, which housed the Court of Justice. Guards at the gate confronted Reiko's entourage. "State your names," they ordered. "Show your identification documents."

As her escorts complied, other guards peered suspiciously into her palanquin. Recently an outlaw had disguised himself as a porter, sneaked into an estate, pulled a dagger from the crate he carried, and slain five people before he was captured. Security had tightened everywhere. Now the guard recognized Reiko and let her procession through the gate. In the courtyard she climbed out of her palanquin. More police than usual stood guard over more than the usual number of prisoners awaiting trial. The prisoners were mostly samurai who appeared to be troops from Yanagisawa's army. Shackled by heavy chains, they were disheveled and bloody, as if they'd fought savagely while resisting capture. No matter that Yanagisawa had been an evil, harsh master, Bushido—the samurai code of honor—demanded their unwavering loyalty to him. Reiko's bodyguards led her past them and other prisoners, tough-looking commoners. Crime was rampant among the townspeople; many had taken advantage of the general disorder and an overworked police force.

Inside the low, half-timbered mansion, Reiko entered the Court of Justice and found the trial ready to begin. On the dais at the end of the long hall sat her father, Magistrate Ueda, portly and dignified in his black ceremonial robes, one of two magistrates who maintained law and order and settled disputes in Edo. A secretary, equipped with a desk and writing implements, sat on either side of him. Except for the courtroom guards, only two other people were present. One was a *doshin*—a police patrol officer. Clad in a short kimono and cotton leggings, he knelt near the dais. At his waist he wore a single short sword and a *jitte*—a steel wand with two curved prongs above the hilt, used for parrying and catching the blade of an attacker's sword. The other was the defendant, a woman dressed in a hemp robe. She knelt before the magistrate on a straw mat on the *shirasu,* an area of floor covered by white sand, symbol of the truth. Her hands were chained behind her; her long black hair straggled down her back.

Magistrate Ueda acknowledged Reiko's presence with a slight nod. He signaled one of his secretaries, who announced, "The defendant is Yugao from Kanda district."

Reiko knelt at the side of the room, where she had a view of the woman's face. It was sternly beautiful, with a high forehead and cheekbones, a thin, elegant nose, and carved lips. Yugao seemed a few years younger than Reiko's own age of twenty-five. She sat with her head bowed, her gaze fixed on the white sand. Her slender body was rigid under the baggy robe.

"Yuago is charged with the murders of her father, her mother, and her sister," the secretary said.

Shock jarred Reiko. Murdering one's family was a heinous crime that repudiated the morals of society. Could this young woman have really done it? Reiko wondered why her father had wanted her to see this trial.

"I will hear the evidence against Yugao," said Magistrate Ueda.

The *doshin* came forward. He was a short man in his thirties, with blunt, weathered features. "The victims were found lying dead in their house," he said. "Each had been stabbed many times. Yugao was found sitting near the bodies, holding the knife. There was blood all over her."

That a daughter could commit such an atrocity against her parents, to whom she owed the utmost respect and affection! For one sister to slay another! Reiko had seen and heard of many terrible things, but this exceeded them all. Yugao neither moved nor changed expression; she gave no sign of innocence or guilt. She appeared not to care that she was accused of a crime for which the penalty was death and that most trials ended in convictions.

"Did Yugao say anything when she was arrested?" said Magistrate Ueda.

"She said, 'I did it,' " the *doshin* replied.

"Is there any evidence to the contrary?" Magistrate Ueda said.

"None that I saw."

"Have you any witnesses who can prove that Yugao did indeed commit the crime?"

"No, Honorable Magistrate."

"Have you looked for or identified any other suspects?"

"No, Honorable Magistrate."

Reiko began to have a strange feeling about this trial: Something wasn't right.

"The law allows accused persons to speak in their own defense," Magistrate Ueda told Yugao. "What have you to say for yourself?"

Yugao spoke in a flat, barely audible voice: "I killed them."

"Is there anything else?" Magistrate Ueda asked.

She shook her head, apparently indifferent to the fact that this was her last chance to save her life. The *doshin* looked bored, waiting for Magistrate Ueda to pronounce Yugao guilty and send her to the execution ground.

A frown darkened Magistrate Ueda's face. He contemplated Yugao for a moment, then said, "I will postpone my verdict. Guards, take Yugao to an audience chamber." He turned to his secretaries. "There will be a recess before the next trial. Court is adjourned."

Now Reiko knew something unusual was going on. Her father was a decisive man, and as quick to serve justice as the law demanded. She'd watched many of his trials and never before seen him delay a verdict. Nor, it seemed, had the secretaries and the *doshin,* who gazed at him in surprise. Yugao's head jerked up. For the first time Reiko got a full view of her eyes. They were flinty black, inside curved slits beneath smooth lids. They blinked in confusion. As the guards led her from the courtroom, she went meekly. The secretaries departed; Magistrate Ueda stepped off his dais. Reiko rose, brimming with curiosity, and hurried over to join him.

"Thank you for coming, Daughter," he said with a fond smile.

They'd always been closer than most fathers and daughters, and not just because Reiko was his only child. Reiko's mother had died when Reiko was a baby, and the magistrate cherished her as all that remained of the wife he'd adored. Early in her life, he'd noticed her intelligence and given her the education normally reserved for sons. He'd employed tutors to instruct her in reading, calligraphy, history, mathematics, philosophy, and the Chinese classics. He'd even hired martial arts masters to teach her sword fighting and unarmed combat. Now they shared an interest in crime.

"What did you think of the trial?" Magistrate Ueda asked.

"It was certainly different from most," Reiko said.

The magistrate nodded agreement. "In what way?"

"To begin, Yugao confessed so readily," Reiko said. "Many defendants claim they're innocent even if they're not, to try to avoid punishment. Yugao didn't even speak in her own defense. Maybe she was too shy or frightened, as women sometimes are, but if so, I couldn't tell. She showed so little emotion." Most defendants were beset by remorse, hysteria, or otherwise agitated. "She didn't seem to feel anything at all, until you delayed the verdict. I sensed that she didn't exactly welcome a reprieve, which is also strange."

"Go on," Magistrate Ueda said, pleased by Reiko's astute observations.

"Yugao never said why she killed her family, if in fact she did. Criminals who confess tend to make excuses to justify what they've done. This is the first trial I've seen where a motive for the crime wasn't presented. The police don't seem to have looked for it." Puzzled and disturbed, Reiko shook her head. "They seem to have arrested Yugao because she was the obvious suspect, despite the fact that the evidence against her isn't proof of her guilt. In fact, they seem to have done no investigation at all. Have they become so negligent lately?"

"This is a special case," Magistrate Ueda said. "Yugao is a *hinin*."

"Oh." Comprehension flooded Reiko.

The *hinin* were "non-humans"—citizens demoted to an outcast class near the bottom of the social order as punishment for crimes that were serious but not bad enough to warrant the death penalty. These crimes included theft and various moral transgressions. *Hinin* were prohibited from dealings with other citizens; the few thousand in Edo lived in settlements on the fringes of the city. The only people who ranked lower were the *eta*—hereditary outcasts due to their traditional link with death-related occupations, such as butchering, which rendered them spiritually unclean. One major distinction separated *hinin* from *eta*: The *hinin* could finish their sentences or be pardoned, obtain amnesty, and regain their former status, while the *eta* were permanent outcasts. But both classes were shunned by higher society.

"I suppose the police don't waste their time investigating crimes among the *hinin*," Reiko said.

Magistrate Ueda nodded. "Not when a case seems as clear-cut as this one. Especially these days, when the police are busy rounding up renegades and quelling disturbances." Concern deepened the lines in his face. "My verdicts depend on information from them. When they provide so little, I find it difficult to render a just decision."

"And you can't tell any better than I can whether Yugao is guilty or innocent based on the testimony at her trial," Reiko deduced.

"Correct," said Magistrate Ueda. "Nor can I tell from what I was able to learn beforehand. When I heard of the case, I knew the police wouldn't have conducted a thorough investigation, so I made a point of questioning Yugao myself. All she would say was that she killed her parents and sister. She declined to explain. Her demeanor was the same as you saw."

He expelled a breath of frustration. "I can't let a confessed murderess go free just because I'm not satisfied with the case against her. My superiors would disapprove."

And his position depended on their good will, Reiko knew. Should they think him lenient toward criminals, he would be expelled from his post, a calamitous disgrace.

"Yet I can't convict a young woman and sentence her to death on such incomplete information," he said.

Reiko knew her father had a soft spot in his heart for young women; she supposed that he saw her in them. And unlike many officials, he cared about serving justice even when an outcast was involved.

"This brings me to the reason I invited you to the trial," Magistrate Ueda continued. "I sense there's more to this case than meets the eye. And I want to know the truth about the murders, but I haven't the wherewithal to seek it myself. My schedule is packed with trials; my staff is fully occupied. Therefore, I must ask you a favor: Will you investigate the crime and determine whether Yugao committed it?"

Joy and excitement leapt in Reiko. "Yes!" she exclaimed. "I would love to!" Here was a new, unprecedented opportunity—a whole mystery of her own to solve, not just a part of one of Sano's cases.

Magistrate Ueda smiled at her enthusiasm. "Thank you, Daughter. I know you've had time on your hands lately, and I decided you are the right person for the task."

"Thank you, Father," Reiko said, warmed by the respect that his words implied. Once he'd disparaged her detective abilities and thought she belonged at home tending to domestic duties; back then, he wouldn't have allowed her to undertake a job usually reserved for men. No ordinary official would ask his daughter to do such a thing. No one except her father, who understood her need for adventure and accomplishment, would expect such a favor from the chamberlain's wife.

"I'll begin immediately," Reiko said. "First I'd like to talk with Yugao. Maybe I can get her to tell me what really happened the night of the murders."

Maybe Reiko would also have the satisfaction of proving a young woman innocent and saving her life.

3

Sano and Detectives Marume and Fukida hastened through the stone-walled passages that led down the hill from the palace, past checkpoints manned by sentries. They found two of Lord Matsudaira's soldiers guarding the gate to the racetrack. The soldiers let them inside. As the gate shut behind them, they surveyed their surroundings.

A crowd of men, who looked to be spectators at the race, loitered in clusters or sat in the stands. Their gaudy robes made bright spots of color against the backdrop of dark green pines that fringed the premises. Lord Matsudaira's soldiers hovered, watching everyone. A small band of them stood in a circle at one end of the bare, dusty oval track. Sano presumed they were guarding the corpse. Horses neighed in stables arrayed along one wall. The sky was still bright, but the sun had descended, and the hill above the compound cast a shadow over the track. The afternoon's warmth had begun to cool as evening approached.

Now the spectators noticed Sano and rushed toward him. He recognized some as minor bureaucrats, the sort with vague duties and enough idle time to watch horse races. He experienced the surge of excitement with which he'd begun each new investigation when he'd been *sōsakan-sama*. But he also felt sad because he missed Hirata, his chief retainer, who'd once lent his expert, faithful assistance to Sano's investigations. Hirata now had other duties besides being at hand whenever Sano needed him.

A man stepped forward from the crowd. "Greetings, Honorable Chamberlain." He was a muscular samurai in his forties, with a tanned, open face and a deferential yet confident manner. Sano recognized him as the master of the racetrack. "May I ask why we've been kept here?" Irate mutters from the spectators echoed his question. "What's going on?"

Sano said, "Greetings, Oyama-*san*," then explained, "I'm here to investigate Chief Ejima's death. Lord Matsudaira thinks it was murder."

"Murder?" Oyama frowned in surprise and disbelief. Low exclamations rose among the spectators. "With all due respect to Lord Matsudaira, that can't be. Ejima fell off his horse during the race. I saw. I was standing by the finish line, not five paces away from him when it happened."

"He seemed to faint in the saddle just before he dropped," said a spectator. "It looked as if his heart had suddenly given out."

Sano saw heads nodding, heard murmurs of agreement. Contradictory feelings beset him. If these observers were correct, then the death wasn't murder, the other three probably weren't either, and his inquiry would be short. He felt a letdown coming. Then he reasoned that at least this would mean the regime was safe, and he would be glad to put Lord Matsudaira's fears to rest. But for now he must keep an open mind.

"My investigation will determine whether Ejima was a victim of foul play or not," Sano said. "Until it's finished, this is a case of suspicious death. The racetrack will be treated as a crime scene, and you are all witnesses. I must ask you all to remain here and give statements about what you observed."

He saw irritation on the men's faces. He sensed them thinking that Lord Matsudaira was too quick to see evil schemes everywhere and that he himself was wasting his time as well as theirs. But no one dared argue with the shogun's second-in-command. Sano reflected that his new status had its advantages.

"Fukida-*san,* you start taking the witnesses' statements. Marume-*san,* you come with me," Sano told his men.

The thin, scholarly, serious detective began herding the crowd into a line. The brawny, jovial detective accompanied Sano as he strode along the track. The racetrack master followed them. As they neared the body, the soldiers surrounding it stepped aside. Sano and his companions halted and looked down at the dead man.

Ejima lay sprawled on his back, his arms and legs bent, against a wide, smudged black line painted across the track. His iron helmet covered his head and face. Sano could see his eyes, dull and vacant, through the open visor. Ejima's metal armor tunic was dented. Blood and grime stained his blue silk kimono, trousers, white socks, and straw sandals.

"He looks like he's been beaten," Marume said.

"The horses trampled him," Oyama explained. "He fell right under their hooves. It happened so fast, and the other riders were so close behind him, there was no time for them to steer clear."

"At least he won his last race," Marume said.

"Has his family been notified of his death?" Sano asked Oyama.

"Yes. My assistant went to tell them."

"Did anyone touch him after he fell?" Sano said.

"I turned him over to see how badly he was hurt and try to help him. But he was already gone."

"Has the track been cleaned since he died?"

"No, Honorable Chamberlain. When I sent the news to Lord Matsudaira, his troops came and brought orders that nothing was to be disturbed."

Sano felt hindered by the troops, who lingered too close, waiting to see what he would do. "Wait over there," he told them and Oyama, gesturing down the track.

When they'd moved off, Sano said to Marume, "Supposing Ejima didn't die of a bad heart, the fall could have killed him. But then the question is, what caused the fall?"

"Maybe someone in the stands threw a rock at him, hit his head, and knocked him unconscious. Everyone else there would have been too busy watching the race to notice." Marume paced around the body, kicking at a few stones that lay scattered on the dirt. "One of these could be a murder weapon."

Sano listened to sporadic gunfire that emanated from the distant martial arts training ground. He rotated, looking beyond and above the track. Soldiers peered down at him from windows in covered corridors and watchtowers atop the walls that enclosed the compound and rose up from the slope higher on the hill. "Someone up there could have shot a gun at Ejima."

"Who would have noticed one more shot?" Marume agreed.

"I don't see a bullet wound on him, but he could have been hit on his helmet and stunned." Crouching, Sano examined Ejima's helmet. Its metal surface was covered with scratches and dents.

"I'll have the area searched for a bullet," Marume said.

"In any case, the witnesses aren't limited to the people inside the compound when Ejima died," Sano said. "We'll have to round up all the soldiers who were on duty anyplace with a view of the racetrack. But first I want to question the other witnesses who were closest to Ejima."

He and Marume walked over to the racetrack master.

"Are you finished inspecting the body?" Oyama asked. "May I have it removed?" He sounded anxious to rid his domain of the physical and spiritual pollution conferred by death.

"Not yet," Sano said, because he needed a more thorough examination of the corpse than could be done here, and he didn't want it whisked off for the funeral and cremation. "I'll take care of its removal. Right now I want to talk to the riders who were in the race with Ejima. Where are they?"

"In the stables," Oyama said.

Inside the long wooden barns with thatched roofs, horses stood in stalls while grooms washed and wiped them, combed their manes, and bandaged wounded legs. Manure and hay scented the air. The five riders squatted in a corner, conversing in low voices. They'd stripped off their armor, which hung on racks that also held their riding gear. When Sano approached them, they hastily knelt and bowed.

"Rise," Sano said. "I want to ask you some questions about Chief Ejima's death." He observed that the riders were all robust samurai in their late twenties or early thirties. They were still grimy from the race, and reeked of sweat. As they rose, he said, "First, identify yourselves."

Among them were a captain and a lieutenant from the army, a palace administrator, and two distant cousins of the shogun. When Sano asked them to describe what they'd seen during the race, the army captain spoke for them: "Ejima crumpled in his saddle. He fell off his horse. Our horses ran him over. By the time we'd stopped and dismounted, he was dead."

This matched the story told by the spectators. "Did you see anything hit him before he crumpled?" Sano said. "Such as a rock or a bullet?"

The riders shook their heads.

"Did you touch Ejima?"

They hesitated, eying one another with uneasy expressions. Sano said, "Come on. I know that horse racing is a rough sport." He moved to the rack and fingered a riding crop, which consisted of a short, stout leather whip with an iron handle. "I also know that the horses aren't the only ones to take the brunt of these. Now speak up."

"All right. I hit him," the captain said reluctantly.

"So did I," said the lieutenant. "But we were just trying to slow him down."

"We didn't hit him that hard. He got me a lot worse than I got him." The captain gingerly touched his face, which was swollen around his jaw.

"We play rough, but we never intentionally hurt a fellow rider," said the lieutenant. "That's the code of honor at the racetrack." The other men nodded, united against Sano's implied accusation. "Besides, he was a friend. We had no reason to kill him."

"Although I bet that a lot of other people did," the captain said.

Sano thanked the men for their help. As he and Marume walked away from the stables, Marume said, "I think they're telling the truth. Do you believe them?"

"For now," Sano said, reserving judgment until evidence should indicate otherwise. "The captain was right when he hinted that Ejima was a good candidate for murder."

"Because he was one of Lord Matsudaira's top officials?"

"Not only that," Sano said. "His position made him a target. He headed an organization that spies on people."

No one was safe from the *metsuke,* especially in this dangerous political climate, when a man's most innocuous words or deeds could be twisted into evidence of disloyalty to Lord Matsudaira and cause for banishment or execution.

"If Ejima was murdered," Sano said, "the killer may be connected to someone destroyed by a *metsuke* investigation." And Sano recalled that Ejima had enjoyed his dirty job a little too much. The relish he'd taken from ruining people might have angered their relatives and friends.

"Talk about a man with a lot of enemies," Marume said.

"But motive doesn't necessarily mean murder," Sano reminded them both. "Not when there's so little evidence." He resisted his hunch that Ejima had been a victim of foul play: Even samurai instinct was susceptible to influence by personal bias. "Before we go any further, we should finish interviewing all the witnesses."

He looked across the track, where Detective Fukida was still busy with the spectators, then up at the soldiers along the walls and in the turrets. "Even more important, we have to determine the exact cause of Ejima's death."

This was something that Sano, despite all his past experience and newfound authority, couldn't do himself. And the scope of the investigation extended far beyond the racetrack, past the men present at the scene of the death, to include Ejima's foes as well as Lord Matsudaira's. That could mean hundreds of potential witnesses—and suspects. Sano needed more help than Marume and Fukida could provide, from someone he could absolutely trust.

"Send for Hirata-*san,*" he told Marume. "Tell him to meet me here right away."

4

Hirata sat behind the desk in the office that had once belonged to Sano, inside the estate where he was now master. Into the room filed ten members of the hundred-man detective corps that he'd once supervised for Sano and now commanded for himself.

"Good evening, *Sōsakan-sama*," the detectives chorused as they knelt and bowed to Hirata.

"What have you to report?" Hirata asked.

The men described their progress on various cases he'd assigned them—a theft of weapons from the Edo Castle arsenal; a search for a rebel band suspected of plotting to overthrow Lord Matsudaira. The political climate had spawned many crimes to occupy the shogun's new Most Honorable Investigator of Events, Situations, and People. As he listened, Hirata tried to ignore the pain from the deep, barely healed wound in his left thigh. He tried to never let his expression reveal his suffering. But Hirata couldn't hide that he'd lost much weight and muscle after the injury that had almost killed him. He couldn't deny that all the honors that had resulted from his valor in the line of duty had come with a terrible price.

Six months ago he'd stopped an attack on Sano and saved Sano's life. The cut from the attacker's sword, meant for Sano, had gashed Hirata's leg so badly he'd thought his death was certain. As blood poured from him and he lost consciousness, he thought he'd performed the ultimate act of samurai loyalty—sacrificing himself for his master.

Three days later Hirata had awakened, and learned that Lord Matsudaira had defeated Yanagisawa, Sano was the new chamberlain, and he himself was a hero. The shogun had declared that if Hirata lived, he would be promoted to Sano's former post. Hirata had been thrilled by the honor, and amazed that he—a onetime police patrol officer—had ascended to such a high rank. But for two long months, the pain had been so bad that the doctors gave him large doses of opium, which kept him in a drowsy daze. Fever sickened and weakened Hirata. Once robust and active, he was an invalid until the New Year, when the evil spirits of disease finally left him, and he began to recover. Everyone said his cure was a miracle, but Hirata wasn't so sure.

Now the detectives finished their reports. Hirata gave his orders: "Find out if any of the missing weapons have turned up on the market. Put a secret watch on the teahouse where the rebels have friends."

The detectives bowed and departed. Hirata clenched his teeth against the pain. Today he would gladly trade his new post for the good health he'd once taken for granted. He was ashamed because he did little besides hear reports and give orders. Sano had done much more. Hirata knew that what he told the detectives to do, they probably could think of themselves, although they always pretended they needed his guidance. Loyal friends, they never showed that they knew he depended on them for everything; they acted as though he was in charge. They did the investigations he'd once done—because he no longer could.

Walking or riding a horse was so uncomfortable that Hirata seldom went outside the estate. A brief martial arts practice each day exhausted him. Even sitting for long taxed his energy. At age twenty-eight, he was as feeble as an old man.

His wife Midori entered the room. Young, plump, and pretty, she smiled at him, but her face had the worried look she'd worn ever since his injury. She said, "Taeko wants her papa. Can you come and see her?"

"Of course."

Hirata rose laboriously. He leaned on his wife as they walked down the corridor. She was the only person he allowed to see his weakness. She loved him too much to think less of him. He loved her for her loyal, tender care. That his injury had brought them closer together was the only thing for which he was truly glad. He didn't regret that he'd ruined himself to save Sano; he would again, if need be. But as much as he appreciated the honor and acclaim, he sometimes wondered if it would have been better if he hadn't lived. Death would have gotten him all the glory and none of the suffering.

In the nursery, his daughter Taeko sat on the floor, dressed in a red kimono, surrounded by toys and attended by a nursemaid. Eleven months old, she had round, bright black eyes and downy black hair. She cooed and bounced when she saw Hirata. His spirits lifted.

"Come to Papa," he said, kneeling down to hug her.

Taeko flung herself into his arms. She landed hard on his bad thigh. Hirata yelled in pain. He shoved Taeko off him. Confused and hurt, she began to cry. Hirata hobbled into the corridor and lay gasping on the floor. He listened while Midori and the nursemaid soothed Taeko. When she'd quieted, Midori came to him.

"Are you all right?" Midori said anxiously.

"No! I'm not all right! What kind of man can't even hold his own child?" Hirata spoke with the frustration and self-pity that he usually tried not to show or feel: "If Taeko can hurt me so badly, then what if I should have to fight a criminal who's much bigger and stronger? I would be cut down like a blade of grass!"

Midori knelt beside him. "Please don't get upset," she said. "Don't think about fighting yet."

Her voice quaked with fear because she'd almost lost him once and she didn't want him in danger again. She took his hand. "You must be tired. Come to bed and take a nap. I'll bring your sleeping potion."

"No," Hirata said, although he craved the opium that brought blessed relief from the pain. He resisted using the drug because it stupefied his mind, the only part of him not damaged.

"It's only been a short time since you were injured," Midori said. "Every day you're getting stronger—"

"Not strong enough," Hirata said bitterly.

"You'll soon be able to fight as well as ever," Midori persisted.

"Will I?" Despair filled Hirata.

Midori hung her head; she couldn't promise that he would ever be himself again. The doctors had told them he should be satisfied just to be alive. But she said sensibly, "There's no need for you to fight, anyway."

Hirata exhaled. If he couldn't fight, how could he call himself a samurai?

"The detectives can do whatever needs to be done," Midori said, "until—"

"Until something important comes up that they can't handle by themselves and I can't manage from home," Hirata said. "Then what?"

He heard someone call, "*Sōsakan-sama.*" He sat up as Detective Arai, his chief retainer, came toward him along the passage.

"There's a message from the chamberlain," Arai said. "He requires your assistance on an urgent matter. He wants you to meet him at the Edo Castle racetrack immediately."

Honor, duty, and friendship propelled Hirata to the racetrack. It wasn't far from his estate, but by the time he arrived with two detectives and they dismounted from their horses inside the gate, his wounded leg ached even worse than usual. He looked across the compound and saw Sano at the opposite end, talking to a group of officials. Hirata drew a deep breath. His infirmity magnified the distance between him and Sano tenfold. He gathered his strength.

"Come on," he told Detectives Arai and Inoue.

As they began the long walk, Detective Arai spoke in a quiet, offhand voice, "We could ride."

His men always tried to make things easy for him. "No," Hirata said.

This was one of his rare public appearances. Most of his colleagues hadn't seen him since he'd been injured, and he had to demonstrate that he'd made a full recovery. To show any weakness would diminish his status. While he labored toward Sano, the officials scattered around the track bowed to him, and he nodded in acknowledgment. He feared that everyone could see how hard he was struggling not to limp. Sano, Marume, and Fukida hurried to meet Hirata and his detectives.

"Honorable Chamberlain," Hirata said, trying not to gasp for breath.

"*Sōsakan-sama,*" said Sano.

They exchanged bows; their men, once comrades in the detective corps, greeted one another. Hirata was glad to see Sano because he rarely did; perhaps a month had passed since they'd last met. Although Hirata was technically still Sano's chief retainer, their new duties kept them apart. Now, a stiff formality had replaced the camaraderie they'd once shared. Relations between them had been awkward since Hirata's injury.

Sano signaled their men to move off and allow them some privacy. "I hope all is well with you?" Sano said. Concern sobered his gaze as he regarded Hirata.

Perhaps the fact that Hirata had saved Sano's life should have brought them closer together, but it had had the opposite effect. That Hirata had done only what a samurai owed his master didn't exempt Sano from guilt because he was whole and Hirata maimed. Sano's guilt and gratitude, and Hirata's loss, filled a wide gulf between them.

"All is very well with me." Hirata stood as straight as he could; he hoped Sano wouldn't read his pain etched on his face. He didn't want Sano to feel worse; for Sano to suffer distressed Hirata deeply. "And you?"

"Never better," Sano said.

Hirata noticed that Sano had lost the anxious, careworn air that had marked him in his early days as chamberlain. Indeed, he looked like himself in the old days when he and Hirata had first worked together. But Hirata didn't want to think about those days.

"What happened?" Hirata said, gesturing around the track.

"Ejima Senzaemon, chief of the *metsuke,* died during a race," Sano said. "Lord Matsudaira suspects foul play and has asked me to investigate." He described his meeting with Lord Matsudaira, and the preliminary inquiries he'd conducted.

"So far it doesn't sound as if Ejima's death was murder," Hirata said, interested yet skeptical. "Can it and the earlier deaths really be part of a plot against Lord Matsudaira, or is he imagining a plot in a set of coincidences?"

"That's what I mean to find out," Sano said. "I called you here because I need your help."

Even as Hirata experienced an ardent wish to work with Sano on such an important case, he worried that it would require more strength than he had. Hirata saw Sano appraising his gaunt figure, and realized that Sano feared he was physically unable to work. Mortification sickened Hirata. He couldn't let Sano think him weak and useless.

"It will be an honor to serve you," Hirata said. He would help Sano or die trying. "Where do you want me to start?"

"You can start by taking Ejima's body to Edo Morgue," Sano said in a low voice that the witnesses and soldiers wouldn't overhear. "Ask Dr. Ito to examine it."

Once a prominent, wealthy physician, Dr. Ito had been sentenced to lifelong custodianship of Edo Morgue as punishment for conducting scientific experiments that derived from foreign lands, a crime strictly forbidden by Tokugawa law. He'd helped Sano on past investigations.

"Have him find out the exact cause of death," Sano clarified. "That's key to establishing whether it was murder."

"I'll go right away," Hirata said.

He sounded as eager as ever to do Sano's bidding. But Sano saw the pain and worry he tried to hide, and sensed him wondering if he could withstand the journey to Edo Morgue, all the way on the other side of town. Sano, who hadn't seen Hirata in a while, had been dismayed to observe how fragile he still was. Sano didn't want Hirata taxing his health or getting hurt again for Sano's sake. But although Sano would rather go to Edo Morgue himself, it was too big a risk: Should the chamberlain of Japan be caught participating in the forbidden science of examining a corpse, he would fall much farther than Dr. Ito had. Nor could Sano take back his request and shame Hirata. He needed Hirata as much as Hirata apparently needed to prove himself capable of the duty that the bond between samurai and master required.

"Bring the results of Dr. Ito's examination to me as soon as possible," Sano said. "If I've finished questioning witnesses by then, I'll be at my estate." He couldn't let the government collapse while he investigated a murder that might not be murder. "Then we'll report to Lord Matsudaira. No doubt he's anxious for news."

5

One wing of the Court of Justice contained rooms where the magistrate and his staff conferred with citizens seeking to resolve disputes that involved money, property, or social obligations. Here Magistrate Ueda had sent Yugao. As Reiko walked down the passage, she heard raucous male laughter from an open door. She peered inside.

The room was a cell enclosed by sliding paper-and-lattice walls, furnished with a *tatami* floor and a low table. Yugao stood between the two guards that Reiko liked the least in her father's retinue. One, a thickset man with squinty eyes, pawed Yugao's cheek. The other, athletic and arrogant, groped under the skirt of her hemp robe. Yugao scrambled away, but the men caught her. They yanked at her robe, squeezed her buttocks and breasts. She strained at the shackles that bound her hands while she kicked her bare feet at the men. They only laughed more uproariously. Her face was tense with helpless anger.

"Stop that!" Reiko exclaimed. Bursting through the door, she ordered them, "Leave her alone!"

They paused, annoyed at the interruption. Their faces showed dismay as they recognized their master's daughter.

"The magistrate will be displeased to hear that you've been taking advantage of a helpless woman in his house," Reiko said, her voice sharp with ire. "Get out!"

The guards slunk off. Reiko shut the door and turned to Yugao. The woman slouched, her face concealed behind her tousled hair, her robe hanging off her shoulder. Pity filled Reiko.

"Here, let me fix your clothes," she said.

As she touched Yugao, the woman flinched. She tossed back her hair and stared at Reiko. "Who are you?"

Reiko had expected Yugao to be thankful for her protection from the guards, but Yugao was wary, hostile. Seeing her at close view for the first time, Reiko noticed that her complexion was ashen from fatigue and malnourishment, her flinty eyes shadowed underneath, her lips chapped. Harsh treatment by the jailers had surely taught her to be leery toward everyone. Although she was accused and perhaps guilty of a serious crime, Reiko felt her sympathy toward Yugao increase.

"I'm the magistrate's daughter," Reiko said. "My name is Reiko."

A long gaze of mutual curiosity passed between them. Reiko watched Yugao appraise her tangerine-colored silk kimono printed with a willow tree pattern, her upswept coiffure, her carefully applied white makeup and red lip rouge, her teeth blackened according to fashionable custom for married women of her class. Meanwhile, Reiko perceived Yugao's jailhouse stink of urine, oily hair, and unwashed body, and saw resentment and envy in Yugao's eyes. They looked at each other as though across a sea, the highborn lady on one shore, the outcast on the opposite.

"What do you want?" Yugao said.

Her rude tone surprised Reiko. Maybe the woman had never been taught good manners. Reiko wondered what station in society Yugao had originated from and what she'd done to become a *hinin,* but it didn't seem a good time to ask.

"I want to talk to you, if I may," Reiko said.

Suspicion hooded Yugao's gaze. "About what?"

"About the murder of your family," Reiko said.

"Why?"

"The magistrate is having trouble deciding whether to convict you," Reiko said. "That's why he postponed his verdict. He's asked me to investigate the murders and find out if you're guilty or innocent."

Yugao wrinkled her brow, clearly perplexed by the situation. "I said I did it. Isn't that enough?"

"He doesn't think so," Reiko said, "and neither do I."

"Why not?"

This conversation reminded Reiko of the time when Masahiro had stepped on a thistle and she'd had to pull the spines from his bare foot. "One reason is that we need to know why your parents and sister were killed," Reiko said. "You didn't say."

"But . . ." Yugao shook her head in confusion. "But I was arrested."

Reiko could sense her thinking that her arrest should have guaranteed a conviction, as everyone knew it would have under ordinary circumstances. "Just because you were caught at the scene of the crime doesn't prove you did it," Reiko explained.

"So what?" Anger tinged Yugao's query.

"That's another reason my father wants me to investigate the crime." Reiko was increasingly puzzled by the woman's attitude. "Why were you so eager to confess? Why do you want us to believe you killed your family?"

"Because I did," Yugao said. Her tone and expression implied that Reiko must be stupid not to understand.

Reiko stifled a sigh of frustration and a growing dislike of the ill-natured woman. "All right," she said, "let's suppose for the moment that you stabbed your parents and sister to death. Why did you?"

Sudden fear glinted in Yugao's eyes; she turned away from Reiko. "I don't want to talk about it."

Reiko deduced that whether or not Yugao had killed her family, the motive for the murders lay at the root of her odd behavior. "Why not? Since you've already confessed, what harm is there in explaining yourself?"

"It's none of your business," Yugao said, her profile stony and unrelenting.

"Were there problems between you and your mother and father and sister?" Reiko pressed.

Yugao didn't answer. Reiko waited, knowing that people sometimes talk because they can't bear silence. But Yugao kept quiet, her mouth compressed as though to prevent any words from leaking out.

"Did you quarrel with your family that night?" Reiko asked. "Did they hurt you in some way?"

More silence. Reiko wondered if there was something wrong with Yugao besides a bad attitude. She seemed lucid and intelligent enough, but perhaps she was mentally defective.

"Maybe you don't understand your situation. Let me explain," Reiko said. "Murder is a serious offense. If you're convicted, you'll be put to death. The executioner will cut your head off. That will be the end of you."

Yugao responded with a sidelong glance that deplored Reiko for treating her like an imbecile. "I know that. Everybody does."

"But sometimes there are circumstances that justify killing," Reiko said, although she had difficulty imagining what could justify these murders. "If that's true in your case, you should tell me. Then I can tell the magistrate, and he'll spare your life. It's in your interest to co-operate with me."

Sardonic laughter pealed from Yugao. "I've heard that story before," she said as she faced Reiko. "I've been in Edo Jail for nine days. I listened to the jailers torturing other prisoners. They always said, 'Tell us what we want to know, and we'll set you free.' Some of the poor, stupid idiots believed it and spilled their guts. Then later, I heard the jailers talking and laughing about how they'd been executed."

Yugao tossed her head; the long, oily strands of her hair whipped at Reiko. "Well, I won't fall for your lies. I know that I'll be executed whatever I say."

"I'm not lying," Reiko said urgently. "If you had a good reason for killing your family—or if you help me determine that you didn't do it—you will be set free. I promise."

The disdain on Yugao's face said how much she thought a promise from Reiko was worth. Jail must have taught Yugao harsh lessons she wouldn't be coaxed into forgetting. Still, Reiko persisted: "What have you got to lose by trusting me?"

Yugao only shut her mouth tight and hardened her obstinate gaze. Reiko had often prided herself on her ability to draw information from people, but Yugao wore resistance like the shell of a turtle, hoarding her secrets underneath it. She vexed yet intrigued Reiko.

Switching tactics, Reiko said, "I'm curious about the night of the murders. Were you alone in the house with your family?"

No reply came from Yugao, except a frown as she tried to figure out where Reiko's conversation was going.

"Or was there someone else?" Reiko said. When Yugao still didn't answer, Reiko said, "Did someone else come and stab your family to death?"

"I'm sick of all these questions," Yugao muttered.

"Are you trying to protect whoever it was by taking the blame yourself?" Reiko said. "What really happened that night?"

"What do you care? Why do you keep pestering me?"

Reiko began to explain again, just in case she hadn't made her purpose clear at first: "The magistrate—"

"Oh, yes," Yugao interrupted with a snort. "The magistrate set you on me. And of course you obliged him, because you're a good little daughter who always does whatever Papa says."

Her insulting tone seemed an overreaction to a few simple questions. "I just want to find out the truth about a terrible crime," Reiko said, controlling her temper. "I want to make sure the wrong person isn't punished."

"Oh. I see." Scorn curled Yugao's lip. "You're a spoiled rich lady who's bored with her life. You entertain yourself by poking your nose in other people's business."

"That's not so," Reiko said, stung by this accusation, not the least because there was a smidgen of truth to it. "I'm trying to see that justice is served."

"How noble you are," Yugao mocked. "I suppose it amuses you to toy with a *hinin*. Don't you have anything better to do, you silly, worthless little goose?"

"Don't you speak to me that way! Show some respect!" Reiko ordered, now hot with fury. That an outcast dared to insult her, the wife of the chamberlain! "I'm trying to help you."

"Help me?" Yugao's voice rose with incredulity. "Don't make me laugh. What you really want is for me to tell you something that makes me look guilty. Then the magistrate can sleep easy after he sentences me to death." A snide grimace twisted her lips. "Well, too bad for him. I refuse to go along with you."

Reiko couldn't deny that she was honor-bound to follow her investigation either way it went, and any incriminating information Yugao gave would be used against her. In that case, Magistrate Ueda would condemn her with a clear conscience. Yugao might be deranged, but her logic was sound.

"Whether you believe me or not, I'm your last chance to save your life," Reiko said. "If you're as smart as you think you are, you'll tell me about the night your family was murdered."

"Oh, quit bothering me," Yugao snapped. "Go away."

"Not until you answer my questions." Reiko advanced on Yugao. "What really happened?"

Yugao took a few paces backward. "Why don't you just go home and write poetry or arrange flowers like the rest of your kind?"

"Why did your parents and sister die?" Reiko said.

She backed Yugao against the wall. Their antagonism heated the room as they stared at each other. Yugao's mouth worked while her eyes gleamed with feral mischief. She spat straight into Reiko's face.

Reiko cried out as the gob of saliva hit her cheek. Recoiling from Yugao, she stumbled backward across the room. She wiped her hand across the warm wetness that slithered down her skin. It was as much a defilement as an insult. Such shock, outrage, and disgust filled her that she could only stammer and gasp. Yugao burst into jeering laughter.

"That'll teach you to pester me," she said.

Reiko experienced an overwhelming urge to draw the dagger from under her sleeve and teach Yugao a lesson of her own. Afraid she would kill the woman if they remained together a moment longer, Reiko stormed out the door.

Yugao's taunting voice followed her down the passage: "Yes, run away! Don't ever come near me again!"

The sun descended over the wooded hills west of Edo. Its fading light gilded the tile rooftops spread across the plain below the castle, the river that curved around the city, and the pagodas in the temple district. Wisps of black smoke rose from points scattered across the panorama. In the Nihonbashi merchant quarter, fire brigades comprised of men dressed in leather capes and helmets and equipped with axes raced through the narrow, winding streets on their way to fight blazes set by outlaws as well as caused by common accidents. Shopkeepers were busy dismantling their roadside displays of merchandise and taking them indoors. They closed and locked the shutters that covered their storefronts. Housewives leaned from balconies, calling their children inside. Laborers and craftsmen hurried home. At the gates between neighborhoods, sentries stood armed with clubs and spears. In the wake of the political upheaval, the city shut down early, anticipating the trouble that night often brought.

Three samurai, dressed in plain, drab cotton garments and wicker hats, rode together on horseback through the rapidly emptying quarter. At a distance trailed a peasant pushing a wooden barrow used to transport night soil from the city to the fields. Two more mounted samurai followed the night soil collector. From his position between Detectives Arai and Inoue in the lead, Hirata glanced over his shoulder to make sure the barrow was still in sight. It contained Chief Ejima's body, which he'd smuggled out of Edo Castle, hidden under a false bottom covered by a load of feces and urine from the castle's privies. The guards at the checkpoints hadn't bothered to inspect the malodorous barrow for stolen treasure. Nor had they recognized Detective Ogata, disguised as a night soil collector, who pushed the barrow. The two samurai behind it were also Hirata's detectives, assigned to watch for spies following their party. They'd all left the castle separately, then joined up in town. Such were the precautions necessary for a clandestine trip to Edo Morgue.

Hirata shifted in his saddle, trying in vain to find a comfortable position, as his horse's every footfall jarred him. A part of his mind whispered that he shouldn't have taken on this investigation. He gripped the reins and tried to concentrate on his duty to Sano, but other problems besides pain troubled him. Only six months ago he'd moved boldly through the world, but the world was a dangerous place for a cripple.

Now he and his party entered Kodemmacho, the slum that housed Edo Jail and the morgue within it. Rundown shacks lined streets deserted except for a few wandering beggars and orphans. Hirata heard squabbling voices inside the shacks; they fell silent as his party passed, then resumed. Frightened faces peered at him from doorways. The late afternoon seemed darker here, the dusk hastening. The odors of cesspits, greasy fried fish, and garbage tainted the air.

Hirata's instincts suddenly tingled, warning him of a threat. Up the street, a band of six samurai rounded a corner, their dirty, worn-out clothes and unshaven faces marking them as *rōnin*. They walked with stealthy intent, like a pack of wolves on the prowl. As they spied Hirata's party, their stride quickened to a run toward him. Steel rasped as they drew their swords. Hirata realized that they must be fugitive, low-level troops from Yanagisawa's army. They were upon him so fast that he barely had time to draw his own weapon before one of them grabbed his ankle.

"Get off your horse!" the outlaw shouted.

Two of his comrades assailed Detectives Inoue and Arai, trying to pull them from their mounts. Hirata knew that horses were a valuable commodity to the outlaws, many of whom had lost their own during the battle. They could be used as transportation or sold for cash to buy food and shelter. Hirata lashed his sword at the outlaw, who at the same moment tugged hard on Hirata's ankle. A fireball of pain shot up his leg and tore a yell from him. He went tumbling off his horse. He let go of the sword and flung out his hands to break his fall.

Hirata's body thudded on the dirt. More pain jarred him; he groaned and clutched his leg while a spasm knotted the muscles. The outlaw hooted with derisive laughter. He grabbed the reins of Hirata's horse, which shied and whinnied. Hirata labored to pick up his fallen sword; he clambered to his feet. Detectives Inoue and Arai were still on horseback, fighting the other outlaws, who lunged, struck, retreated, and lunged anew. Steel blades clanged. Hirata swiped at the outlaw who was trying to mount his horse, but his blow lacked speed and force. The outlaw easily parried it. The counterblow knocked Hirata to the ground again. Arai and Inoue leapt from their mounts and rushed to help him, but the other outlaws surrounded them in a storm of blades that they fought fiercely to repel. Hirata swung again at his outlaw, who parried and laughed, still holding his horse by the reins. Overcome, Hirata lay on the dirt and rolled from side to side in a frantic attempt to avoid his tormenter's sword that whizzed and sliced at him.

Detective Ogata, who'd abandoned the night soil cart, came rushing to rescue him, dagger in hand. His two mounted men of the rear guard also galloped to his aid, swords drawn. The outlaws saw they had more opposition than they'd thought, fled down the road, and scattered into the alleys. The detectives gathered around Hirata.

"Are you all right?" Inoue asked anxiously.

Gasping and exhausted, his heart pounding from his close call, Hirata pushed himself upright. "Yes," he said, his voice brusque. "Thank you."

He was mortified that he'd been unable to defend himself—or capture the gang as he should have done. Inoue and Arai held out their hands, offering to help him rise, but he ignored them and struggled to his feet. He avoided his men's gazes, lest he see pity in them. He sheathed his sword and climbed onto his horse.

"Let's go. We've got work to do." He added, "Don't mention this to Chamberlain Sano."

As they resumed their progress, Hirata wondered how he would get through this investigation, or the rest of his life.

6

"How did you fare with Yugao?" Magistrate Ueda asked Reiko.

They were seated in his private office, a sanctuary lined with shelves and cabinets that contained court records. A maid poured them bowls of tea, then withdrew.

"I must say she wasn't very cooperative," Reiko said ruefully. She dabbed her cloth tea napkin against her face. Although she'd washed off Yugao's saliva, she still felt its moist slime on her skin, as though the *hinin* had permanently contaminated it. "In fact, she did her best to make me think the worst of her and discourage me from doing anything that might save her."

Reiko gave her father an edited version of her talk with Yugao. She told him that Yugao had been rude to her, but didn't repeat the insults; nor did she mention how Yugao had spat on her. She felt chagrined because she should have handled the situation better, although she didn't know what she could have done differently. And she didn't want her father to become offended on her behalf and punish Yugao. Despite Yugao's behavior, Reiko still pitied the woman, for Yugao must have suffered much degradation in her life as an outcast, whether she was a murderer or not. Even a *hinin* deserved justice.

"I'll send Yugao back to jail for the time being. What was your overall impression of her character?" Magistrate Ueda said between sips of steaming tea.

"She's quite a nasty, bad-tempered person," Reiko said.

"Do you think she's capable of murder?"

Reiko pondered, then said, "I do. But I wouldn't place much faith in a personal opinion based on one short meeting." Now that her own temper had cooled down, her sense of honor required that she put aside her emotions and conduct a thorough, fair inquiry. And she had too much pride to fail. "I need to do more investigation before I can determine the truth about Yugao." Too many unanswered questions remained. "And since she won't help me, I'll have to look elsewhere."

"Very good." Magistrate Ueda glanced at the window. The sun, fading with the approach of twilight, shone golden through the paper panes. He set down his tea bowl and rose. "I must return to the courtroom. I have three more trials today."

"And I should be going home." Reiko also stood.

Traveling through the city after dark was even more dangerous than usual. At night the outlaws marauded, and prudent citizens stayed indoors. Reiko wondered when she would see Sano and hoped he wouldn't be home too late, for she was eager to tell him about her new investigation.

"Tomorrow, maybe I'll find evidence that someone other than Yugao killed her family," Reiko said. But at this moment, she had to admit she wouldn't mind proving that Yugao was as guilty as she claimed to be.

Although Hirata had been a frequent visitor to Edo Jail during his police days, he hadn't seen the Tokugawa prison for a while. Now, as he and his detectives approached it, he observed that it hadn't improved. The fortress-like structure still loomed above a canal that smelled like sewage; the water murkily reflected the setting sun's orange rays. The high stone walls still wore a coat of moss. The same sullen guards peered from the watch turrets. The same aura of despair hung over the gabled rooftops within. Hirata and his men brought the cart that contained Ejima's corpse across the bridge to the iron-banded gate. There, lanterns burned and a guardhouse sheltered two sentries.

"We want to see Dr. Ito at the morgue," Hirata told them.

They promptly opened the gate. Hirata knew that Sano paid them a generous salary to admit visitors for Dr. Ito, ignore their business in the morgue, and tell no tales. Hirata led his men into the compound, past dingy barracks and the warden's office building that surrounded the dungeon. He knew where the morgue was, but he'd never been inside; most people shunned it in fear of physical and spiritual contamination. Entering a courtyard enclosed by a bamboo fence, he found a low building with scabby plaster walls and a ragged thatched roof. As he and the other men dismounted, he looked through its barred windows.

Its interior was furnished with cabinets and waist-high tables. Three male *eta*—the outcasts who staffed the jail—were washing naked corpses in stone troughs. A man came out the door. He was tall, in his late seventies, with white hair, prominent facial bones, and a shrewd expression; he wore a long, dark blue coat, the traditional uniform of a physician.

"Dr. Ito?" said Hirata.

"Yes?" the doctor said. "To whom do I have the pleasure of speaking?" When Hirata identified himself and his men, Dr. Ito's face relaxed into a smile. "I'm honored to make your acquaintance, Hirata-*san*," he said with a courteous bow. "Your master has spoken highly of you."

"He speaks highly of you, too," Hirata said.

"Is he well?" When assured that Sano was, Dr. Ito said, "I am glad to hear that. It has been over six months since I last saw him."

Hirata detected a wistful note in the doctor's voice. As chamberlain, Sano was so closely watched that he didn't dare associate with a convicted criminal. Hirata knew that Sano missed his friend and observed that the feeling was mutual.

"How may I be of service?" Dr. Ito asked.

"Chamberlain Sano has sent a body he'd like you to examine." Hirata explained about Chief Ejima's death.

"I'm happy to oblige. Where is it?"

Detective Ogata took the lid off the night soil cart. He lifted out the bin of stinking human waste and exposed Ejima, still dressed in his clothes, armor, and helmet, wedged in the hidden compartment. Dr. Ito called two of the *eta* outside to empty the waste bin. He told the third to carry the corpse indoors.

"This is my special assistant. His name is Mura," he introduced the man.

Mura was gray of hair and stern of face. Hirata remembered Sano telling him that Dr. Ito had befriended Mura even though he was an outcast, and Mura performed all the physical work associated with Dr. Ito's examinations. Now Mura laid Ejima's corpse on a table. He positioned lanterns on stands near it. As Hirata, Dr. Ito, and the detectives grouped around the table, the smoky, flickering flames lit their faces and the dead man. Hirata thought they must look as if they were gathered to perform some weird religious ritual. His leg ached, and he hoped he could remain standing for the duration.

"Please undress the body, Mura-*san*," said Dr. Ito.

The *eta* removed Ejima's helmet. The face that appeared was almost boyish, with sleek, unlined skin, although Hirata knew that Ejima had been in his forties. In life he'd worn a habitual sly look that proclaimed secret knowledge; in death, his countenance was blank.

"Can you figure out how he died without cutting him?" Hirata asked Dr. Ito. "I have to return him to Edo Castle. It wouldn't do for people to guess he'd been examined."

"I'll try," Dr. Ito said.

Everyone watched Mura work the armor and robes off the body. So far, there seemed nothing gruesome about the examination. Mura handled Ejima with gentle, respectful care. Soon Ejima lay naked, his torso marked with bloody red hoofprints and gouges where the horses had trampled on him. Dr. Ito donned white cotton mitts to protect himself from bodily excretions and spiritual pollution. He inspected Ejima's head, turning it from side to side. His hands moved, pressing and probing, over the torso.

"I feel broken ribs and ruptured internal organs," he told Hirata.

"But did I understand you to say that the witnesses saw Ejima collapse in the saddle?"

"Yes," Hirata said.

"Then he was probably dead before he fell, and these injuries are not what killed him," Dr. Ito said. "Mura-*san,* please turn the body."

Mura rolled Ejima onto his stomach. A dark stain had spread across his back. "The blood has pooled," Dr. Ito explained, then carefully examined Ejima's scalp. "There are no injuries here. The helmet protected his head." Circling the table, he pored over the body; he told Mura to turn it again, then continued his scrutiny. He shook his head and frowned.

"Can't you tell what caused his death?" Disappointment filled Hirata at the thought of returning to Sano empty-handed.

Dr. Ito suddenly halted near the right side of Ejima's head. He stooped, his gaze intent. An expression of surprise and heightened interest came over his face.

"What is it?" Hirata said.

"Observe this mark." Dr. Ito pointed to a hollow in the facial bones between the eye and the ear.

Hirata leaned close. He saw a small, bluish, oval spot, barely visible, on Ejima's skin. "It looks like a bruise."

"Correct," said Dr. Ito. "But it's not from the injuries at the track. This bruise is more than a day old."

"Then it must have nothing to do with his death," Hirata said, feeling let down. "Besides, a little bruise like that never hurt anybody."

But Dr. Ito ignored Hirata's words. "Mura-*san,* please fetch me a magnifying lens."

The *eta* went to a cabinet and brought a round, flat piece of glass mounted in a black lacquer frame with a handle. Dr. Ito peered closely through it at the bruise, then gave Hirata a look. Enlarged, the bruise showed an intricate pattern of parallel lines and whorls. Hirata frowned in disbelief.

"It's a fingerprint," he said. "Someone must have pressed against Ejima's skin hard enough to bruise it. But I've never seen such fine detail in a bruise. What's the meaning of this?"

As Dr. Ito contemplated the strange bruise, wonderment shone in his eyes. "In all my thirty years as a physician, I've never personally seen this, but the phenomenon is described in the medical texts. It sometimes appears on victims of *dim-mak*."

"The touch of death?" Hirata saw his own amazement reflected on his men's faces. The atmosphere in the room chilled and darkened.

"Yes," Dr. Ito said. "The ancient martial arts technique of delivering a single tap that is so light that the victim might not even feel it but is nonetheless fatal. It was invented some four centuries ago."

"The force of the touch determines when death occurs," Hirata recalled from samurai lore.

"A harder tap kills the victim immediately," Dr. Ito clarified. "A lighter one can delay his death for as long as two days. He can seem in perfect health, then suddenly drop dead. And there will be no sign of why, except an extremely clear fingerprint where his killer touched him."

"But *dim-mak* is so rare," said Detective Arai. "I've never heard of anyone using it—or killed by it—in my lifetime."

"Neither have I," said Detective Inoue. "I don't know of anyone in Edo who's capable."

"Remember that anyone who is would not publicize the fact," Dr. Ito said. "The ancients who developed the art of *dim-mak* feared that it would be used against them, or for other evil purposes. Hence, they passed down their knowledge to only a few favored, trusted students. The techniques have been a closely guarded secret, kept by a handful of men whose possession of it is known only among themselves."

"Doesn't it take an expert martial artist to master the techniques?" Hirata asked.

"More than that," Dr. Ito said. "The successful practitioner of *dim-mak* must not only learn to concentrate his mental and spiritual energy and channel it through his hand into his victim; extensive knowledge of anatomy is required to target the vulnerable points on the body. The points are generally the same as those used by physicians during acupuncture. The energy pathways that convey healing impulses through the body can also convey destructive forces."

He touched the bruise with his gloved hand. "This bruise is located on a junction along a pathway that connects vital organs." He continued, "The need for anatomical knowledge explains why the practitioners study medicine as well as the mystic martial arts."

"Do you really think Ejima died of murder by *dim-mak*?" Hirata said, skeptical though intrigued.

"In the absence of any other symptoms besides the bruise, where the killer's energy entered the body, it is probable," Dr. Ito said.

Hirata expelled his breath, awed by the import of Dr. Ito's finding. "Chamberlain Sano will be interested to hear this."

"We should not be too hasty to inform him," Dr. Ito cautioned. "The bruise isn't definitive proof. If my theory is wrong, it could misdirect Chamberlain Sano's inquiries. Before I can pronounce the cause of death, it should be confirmed."

"Very well," Hirata said. "How do we do that?"

Dr. Ito's expression turned grave. "I must dissect the head and look inside."

A serious dilemma faced Hirata. He needed to tell Sano exactly how Ejima had died and establish beyond doubt that the death had resulted from foul play, but mutilating the corpse was a big risk. Hirata and Sano both had enemies who were waiting and watching eagerly for them to make a mistake. Should anyone notice signs of an illegal autopsy on a corpse from a case under their investigation, their enemies might get wind of it. Yet Hirata couldn't fail in his duty to Sano. Casting about for a solution to his problem, Hirata found one that he thought would work.

"Go ahead," he told Dr. Ito. "I'll take the responsibility. But please do as little damage as you can."

Dr. Ito nodded, then said, "Proceed, Mura-*san*."

Mura fetched a razor, a sharp, thin knife, and a steel saw. He trimmed and shaved Ejima's hair in a narrow band from ear to ear across the back of the scalp, then made a cut that circled the head just above the eyebrows. He peeled back the flesh, exposing the moist, bloody skull, then began sawing the bone. The rasp of the saw grated loud in the silence that fell over his audience. Hirata watched, fascinated and repelled.

In his lifetime he'd seen all kinds of gory spectacles—men's faces cleaved in half and their bellies slit wide open during swordfights, their heads lopped off by the executioner, blood and innards spilled. Yet this methodical butchery disturbed him. It transformed a human into a piece of meat. It seemed the ultimate disrespect for life. Hirata began to understand why foreign science was outlawed, to protect society and its values, at the cost of advancing knowledge.

Now Mura finished cutting the skull all the way around and through the bone. He took hold of Ejima's head and worked the top free, as though removing a tight lid from a jar. He inserted the knife blade into the skull and scraped the tissue that held its cap in place. Hirata watched Mura lift off the skullcap. Blood oozed out, red and viscous, thickened with clots. It bathed the grayish, coiled mass of the brain, glistened wetly in the lantern light, and soiled the table.

"Here is our proof," Dr. Ito said with satisfaction as he pointed to the blood. "When a death-touch is struck, its energy travels along the internal pathway that connects the point of contact to a vital organ. Ejima's murderer targeted his brain. The touch on his head caused a small rupture to a vessel inside his brain, which gradually leaked blood and enlarged until it burst and killed him."

"And he had no other injuries that could have caused the bleeding?" Hirata said.

"Correct," said Dr. Ito. "*Dim-mak* was the cause of death."

Hirata nodded, but he felt as much apprehension as relief that they knew how Ejima had died. "We'll go back to Edo Castle and report the news to Chamberlain Sano," he told the detectives.

"What about the body?" Inoue said. He glanced at Ejima's corpse, which lay with its brain exposed, the skullcap beside it on the bloody table.

"It goes with us." Hirata turned to Dr. Ito. "Please have your assistant put Ejima's head back together, wrap a bandage around it, clean him up, and dress him."

This was only the beginning of the effort to cover up the examination.

7

When Sano finished inspecting the racetrack and questioning the witnesses there, he and Marume and Fukida interviewed the
sentries and patrol guards who'd been in the vicinity at the time of
Ejima's death. By the time they returned to his estate, night had fallen.
Sano was glad to see that the crowd of people outside his gate and in
his anteroom had disappeared—they'd given up on seeing him today.
But when he stopped at his office to see what had happened during his
absence, his aides besieged him with urgent queries and problems.
Sano found himself sucked back into the whirlwind of his life, until a
servant brought him two messages: Lord Matsudaira demanded to
know what was taking him so long, and Hirata had arrived.

Sano went to his audience chamber and found Hirata kneeling on
the floor. He was shocked to see how ill Hirata looked. Fresh guilt
needled Sano.

"Would you like some refreshment?" Sano said. He regretted that
the usual courtesy due any guest was all he could offer Hirata; apology
or sympathy would only hurt Hirata's pride.

"No, thank you, I've already eaten." Hirata tacitly denied his obvious discomfort while reciting the polite formula.

"Well, I haven't, and I insist that you join me," Sano said, although
time was short. He summoned a maid and told her, "Bring us dinner,

and put some healing herbs in the tea. I've got a headache." He didn't, but perhaps the medicine would make Hirata feel better. After the maid departed, Sano said, "What did Dr. Ito find out?"

As Hirata told him, astonishment filled Sano. "Ejima was killed by *dim-mak*? Is Dr. Ito certain?"

Hirata described the fingerprint-shaped bruise, the dissection, and the blood in the brain.

"Well, I suppose there's a first time for everything," Sano said. "And Dr. Ito's news jibes with what I've learned. All the witnesses say Ejima dropped dead for no apparent reason. The guards who were watching him through spyglasses during the race didn't see anything hit him. No one fired a gun anywhere near the track; no bullet was found. Ejima wasn't killed by any conventional means." Sano felt trepidation as well as excitement. "We now know that Ejima was murdered, and how it was done. But this seriously complicates the case."

Hirata nodded. "It means that the racetrack isn't necessarily the crime scene. The death-touch could have been delivered to Ejima hours or days before it took effect."

"And the suspects aren't limited to the people who were around the track when Ejima died," Sano said.

He and Hirata sat in silence, listening to the temple bells ringing and dogs barking in the night, the wind rising and insects singing in the garden. Sano said, "The killer is out there." He anticipated the thrill of the hunt, but also an unprecedented challenge in the shape of an adversary who was far more skilled at martial arts than himself. "And we have no idea who he might be."

The maid brought them a dinner of rice balls, sashimi, and pickled vegetables. Sano noticed that Hirata hardly touched the food, but he gulped the tea and seemed to revive a bit. "We have two problems that are more immediate than catching the killer," Sano said. "First, how are we going to hide the fact that Ejima's body was dissected?"

"I've already taken care of that," Hirata said. "I had Dr. Ito's assistant wrap up its head. Then I took it home and had my servants dress it in a white silk robe and lay it in a coffin filled with incense. When I delivered it to Ejima's family, I told them that I'd prepared it for the funeral. The reason I gave was that I wanted to spare them the sight of Ejima's terrible wounds. I also said I would pay for a grand funeral. I gave the family a quick look at Ejima, then sealed up the coffin. They were so grateful that I don't think they'll open it for a closer look."

"Well done," Sano said, impressed by Hirata's ingenuity. "But I'll pay for the funeral." That was a small price for keeping the examination a secret.

"What's the second problem? How to tell Lord Matsudaira that Ejima was murdered by *dim-mak* without saying how we found out?" Hirata said.

Sano nodded as he set aside his chopsticks. "But I have a solution. I'll tell you on the way to the palace."

A waxing crescent moon adorned the indigo sky over the peaked tile roofs of the palace. Flames glimmered in stone lanterns around the complex of half-timbered buildings and along the white gravel paths that crossed its lush, still gardens. Frogs sang in ponds while gunshots echoed from night target practice at the martial arts training ground. Patrolling guards wore Lord Matsudaira's crest, asserting his place in the heart of the Tokugawa regime.

When Sano, Hirata, and detectives Marume and Fukida arrived in search of Lord Matsudaira, the sentries at the palace door directed them to the shogun's private quarters. There they found a party in progress. Handsome boys dressed in gaudy silk robes played the samisen, flute, and drum; others danced. The shogun lolled on cushions while more boys chattered around him and plied him with wine. His taste for young males was public knowledge. That he preferred them to his wife and concubines explained why he'd failed to produce a blood heir. Near the shogun sat Lord Matsudaira and two members of the Council of Elders, which comprised the shogun's chief advisors and the regime's principal governing body. Lord Matsudaira knelt with his arms folded and his expression grim: He disapproved of such frivolous entertainment. The elders sipped wine and nodded their heads in time to the music.

"Well?" Lord Matsudaira said eagerly as Sano and his companions approached, knelt, and bowed. "Was it murder?"

"It was," Sano said.

The elders frowned in concern. The shogun dragged his attention away from the dancers and regarded Sano with befuddlement. His face was flushed from the wine; his hand fondled the knee of the boy seated beside him.

This was Yoritomo, the shogun's current favorite. He was a youthful, strikingly beautiful likeness of his father, the former chamberlain. Although Lord Matsudaira had exiled Yanagisawa and his family, Yoritomo remained in Edo because the shogun had insisted on keeping him. He had Tokugawa blood—from his mother, a relative of the shogun—and rumor said he was heir apparent to the dictatorship. The shogun's fondness protected Yoritomo from Lord Matsudaira, who wanted to eliminate everyone connected to his rival. Yoritomo smiled shyly; his large, liquid black eyes, so like his father's, glowed with happiness at seeing Sano.

"So I was right." Gratification swelled Lord Matsudaira's countenance. "I knew it."

"Who are you talking about?" the shogun said.

"Ejima, chief of the *metsuke*." Lord Matsudaira barely hid his impatience. "He died this morning."

"Ahh, yes," the shogun said with an air of dim recollection.

"I thought Ejima took a fall at the racetrack," said one of the elders. He was Kato Kinhide, who had a broad, leathery face with slit-like eyes and mouth. The other was Ihara Eigoro. They'd opposed Lord Matsudaira and supported Yanagisawa during the faction war. They, and some of their allies, had survived the purge by latching onto Yoritomo, who was alone at court and depended on his father's friends for protection. But Sano knew that the protection worked both ways: Yoritomo's influence with the shogun protected Kato, Ihara, and their clique from Lord Matsudaira. He was their foothold in the regime, the promise of another chance at gaining control over it.

"The fall didn't kill Ejima," Sano said.

"Then what did?" Ihara said. Short and hunched, he had a vaguely simian cast. He and Kato resented Sano because he'd declined to take their side during the faction war, and now worked closely with Lord Matsudaira. They envied him for rising above them in rank.

"Ejima was a victim of *dim-mak*," answered Sano.

"The death-touch?" Lord Matsudaira stared in amazement, as did the elders and Yoritomo. The shogun merely looked confused. The music and dancing continued while the boys joked and laughed together.

"That's difficult to believe," Kato said, always ready to deride Sano and raise doubts about his judgment. "*Dim-mak* is a lost art."

"What evidence do you have?" Ihara said.

"When Ejima's body was prepared for the funeral, a bruise was observed on his head. It had the shape and markings of a fingerprint." This was the story Sano had invented to cover up the illegal dissection. "According to the martial arts literature, this is a sure sign of the death-touch."

"Books are hardly adequate confirmation," Kato scoffed.

"One can find something in them to support any argument whatsoever," Ihara said, backing up his comrade.

Sano understood why they were so anxious to dispute that Ejima's death was murder. "Nonetheless, I stand by my opinion. But let us defer to His Excellency to settle the issue."

The shogun looked pleased to be consulted, yet daunted. He turned to Lord Matsudaira.

"Chamberlain Sano is the expert on crime," Lord Matsudaira said. "If he says it was *dim-mak,* that should suffice."

Sano also understood that Lord Matsudaira was so eager to confirm that Ejima was murdered that he would accept an unusual method whether or not he believed in it.

"Well, ahh, then so be it," the shogun said, clearly glad that Lord Matsudaira had spared him the need to think. "The, ahh, official cause of the death is as Chamberlain Sano says."

Lord Matsudaira nodded in approval. Kato and Ihara tried to hide their displeasure, and Sano his relief that his ploy had worked and the

Check Out Receipt

Saline District Library
734-429-5450
http://salinelibrary.org

Saturday, September 24, 2016 2:03:30 PM

Title: Four : A Divergent collection
Call no.: Teen Rot v.4 c.4
Due: 10/22/2016

Title: Girl on the run
Call no.: Teen Mye
Due: 10/22/2016

Title: The assassin's touch
Call no.: Mystery Row
Due: 10/22/2016

Total items: 3

****
You can now pay your library fines
online at http://salinelibrary.org

autopsy remained a secret. He wondered how long his luck would hold.

Yoritomo flashed a congratulatory smile at Sano. During the past six months they'd become friends, despite the fact that Sano had once been Yoritomo's father's enemy. Sano had taken pity on Yoritomo, and had found him to be a decent, thoughtful young man who deserved better than a life as the shogun's sexual plaything and a pawn of his father's cronies, especially since his status as heir to the regime was by no means certain. That Yanagisawa had produced such a fine son amazed Sano, who had acquired yet another responsibility—as mentor to his former enemy's child.

"What about the three other recent deaths?" Lord Matsudaira asked Sano. "Were they also caused by *dim-mak?*"

Kato interrupted, "Do you mean the supervisor of court ceremony, the highway commissioner, and the treasury minister?"

"I do," said Lord Matsudaira.

"All those deaths can't possibly be murder," Ihara protested.

Sano observed Ihara and Kato growing nervous at the turn the discussion had taken.

"We'll see about that," Lord Matsudaira said in an ominous tone. "Chamberlain Sano?"

"Whether Supervisor Ono, Commissioner Sasamura, or Treasury Minister Moriwaki were murdered hasn't been determined yet." Sano earned a grunt of disappointment from Lord Matsudaira, and relieved looks from the elders.

"I'll investigate their deaths tomorrow," Hirata spoke up.

"At least someone recognizes the need to investigate before jumping to conclusions," Kato said under his breath.

Lord Matsudaira asked Sano, "Have you any idea who killed Ejima?"

"Not yet. Tomorrow I'll begin looking for suspects."

"Maybe you needn't look very far." Lord Matsudaira fixed an insinuating gaze on the elders.

They tried to hide their consternation. "Even if you believe that someone in this day and age has mastered the technique of *dim-mak,* you can't think it's anyone in the regime," Ihara said. Sano knew that he and Kato had feared all along that Lord Matsudaira would accuse them of killing his officials in order to undermine him.

"Anyone who doesn't have the skill or the nerve to commit murder could have hired an assassin who does," Lord Matsudaira said.

"The same goes for anyone who accuses others," Kato retorted. "Some men are not above committing crimes in order to strike at their enemies."

Lord Matsudaira's gaze turned wary because Kato had fired his accusation back at him.

"Maybe we should examine Chamberlain Sano's own motive for designating the deaths as murders and conducting an investigation." Ihara eyed Sano.

The shogun frowned in baffled annoyance as he divided his attention among the music, the dancing, and the conversation. Yoritomo looked unhappy because Sano had come under attack. Sano knew that Kato and Ihara feared his friendship with Yoritomo, which undermined their own influence over the young man. Without Yoritomo, and his connection with the shogun, they would be exposed targets for Lord Matsudaira. Better for them to strike at Sano even though he'd tried to make peace with them.

"My sole aim is to discover the truth," Sano said.

"The truth as it suits you and Lord Matsudaira," Kato said with a grimace of disdain, then addressed the shogun: "Your Excellency, the murders—if such they are—should be investigated by someone who has no personal stake in the outcome and can be objective. I propose to lead a committee to get to the real truth of the matter."

"You have at least as much at stake as anyone else," Lord Matsudaira said scornfully.

"A committee is a fine idea," said Ihara. "I'll be on it."

Sano wondered if they wanted to take over the investigation because they feared that he would expose them as murderers, or try to frame them if they weren't guilty. Sano couldn't let them sweep one crime, and possibly four, under the *tatami,* or frame Lord Matsudaira and take him down in the process. It was time to pull rank.

"I'm glad to hear that you're so willing to investigate Chief Ejima's murder," Sano said to Kato and Ihara. "I always welcome such dedication from my subordinates." The elders were technically subordinate to him, even though their age and seniority gave them special standing. "If I need your help, I'll ask for it. Until then, you will restrict your role to advising His Excellency in your usual capacity."

Rage at this putdown clenched Kato's and Ihara's jaws, but they couldn't openly defy a direct order.

"You've always been satisfied with Chamberlain Sano's service," Lord Matsudaira told the shogun. "He's the man best qualified to investigate. Let him continue."

"Well, ahh, that sounds like a good idea," said the shogun. Disagreements bothered him, and he spoke with a timid desire to have this one settled.

"Just because Sano has succeeded in the past doesn't mean he's guaranteed not to fail you now, Your Excellency," Kato said with an urgency born of panic.

"This case is too serious for him to handle alone, no matter his expertise," Ihara added.

Sano sensed them thinking that if Lord Matsudaira had his way, and they were implicated in the deaths of four high Tokugawa officials, they would be executed for treason. Not even their connection to Yoritomo would save them.

"Enough of all this advice!" the shogun suddenly exclaimed. Perhaps he sensed the undercurrents in the conversation, Sano thought; perhaps he felt a need to assert his authority. "I shall decide who investigates the murder of, ahh—" He fluttered his hands in confusion. "Whoever those people were. Everyone just be quiet and let me think!"

The musicians ceased playing; the dancers froze in mid-step; the boys' chatter faded. An uncomfortable hush descended upon the room. Lord Matsudaira's face was stern with displeasure at losing control over the situation. The elders sat as still as if in deep meditation, willing the shogun to favor them. The shogun fidgeted with self-doubt and his dread of making a mistake. Sano saw his fate teetering on his lord's whim. The murder investigation now involved much more than the quest for a killer. Sano's own survival was at risk.

Yoritomo leaned close to the shogun and whispered in his ear. Sano frowned, as startled as Lord Matsudaira, the elders, Hirata, and the detectives looked. The shogun raised his eyebrows while he listened to Yoritomo; he nodded.

"I've made my decision," he said, confident now. "I will allow Chamberlain Sano to investigate the murder and apprehend the killer."

Relief, but also misgivings, filled Sano. Hirata and the detectives nodded at him in approval. Lord Matsudaira's face expressed a mixture of gratification at getting his way and vexation that his former rival's son had such influence over the shogun. The elders tried to hide their disgruntlement. Yoritomo beamed at Sano.

"That's enough of this, ahh, serious talk," the shogun told Sano, his companions, Lord Matsudaira, and the elders. "You're all dismissed. Keep me informed on the, ahh, progress of the investigation." He gestured at the musicians, dancers, and other boys. "Let the party resume."

In the corridor outside the shogun's private chambers, Lord Matsudaira and the elders marched past Sano. "I trust that you'll solve this case to my satisfaction," Lord Matsudaira said. His tone emphasized their comradeship, yet hinted at dire consequences for Sano if he failed.

The elders bowed to Sano. Their courtesy said they feared he would incriminate them; the hostility in their eyes said this wouldn't be the last time they opposed him as long as he was allied with Lord Matsudaira.

"You would do well to remember how you got where you are," Kato said. Sano had been appointed chamberlain because his independent spirit had made him the one man that Lord Matsudaira and the remnants of Yanagisawa's faction could agree upon. Kato was telling

Sano that they'd helped put him in power and they could cut him down if he caused trouble for them.

Yoritomo emerged from the doorway. Ihara said to him, "Are you coming with us?"

"No. I'll see you later." Yoritomo halted beside Sano.

Disapproval colored the elders' faces. "Don't forget who your real friends are," Ihara said.

The elders departed in a huff. Sano and Yoritomo walked down the corridor together. Hirata and the detectives trailed them. Sano said, "I must thank you for putting in a word for me with the shogun."

Yoritomo blushed with pleasure at Sano's gratitude. "After all you've done for me, it was the least I could do," he said.

He looked so happy, so eager for approval, that Sano hated to say what he must. "But you shouldn't have interfered. You can't afford to upset Kato or Ihara for my sake. That was foolish. Never do it again."

"Please forgive me. I guess I wasn't thinking." Yoritomo hung his head, mortified by Sano's criticism. "I only wanted to help you."

"Helping me is not your duty," Sano said gently but firmly. That the father had once done everything possible to ruin him, and the son risked his own safety to protect him! "And you should stay out of politics. They can be deadly."

"Yes . . . I understand what you mean."

Yoritomo's chastened tone said he'd caught Sano's allusion to his banished father. Sano knew that although Yoritomo adored and missed his father, he hadn't been blind to Yanagisawa's faults. As they stopped at the door that led out of the palace, Yoritomo gazed earnestly at Sano.

"But if you ever need me to do anything for you . . ." Yoritomo's eyes shone with the love and hero-worship that he'd transferred from his absent father to Sano. "Just ask me."

His devotion made Sano uncomfortable even as it moved him. All he'd done to win it was spend a little time chatting with the boy over a drink or on a walk through the castle now and then. But this was more kindness than anyone else had paid him without expecting anything in return. "Well, let's hope that won't be necessary."

Yoritomo went back to the shogun's party. Sano and his retinue headed through the dark, winding passages of Edo Castle toward his compound. He looked forward to telling Reiko about his new case, and he felt a sharp nostalgia for the days when they'd investigated crimes together. This wouldn't be just like old times. Everything had changed.

"Watch, Mama, watch!"

Masahiro pranced along the corridor in the private quarters of the chamberlain's compound. The floor emitted loud squeaks where his little feet trod. Reiko strolled after him, wincing at the noise. One of her son's favorite pastimes was playing with the nightingale floor, designed to give warning that an intruder was in the house. When Sano and Reiko had moved into Yanagisawa's former residence, they'd discovered that it was riddled with nightingale floors. And soon Masahiro had memorized all the places they squeaked.

"Look, Mama!" he cried. As he backtracked down the passage, the floor made not a sound.

"Very good." Reiko smiled, proud that he'd also memorized the places where one could tread silently. She thought him very clever for a boy not quite three years old. "Now it's time to get ready for bed."

After they'd bathed together, while she was tucking him in bed, Sano came and joined them. "You're home early," she said. "I'm glad to see you."

Sano looked tired yet alert. "I'm glad to see you, too."

Masahiro jumped into Sano's arms. Sano tossed him into the air. They laughed and played tag around the room.

"Please don't excite him," Reiko said. "He'll never go to sleep."

"But I hardly ever see him," Sano said regretfully, as he held their son on his lap and Masahiro chattered happily. "I want to be a good father, but every day just slips by without a chance. I want to teach Masahiro about life, martial arts, and the Way of the Warrior, like my father did me." Sano's father had operated a martial arts school in which Sano had spent most of his childhood. "But time is going to be even tighter than usual."

After much fuss, Reiko and Sano finally settled Masahiro in his bed. They went to their chamber, where Reiko poured sake for them.

"The chief of the *metsuke* has been murdered," Sano said. "Lord Matsudaira has ordered me to investigate."

As he explained the particulars of the crime, and the dangers involved, and the consequences of not solving it, Reiko felt as much excitement as alarm. Sano said, "This murder case has the potential to fan the flames of political conflict into another war. Lord Matsudaira is vulnerable because his officials are under attack. I'm once again caught between the two factions."

He had farther to fall nowadays, but Reiko knew he'd never failed to solve a case in the past, and a murder investigation was something they could share, unlike the administrative work that usually occupied him. "It sounds like a most fascinating case," she said. "Is there anything I can do to help?" Working on his case as well as her own would keep her very busy, but having too much to do was far better than not enough.

"Maybe later." Sano drank his sake, then said, "What did you do today?"

Reiko noted how quickly he'd changed the subject; she felt the distance that had grown between them. Why didn't he want to discuss the case any further? He sounded almost as if he didn't want her involved. But they'd been partners in detection during nearly four years of marriage. Reiko decided to take Sano's words at face value and assume that he would let her help if she could.

"I have a new case of my own," she said.

As she told him about Yugao, the trial, and her father's request,

Sano looked as much troubled as interested. "This woman Yugao is a *hinin*?"

"Yes. That's why the police didn't really investigate the murder of her family and she didn't get a fair trial."

"And you're going to look for evidence that may prove she's innocent despite the fact that she confessed?"

Reiko was puzzled by the note of disapproval she heard in Sano's voice. "Yes."

Chin in hand, Sano said, "I don't know if this is such a good idea."

"Why not?" Reiko asked in surprise. She'd thought Sano would be glad she had something as worthwhile to do as defending a downtrodden member of society.

He spoke with reluctance. "Our situation has changed since I was *sōsakan-sama*. I'm much more closely watched than I was then. So is my family. We're all held to a higher standard of behavior nowadays. Things we used to do won't go unnoticed anymore. The consequences of associating with the wrong people are the same, but the risk is far greater."

"Are you saying that I shouldn't associate with Yugao because she's an outcast and it will reflect badly on you?" Reiko could hardly believe what she was hearing.

"For you to befriend and assist her goes against the taboo that bans contact between *hinin* and ordinary citizens," Sano said. "And for my wife to defy the ban will give the impression that I don't respect the customs that govern society. But that's only part of the problem."

Reiko stared at him in open-mouthed amazement. Was this her husband talking? Sano had never used to care so much about public opinion. He certainly wouldn't have put it ahead of justice. She began to understand why he didn't want her involved in his investigation.

"The main problem is that your father has asked you to interfere with the justice system," Sano went on. "I have much respect for him, but he's pushing the limits of his authority by ignoring the evidence against Yugao—as well as her confession—and asking his daughter to investigate the murders."

"I guess I hadn't thought of it in that light." Reiko had been focused on helping her father, preventing a possible miscarriage of justice, and her own desire for detective work. Although Sano had a good point, she protested: "But the murders should be investigated. There's no one else to do it, and I have experience with matters of this sort."

"I know you do." Sano's tone was placating, reasonable. "But you have no official standing. And in spite of that fact, the magistrate clearly intends for the results of your investigation to override those of the police." He shook his head. "This is bending the law. I can't condone it. I can't afford to look as if I favor outcasts and let off self-admitted criminals."

"Are you telling me I should drop my investigation?" Reiko was aghast, but not just because she realized that his position was insecure enough that his wife's behavior could be used against him.

"I'm hoping you'll understand why you should drop it voluntarily," Sano said.

Reiko sat silent until she marshaled her thoughts. "I understand that your enemies are looking for any weapon to destroy you. I understand that it could be me."

In the combat zone of politics, even such a minor fault as a wife who flouted tradition was a serious liability for an official. She didn't want to jeopardize Sano's position and risk bringing disgrace on him and their family, but neither did she want to give up her investigation. Moreover, she was disturbed by the change in Sano, who once might have eagerly taken up Yugao's cause himself.

"But a woman's life is at stake, and there are enough unanswered questions to raise doubts about her guilt. Don't you think it's important to find out what really happened the night her family was murdered?" Reiko hated to think Sano had altered so much that he didn't. "Do you not care anymore about making sure that the real culprit is punished?"

"Of course I do," Sano said, annoyed and impatient.

Pursuing the truth and serving justice were cornerstones of his honor, as critical in his mind to Bushido as courage, duty to his master, and skill in the martial arts. Certainly he was observing his principles in his current case. But Reiko's words gave him pause. Had six months as chamberlain made him care more for politics and position than for honor? Did he follow his path through the Way of the Warrior only when orders from above gave him permission? The idea dismayed Sano.

"Then do you think that Yugao should die for a crime that she might not have committed because she's a *hinin* and therefore doesn't deserve fair treatment?" Reiko said.

"Her social status has nothing to do with my doubts about the wisdom of your investigation. As far as I'm concerned, she's as entitled to justice as any other citizen." Yet Sano heard his tone grow defensive; he wondered if this personal belief he claimed still held true. Had his higher rank made the people far below him seem not worth any inconvenience to himself? "But I don't have as much room to operate outside the law as I used to."

"You have much more power than you did before," Reiko reminded him. "Shouldn't you use it to do good?"

"Of course." Sano hadn't forgotten that was his goal as chamberlain. "But it's debatable whether giving Yugao a second chance qualifies as doing good. She sounds guilty to me, and if she is, an investigation would only delay justice. And the trouble with power is that it can corrupt those who believe they're doing what's right as well as those who try to do evil."

The specter of Yanagisawa haunted the mansion in which he'd once lived and Sano and Reiko now sat. Now Sano had Yanagisawa's same position of influence and faced the same temptations.

"Power makes men think they're above the law, free to act as they please," Sano said. "Things I do might seem good at the time—but they may have bad consequences I never expected. In the end, I may have done more harm than good. I'll have abused my power and disgraced my honor."

And I'll become Yanagisawa, who schemed, embezzled, slandered, and killed to advance his own interests. Then one day I'll be shipped off to the same island of exile.

Appalled enlightenment dawned on Reiko's face as she read his thoughts. "But you would never be as bad as that. And the case of Yugao is just one small though important matter. It could hardly ruin your political career—or your honor. I think you're blowing it out of proportion."

She might be right, but Sano didn't like to be wrong; nor did he want to back down. He felt vexed at Reiko for challenging him and raising issues about himself that were uncomfortable to face. He followed the impulse to take the offensive.

"Now that we've discussed my reasons for not wanting you involved with Yugao, I'd like to know why you're so eager to take on this investigation," he said. "Has your sympathy for her prejudiced you in her favor? If so, this won't be the first time that's happened."

Reiko's eyes widened. He was alluding to the Black Lotus Temple case, when she'd tried to help another young woman accused of murder. They seldom discussed it because it had almost ruined their marriage, and was still a sensitive issue. "I have no particular sympathy for Yugao. If you had seen how hostile she was to me, you would know that I have every reason to want to prove she's guilty."

Sano nodded, although unconvinced. "But I must ask you to reconsider taking on this new case."

Reiko was silent, her expression conflicted. Sano sensed how much she wanted to conduct this investigation; he saw her trying not to be angry at him. At last she said, "If you forbid me, I will honor your wishes."

Now Sano had a dilemma. If he gave in because he loved Reiko, wanted her to be happy, and stood by his principles, he would jeopardize his position, and woe betide them should something go wrong. The threat of death had constantly haunted Sano since he'd joined the *bakufu,* but now he had even worse to fear. He looked toward the room where Masahiro lay asleep. As his son grew, Sano became more aware of his role as a father and how much his son's fate depended on him. The son of a disgraced official would face a bleak future.

Yet if he forbade Reiko, he would be turning his back on honor and proving himself a coward. Caught between fire and plague, he erred on the side of honor, as he always had.

"I won't forbid you," he said. "Go ahead with your investigation if you insist. But be careful. Try not to attract attention or do anything that could hurt us."

Reiko smiled. "I will. I promise to be discreet. Thank you."

Sano saw that she was glad he'd given her his permission, if not his blessing; he could also tell she wasn't surprised by his decision. Somehow she'd maneuvered him into a position where he couldn't say no without compromising himself. He felt a grudging yet fond admiration for her cleverness. Reiko could certainly handle him better than he could her. But tonight had shown him that he needed someone to help him stay true to his ideals, and he was glad he could count on Reiko.

"How do you propose to begin your investigation?" he said.

"I thought that tomorrow I would examine the place where Yugao's parents and sister were murdered, then talk to people who knew the family," Reiko said. "Maybe I can turn up evidence that will prove whether she's innocent or guilty."

"That sounds like a good approach." Sano hoped he wouldn't come to regret his decision.

"What's the next step in your investigation?" Reiko sparkled with vivacity, as she always did when looking forward to an adventure.

"I need to reconstruct the murder of Chief Ejima." Sano mused. "Your investigation is ahead of mine in some respects. At least you have a primary suspect, and you know where the crime occurred. My first task is to find the actual crime scene where the death-touch was delivered to Ejima. Maybe then I can learn who did it."

9

Sano rose the next morning before the sun ascended over the hills east of Edo and the night guards went off duty at the castle. Before he resumed investigating the murder, he ate a hasty meal in his office while his staff briefed him on news dispatches from the provinces. The anteroom was already crowded with officials, but today he couldn't let his daily routine steal all his time; he couldn't shuffle paper while a killer was at large and the balance of power depended on him. It was high time to close his open door.

He dismissed his staff and told his principal aide, "I'm going out."

"People are waiting to see you, Honorable Chamberlain," the aide politely reminded Sano. He was a clever, capable, honest man named Kozawa, of scholarly appearance and deferential manner. "And here is more correspondence for you to read and answer." Kozawa indicated an open chest full of scrolls that had materialized beside Sano's desk.

There was no time like the present to start anew. Sano took a deep breath, then said, "Sort out everything and everybody. Save the important matters for me. Handle the minor ones yourself."

"Yes, Honorable Chamberlain," Kozawa said, taking the order in stride.

"I want any case of sudden death among the *bakufu* officials reported to me, directly and at once," Sano said. If there was another murder in a plot against Lord Matsudaira, he wanted to know as soon as possible. "The body is not to be touched. No one leaves or enters the scene of death before I arrive."

"As you wish, Honorable Chamberlain. Where can I reach you if need be?"

"I'll be at Chief Ejima's estate for a while," Sano said. "After that, I don't know."

As Sano left his office, Detectives Marume and Fukida and his other attendants fell into step with him. He fought the feeling that he'd just let go the reins and disaster lay ahead whether he solved the murder case or not.

Chief Ejima's estate in the Hibiya administrative district was large and imposing, as suited his high rank. A two-story mansion enclosed by a high wall dwarfed other nearby houses; the gate had double portals and two tiers of roofs. When Sano arrived there with his entourage, he found that a strange vacuum surrounded the estate. Officials, clerks, and soldiers thronged the streets of the district, but the ones outside Ejima's house were deserted, as if everybody was shunning the place in which the master lay recently dead, avoiding contamination by the evil spirits. Sano and his men stopped at the gate as servants hung mourning drapery over it. The black cloth flapped in the breeze; funereal incense smoke tainted the bright spring day.

Detective Marume addressed the two guards in the booth; "The honorable chamberlain wants to speak with your master's family. Take us to them."

One advantage Sano enjoyed as chamberlain was that his rank commanded instant respect and unquestioning obedience. The guards quickly summoned servants who escorted Sano, Marume, Fukida, and the rest of their party into the house. They removed their shoes and swords in the entryway, then walked down a corridor that smelled of incense smoke that drifted from the reception room. As Sano approached this, he heard voices inside. Through a lattice-and-paper partition he saw the glow of lanterns and the blurry shadows of two human figures.

"You have no claim to his estate," said a man's voice, raised in anger.

"Oh, yes, I do," shrilled a defiant female voice. "I was his wife."

"*His wife.*" The male voice dripped scorn. "You're nothing but a whore who took advantage of a lonely man."

A shriek of laughter came from the woman. "I'm not the only one who took advantage of my husband. You're just a poor relation that he adopted as his son. He never would have if you hadn't played up to him so that you could get your hands on his money."

"Be that as it may, I am his legal son and heir. I control his fortune now."

"But he promised me a share of it," the woman said, her anger now tinged with desperation.

"Too bad for you that he never wrote his promise into his will. I don't have to give you a single copper. It's all mine," the man said triumphantly.

"You filthy bastard!"

The servant who'd escorted Sano into the house knocked on the door frame and called in a polite voice, "Excuse me, but you have visitors."

The man cursed under his breath. His shadow moved close to the partition. He slid the door open, revealing himself as a thickset young samurai in his late twenties. He gaped at Sano.

"Honorable Chamberlain," he said. "What—why—?"

Chief Ejima's adopted son had thick eyebrows and a low, heavy forehead that gave him a primitive appearance despite the black silk ceremonial robes he wore. He was obviously upset to realize that Sano had overheard the quarrel.

"Forgive me for the intrusion," Sano said, "but I must talk to you about your father's death."

The woman appeared beside the son. She was near his age—and perhaps two decades younger than her husband had been. Glossy black hair hung in a plait over her shoulder. She had pretty features sharpened by cunning. She wore a modest but expensive gray satin kimono.

"Of course. A thousand apologies for my poor manners," said the son, bowing to Sano. "My name is Ejima Jozan."

Lady Ejima also bowed. Her tilted black eyes sparked with wariness as they regarded Sano.

"Please come in." Apparently mystified as to the reason for this visit from the shogun's second-in-command, Jozan backed into the room to let Sano and his men enter.

The room's shutters were closed against the sunshine. The sealed oblong wooden coffin lay on a dais. Smoking incense burners adorned a table that also held a vase of Chinese anise branches, offerings of food, and a sword to avert evil spirits. Jozan and Lady Ejima had been quarreling over Ejima's estate while holding a vigil over his corpse, like scavengers fighting over carrion.

"My condolences on your loss," Sano said.

Jozan thanked him. Lady Ejima said, "May I offer you some refreshments?"

Her manner was more forward than usual for a high-ranking woman. Sano recalled hearing that Ejima had married a courtesan from the Yoshiwara pleasure quarter. After Sano had politely declined her offer, he said, "Are there any family members in this house besides the two of you?"

"No," Jozan said. "The others live away from Edo."

"I'm sorry to say that I have bad news," Sano said. "Ejima-san's death was murder."

A gasp of surprise issued from Lady Ejima. "But I thought he was killed in an accident during a horse race."

Jozan shook his head, dazed. "What happened?"

"He was a killed by a death-touch. Someone has apparently mastered the ancient martial arts technique and used it on your father." Sano watched the widow and adopted son. Lady Ejima's pretty face took on a frozen, opaque look. Jozan blinked. Sano wondered if they were upset or thinking how the murder would affect them.

"Who was it?" Jozan said. "Who killed my father?"

"That's yet to be determined," Sano said. "I'm investigating Ejima-san's murder and I need your cooperation."

"I'm at your service." Jozan made an expansive gesture, as though glad to give Sano anything he asked.

"I, too, will do whatever I can to help find my husband's murderer," said Lady Ejima.

Jozan's features crumpled. He averted his face, hiding it behind his sleeve. "Please forgive me," he said as a sob choked him. "My poor father's death was enough of a shock, but now this! It's a terrible tragedy."

Lady Ejima seized Jozan's arm and yanked it away from his face. "You hypocrite! What do you care how he died, as long as you inherit his money?"

"Shut up! Get away from me!" Jozan flung the woman off him and turned to Sano, obviously aghast that the chamberlain of Japan should hear him accused of such lack of filial devotion. "Please pay no attention to her. She's hysterical."

Sano observed that Jozan's eyes were devoid of tears and black with fury at Lady Ejima.

"My dearest, darling husband, gone forever!" she wailed. "I loved him so much. How shall I live without him?"

Jozan scowled at her. "You're the hypocrite. You pretended to love my father, but you only married him because of his rank and wealth."

"That's not true!" Lady Ejima shouted. "You were always jealous because I came between you and him. Now you're trying to slander me!"

Sano reflected that the culprit in a murder case was often to be found within the victim's family. Jozan and Lady Ejima seemed unlikely to know the technique of *dim-mak,* but a past case involving a murder in the imperial capital had taught Sano that martial arts skills came in unexpected-looking packages.

"That's enough out of you," Jozan said, his patience snapped. "Leave the room."

"You don't give the orders around here," Lady Ejima huffed. "I'll stay. Any business regarding my husband is my concern."

"Actually, I want you both to stay," Sano said.

Lady Ejima gave Jozan a smug, vindicated smile. He hissed air out his mouth, flung her a look that promised she would be sorry later for insulting him, and turned, shamefaced, to Sano. "A thousand apologies for our disgraceful behavior," he said. "We meant you no offense. How can we help you?"

"I need to know who was with Ejima and every place that he went during the past two days," Sano said. "Can you reconstruct his movements for me?"

"Yes," Jozan said. "I served as his secretary. I kept his schedule."

"Let's start with the time before the horse race."

"My father and I had breakfast together, then worked on reports and correspondence in his office here at home."

"How did he spend the previous night?" Sano asked.

Lady Ejima answered: "He was with me. In our bedchamber."

"The whole night?"

"Well, no. He came home very late."

"We went to a banquet at the chief judicial councilor's estate," Jozan said.

Sano saw the scope of his investigation expand to include many people besides Ejima's family and the horse race crowd. "And before that?"

"We spent the day at *metsuke* headquarters." This was a complex of offices in the palace. "My father had meetings with subordinates and appointments with visitors."

More questioning revealed that Ejima had spent the previous night with his wife and the evening at another banquet.

"In the afternoon, we went into town so that my father could meet with informants," Jozan continued. "It wouldn't do for them to come here or to headquarters."

Sano understood why they wanted to keep their role as informants a secret: They were *bakufu* underlings hired to report on their superiors, who would punish them harshly for spying. "Where did these meetings take place?"

"At six different teahouses in Nihonbashi."

The investigation now expanded across even more territory, to include countless potential suspects. "I need the locations of those teahouses," Sano said. "Also the names of everyone that Ejima saw."

"Certainly."

Jozan fetched his record book. Sano skimmed the neatly written characters. Jozan had recorded the names of the fifteen banquet guests, the twenty men who had meetings and appointments with his father, and Ejima's informants.

"Did you see any of these people touch your father here?" Sano tapped a finger against his head where the fingerprint bruise had appeared on Ejima.

"No. But I wasn't watching him every moment. I suppose they could have. And these appointments were private." Jozan pointed to the names of three men Ejima had seen at *metsuke* headquarters and of all the informants. "He talked to them alone, while I stayed outside his office and the teahouses."

"Who else besides the people listed in this book was around your father during the past two days?" Sano said.

Jozan visibly quailed at the prospect of trying to recollect. "His staff. Servants and guards, here and in the palace. People at the teahouses."

And the crowds in the city streets, Sano thought. "Write down everybody you can remember. Send me the list."

"Certainly," Jozan said, daunted but game.

Sano addressed Lady Ejima: "Can you think of anyone else who could have touched your husband?" She shook her head. Sano didn't fail to note that she and Jozan had spent time alone with Ejima and had had the best opportunity to touch him. "Did any of the people Ejima saw have any reason to want him dead?" Sano asked them both.

Jozan's expression turned dubious; he clearly didn't want to accuse important officials. "Not that I know of."

"I want the *metsuke* records on everyone who's been executed, demoted, exiled, or otherwise harmed as a result of investigations by Ejima since he became chief. Get them to my office today."

Jozan hesitated; the *metsuke* was loath to turn over confidential documents, share secrets, and diminish their unique power. But he couldn't refuse an order from the shogun's second-in-command. "Certainly."

And Sano thought him smart enough to realize he was a suspect and it would behoove him to cast suspicion elsewhere. Sano foresaw much tedious work investigating people who'd had contact with Ejima or grudges against him. Fortunately, he could delegate much of it.

"I must borrow your records," he told Jozan, who nodded. Upon taking a second look at them, he recognized many names. One jumped out at him: Captain Nakai, a soldier in the Tokugawa army. Nakai had fought for Lord Matsudaira during the faction war. Sano recalled that he was a star martial artist who'd distinguished himself by killing forty-eight enemy troops. And he'd had a private appointment with Ejima.

Outside on the street, after thanking Jozan and Lady Ejima for their cooperation, Sano said to his detectives, "The officials who were at the banquet all live here in Hibiya or inside the castle. I'll drop in on them, then go to *metsuke* headquarters to talk to Ejima's subordinates. Marume-*san* and Fukida-*san,* you'll come with me. In the meantime—" He handed the record book to another aide, a young samurai named Tachibana, also a former detective. "You and the others round up these men who had private appointments with Ejima and send them to my estate." Another advantage to being chamberlain was that almost everybody's presence was Sano's to command. He would save the informants for later. "Make Captain Nakai your top priority."

"Yes, Honorable Chamberlain," Tachibana said, eager to prove his worth.

As Sano rode off with Marume and Fukida, he felt elated that his investigation was making progress. Maybe he could solve the case and appease Lord Matsudaira and the opposition before war broke out. But he wondered uneasily whether Hirata would hold up long enough to investigate previous murders. And Sano wondered what Reiko was doing.

10

The *hinin* settlement where Yugao and her family had lived was a slum that infested the bank of the Kanda River, northwest of Edo Castle. Tents made of tattered cloth and bamboo poles, inhabited by recent arrivals, surrounded a village of hovels built from scrap wood. A wasteland occupied by a vast garbage dump separated the settlement from a rundown neighborhood of houses and shops on the outskirts of Edo proper. Smoke rose from within the settlement, darkening the sky and sun. A procession that consisted of four samurai, a palanquin, and its bearers halted near the dump.

Reiko climbed out of the palanquin. As she looked around, her face flinched at the stink of the garbage heaps where buzzing flies swarmed and children, rats, and stray dogs foraged. But curiosity stirred within her. She'd seen *hinin* settlements but never been in one; polite custom kept ladies of her class out of them as strictly as the law divided the outcasts from the rest of society. Eager to explore and learn whatever she could here about Yugao and the murders, Reiko started across the weedy, muddy ground toward the settlement. She gathered her plain gray cotton cloak around her. She wore straw sandals instead of her usual clogs made of lacquered wood. Her hair was done in a simple knot with no ornaments, her face adorned with minimal powder and rouge. Her guards wore swords and armor tunics, but no crests to signify who their master was. Reiko intended their mission to be as covert as possible, thus keeping her promise to Sano.

Voices raucous with laughter and argument resounded from the tents as Reiko neared the settlement. Outcasts, mainly men, loitered around campfires where rotting fish sizzled in rancid grease. Five of the men hastened toward Reiko's party. They wore tattered short kimonos and leggings, with clubs and daggers at their waists. They had shaggy hair, grime ingrained in their skin, and hostile faces.

"What do you want?" one of the men said to Reiko's guards. His arms were covered with tattoos, the mark of gangsters. He and his companions blocked the path.

"Greetings," Reiko's chief escort said politely. He was Lieutenant Asukai, a tough young samurai who would have ordinarily told these ruffians to step aside, and dispersed them by force if necessary. But Reiko had ordered him and the others to be discreet. "My master's lady wants to talk to a few people here."

The tattooed man scowled. "Sure, and I'm His Excellency the shogun. You samurai come here to pick on us *hinin*. You think you can kill us just because the law lets you get away with it." Reiko realized that this must be a common problem for the outcasts. "Well, not today." He and his men drew their daggers. Other outcasts emerged from the tents, brandishing clubs, spears. "Get lost."

"Wait." Lieutenant Asukai raised his hands in a placating gesture while his comrades clustered protectively around Reiko. "We're not here to make trouble. We just want to talk." His manner was calm, but although he and his comrades were trained, expert fighters and the outcasts were unskilled thugs, they were outnumbered. Reiko felt a pang of fear. She'd been caught in fights before, and she didn't want to repeat the experience.

"I said, get lost." The tattooed leader spoke with the brazen air of a man who was angry at the world and hadn't much to lose. "Go, or die."

The other outcasts echoed him with savage, enthusiastic roars. They didn't wait to see if Reiko and her guards would leave, but quickly surrounded them. Blades pointed toward Reiko; clubs rose to strike; faces avid for a fight stared down her guards. Metal rasped as the guards drew their swords. People hurried from the dump and the settlement to watch. Dismay filled Reiko because her investigation had barely begun, and already she'd landed in trouble.

A loud, authoritative male voice demanded, "What's going on here?"

The outcasts turned toward the settlement. Their circle loosened, and Reiko saw a man, followed by two others, striding toward her. Perhaps forty years of age, he had surly yet handsome features shadowed by whisker stubble; he carried a spear upraised in his fist. His kimono, trousers, and surcoat had the same grimy look as the other outcasts' clothing, but were made of silk. His hair was combed and oiled into a neat topknot. He had the noble bearing of a samurai, even though his crown wasn't shaved and he wore no swords. His men resembled the other outcasts; they were clearly commoners. He halted and panned his dark gaze over the crowd.

"We're just trying to get rid of these trespassers before they hurt somebody," said the tattooed ruffian.

The man studied Reiko's party with suspicion. "I'm Kanai Juzaemon, the headman of this village." Everyone in society was regimented and every neighborhood had its appointed official, no less the *hinin* settlement. His two names identified Kanai as a member of the warrior class. "Who are you?"

Lieutenant Asukai muttered to Reiko, "Maybe we'd better tell the truth."

Reiko didn't see much other choice. "I'm the daughter of the magistrate," she said. But at least she could hide her connection with Chamberlain Sano. "My name is Reiko. We're here because my father asked me to investigate the murder of the family of a woman named Yugao."

The headman looked at her as if surprised that she'd spoken for herself as well as by what she'd said. He signaled the outcasts to lower their weapons; they obeyed. As Reiko wondered how a samurai had become their leader, he said, "Would your father be Magistrate Ueda?"

"Yes," Reiko said, cautious because she heard distrust in his voice.

"Magistrate Ueda demoted me to *hinin* status. He did the same to many people here."

Unfriendly echoes of agreement arose from the crowd. Reiko regretted mentioning her father, whose name was unlikely to win her favor among the outcasts. Her guards braced for an attack.

"But the magistrate's word is the law," Kanai said with fatalistic gloom. "I suppose that means we have to accommodate his daughter." He waved his spear at the crowd. "Go about your business."

The ruffians and spectators slunk away. Relief overwhelmed Reiko. Her guards let out their breath while they sheathed their swords.

"What exactly does she want to do?" the headman asked Lieutenant Asukai.

"You'll have to ask her."

Kanai looked increasingly baffled by the unconventional circumstance of a magistrate's daughter investigating a crime. He turned his quizzical gaze on Reiko.

"First I'd like to see the place were the murders happened," Reiko said.

"Suit yourself." The headman shrugged, perplexed yet resigned. "But I'd better take you. It should be obvious by now that you're not especially welcome here."

He led the way into the settlement. Two of Reiko's guards preceded her and the others; the headman's comrades brought up the rear. As they wove between the tents, the occupants stared at them with sullen curiosity. Some followed Reiko and her party; soon she had a long entourage. So much for a discreet investigation; Reiko could only hope that news of her doings wouldn't reach anyone in a position to hurt Sano.

The ground under her feet was trampled flat and hard, its surface muddy and slick from water spilled by women washing laundry or cleaning fish. The foul odor of human waste and stagnant cesspools sickened Reiko. There was obviously no night soil collection here. Bonfires burned garbage that hadn't made its way to the dump; there was no trash collection here, either. Reiko felt filth wetting her socks and hem. How could these people bear living in such squalor?

Her party reached the hovels. Each tiny structure was a patchwork of boards scavenged from burned buildings and construction sites, barely high enough for a man to stand up inside. Their windows were holes covered with dirty paper, their roofs composed of thatch or cracked, broken tiles. Voices argued; a baby squalled. Reiko ducked under ragged clothes strung on lines between the hovels. She and her escorts squeezed past men playing cards in the narrow lanes. They stepped over a drunk who lay unconscious. At one hovel, a man counted coins into the hand of a slovenly woman.

The vices flourished here.

Smoke darkened the atmosphere like a perpetual twilight. The stench was concentrated, as if the outside air couldn't penetrate. The fact that her father had sentenced people to this life made Reiko uncomfortable even if they'd deserved the punishment.

"Here it is," Kanai said, stopping outside a hovel. Two features distinguished it from the others—a lean-to built on one side, and a sprinkling of white salt crystals at the threshold, to purify a place where death had occurred. "There's not much to see, but look all you want." He held back the faded indigo cloth hung over the doorway.

While the outcasts avidly watched, Reiko stepped inside. Murky daylight filtered through two windows. The sweet, metallic, and foul odors of rotting blood and flesh tainted the air. Reiko's throat closed; nausea gripped her stomach. On the floor she saw dark patches where blood and viscera had been wiped up but had sunk into the packed earth. The hovel had one room plus an alcove formed by the lean-to; the whole space was smaller than her bedchamber at home. She could hardly believe that four people had lived here. It was empty except for a ceramic hearth in a corner.

Kanai spoke from the door: "The neighbors looted everything that wasn't too heavy to move—dishes, clothes, bedding. People here are so poor, they don't mind robbing the dead."

Reiko saw that she wouldn't find any evidence here. But although she felt the pollution of death seeping into her, and she was desperate to breathe pure air, she stayed, hoping to absorb clues from the crime scene. On one wall were jagged notches cut with a knife. Reiko counted thirty-eight, perhaps scores from card games. She sensed lingering emotions—rage, terror, despair.

"Pardon my curiosity," Kanai said, "but why did the magistrate send you to investigate the murders?"

"I have some experience with such things." Reiko forbore to mention her work for Sano.

The headman frowned in disbelief; women didn't ordinarily investigate crimes. Then he shrugged, too indifferent to press for an explanation. "But isn't the case already solved? Yugao has been arrested."

"The magistrate and I both have doubts about whether she killed her family."

"Well, I don't," Kanai declared. "As far as I'm concerned, Yugao is guilty."

"Why is that?"

"I was here that night. I discovered the murders. I caught Yugao."

Reiko had planned to search for the first witness at the scene after the murders; now luck had saved her the work. "Tell me what happened."

The headman's expression said he didn't understand why she wouldn't just accept his word as truth instead of bothering herself with *hinin* business, but again he shrugged. "My assistants and I were patrolling the settlement. Constant vigilance is the only way to keep order." Reiko noted his upper-class diction. "We heard screams coming from this area."

Reiko pictured him and his men carrying torches through the dark settlement, the bonfires burning and the residents brawling in the night; she heard women screaming.

"By the time we reached this house, the screams had stopped. The man was lying there." Kanai pointed at a blood-soaked patch on the floor. "I think he died first. He was in bed. His wife lay there, and his younger daughter there." Reiko followed his pointing finger to two other spots, across the room, where the floor was stained reddish-brown. "They'd been chased. You can see the bloody footprints."

Reiko also saw blood spattered on the plank walls and envisioned two terrified women running while a blade slashed them.

"All the victims had been stabbed many times all over their bodies. They had cuts on their hands because they'd tried to defend themselves." Kanai entered the hovel, stood in the center. "Yugao was sitting here, surrounded by the corpses. There was blood smeared on her face. Her clothes were drenched with it. She was holding the bloody knife." He shook his head. "I've seen murders before—they're not exactly rare here—but this one shocked me. I said to Yugao, 'Merciful gods, what happened?' " Emotion colored his dispassionate tone. "She looked up at me, perfectly calm, and said, 'I killed them.' Well, that seemed obvious. So I turned her over to the police."

He'd confirmed what the *doshin* had said at Yugao's trial. His description of that night brought it to vivid life for Reiko, who felt more inclined than ever to believe that Yugao was as guilty as she said. Yet Reiko couldn't conclude her investigation based on the testimony of a witness who'd arrived at the scene after the murders were done.

"When you came here that night, did you see anyone around besides Yugao?" Reiko asked.

"Only some folks who'd come out of their houses to see what the commotion was."

Reiko must later determine whether the neighbors had noticed anyone near the house before the murders, or fleeing it afterward. "How well did you know the family?"

"Well enough. They'd been here more than two years. They had about six more months left of their sentence."

"What can you tell me about them?"

"The man's name was Taruya. He once owned an entertainment hall in Ryōgoku. He was a wealthy, important merchant, but when he became a *hinin,* he got a job as an executioner at Edo Jail." That was one of the lowly occupations assigned to the outcasts. "His wife O-aki and Yugao earned a little money by sewing. The younger daughter, Umeko, sold herself to men." The headman pointed at the alcove. "That's where she serviced them."

"I need to know why Yugao killed her family, if she did," Reiko said.

"She didn't tell me, but she didn't get along with them particularly well. They quarreled a lot. Neighbors were always complaining about the noise. Of course that's nothing unusual here. If there's one thing I've learned in my seven years in this hell, it's that when people are miserable and cooped up together, fights are bound to break out. Some little thing probably tipped Yugao over the edge."

Here Reiko saw a chance to answer at least one question. "Why did Yugao and her family become outcasts?"

"Her father committed incest with Yugao."

Reiko knew that incest with a female relative was one of the crimes for which a man could be demoted to *hinin,* but she was nonetheless shocked. She'd heard gossip about men who satisfied their carnal lust on their daughters, but couldn't understand how a father could do such a perverted, disgusting thing. "If Yugao's father was the criminal, what were Yugao and her mother and sister doing here?"

"They were three helpless women without any money to their own names. They depended on Taruya to support them. They had to move here with him or starve to death."

Which meant that the whole family—including Yugao—had shared his punishment. That seemed unfair, but Tokugawa law often punished a criminal's family for his transgression. Reiko's heartbeat quickened because she spied a possible motive for at least one of the murders. Had Yugao felt so soiled and shamed by the incest that she'd come to hate the father that tradition commanded her to respect and love? Had her hot temper ignited into murderous rage that night?

Reiko gazed around the hovel. Her imagination populated the room with a man and three women seated at their evening meal. The faces of Yugao's father, her mother, and the sister were indistinct; only Yugao's features were in clear focus. Reiko heard their angry voices rise in a quarrel fostered by living in crowded conditions, not having enough to eat, and their mutual disgrace. She envisioned them hurling blows, dishes, and curses at one another. And perhaps the crime that had condemned them to their fate hadn't stopped. Reiko

imagined the hovel in the dark of that night. She saw two shadowy figures, Yugao and her father, in a bed superimposed over the largest
blood-stained patch on the floor.

*He pins her down, his hand held over her face to muffle her cries as he
thrusts himself against her. Nearby, her mother and sister lie asleep in their
beds. After the illicit coupling is done, the father rolls off Yugao and falls
asleep, while she seethes with ire. This night's indignity has been one too
many. Yugao has had enough.*

*She rises, fetches a knife, and plunges it into her father's chest. He awakens,
howling in pain and surprise. He tries to seize the knife from her, but she slashes
his hands and stabs him again and again. His cries rouse Yugao's mother and
sister. Horrified, they grab Yugao and pull her away from her father, but too
late—he is dead. Yugao is so frenzied that she goes mad. She turns the knife on
her mother and sister. She chases them, slashing and stabbing, while they scream
in terror. Their feet leave bloody prints on the floor, until they fall lifeless.*

*Yugao surveys her work. Her thirst for vengeance is satisfied; her frenzy
turns to unnatural serenity. She sits down, the knife in her hands, and waits for
whatever will come.*

The headman's voice interrupted Reiko's thoughts. "Have you seen
enough?"

The vision faded; Reiko blinked. She now had a plausible theory of
why, and how, the murders happened, but it was mere speculation.
She needed more evidence to support it before she told her father that
Yugao was guilty and he should sentence her to death.

"I've seen enough here," she said. "Now I must talk to the family's
neighbors." Maybe they'd seen something Kanai hadn't. Had someone
else entered the hovel and committed the murders? Had Yugao been
an intended victim? That would leave questions as to why she'd
survived—and confessed—but Reiko still sensed that there was more
to the crime than she'd learned. "Will you guide me around the settlement and introduce me?"

Kanai gave her a look of forbearance. "Whatever you want, but I
think you're wasting your time."

Reiko's curiosity about the *hinin* extended to this man who'd become her willing, albeit skeptical, assistant. "May I ask how you became a *hinin*?"

His face darkened with emotion; he turned away from her. "When I was young, I fell in love. She was a maid at a teahouse." He spoke as though each word flayed him with a whip. "I was a samurai from a proud, ancient family." Yet a hint of a smile said he took pleasure from wounding himself. "We wanted to marry, but we belonged to different worlds. We decided that if we couldn't live together, we would die together. One night we went out to the Ryōgoku Bridge. We tied ourselves together with rope. We pledged eternal love. Then we jumped."

This was an old story, the subject of many Kabuki plays. Suicide pacts were popular among illicit lovers. Reiko said, "But you're—"

"Still alive," Kanai said. "When we fell in the river, she drowned almost at once. She gave up her life easily. But I—" He drew a wavering breath. "It was as if my body had a will of its own, and it didn't want to die. As the current swept us away, I struggled until the ropes that tied me to her came loose. I swam to a dock. A police officer found me there. Her body washed up downstream the next day. And I was made an outcast."

That was the standard punishment for survivors of love suicide pacts. As Reiko studied his bleak posture, she realized that Kanai still mourned his beloved. "I'm sorry. Maybe if I put in a good word for you with my father, he'll pardon you."

"Thanks, but don't bother," Kanai said, his expression morose as he faced her. "My sentence was one year. I can leave any time I want. I choose to stay."

"Why?" Reiko couldn't believe that anyone would voluntarily live here.

"I was too much a coward to die. What kind of poor excuse for a samurai does that make me?" Kanai's tone was scathing. "She's dead. I'm alive. Staying here is my punishment."

With a visible effort he donned his usual, indifferent attitude. "But you didn't come here to listen to my pitiful story. Come with me—

I'll introduce you to Yugao's neighbors." As they exited the hovel, he said, "There's one lesson you can learn from my example, that you should keep in mind while you investigate these murders: Some people accused of crimes truly are guilty."

11

Cannons and gunshots blasted around Hirata. He stood alone on a battlefield, his body clothed in armor, his sword in his hand. Amid clouds of smoke and mist, shadowy figures engaged in fierce combat. Their cries rang above the blare of conch trumpets and the thunder of war drums. A soldier on horseback galloped through the mist, his lance aimed at Hirata. Hirata dodged and swung his sword. It cut the soldier across the belly. The soldier dropped from his mount, spurting blood. A swordsman charged Hirata from the rear. Hirata whirled; his blade lashed open the man's throat. More soldiers assailed Hirata. He slew them with effortless grace. His blade seemed an extension of his will to win. Exhilaration filled him.

Suddenly the battle sounds faded; the armies dissolved in the mist. Hirata awakened to find himself lying in bed, his wounded leg throbbing. The war-cries became the chatter of servants in his estate; the gunfire emanated from the Edo Castle shooting range. Morning sunlight from the window stabbed his eyes. His head ached and his stomach was sour—after-effects of his sleeping potion. Every night he dreamed that he was whole and strong; every morning he awakened to the nightmare of his true existence. But he stoically heaved himself out of bed. He had important work to do, and he'd already slept too long.

"Midori!" he called.

After she helped him dress and coaxed him to eat some rice gruel and fish, he went into his office and sent for his detectives. He assigned men to take charge of ongoing investigations, dismissed them, and told Arai and Inoue to stay.

"Today we'll investigate the previous deaths that Lord Matsudaira thinks were murders," he said.

"That would be Ono Shinnosuke, the supervisor of court ceremony, Highway Commissioner Sasamura Tomoya, and Treasury Minister Moriwaki?" said Arai.

Hirata nodded. "We'll try to find out whether they were victims of *dim-mak*. If so, we'll look for suspects."

"Where do we start?" said Inoue.

"At their homes. That's where Ono and Sasamura died."

All three men had lived in estates in the Hibiya administrative district. Hirata hoped he wouldn't have to travel any farther. The pain was especially severe this morning, due to yesterday's exertions. Maybe he could connect the previous deaths to Chief Ejima's and uncover some leads before his strength gave out. He tucked a vial of opium under his sash in case he should need relief.

Two hours later, he and the detectives walked out the gate of Treasury Minister Moriwaki's residence. They mounted their horses while clerks, officials in palanquins, and foot-soldiers streamed past them in the street.

"Another dead end," Inoue said regretfully.

"It's too bad that no one here, or at the court supervisor's or the highway commissioner's estates, noticed a fingerprint-shaped bruise on any of the victims," Arai said.

Hirata had questioned the men's families, retainers, and servants, to no avail. Because the bodies had been cremated, they couldn't be examined. "Moriwaki's wife did tell us some interesting facts about what happened after he died," Hirata remarked.

"But we've learned nothing to prove that Ono and Sasamura didn't die natural deaths in their sleep," said Inoue.

"Maybe Ejima's murder was an isolated incident and there's no conspiracy against Lord Matsudaira," Arai said.

"In which case, this list of people that the men saw during the two days before they died won't do us much good because there's no reason why the name of Ejima's killer would appear on it." Hirata tucked the scroll in his saddlebag. He felt sick and weak, as well as frustrated.

"What do we do now?" Inoue said.

Hirata didn't want to give up and return empty-handed to Sano. "Treasury Minister Moriwaki's case is different from the other two. He wasn't found dead in bed at home. And our list of his contacts and places he went is incomplete." Moriwaki's former secretary had said that the treasury minister had been an eccentric, secretive man who'd liked to arrange his own appointments and go off by himself. "Maybe if we trace his movements, we'll turn up some evidence that he was murdered, and some clues as to who killed Chief Ejima as well as him."

Even though the stiffness in Hirata's leg had eased somewhat, he spoke with as much reluctance to take another journey as anticipation of success: "The one place we know for sure that Moriwaki went is the bathhouse where he died. We'll go there."

The journey took Hirata to the Nihonbashi merchant district. The canals that traversed the neighborhoods brimmed with spring rain. Into them, willows trailed their boughs like girls washing their hair. Plum trees blossomed in pots outside doorways and on balconies. Hirata and his men rode past a funeral procession of lantern-bearers; priests ringing bells, beating drums, and chanting prayers; and white-robed mourners who accompanied a coffin decorated with flowers. Funerals were a disturbingly common sight since the war.

The bathhouse was located in a half-timbered building with a gleaming tile roof. It occupied an entire block in a neighborhood composed of stately houses near shops that sold expensive art objects. Clean indigo curtains, printed with the white symbol for "hot water," hung over the entrance. Pretty maids dressed in neat kimonos stood there to welcome customers. When Hirata and his detectives dismounted outside, servants hurried to tend their horses. He deduced that the place catered to folk who were wealthy enough to have bath chambers at home but came here for other reasons besides washing themselves.

A samurai strode out the door. He was tall, with a muscular build and arrogant bearing; he wore opulent silk robes, a fancy armor tunic, and two elaborate swords. Two samurai attendants followed him. As he caught sight of Hirata, a sneer appeared on his handsome, angular face.

"Well, if it isn't the *sōsakan-sama,*" he said.

Hirata bristled at the man's insulting tone. "Greetings, Police Commissioner Hoshina."

The police commissioner had been the lover of Yanagisawa, and a staunch ally of his faction, until a bitter quarrel had split them up. Hoshina had then taken revenge by joining Lord Matsudaira and thus kept his position at the head of the police force. He was a longtime enemy of Sano, and their bad blood extended to Hirata.

"I'm surprised to see you. The last I heard, you were on your deathbed." Hoshina's insolent gaze raked Hirata. "I think you got up a little too soon."

Hirata found it humiliating to stand withered and frail before his strong, healthy adversary. "I'm just as surprised to see you," he retorted. "The last I heard, you and Lord Matsudaira were like this." He held up two crossed fingers. "Why aren't you with him? Have you fallen out of his favor?"

Hoshina's jaw tightened, and Hirata was gratified to see that he'd hit the mark. "What are you doing here?" Hoshina said, then raised his palms. "Don't tell me: You've come to investigate the death of Treasury Minister Moriwaki. Chamberlain Sano is too important to do it himself, so he sent his faithful dog."

"I bet you're here for the same reason." Hirata controlled his temper with difficulty. As Hoshina nodded, Hirata recalled the facts that the treasury minister's wife had told him. "But didn't you already investigate his death? Didn't you arrest somebody who was executed for murdering him?"

Sullen silence was Hoshina's reply. His attendants looked abashed for his sake.

"Then Chief Ejima died," Hirata went on. "Now it appears that he may have been murdered by the same person who killed the treasury minister and you made a mistake."

"So what if I did?" Hoshina said, flustered and defensive. "Anyone else might have done the same."

"But you were the unlucky one. That's why you're in disgrace with Lord Matsudaira. The instant he heard that Ejima was dead and realized he'd just lost another high official, he knew you'd botched the investigation and he threw you out of his inner circle. My condolences." Hirata pitied Hoshina not at all. "Now, if you'll excuse me, I'm going to do a proper investigation of Treasury Minister Moriwaki's death."

He and his detectives started toward the bathhouse door, but Hoshina blocked their way. "You're wasting your time," Hoshina said. "I've already reexamined the scene of death."

"What, are you trying to correct your mistake by going over the same ground where you slipped up?" Hirata said.

Hoshina scowled. "There's nothing to see in there," he insisted, which convinced Hirata that the bathhouse contained important clues. Hirata and his men kept walking. Hoshina followed them into the bathhouse. Inside a vestibule, a woman dressed in a gray and white floral kimono knelt on a platform. Racks on the walls contained towels and cloth bags of rice-bran soap.

"Good day, masters," she said, bowing to Hirata and the detectives. She looked to be in her fifties, stooped and slight, her hair dyed an unnatural shade of black, her face heavily powdered and rouged. But her eyes were bright, her features still pretty. When she saw Hoshina, her smile faded. "Back again so soon? Haven't you caused enough trouble here already?"

She was the type of older woman who spoke her mind, even to male social superiors, who were probably intimidated because she reminded them of their strict mothers or childhood nursemaids. Now, as Hoshina glowered, she said to Hirata, "Welcome to my establishment. You and your men can undress in there." She pointed to an adjacent room behind a curtain, where dressing gowns hung on hooks, clothes were folded into compartments on the wall, and shoes stood on racks.

"Thank you, but we don't want a bath." Hirata introduced himself, then said, "We're here to investigate the death of one of your customers—Treasury Minister Moriwaki."

The proprietress flicked her shrewd gaze from Hirata to Hoshina. "I'm glad somebody else has taken charge. How may I help you?"

"You can show me where the treasury minister died."

"Come right this way." Stepping off the platform, she smiled at Hirata and cut her eyes at Hoshina.

Hirata and his men followed her through a curtained doorway and along a corridor. Steamy air and splashing noises issued from chambers divided by lattice-and-paper partitions. Each contained a large, square sunken tub surrounded by a raised floor made of wooden slats. Naked men soaked in the tubs or crouched beside them. Female attendants scrubbed backs, poured buckets of water over the men, or sat naked beside them in the tubs. Some of the doors were closed; from these issued giggles and moans. Hirata knew that bathhouse prostitution was illegal but common, and the proprietress surely must pay the police to let her operate outside the law.

She opened a partition. "This is it." The tub was empty, the floor dry. She stepped inside and opened the bamboo blinds. Dust motes glistened in the sunshine. "We haven't used this room since Moriwaki-*san* died. None of the girls will work in here. They think it's haunted by his ghost."

"Were you on the premises when he died?" Hirata asked.

"Yes. I told *him* what happened." The proprietress cast a baleful look at Hoshina. "But he wouldn't listen."

Hoshina slouched against the wall, his hands in his armpits, his expression stormy. But Hirata knew he'd stick around to see if Hirata would turn up something he'd missed, which he could use to get back in Lord Matsudaira's good graces. He was the sort of man who would rather take credit for someone else's work than take pains to do his job right in the first place.

"I'll listen," Hirata said. "Tell me."

"I was out front when Moriwaki came for his bath," the woman explained. "He was a regular customer. Came in almost every day. I called Yuki to wait on him. She was his favorite girl. She brought him in here. After a while, I heard a loud crash. Yuki screamed. I ran to see what was wrong. I found Moriwaki-*san* lying there, naked." She pointed at the floor beside the tub. "Yuki said he'd fallen down. His head was bloody where it had hit the floor."

She pursed her lips. "First time a customer ever died here. Very bad for business. But it was an accident."

Hirata observed that this sounded just like Chief Ejima, suddenly dropping dead for no clear-cut reason. Had the treasury minister been another victim of *dim-mak*?

"I sent a message to Moriwaki's family. His retainers came and told Yuki and me not to worry; they didn't blame us. They took his body home. But the next day, *he* showed up." She shot a bitter glance at Hoshina. "He took Yuki into a room and asked her what had happened to Moriwaki. When she tried to tell him she hadn't done anything wrong, he called her a liar. I heard him hitting her. I heard her crying."

"That's enough," Hoshina interrupted angrily.

"Go on," Hirata said.

The woman gave Hoshina a vindictive smirk. "He thought Yuki had pushed Moriwaki. He made her say so. He arrested her and took her to jail, even though I told him Yuki was a good girl who'd never hurt a fly. Next day, her head was cut off."

Hirata regarded the police commissioner with disgust. "That was good, quick detective work."

Nettled, Hoshina hurried to justify himself. "It was standard procedure." Torture of suspects was legal and often used to obtain confessions. The disadvantage was that it tended to produce as many false confessions as true ones.

"And today he comes back," the woman said. "It's plain to see that he's found out that Yuki didn't kill the treasury minister, because he's poking around again, looking for some other innocent person to blame."

"Shut up, old woman!" Hoshina said, goaded to a rage. "I'll close down your bathhouse, or—"

Fists clenched, he advanced on her. Hirata's detectives pushed him away. Hirata said, "This woman is an important witness, and if you do anything to hurt her, you'll be in more trouble than you already are."

Hoshina subsided, impotent but seething. Hirata took a petty pleasure in making Hoshina pay for insulting him today and sabotaging Sano in the past. He addressed the woman: "I intend to see that the real killer is caught. I need to ask you some questions about Treasury Minister Moriwaki."

Smug under his protection, the woman said, "Go right ahead."

"Did Moriwaki have any unusual bruises that you saw?"

"As a matter of fact, he did."

Hoshina spoke through gritted teeth: "I ordered you to keep quiet about everything pertaining to this investigation."

"I can't refuse to talk to the shogun's detective, can I?" The woman feigned helpless innocence. She told Hirata, "He had a bruise right here," and pointed to a spot near her temple.

Hirata felt a ripple of excitement. "What did it look like?"

"It was blue. Oval-shaped. Kind of like a fingerprint."

At last Hirata had definite evidence that connected one of the previous murders to Chief Ejima's. Hoshina looked displeased; obviously, he'd wanted to hoard this important fact for his own use.

"When did you see the bruise?" Hirata said.

"Right after Moriwaki died. I washed the blood off him before his retainers took him home." She added, "Whenever I bathed him, he would suckle on my breasts while we sat in the tub. Some men his age like to do that, you know. I'd spent so much time looking down at his head that I couldn't help but notice the bruise because it hadn't been there before."

That was more detail than Hirata needed, but it added veracity to her statement. "You said the treasury minister was a regular customer. Had he come here during the two days previous to his death?"

Hoshina made angry, shushing gestures. The woman ignored him. "As a matter of fact, he was here just the day before."

Now Hirata could account for some of the time Moriwaki had spent away from Edo Castle. "Did you see anyone with him that day?"

"I already asked her that," Hoshina interrupted. "She doesn't know anything. She's inventing lies to please you."

The woman put her hands on her hips while her eyes shot angry sparks at Hoshina. "I'm not a liar. And if you think I am, then why were you so excited when I told you who I'd seen with Moriwaki?"

Hoshina spat out a breath of frustration. Amused, Hirata said, "Tell me what you told the police commissioner."

"A samurai came into the bathhouse with Moriwaki. He begged to talk to him. Moriwaki said he was busy, but the samurai followed him into the dressing room. They started arguing. I didn't notice what they said, but I think the samurai wanted a favor. Moriwaki told him to leave. He did."

Hirata sensed that he was on the verge of learning something critical. "Do you know who this samurai was?"

"Yes. I asked Moriwaki, 'Who was that rude fellow?' He said it was a Captain Nakai, from the Tokugawa army." She grinned triumphantly at Hoshina.

He stalked, cursing and furious, out of the room. Now Hirata understood why he'd wanted to keep the proprietress's information a secret. Captain Nakai was an excellent suspect, who'd demonstrated his martial arts skills during the faction war. Connecting him with Treasury Minister Moriwaki was a stroke of luck, for he hadn't appeared on the lists of people who'd had contact with any of the previous victims.

"Was Captain Nakai alone with the treasury minister?" Hirata asked.

"Yes. While Moriwaki was undressing."

"Did he touch Moriwaki?"

"I don't know. The curtain was closed."

Hirata was elated nonetheless. When he and the detectives left the bathhouse, he found Police Commissioner Hoshina waiting for him in the street, still fuming.

"I just wanted to tell you that you won't get away with making a fool of me in there," Hoshina said. "And if you think you and Chamberlain Sano are going to solve this case and win more honors at my expense, you're sadly mistaken. I'm going to ruin you both."

He shoved his hand against Hirata's chest. Hirata lost his balance; his lame leg buckled. He fell into a pile of horse manure. A cry of indignation burst from him at this public humiliation. Hoshina and his attendants laughed.

"That's right where you belong," Hoshina said as the detectives helped Hirata to his feet and wiped the manure off him. "Next time I strike, you'll stay down."

Hoshina and his men mounted their horses and rode away. Detective Inoue said, "Don't pay any attention to that loser, Hirata-*san*. He's not worth worrying about."

But Hirata knew that Hoshina was dangerous as well as desperate to regain his status at court. Their skirmish was only the first round in what promised to be bloody political war. Hirata limped toward his horse. "Come on, we're going back to Edo Castle. I want to tell Chamberlain Sano about Captain Nakai." And he'd better warn Sano to expect trouble from his old enemy.

12

The weather turned warm and muggy as Reiko and her escorts trudged through the *hinin* settlement. Smoke and sweat filmed her skin; ashes stung her eyes and parched her throat; and she felt as though she was absorbing contamination from the outcasts. Her visits to the first few houses nearest Yugao's produced no new suspects or witnesses.

"If you want to find the killer, you should look no further than Edo Jail," the headman said as he and Reiko skirted a garbage heap in an alley.

Reiko had begun to think Kanai was right. The rising temperature increased the stench; she was more than a little tempted to give up. The insolent Yugao hardly seemed worth this effort. But Reiko said, "I'm not finished here yet."

They circled, through lanes where ragged laundry dripped from clotheslines into overflowing gutters, around to the hovel behind Yugao's. A yard filled with washtubs, broken tools, and other junk separated the two properties. The outcast who lived in the hovel was an old man who sat in his doorway, fashioning sandals out of scrap straw and twine. When Reiko asked him if he'd seen anyone at Yugao's house besides her family on the night of the murder, he said, "There was the warden."

"From Edo Jail?" Reiko said.

The old shoemaker nodded; his gnarled hands deftly plaited the straw. "He was Taruya's boss."

"He's a former gangster," the headman told Reiko. "He was demoted for extorting money from merchants in the vegetable market and beating them up when they didn't pay."

"When did you see him?" Reiko asked, excited because she'd discovered a new suspect, and one with violent tendencies.

"I didn't see him," the shoemaker said, "but I heard his voice. He and Taruya were arguing. It was just after sundown."

"When did he leave?"

"The shouting stopped a little while later. He must have gone."

Reiko felt a pang of disappointment because the timing of his visit didn't coincide with the crime. Yet perhaps the warden had returned later to settle his score.

"Where can I find the warden?" Reiko asked.

"Where everybody in this place eventually shows up." Kanai's expression indicated that he was losing patience with her, but he said, "Come along; I'll take you."

They resumed traipsing through the settlement. Reiko questioned the inhabitants at hovels and passersby they encountered, to no avail. Her escorts looked bored and glum. A water-seller appeared, carrying buckets suspended from a pole on his shoulders, and Reiko longed for a drink but couldn't bear to swallow water from this filthy place. She dabbed her perspiring face with her sleeve and squinted up at the sun that shone high and bright through the smoke. Against the sky rose the skeletal wooden structure of a fire-watch tower. On the platform under the bell that hung from its top stood a boy.

Reiko called to him, "Excuse me, were you on duty the night the Taruya family was murdered?"

Peering down at her, he nodded.

"Can you come down for a moment and talk?" Reiko said.

He shimmied down the ladder, agile as a monkey. He was perhaps twelve years old, with an elfin face and knobby bones. Reiko asked him to describe what, if anything, he'd observed that night.

"I heard screams," he said. "I saw Ihei run away from the house."

"Who is Ihei?" Reiko asked. Interest revived her energy.

"He lives by the river," said the boy. "He used to visit Umeko."

"He was a thief in his former existence," Kanai explained. "Now he's a street-cleaner."

Reiko looked up at the tower, gauged its distance from Yugao's house, and imagined how the settlement must look at midnight. "How did you recognize him?" she asked the boy. "Wasn't it dark?"

"There was lightning. And Ihei walks like this." He hunched his back and shuffled.

Reiko didn't know whether to be glad or sorry that she now had two suspects placed at the crime scene besides Yugao. She thanked the boy, who bowed and darted around her guards.

Kanai shouted, "Wait just a moment!" He ran after the boy and grabbed him by his collar. "Give it back."

The boy reluctantly took a leather drawstring pouch from his pocket. It was the kind in which men carried money, medicines, religious items, or other small valuables.

"Hey, that's mine," Lieutenant Asukai said, groping the empty place where the pouch had once dangled from his sash. He snatched it from the boy's hand.

"You have to be careful around him, his parents, his brothers, and his sisters," Kanai said. "Every one of them is a sneak-thief." He released the boy and swatted his rear end. "Behave yourself, or I'll have another year added to all your sentences."

Soon Reiko and her companions reached their destination—a teahouse located in a large shack, enclosed by a thatched roof and plank walls, on the riverbank. Its front and back doors stood open to let the breeze refresh the men who lounged on the raised floor. The proprietor served liquor out of crude ceramic jugs. The teahouse appeared to be the social center of the outcast world. Down the river, boats housed brothels and teahouses for ordinary citizens; bridges led to neighborhoods on the opposite bank.

The headman called to one of the customers: "What are you doing here so early, Warden? Did Edo Jail shut down, or are you sneaking a holiday?"

"What's it to you if I am?" said the warden. He was short, muscular, in his forties. His head was shaved bald and circled by a dirty white cotton band. He had heavy black eyebrows and whisker stubble, and a complexion rough with pits, swollen pores, old scars. Tattoos covered his arms.

Ignoring his rudeness, the headman said, "This lady is the daughter of Magistrate Ueda. He's sent her to investigate the murder of Taruya and his family. She wants to talk to you."

The warden turned his unblinking eyes on Reiko. The pinpoints of light reflected in them seemed abnormally bright. "I know who your father is." He grinned, showing decayed teeth. "Not that I've ever met him, but I work for him."

Reiko noted the stains on his blue kimono and straw sandals, and the grime under his fingernails. Was it blood from criminals he'd tortured at the prison? A shudder rippled through her. This investigation was showing her the dark side of her father's job as well as the underbelly of Edo.

"Did you go to visit Taruya that night?" she asked.

"So what if I did?"

"Why did you?"

"I had business with him." The warden ogled Reiko and licked his lips.

"What kind of business?" she said, trying not to flinch.

"Taruya had started a gambling ring at the jail. He'd been cheating people who work there." The ire in his voice told Reiko that the warden himself had been one of Taruya's marks. "I went and ordered him to give back the money he'd stolen. He said he'd won it honestly, and he'd already spent it. We got into a fight. I beat him up until his wife started hitting me with an iron pot and chased me out."

He grimaced in disgust, then smirked. "But now Taruya is dead. He'll never cheat anybody again. His daughter did the world a favor when she took a knife to him."

His daughter wasn't the only person who'd had reason to kill him, Reiko thought. "Where did you go after you left the house?"

"I went to see my lady friend."

"She's a nighthawk in the tent village," the headman said.

Leeriness shrank the bright pinpoints in the warden's eyes. "If by some chance Magistrate Ueda is thinking of pinning the murders on me instead of Yugao, tell him that I didn't do it. I couldn't have. I was with my lady all night. She'll swear to it."

Yet Reiko knew that a man who'd extorted money from merchants and beat them into paying wouldn't balk at murder, and he looked capable of intimidating a woman into lying for him.

"Any more questions?" His grin mocked Reiko; his gaze wandered over her body.

"Not at the moment," Reiko said. Unless she could find evidence against him, she had to let him go.

"Then if you'll excuse me . . ." The warden ambled to the back door, reached under his kimono, and pulled his organ from his loincloth. After giving Reiko a good view of it, he urinated into a slop jar outside the teahouse. "Give Magistrate Ueda my best regards."

Offense and embarrassment burned inside Reiko. The headman said, "I apologize for his bad manners." He glanced down the street. "If you want another chance to save Yugao, here he comes now."

A young man approached the teahouse, shoulders hunched, feet scuffling. He wore faded, torn clothes; a wicker hat shaded his face, which was scrunched in a frown that looked permanent. He carried a broom, dustpan, and trash basket.

"That's Ihei," the headman said.

The street-cleaner looked up as Reiko and her guards advanced on him. His face took on a look of alarm. He turned and scuffled rapidly away.

"Stop him!" Reiko ordered her guards.

They raced after the young man. Dropping his tools, he hastened down the street, but his awkward gait hampered his flight. The guards easily caught him and propelled him toward Reiko.

"Let me go!" he cried, struggling in their grasp. "I didn't do anything wrong!" His voice was high and weak, his grimy face taut with panic.

"If you didn't do anything wrong, then why did you run?" Reiko said.

His frown deepened with his surprise at seeing a lady of her class in the settlement. He glanced at her guards. "I—I was afraid they would hurt me."

"Some samurai thugs beat him up," Kanai said. "They broke a lot of bones. That's why he's deformed."

Reiko was appalled by yet another tale of the *hinin*'s cruel existence. "No one's going to hurt you. I just want to talk. If you promise not to run, they'll let you go."

His expression said he didn't trust her, but Ihei nodded. The guards released him but stood ready to restrain him again if necessary. "Talk about what?"

"About the night that Umeko and her parents were murdered," Reiko said.

Panic flashed in Ihei's eyes. He backed away. The headman said, "Whoa!" and the guards grabbed Ihei, who cried, "I don't know anything about that."

"You were seen running away from the house," Reiko said.

His features drooped in dismay. "I had nothing to do with it." Guilty bravado tinged his voice. "I—I swear!"

"Then what were you doing there?"

"I went to see Umeko."

"Why?" Reiko considered the possibility that Umeko had been the intended victim, despite the clues at the crime scene that indicated her father was killed first. She recalled that Yugao's sister had been a prostitute. When Ihei hesitated, Reiko said, "Were you one of her customers?"

"No!" Ihei exclaimed, offended.

"Yes, you were," Kanai said. "Don't lie; you'll get yourself in trouble."

Ihei sighed in resignation. "All right—I was Umeko's customer. But it was more than the usual thing. I loved her." His voice trembled; tears trickled lines through the grime on his cheeks. "And now she's gone!"

His grief seemed genuine, but sometimes killers did mourn the loss of loved ones they'd murdered. Reiko had watched them sob during their trials in her father's court. "Why did you go to see her?"

"That morning I'd asked her to marry me. She—she said no. She laughed at me." Ihei's eyes burned with humiliation. "She said she would never lower herself to marry a hunchback outcast. I said I knew she was born higher than me, but I told her that we were both *hinin* now. Fate had brought us together here. I told her how much I loved her. I said I would make her happy. I earn enough money that she could have moved into my hut and not have had to sell herself. But then she got angry."

His tone reflected the hurt and surprise he must have felt. "She said she wasn't going to be here forever. She was mad at me for suggesting it. She said she was going to wait until her father had served his sentence, got his business and his house back, and then marry some rich man. She told me to leave her alone because she never wanted to see me again."

She sounded callous and ill-tempered enough to provoke murder. "But you didn't leave her alone," Reiko deduced. "You went back that night. What happened?"

"I had to see her. I thought I could make her change her mind. That night I went to her house. I knocked on the door frame. When she answered, I tried to talk to her. She told me to be quiet—her family was sleeping. She said I could come in—for the usual price. All she wanted from me was my money." The street-cleaner hung his head in woe. "I wanted her so badly that I agreed. She took me into her room. I made love to her."

Reiko pictured them in the lean-to at the house. As Umeko serviced him, had his passion for her fueled his rage at her rejection? Had his love turned to hatred?

"After we finished, we fell asleep. I don't know for how long. I was wakened by screaming and noises. Her mother shouted, 'What are you doing?' then 'Stop!' She was crying. There were loud thumps, and sounds like fighting and running, in the other room." Ihei's face showed confusion at the memory. "Umeko jumped up and ran out there. I heard her say, 'What's going on?' Then she started screaming, 'No!' and calling me for help. I pushed aside the curtain. Umeko ran past me. Someone was chasing her. Stabbing her." He raised his fist and pantomimed the frenzied, downward slashes. "I rushed out, and Umeko fell at my feet. The screaming stopped. I smelled blood."

Ihei swallowed a retch; his eyes shone with remembered fear. "It was quiet except for the sound of someone panting. Then suddenly a shadow rushed at me. I saw the knife gleam in its hand." He reeled backward, pantomiming his reaction. "I turned and ran out the door. I kept running all the way home."

His broken body trembled; he sobbed into his hands. "Umeko is dead. If only I could have saved her! But all I did was run like a coward."

Reiko could picture the scene he'd described; she could imagine his terror as he realized that his beloved and her family had been slain and he would be the next to die unless he fled. She could also imagine a different scenario. Maybe, after he and Umeko had made love, he'd again asked her to marry him, and again she'd refused. Maybe they'd argued, and he'd become so furious that he'd stabbed her, and when her parents tried to intervene, he'd turned the knife on them.

"Who was this person that you saw stabbing her?" Reiko asked.

"I don't know." The street-cleaner dropped his hands and raised his red, tear-swollen eyes to her. "It was dark; I couldn't see much. At the time I thought some madman had broken into the house while I was asleep. But it must have been Yugao. I mean, she was arrested, wasn't she?"

"Yes," Reiko said. If she was the killer, that would explain the fact that she was the sole survivor of her family, not a wound on her. The murders could have happened the way he'd said; maybe he'd caught Yugao in the act. But Ihei wasn't exactly a reliable witness; he'd had ample cause and perfect opportunity to commit murder himself.

"I've told you everything," he said. "Can I go now?"

Reiko hesitated. He was as good a suspect as Yugao; there was enough evidence to convict him in court. She was tempted to have her guards take him to jail, but she remembered what Sano had said about her interfering with the law. It wasn't her place to arrest suspects. Furthermore, she wasn't particularly eager to clear Yugao, since she still hadn't made up her mind about the woman's guilt or innocence.

"You can go," Reiko said, "as long as you stay in Edo. You may be needed for more questioning."

"Don't worry," the headman said, "he's not going anywhere. He hasn't anywhere to go."

The street-cleaner scurried off, picking up his broom, basket, and dustpan. Reiko asked Kanai, "Are you still convinced that Yugao killed her family?"

He wrinkled his brow and scratched his scalp. "I must admit I'm not so sure anymore. You've poked a couple of holes in my confidence. It's obvious now that there was more going on that night than I thought." He pondered a moment. "But suppose that Ihei or the warden, or somebody else, killed those people. Then why did Yugao confess?"

"That's a good question," Reiko said.

Yugao was a mystery that she must solve before she could solve the crime. Maybe the woman's secrets lay in the life she'd led before she came to the *hinin* settlement.

"How are you going to answer it?" Kanai asked.

"I think I'll take a journey into the past," Reiko answered.

13

Temple bells boomed in a dissonant music across Edo, heralding noon. Colorful kites spangled the sunlit sky above the rooftops. On the street children played with broken spears dropped by warriors fallen during a clash between rebel outlaws and the army. Inside Edo Castle, Sano sat in his office, interviewing people who'd had contact with Chief Ejima in the two days before his death. He'd already spoken with the guests from the banquet as well as Ejima's subordinates at *metsuke* headquarters. Now he dismissed the last of the men who'd had private appointments with Ejima. He turned to Detectives Marume and Fukida, who knelt near his desk.

"Well, this has certainly turned up enough potential suspects," Sano said.

Fukida consulted notes he'd taken during the interviews. "We've got subordinates who were mad at Ejima because he was promoted over them. We've got the new *metsuke* chief, who benefited from his death. We've got names of men who were demoted or executed because of flimsy evidence that he brought against them, who left sons and retainers eager for blood."

"He had lots of enemies," said Marume, "even though they won't admit knowing *dim-mak*. Any of them could have sneaked up on Ejima and touched him."

"Everybody claims he's innocent, as we might have predicted," Fukida said. "Almost all of them dropped hints that incriminated somebody else. There are so many feuds left over from the war that I'm not surprised to hear people accusing each other."

Sano was troubled because already the murder was fueling political strife that could lead to another war, and he was no closer to solving the case. "Too many suspects are as bad as too few. And we've had neither sight nor word of Captain Nakai, our best candidate."

"I wonder why it's taking so long to locate him," Fukida said. "He should be on duty at his post in the Edo Castle main guard station."

"Shall we start tracking down Ejima's informants?" Marume asked.

Sano's principal aide peeked in the door. "Excuse me, Honorable Chamberlain. The *sōsakan-sama* is here to see you."

When Hirata entered the office, Sano was again dismayed at how ill he looked. He saw sympathy, quickly veiled, on Marume's and Fukida's faces as Hirata awkwardly knelt and bowed. But the most they all could do was ignore Hirata's condition.

"What have you to report?" Sano said.

"Good news," Hirata said, weary but satisfied. "I've investigated the deaths of Court Supervisor Ono, Highway Commissioner Sasamura Tomoya, and Treasury Minister Moriwaki. And I've discovered a suspect." He described his visit to the bathhouse where Moriwaki had died.

Sano leaned forward, elated. "Now we know that at least one of those men was killed by *dim-mak.*"

"It's not too far a stretch to believe that so were the others," Fukida said.

"And Captain Nakai's name has come up again." Sano told Hirata that Nakai had had a private appointment with Ejima. "Now we know he had contact with two victims."

"Captain Nakai might have accosted the other men on the street, too." Hirata seemed proud that he'd linked the cases and turned up evidence against the primary suspect.

Sano was moved and pained by how much Hirata still wanted his approval, after everything he'd been through for Sano's sake. "It's more important than ever to find Captain Nakai."

"Something else has come up that I should mention," Hirata said. "Police Commissioner Hoshina is after your blood."

Sano frowned. "Again?"

Hirata described his encounter with Hoshina at the bathhouse.

"Many thanks for the warning," Sano said.

"What should we do about that scoundrel?" Marume said.

"If I were like my predecessor, I would have his head cut off. But I'm not, so there isn't much we can do until he makes his move, and it's more important than ever to solve this case fast. If we don't, Hoshina will have more ammunition to use against me."

Young Detective Tachibana rushed into the office. "Excuse me, Honorable Chamberlain. I've found out where Captain Nakai is. He didn't show up for duty today, so I went to his house. His wife said he went to the sumo tournament. Shall I go fetch him?"

"Good work. But I'll go myself." Sano rose, stretching muscles cramped from sitting. "It'll save time."

Hirata, Marume, and Fukida rose to accompany him. Sano noticed how stiffly Hirata moved. "If you have other important business, you're excused," Sano said, giving Hirata a graceful way out of a long, uncomfortable ride.

"I've nothing else as important as this," Hirata said staunchly. "And I want to see what Captain Nakai has to say."

Although glad for his company, Sano experienced fresh guilt. "Very well."

The sumo tournaments were held at the Eko-in Temple in Honjo district, across the Sumida River. Sano and Hirata rode with Detectives Marume, Fukida, Arai, Inoue, and Tachibana along the canals that veined Honjo. They passed vegetable markets, residences of minor samurai officials, a few Tokugawa warehouses and the suburban villas of *daimyo,* the feudal lords. Smoke rose and heat shimmered from kilns where ceramic roof tiles were baked. Through the streets marched men who beat a huge drum, announcing the sumo tournament. Sano heard a deeper, louder pulse from the drum in the tall scaffold outside the temple. Crowds streamed toward its gates, which loomed ahead.

Eko-in Temple had been built thirty-eight years ago, after the Great Fire of Meireki, to commemorate the hundred thousand people who'd died in the disaster. Its grounds contained the city's official wrestling arena. Sumo had evolved from a Shinto fertility rite to popular entertainment. Since the beginning of the Tokugawa regime almost a century ago, there had been periodic edicts banning sumo because it was violent, bloody, and often fatal. But the authorities had realized that sumo served a purpose. It gave *rōnin* a place in society, and the officially sanctioned, tightly regulated tournaments gave society a way to blow off steam. Sano noted that the crowds seemed bigger than usual after the war.

He and his men left their horses at a stable and walked into the arena, a vast, open-air space. From its walls extended double tiers of balconies covered with bamboo canopies. The lower tiers were already full of people; newcomers climbed ladders to the upper levels. In the center stood the ring, defined by four pillars with cords strung between them. Thousands more spectators sat crammed together on the ground, pressed up against the ring. Straw rice bales filled with clay had been placed around it to keep the wrestling area clear. Referees and judges knelt at its edge. Vendors selling refreshments waded through the crowds.

"How are we ever going to find Captain Nakai in this?" Hirata asked as he and Sano scanned the noisy, chaotic arena.

"Maybe we'll get lucky," Sano said.

The drumbeats quickened. Into the ring paraded the wrestlers. Their naked chests and limbs bulged with muscle and fat. They wore ceremonial fringe and silk ropes around their waists, and brocade aprons that sported the family crests of the lords of Kishu, Izumo, Sanuki, Awa, Karima, Sendai, or Nambu. Those lords recruited wrestlers for their private stables. Sano noticed larger teams than usual: The war had created more *rōnin,* who swelled the ranks of the sumo wrestlers.

The audience cheered as the wrestlers threw down salt to purify their sacred battlefield. They stamped their feet and clapped their hands to show off their strength and drive off evil spirits. A referee held up placards bearing their names. Gazing up at the balconies, Sano noticed a strange phenomenon. The top tiers were packed except for a vacant spot directly opposite the ring. In its middle sat a lone samurai.

"There he is," Sano said, pointing.

He and his men jostled through the mob; they scaled a ladder. As they edged along the balcony, past the audience who knelt on its floor, a group of commoners seated themselves in the empty space around Captain Nakai.

"You're too close," he said. "Move." His voice was belligerent, threatening. The commoners hastily decamped.

Sano had seen Nakai only once before—at a ceremony after the war, when the victorious army had paraded before Lord Matsudaira, carrying the severed heads of slain enemy troops—but Nakai had made a memorable impression. With his tall, athletic build and noble manner, he epitomized the warrior race.

Although Nakai was in his thirties, past his prime, Sano had easily imagined him single-handedly killing forty-eight men in battle. But today he sat idle, dressed in a brown silk robe, trousers, and surcoat instead of armor; his posture was slouched instead of proudly upright. Discontent shadowed his strong, carven features as he stared down at the ring.

"Captain Nakai?" Sano said.

Nakai turned. Recognition cleared the glum look from his face as he beheld Sano and Hirata. "Honorable Chamberlain. *Sōsakan-sama*." He bowed, alert and animated. "Please sit down." With a smile that showed broad white teeth, he offered them the space he'd kept clear.

"Many thanks," Sano said. He and Hirata and their men sat.

"Are you fond of sumo?" Nakai said.

"Yes," Sano said, "but that's not why we're here. We came to talk to you."

"Me?" Nakai sounded awed and confused. Seeing him at close range, Sano noticed a flaw in his perfection. It was his eyes. Their expression lacked something—perhaps not so much intelligence as self-possession. "But why . . . how did you know to find me here?"

When Sano told him, Nakai's face reddened. "Well, I know I should be at my post, but it's not as if I'm really needed there. Besides, making up duty rosters and inspecting troops is dull work compared to fighting a battle."

Sano knew that many soldiers had had problems readjusting to ordinary life after the war; they were restless, inclined to brawl among themselves and drink too much. But he didn't care for Nakai's attitude. Hirata and the detectives looked askance at Nakai: Samurai were supposed to follow orders and not complain.

"After all I've done for Lord Matsudaira, I deserve more." Nakai obviously thought his accomplishments entitled him to a reward, even though his lord didn't owe him a thing for doing his duty. He seemed unaware of his audience's disapproval. "Many men who killed fewer enemy troops than I did have been promoted, but not me." Bitterness colored his tone. "My family has distant cousins who fought on Yanagisawa's side. I'm tainted by bad blood, through no fault of my own."

Sano thought that was possible, for political ties mattered. But most likely Nakai's superiors had passed him over in favor of men less skilled at combat with better social graces, who had the sense not to show themselves in a bad light to the shogun's second-in-command.

"I've been a faithful servant to Lord Matsudaira. All I want is for him to recognize that. I don't care about a bigger stipend." Nakai donned a noble, martyred air. "All I ask is a chance to serve Lord Matsudaira in a higher capacity, where I can do even more for him than I already have."

Sano seized the opening in his tirade: "Now is your chance. Lord Matsudaira has ordered me to investigate the death of Chief Ejima. I would appreciate your help."

"Of course," Nakai said, disconcerted; he obviously hadn't expected to get his wish in this way. "What can I do for you?"

Below the balcony, across the audience that covered the ground, the wrestlers finished their ritual and marched out of the ring. The announcer shouted the names of the wrestlers who would fight the first match. The drums clamored. Two massive wrestlers, stripped to their loincloths, crouched at opposite ends of the ring. Anticipation stirred the crowds.

"I'm questioning everyone who came in contact with Ejima shortly before he died," Sano began. "The records show that you had a private appointment with him."

Nakai frowned as though trying to figure out the point of the conversation. "Yes, I asked Ejima to help me get a promotion. He was close to Lord Matsudaira, and I thought he could put in a good word for me."

"What happened?"

Anger glinted in Nakai's eyes. "Ejima said no. It was just a little favor, and he could have done it with no trouble to himself. People use their influence for other people all the time—that's how one gets ahead in the *bakufu*. But Ejima said he didn't know me well enough to recommend me to Lord Matsudaira. He said if I wanted to rise in the world, I had a lot to learn. Then he kicked me out."

Sano had met many men like Nakai, good at their jobs but stuck in low ranks because they were grossly inept at politics. They didn't understand the subtle techniques of courting friendship and placing other men under their obligation. They needed to learn that if one wanted favors from strangers, one had better have something to hold over their heads.

"Ejima was the same as the other men I asked for help," Nakai said bitterly. "They all treated me as if I were a dog who'd pissed on their shoes!"

Hirata said, "Was Treasury Minister Moriwaki one of them?"

". . . Yes, I did talk to him."

"At the bathhouse?"

Scowling, Nakai nodded. "He wouldn't give me an appointment. I had to follow him around until I caught him off guard."

"What happened?" Hirata asked.

"He said he couldn't help me; it was up to my superior officer to

decide whether I should be promoted. He told me to go away."
Nakai's temper erupted; he pounded the balcony so hard it shook.
"The nerve of those old snobs! They all got their new, high positions
after Lord Matsudaira defeated Yanagisawa. None of them would be
where they are, if not for men like me." He thumped his chest. "I
fought in the battle while they hid at home. And now they won't
throw me a crumb from their banquet!"

Sano had to agree that Nakai had a legitimate gripe. Hundreds of
troops had died, and men who'd never blooded their own swords had
reaped the benefits. Sano thought of more men besides Ejima and
Moriwaki—and himself—who fit that description. "Did you ask
Court Supervisor Ono and Highway Commissioner Sasamura for their
help?"

Nakai snorted out a breath. "For all the good it did."

"When was this?"

"I don't remember exactly. Not long before they died."

Sano also knew Nakai must realize that there was one man in particular who'd benefited most of all from Nakai's efforts and had the
authority to dispense rewards. "Did you ask Lord Matsudaira for a
promotion?"

Nakai shook his head, simmering with resentment. "I would if I
could. I've requested an audience with him. I risked my life to put him
in power, and he won't even grant me the courtesy of a reply!"

Sano and Hirata exchanged a glance; they noted that Captain
Nakai's grudge included Lord Matsudaira as well as all the victims
he'd had contact with during the critical time period. He had plenty
of reason for attacking Lord Matsudaira's new regime. Sano said,
"What did you do when Ono, Sasamura, Moriwaki, and Ejima
brushed you off?"

Nakai grimaced. "I slunk away with my tail between my legs.
What else could I do?"

"You didn't take revenge on them?" Hirata said.

Suspicion crept into Nakai's eyes. "What are you talking about?"

The wrestlers in the ring suddenly charged. The impact shuddered

117

their flesh. Cheers burst from the audience. The wrestlers pummeled each other; they grappled and shoved as each tried to throw his opponent from the ring.

"You're one of the best fighters in the land," Hirata said. "Do you know *dim-mak?*"

"No. Nobody does. It's just a legend. What——?" The puzzlement on Nakai's face gave way to surprised understanding. "You think those men were killed by a death-touch. And you're asking me if I did it."

"Did you?" Sano said.

Nakai uttered a laugh that didn't hide his consternation. "I never laid a hand on them."

"A finger is all it took," Hirata said, tapping his finger against his temple. "And there went four men who'd not only refused to give you what you want, but insulted your pride."

Nakai stared in outrage. "I'm a soldier, not a murderer. The only people I ever killed were enemy troops on the battlefield." Angry enlightenment filled his eyes. "Oh, I see what's going on. You need someone to blame for those deaths. So you thought, 'How about that poor sucker Nakai? He was so anxious to sacrifice himself for Lord Matsudaira. Let's make him the scapegoat and be rid of him.'" Nakai's voice turned raw with animosity. "Well, I won't stand for it." He squared his shoulders and whipped his sword out of its scabbard.

Sano, Hirata, and the detectives instinctively leapt away and drew their own weapons. The spectators around them squealed and scrambled off, not wanting to be caught in a brawl. But Nakai turned his sword on himself, the hilt grasped in both hands, the blade's tip pressed against his abdomen.

"I'll commit *seppuku* before I let you dishonor my name." His eyes blazed with serious intent.

Sano let out his breath in relief that he needn't fight Nakai. Killing his primary suspect wouldn't help his investigation, and he couldn't help pitying the man. He said, "Put away your sword, Captain."

Nakai glared, but he sheathed his blade rather than disobey a direct command from a superior. Sano couldn't tell whether he was glad or sorry to have his suicide prevented. Maybe Nakai himself didn't know. In the ring, the wrestlers broke apart, then charged again. They staggered together. One lost his balance. The other grabbed his loincloth and heaved. He went reeling across the ring, tripped over the bales at its edge, and fell into the audience, which applauded, cheered, and booed. Spectators in the balconies hurled coins and expensive robes at the winner, who strutted and raised his fists.

"I'm not looking for a scapegoat," Sano told Nakai. "If you're as innocent as you claim, you have nothing to fear from me. But you'd better stay alive and in town until I've finished my investigation."

He nodded to his companions, signifying that they were done with Nakai for now. They filed along the balcony and climbed down the ladder. As they gathered at the bottom, Sano looked up at Nakai. The captain stood on the balcony, gazing down at them, his expression as much aggrieved as hostile.

"Do you think he was bluffing?" Hirata said.

"If he was, he put on a good act," Sano said.

Detective Arai said, "Do you think he's guilty?"

"He's still our best suspect." Sano turned to Tachibana. "Go follow him. Don't let him see you, but don't let him out of your sight. I want to know everywhere he goes, everyone he associates with, and everything he does."

"What if he tries to touch somebody?" asked the young detective.

"Stop him," Sano said, "if you can. If he's the killer, we may not be able to prevent another murder, but at least we can catch him in the act."

"Yes, Honorable Chamberlain." The young detective slipped away and lost himself in the crowds.

"In the meantime, we'll go back to my estate," Sano told Hirata and the other detectives. "Maybe Ejima's informants have been brought in, and we'll find more suspects among them." Furthermore, he had a country to run, and he'd been away far too long. As they plowed through the audience and another match began in the ring, Sano wondered if Reiko was faring any better on her investigation. He hoped she'd confined it to the *hinin* settlement and would soon be done.

14

Ryōgoku Hirokoji was Edo's top entertainment district, situated on the bank of the Sumida River. It had grown up in an open space created as a firebreak after the Great Fire of Meireki, during which thousands of people were trapped and burned to death because they were too many to cross the bridges to safety. As Reiko rode through Ryōgoku Hirokoji in her palanquin, she gazed out the window with curiosity. Colorful signs on the stalls along the wide avenue advertised attractions not seen in the officially licensed theater district, such as female performers. She admired the gorgeously elaborate models of Dutch galleons at one stall; others featured live parrots, human giants, and goblins made out of shells and vines. Priests and nuns begged coins from the strolling crowds.

Reiko had heard her servants talk about this place, but had never been here since it was mostly the domain of the lower classes. Now her guards rode close, ready to protect her from the thieves and other evildoers who mingled in the crowds and lurked in the alleyways. But its disreputable air excited her.

A young nun, dressed in a baggy hemp robe, her head shaved bald, hurried up to Reiko's palanquin and thrust her begging bowl in the window. "Alms for the poor!"

Reiko said, "There was a carnival owned by a man named Taruya. Can you tell me where it was?"

The nun pointed down the street. "Through that red gate."

"Many thanks." After Reiko dropped a coin into the nun's bowl, her escorts bore her toward the two wooden posts painted red and crowned by a tile roof. She'd expected to find the carnival closed since Yugao's father had left, but people were lined up at the ticket booth outside. Beyond the gate spread the connected stalls of a "Hundred-Day Theater"—a variety show. As Reiko climbed out of her palanquin and her escorts bought tickets, she had an uneasy feeling that Sano wouldn't be pleased to hear that her inquiries had taken her beyond the *hinin* settlement. But she must serve justice, and she'd already come this far.

She and her escorts passed through the gate and into another world. Hundreds of stalls spread before her. Their roofs overhung a maze of narrow passages, blocking the sunshine. Red lanterns suspended from the ceilings cast a garish glow on eager faces in the throngs that jostled past Reiko. Chatter, music, and laughter resounded; the smells of sweat and urine assailed her. Hawkers, stationed outside the curtains that draped the entrances to the stalls, beckoned and called to potential customers. Some curtains hung open to reveal gaming dens where men shot arrows at straw targets or tossed balls through hoops, and others in which storytellers recited tales for enthusiastic audiences. At other stalls the curtains were closed. Men flocked to them, handing over coins. A hawker opened a curtain to admit a customer, and Reiko glimpsed bare-breasted girls dancing on a stage inside. As the crowds swept her and her escorts along a passage, she saw another curtain lift to expose two men and a woman, all nude. The woman crouched while one man penetrated her from behind and she sucked the erect organ of the other. Moans erupted from men seated below the stage. Shock stunned Reiko.

Lieutenant Asukai shouted to her over the noise: "What shall we do?"

"I want to talk to whoever owns this place," Reiko shouted back. "Find him for me."

While the other guards stood around Reiko, shielding her from the riffraff, Asukai plowed through the crowds and spoke to the nearest hawker. The hawker replied and pointed down the passage. Reiko looked in the direction indicated. Toward her ran a young woman. Her feet were bare, her eyes wild with fear. She clutched a cheap cotton robe around her body. Long hair streamed behind her. She gasped as she fought past the crowds. Two samurai came chasing after her. In their wake trailed a small, tubby, middle-aged man.

"Don't let her get away, you idiots!" he shouted.

Lieutenant Asukai returned to Reiko and said, "That fat man is the owner. His name is Mizutani."

Reiko and her guards joined the pursuit. The crowds hindered them. Startled exclamations arose. They struggled along winding passages, on the heels of the carnival owner. Just as the woman reached a doorway, the two samurai caught her. She screamed. Mizutani yanked open her robe, baring her full breasts and shaved pubis. He removed a cloth pouch from inside the robe, then slapped her hard across the face.

"How dare you steal my money, you little whore?" he shouted, then told the samurai, "Teach her a lesson."

The samurai began beating the woman. As she screamed, wept, and raised her arms in a vain attempt to shield herself, the spectators cheered and laughed. Reiko shouted to her guards, "Stop them!"

The guards stepped in and grabbed the samurai, who appeared to be *rōnin* hired to do dirty work at the carnival.

"That's enough," Lieutenant Asukai said. He and his comrades flung the *rōnin* away from the woman. "Leave her alone."

She hurried, sobbing, out the door. Mizutani exclaimed in outrage. "Hey, what are you doing?" He reminded Reiko of a tortoise—his neck was short, his nose beaked; his eyes had a cold, reptilian stare. "Who are you to interfere in my business?" He turned to his *rōnin*. "Throw them out."

The *rōnin* drew their swords. Reiko was upset that she'd inadvertently created another troublesome, dangerous scene.

Lieutenant Asukai said quickly, "We're from Magistrate Ueda."

The owner's attitude changed abruptly from high dudgeon to startled dismay as he realized he was facing officers of the law. "Oh. Well, in that case . . ." He waggled his hand at the *rōnin*. They sheathed their weapons while he hastened to defend himself: "That dancer was keeping tips from customers instead of turning them over to me. I can't let my employees get away with cheating me, can I?"

"Never mind that," Asukai said. "The magistrate has sent his daughter here on business." He indicated Reiko. "She wants to talk to you."

Puzzlement blinked the owner's cold eyes as they turned in her direction. He said, "Since when does the magistrate's daughter do business for him?"

"Since now," Asukai said.

Reiko was thankful that she had him to back her up, although she wished she had her own authority. "Did you know Taruya?" she asked the carnival owner.

His expression conveyed offense that a woman should interrogate him so boldly. Lieutenant Asukai said, "Whatever she asks, you'd better answer, unless you'd like Magistrate Ueda to conduct an inspection of your carnival."

Visibly daunted by the threat, Mizutani capitulated. "Taruya was my business partner."

"You owned the carnival together?" Reiko asked.

"Yes. Eighteen years ago, we started out with one stall. We built it up into this." His proud gesture encompassed his sprawling, noisy domain.

"And now the carnival is all yours," Reiko said, thoughtful and interested. "How did that come about?"

"Taruya got himself in trouble. He was sleeping with his daughter. Somebody reported him to the police. He was demoted to *hinin* and banned from doing business with the public, so I took over."

Reiko glanced at the hawkers collecting money from customers who flocked to the stalls. Taruya's demotion had been lucrative for his onetime partner. "Did you buy out Taruya's share?"

"No." Mizutani licked his lips; his tongue looked gray and scaly. He seemed uncomfortable, although Reiko didn't think him the kind of man to feel guilty for taking advantage of his partner's trouble. "We made a deal before Taruya went to the *hinin* settlement. I would send him money every month and run the show until his sentence was finished. Then, when he came back, we would be partners again."

"How generous of you," Reiko said. "But he won't be coming back. Did you know he was murdered?"

"Yes, I heard. What a terrible thing to happen." The regret in Mizutani's voice sounded false; his eyes showed no emotion, only his wish to know the purpose of Reiko's visit. "There was some gossip that his daughter Yugao stabbed him and her mother and sister."

"There's some doubt about that. Do you think she did it?"

Mizutani shrugged. "How should I know? I hadn't seen any of them since they moved to the settlement. But I wasn't surprised to hear Yugao had been arrested. That girl was strange."

"Strange in what way?" Reiko said.

"I don't know." Mizutani was clearly growing vexed by the conversation. "There was something just not right about her. But I really didn't pay her much attention." He chuckled. "She probably got fed up with Taruya in her bed."

"But perhaps she wasn't the only person to want him gone," Reiko said. "Were those monthly payments a burden to you?"

"Of course not." Mizutani spoke as though insulted by the suggestion. "He was my friend. I was glad to help him out."

Shouts suddenly erupted down the passage: A fight had started. As men flung punches at each other and spectators egged them on, Mizutani strode toward them; his *rōnin* followed.

"Hey! No fighting in here!" he shouted. "Break it up!"

The *rōnin* waded into the fray, separating the combatants, while he bustled around and supervised.

"Do you want me to fetch him back?" Lieutenant Asukai asked Reiko.

A bright spot of color in the street outside the carnival caught her eye. She saw, through the milling crowds, the woman that Mizutani had beaten, stooped over a horse trough, bathing her face.

"No," Reiko said. "I have a better idea."

She led her entourage out of the carnival. The woman turned at their approach. Her mouth was swollen where Mizutani had hit her; blood trickled from her lip. Reiko took a cloth from under her sash.

"Here," she said.

The woman looked suspicious that a stranger should offer her solicitude, but she took the cloth and wiped her face.

"What's your name?" Reiko said.

"Lily," the woman answered. She was older than Reiko had at first thought—in her thirties. Hardship had coarsened her voice as well as her pretty features. "Who are you?"

When Reiko introduced herself, fear shone in the dancer's eyes. "I only took a few coppers from him. He didn't need it, and I did—he pays me so little." She stepped backward with a nervous glance at Reiko's guards. "I saw you talking to him. Did he tell you to arrest me?" Tears wavered her voice; she clasped her hands in entreaty. "Please don't! I've got a little boy. It's bad enough that I've lost my job, but if I go to jail, there'll be no one to take care of him!"

"Don't worry; you won't be arrested," Reiko said. She pitied the woman and deplored Mizutani. This investigation kept reminding her that many people lived on the brink of survival, at the mercy of their betters. "I only want to talk."

Lily cautiously relaxed. "About what?"

"Your former employer."

"Is he in some kind of trouble?" Hope brightened Lily.

"Maybe," Reiko said. "Were you working at the carnival when his partner Taruya was running it with him?"

"Yes. I worked there fourteen years." A bitter expression came over Lily's swollen, bruised face. "Fourteen years, and he throws me out because I took money that I earned myself!"

"How did they get along?" Reiko asked.

"They were always fighting over money."

And the fight had been resolved in Mizutani's favor. Reiko said, "How convenient for Mizutani that someone reported Taruya for having incestuous relations with his daughter."

"Is that what Mizutani told you—that somebody reported Taruya?" Snide amusement inflected Lily's voice. "It was him. He did it."

This certainly put a different twist on the matter. "How do you know?"

"When Mizutani had parties at his house, I used to wait on the guests. I would overhear things they said. One night his guests were two *doshin*. He told them he'd caught Taruya and his daughter Yugao in bed together."

A thought disturbed Reiko. "Was Mizutani telling the truth when he said he'd witnessed the incest?"

"I don't know. But I'd never heard of anything funny going on between Taruya and Yugao. Neither had anyone else at the carnival. We were all shocked."

Reiko wondered if Mizutani had invented the whole episode. Without the incest, Yugao had no apparent reason for murder.

Lily's expression turned eager. "Can Mizutani get in trouble if he lied?"

"If he did, he'll be punished," Reiko said. Her father abhorred false accusations and wouldn't stand for one that had made outcasts of an entire family.

"I heard that Yugao killed her father. Did she really do it, or could it have been Mizutani?" The dancer practically salivated at the thought of her former boss convicted and executed.

"That's what I'm trying to determine." Now Reiko recalled something the headman of the outcasts had said, and another thought occurred to her. "Taruya's sentence would have been finished in six months if he hadn't been killed. How did Mizutani feel about that?"

"He wasn't looking forward to Taruya getting out of the *hinin* settlement. It was no secret," Lily said with a sardonic laugh. "The carnival had a bad time during the war. Mizutani lost money. He's run up big debts, and the money-lenders have been threatening to break his legs unless he pays them. I've heard him say that the last thing he needed was Taruya coming back and claiming his half of the business. And that's not all he's said."

She paused, and Reiko said, "Well?"

"I can't talk anymore. I have to find a new job, or my little boy will starve." She fixed a nervous, entreating gaze on Reiko. "If I help you, then you should help me."

Reiko hated to imagine herself and Masahiro losing their livelihood and trying to fend for themselves. Furthermore, she sensed that the woman had important evidence to relate. "If you help me, I'll pay you."

Lily nodded, grateful and pleased at her own cleverness. "Last month I saw Mizutani and his two *rōnin* talking inside the dance stall. I stood outside and listened. You never know what interesting things you'll find out." A crafty smile lifted her swollen lip. "Mizutani said, 'I saw Taruya today. He's anxious to get back his share of the carnival. I told him that's not fair, after I've been running it all this time. But he said a deal is a deal.' One of his *rōnin* said that Taruya still has friends here, and they're gangsters who could make trouble for Mizutani if he backed out. Mizutani said, 'There's one way to break that deal. What if he were to die?' "

A thrill of excitement tingled Reiko's blood. "What else did they say?"

"I don't know. Mizutani saw me eavesdropping and told me to go. I didn't hear the rest."

A new vision of the crime took shape in Reiko's mind. *The rōnin steals into the outcast settlement that night. He sneaks into Yugao's house and stabs her father in his bed. When her mother and sister awaken and try to stop him, he kills them. He means to kill Yugao, but the street-cleaner Ihei comes out of the lean-to and surprises him. The street-cleaner flees in terror. The rōnin doesn't want to leave any witnesses, but he hears people gathering in the streets. He slips out of the hovel. He hides in the back yard while the headman arrives, until Yugao has been arrested, then he vanishes into the night. In the morning, at the carnival, he tells his master that the deed is done.*

"Well?" Lily said eagerly. "Are you satisfied?"

"One more thing," Reiko said. Yugao was still a mystery. If she was innocent, then her confession was all the more baffling. "Did you know Yugao?"

"Not really. Taruya kept his children away from us folks who worked for him." Lily gave a contemptuous sniff. "He thought they were too good to associate with us."

"Is there anyone who did know her?"

"There was a girl who used to be her friend. They were always together." Lily frowned in an effort to recall. "Her name was Tama. Her father owned a teahouse around here." Impatience crossed her face. "Do I get my reward?"

Reiko paid Lily from the pouch where she carried money in case she needed to bribe informants. Lily went off looking much happier than before.

"It's getting late," Lieutenant Asukai warned Reiko. She'd been too busy to notice that twilight was darkening the sky. The entertainment district had grown rowdier; the women and children had departed; young toughs and off-duty soldiers swelled the crowds. "We should take you home."

"In a little while," Reiko said. "I must find out where Mizutani and his *rōnin* were the night of the murders. And I want to look for Yugao's friend Tama."

15

When Sano arrived home that night, Reiko and Masahiro met him in their private quarters. "Masahiro has something to show you," said Reiko.

Her manner was too bright, which awakened immediate suspicion in Sano. He said, "Let's go see."

Masahiro led them to an unused wing of the mansion. Cobwebs hung from rafters in an empty room that smelled of dust.

"Look, Papa," he said, pointing to a knife stuck in the wall. "Me find trap."

He demonstrated how he'd triggered the knife by tapping on a certain spot on the floor with a wooden pole. One of his favorite games was searching for traps that Yanagisawa had installed throughout the compound. The day he and Sano and Reiko had moved in, Masahiro had fallen through a trapdoor in a storehouse and into a pit designed to catch thieves. He'd been shaken up at first, but had become fascinated with traps. He loved tiptoeing through the estate, armed with his pole that he banged on the walls and floors. He'd actually found quite a few traps that the servants had missed in their effort to rid the place of them. Living here was great fun for him.

"That's very good, Masahiro." Sano silently thanked the gods that the knife had flown right over Masahiro. Had he been as tall as an adult, he would have been killed. "You're going to be a fine detective someday."

"It's in his blood," Reiko said.

Sano felt his heart swell with pride and affection toward Masahiro. It seemed that his child became more of an individual every day. Sano had dreams that Masahiro would grow up to be an honorable samurai, make a name for himself, and father his own children one day. He told Reiko in a low voice, "I don't want to spoil his fun, but I'd better have my men re-inspect the estate tomorrow." Nothing must harm his precious son.

He and Reiko followed Masahiro out of the mansion to the garden, where crickets sang in the dark landscape of trees, boulders, pond, and stone lanterns. The little boy skipped away chasing fireflies that sparkled above the grass. Fragrance from night-blooming jasmine scented the air.

"This is so pleasant and peaceful, compared to other places in the world. We truly are fortunate to live here," Reiko mused, then asked Sano, "How did your investigation go?"

He told her about interviewing Chief Ejima's family, subordinates, and other people who had contact with him. "I've just talked to his informants. Just like everyone else, they had opportunity to kill him. Just like everyone else, they deny that they did it. And I have cause to believe them."

"They lacked reason to kill him, or means?"

"Both." Sano thought Reiko seemed a little too interested in his case, especially since she wasn't involved in it. "The informants are minor officials who were disgruntled and trying to ruin their superiors by telling tales on them to Ejima. He was on their side. He also paid them generously. And they don't strike me as expert martial artists. They're the kind of samurai who wear swords as a costume and never fight."

"This Captain Nakai sounds like the most likely culprit," Reiko said.

Sano nodded. "I'm waiting to hear the results of Detective Tachibana's surveillance on him." He shook his head. "I almost wish we could put all the suspects under surveillance."

"You can commandeer as many men as you need," Reiko reminded him.

"There aren't enough I can trust to do a good job. There aren't enough men I can trust at all." Sano was learning the limitations of his power. "Besides, it's possible that Ejima and the other victims were killed by someone whose name hasn't surfaced yet."

Masahiro ran toward the pond. Reiko called, "Don't fall in the water!" Sano asked her, "How did your investigation go?"

She tensed; her bright animation faded. "Well . . . I went to the crime scene. I'm afraid I ran into a bit of trouble." She reluctantly described how she and her guards had been set upon by the outcasts.

Sano realized that she'd been dreading to tell him. He was disturbed because she'd not been as unobtrusive about her inquiries as he'd wished.

"I'm sorry," she said contritely. "Please forgive me."

"It's not your fault," Sano said, meaning it. "And I'm more concerned about your safety than about my position. You'd better not go back to the *hinin* settlement. If you do, the headman might not show up to rescue you again."

Reiko nodded in agreement. "I think I've learned as much there as I could." She hesitated, then confessed, "Afterward, I went to the Hundred-Day Theater that Yugao's father once owned."

As she described what she'd learned, Sano was dismayed even further to realize that her inquiries had moved wider geographically and higher up the social scale. Could they remain secret much longer? Yet he couldn't criticize her for doing the things he would have done in her place.

"Now that you've got alternate suspects as well as evidence against Yugao," he said, "what will you do next?"

"I found out that her father's former business partner and his two *rōnin* were at a card game the whole night of the murders. That might or might not clear them. I wasn't able to find Yugao's friend Tama. But before I try again, I'm going to have another visit with Yugao. Maybe, when she hears what I've learned, she'll be shaken up enough to tell me the truth."

Maybe that would be the end of Reiko's investigation. Sano said, "Good luck bringing the killer to justice, whoever it turns out to be."

Reiko smiled, relieved that he wasn't angry. "What about your investigation?"

"I'm going to try out a new theory. I've been examining the victims' lives in search of suspects who might know *dim-mak*. But what if the victims didn't know their killer? He might be a stranger they encountered in the streets. If so, his name wouldn't be in their appointment records."

And he could be someone far beyond Edo Castle and the administrative district. "It'll be a huge job to reconstruct every move those men made and identify everyone who came within touching distance of them. But unless we get a lucky break very soon, we'd better start. And I'll look specifically for men who know *dim-mak*."

Masahiro came running up to Reiko and tugged her hand. "Me hungry. Eat!"

"Will you have dinner with us?" Reiko asked Sano.

Sano could ill afford the time, but it had been ages since he'd eaten with his family. "Yes. But afterward, I have some work to do in my office."

He had to find out what had happened while he'd been gone, and attend to any urgent business. He also expected Lord Matsudaira to summon him to report on the progress of his investigation. His workload had increased a hundredfold since it began. The murder case had rejuvenated him, but his energy was flagging.

As he and Reiko and Masahiro entered the mansion together, Sano looked around and upward. The stars in the black sky sparkled, as bright as the fireflies, above the rooftops. Night hid from his view the palace up the hill. All was serene, but Sano imagined he heard the echo of war drums. The smell of gunpowder mingled with the floral scents.

"At least there hasn't been another murder," he said.

As night deepened, the moon swelled, white and round and luminescent, over Edo. Night-watchmen stood guard outside warehouses, while soldiers on horseback patrolled the rapidly emptying streets. Inside the windows of the houses, lamps winked out as if extinguished by a vast breath that swept through town. Sentries barred the gates to each neighborhood; the howling of stray dogs echoed in the gathering silence. The city slumbered. Darkness spread across hills and rice fields outside town.

But the Asakusa Temple district up the river blazed with light. Colored lanterns hung from the eaves of the temple buildings, shrines, and roofs of stalls in the marketplace. Hordes gathered to celebrate Sanja Matsuri, the festival that honored the founding of the temple a thousand years ago. People streamed into the main hall to pray for a good harvest, while outside, men performed ancient sacred dances. Village elders from the district paraded through boisterous, drunken throngs that jammed the precinct. Men pushed carts that transported huge drums and gongs, which they beat to produce a thunderous, clanging din. Priests led portable miniature shrines, each decorated with tingling brass bells, gilded ornaments, purple silk cords, and crowned with a gold phoenix. Each shrine rode atop stout wooden crossbeams borne on the shoulders of some hundred youths clad in loincloths and headbands. The bearers chanted in loud, hoarse voices as they labored under their heavy burdens. Sweat glistened on their naked flesh. Cheering crowds engulfed and followed the shrines. Beggars roved, their wooden bowls in hand, beseeching rich folk moved to generosity by the festive atmosphere.

One beggar among the legions made no effort to collect alms. His bowl was empty, his voice silent. Costumed in a tattered kimono and a wicker hat that hid his face, he ignored the merrymakers. His feet, clad in frayed straw sandals, trod a straight path through the crowd, following a group of samurai who walked ten paces ahead of him.

The group stopped at a wine vendor's stall. The beggar halted a short distance away. His intent gaze focused on the samurai at the center of the group, a stout man with a fleshy face already red from liquor. He wore lavish silk robes and ornate swords. The others were simply dressed; his attendants. He and his men bought cups of wine, toasted one another, drank, and roared with laughter. Rage ignited inside the beggar while he watched them. The samurai, a high-ranked *bakufu* official, was one of the enemy that had trampled his honor in the dirt. His spirit roiled with the hot, bloodthirsty lust for revenge that had inspired his one-man crusade.

The drums throbbed and the gongs rang in louder, escalating tempo. Two shrines converged upon each other. Shouts erupted from the bearers, who quickened their steps and the cadence of their chants. The shrines rocked and tilted perilously above the cheering spectators. They charged in ritualistic duel. The official and his attendants moved closer to watch. The beggar followed, unobserved by them, just one insignificant man among thousands. Vengeance would be his tonight—if only he could get close enough to touch his foe.

As he walked, he dropped his begging bowl. He inhaled and exhaled deep, slow, rhythmic breaths. His mind calmed, like the smooth, unruffled surface of a lake. Thoughts and emotions fell away from him. His internal forces aligned, and he slipped into a trance that he'd learned to achieve through endless meditation and years of practice. His vision simultaneously broadened and narrowed. He saw the entire, vast, glittery panorama of Asakusa Temple district, with his enemy's moving figure at its center. His senses grew so acute that he heard his enemy's pulse above the chants, the tinkling bells on the shrines, and the general pandemonium.

The official and his attendants slowed down, their progress hindered by shoving, close-packed humanity. But the beggar slipped through it like water flowing between rocks. People glanced in his direction, then made way for him, as if repelled by some threatening aura that he emanated. He curved his spine, rounded his shoulders, and hollowed his chest in a ritual posture that drew energy from the deepest, most primitive part of him. His limbs felt relaxed and fluid, but alertness tingled through them. The energy thrummed in his blood. The moon and stars seemed to slow their journey across the heavens; the world seemed his to command. He sighted on his enemy and closed the distance between them while the energy inside him radiated outward. His intentions manipulated reality. People moved as if they were puppets under his control, shoving against the man he pursued. They separated him from his attendants and bore him along on their tide. He looked backward at his men, who tried in vain to catch up with him, but the crowd deterred them. The beggar easily followed.

The shrines loomed above their heads, beneath the heaving, writhing, shouting bearers. Now the beggar walked four paces directly behind his enemy. Power rose, like steam inside a volcano, up his spine. He was its vessel, his mind its master. His image of his enemy's back expanded to fill his vision; his surroundings faded. His gaze penetrated the garments that his enemy wore. He saw bare skin and the underlying musculature, skeleton, organs, and blood vessels. Nerve pathways formed a glowing, silvery network that united and animated the whole. They intersected at nodes throughout the body. His eye targeted a node between two vertebrae on his enemy's backbone. He hurried his steps until a mere arm's length divided him from his prey. He inhaled a breath so large that his ribs almost cracked. Spiritual and physical power thundered in him, building to a lethal strength.

Time halted.

His prey and everyone except himself froze motionless.

External sounds faded into abrupt, preternatural silence.

He exhaled at the same moment that he unleashed his control over his body. His arm shot out with such speed that it blurred, propelling his fist, which unclenched an instant before reaching its target.

The tip of his index finger touched the node on his enemy's spine with a pressure as light as if from a feather wafted against it by a breeze. The energy exploded from him. The force of its release lifted his feet momentarily off the ground. His vision shattered into bright fragments of light. His body shuddered violently. He swooned as rapture akin to a sexual climax possessed him.

Life reanimated the world. The shrines resumed their dueling; the bearers chanted; the gongs rang, the drums pounded, and the bells tinkled; the crowds applauded and surged. The beggar gasped, spent from his exertion. He saw his foe turn toward him.

The official's expression was one of wary puzzlement: He'd sensed if not actually felt the touch against his back and the presence of danger. It had caused him no pain; he hadn't even flinched. The beggar let the crowd come between them and carry him away. From a distance he watched the official spot his attendants and push through the melee with them. He looked as ruddy, vigorous, and high-spirited as ever. But the beggar imagined the energy from his strike racing along the man's nerve pathways and piercing a vein in his brain. He envisioned the blood beginning to leak, the life-force slowly draining. Triumph elated him.

His enemy was a dead man walking, another casualty of his crusade.

16

Sunrise found Sano at his desk, reading documents by the glow of a lantern that had burned all night. As he affixed his signature seal to a document, he noticed that the crickets had ceased to chirp in the garden outside and birds were singing. He heard chatter and bustle from the servants as his estate awakened to life. Detectives Marume and Fukida entered his office, followed by Hirata and Detectives Inoue and Arai.

"Did you forget to go to bed yesterday?" Marume asked.

Sano yawned, stretched his cramped muscles, and rubbed his bleary eyes. "I had some work to catch up on."

He'd made barely a dent in the correspondence and reports that had filled up his office while he'd been gone, even though his principal aide Kozawa had dealt with much business. And last night, when he'd briefed Lord Matsudaira on the progress of his investigation, Lord Matsudaira had ordered him to continue giving it top priority. Now Sano wished there were two of him, or more hours in the day.

Kozawa appeared, and Sano gave orders that included postponing all his conferences. He dismissed his aide with instructions to attend to minor matters. Then he explained to Hirata and the detectives his plan for today's inquiries.

"We'll focus on identifying people that the victims had contact with but were strangers to them, and finding martial artists who might know *dim-mak*." Sano checked the notes that he and Hirata and the detectives had written. "We've determined that all the victims spent time outside the castle and administrative district during the two days prior to their deaths. Hirata-*san,* I want you and your men to go where they went and find out who, if anyone, besides their friends, families and associates, came close enough to touch them."

He had a disturbing premonition that the killer would strike again unless they worked fast. "Marume, Fukida, and I will go fishing for martial arts experts. I know a good place to start."

Sano and the detectives rode through a gate into a neighborhood on an edge of the Nihonbashi merchant district. The sentry greeted him by name. The district was populated by families of samurai blood who'd lost their status through war and other misfortunes, merged with the commoners, and gone into trade. He led the familiar way across a bridge that spanned a canal lined with willows. Whenever he came here it seemed as if he'd traveled a great distance. Along the street of modest shops, houses, and food stalls, people smiled and bowed to him. Receiving such courtesies here always made him feel like an impostor. Some of those old folks had once scolded him for making mischief. He passed little boys who were playing and laughing. Had it really been thirty years since he'd been one of them?

He dismounted in a narrow side lane. Fences enclosed the rear lots of businesses and the proprietors' living quarters. A gate opened. Two women carrying baskets emerged. One was in her fifties, gray-haired and dressed in a plain gray kimono, the other white-haired and elderly. Sano approached them while his men waited down the lane.

"Hello, Mother," he said.

The gray-haired woman looked up at him in surprise. "Ichirō!" An affectionate smile brightened her lined face.

Sano greeted his mother's maid and companion, who'd worked for his family since before his birth: "Hello, Hana-*san.*"

139

They had just come out of Sano's childhood home. His father had become a *rōnin* when the third Tokugawa shogun had confiscated his master Lord Kii's lands forty years ago, turning the Sano clan and the lord's other retainers out to fend for themselves. Before his death six years ago, Sano's father had approached a family connection, called in a favor, and obtained for his only son a post as a police commander. An extraordinary chain of events had led Sano from there to his present station.

"It's good to see you," his mother said. "You haven't been home for more than two months."

"I know," Sano said, feeling guilty because he'd neglected his duty to her.

When he'd become the shogun's *sōsakan-sama* after a brief stint on the police force, he'd moved to Edo Castle and taken her with him. But the change had upset her so much that Sano had been forced to move her back to the house where she'd spent almost her entire life. Now she lived here contentedly, on the generous allowance he provided.

"How are my grandson and my honorable daughter-in-law?" His mother adored Masahiro, but was awed by Reiko and shy with her. After Sano replied that they were well, she said, "Hana and I were on our way to the market, but we can go later. Come inside and have something to eat."

"Thank you, but I can't stay," Sano said.

She noticed his men waiting on their horses down the street. "Ah. You're busy. I mustn't keep you."

They parted, and Sano walked to the corner. There stood the Sano Martial Arts Academy, which occupied a long, low, wooden building with a brown tile roof and barred windows. Like many *rōnin,* Sano's father had been cut loose with no skills except in the martial arts. He'd founded the academy and scratched out a meager livelihood for himself and his family. During Sano's youth, the school had lacked the prestige to attract samurai from beyond the lower ranks. But today he saw boys and young men who wore the crests of the Tokugawa and great *daimyo* clans streaming in the door. His name, his high position,

140

and the fact that he'd learned his own acclaimed fighting skills here had boosted the school's reputation. Now it was one of the top places to train in Edo.

Sano entered the school. Inside the practice room, students dressed in loose cotton trousers and jackets sparred against one another. Amid a din of clacking wooden swords, stamping feet, and battle cries, instructors shouted directions. The *sensei,* Aoki Koemon, hastened over to Sano.

"Greetings," he said with a welcoming smile.

He was a stocky, genial samurai, near Sano's own age of thirty-six. They'd grown up together, and Koemon had once been an apprentice to Sano's father, who had left the school to him. Sano sometimes envied his friend and childhood playmate the simple life that would have been his if not for his father's ambitions for him.

Koemon pulled two wooden swords from a rack on the wall. "It's been ages since you showed up for a practice session. Are you here to make up for lost time?"

"Actually, I've come in search of somebody," Sano said.

The school was a gossip center of the martial arts world, and a source of news he'd often plumbed. But when Koemon tossed him a sword, he caught it. They faced off, holding their weapons upright. Sano hadn't fought a match in more than a month, and the sword felt good in his hands.

"Who is it?" said Koemon as they circled each other and the class continued nearby.

"A martial artist who has the touch of death."

Koemon lunged, whipping his sword in a fast curve. Sano dodged and barely avoided a smack on the hip.

"With all due respect, your reflexes are a lot slower than they used to be," Koemon said. "I don't know of anyone who practices *dim-mak.*"

They resumed circling. "Well, he exists." Sano launched a series of lashes that Koemon easily parried, while he explained about the murders. "And he's in Edo."

"That's amazing," Koemon said, then attacked Sano with swift, ferocious swordplay that drove him backward against the wall.

Already breathless from exertion, Sano counterattacked, gained himself room to maneuver, and darted around Koemon. Sweat trickled down his brow as they faced off again. The sword now felt heavy in his hands, which hurt where his calluses had grown soft. "Have you heard of any martial arts masters coming to town?" Perhaps the killer numbered among those *ronin* who wandered Japan, fighting duels, teaching lessons, and gathering disciples. There had been legions after the Battle of Sekigahara ninety-four years ago, during which the first Tokugawa shogun Ieyasu had defeated his rival warlords whose armies had then scattered, but their numbers had dwindled over the decades.

"Not recently," Koemon said.

"On the other hand, he could be someone who's been here all along." Sano favored this theory. "Maybe the killer is an enemy of the victims—or Lord Matsudaira—who's hidden his secret knowledge of *dim-mak* until now." Sano charged and slashed.

As Koemon leapt away, Sano's blade grazed his sleeve. "Good, you're warming up," Koemon said. A thought altered his expression. "I just remembered something. Do you know the priest Ozuno?"

"The name doesn't sound familiar," Sano said as they struck and parried. "Who is he?"

"He's a samurai from the old days. When he lost his master, he took religious vows. He entered the monastery at Enryaku Temple on Mount Hiei."

Mount Hiei was the sacred peak near the imperial capital. Enryaku Temple had been a mighty Buddhist stronghold of fighting priests until some hundred years ago, when its political influence and military power had posed a threat to the warlord Oda Nobunaga and he'd leveled it. The temple had since been rebuilt, and traditions died hard.

"The priests taught Ozuno their ancient secrets." Koemon's sword battered Sano's. "By the time he came down from the mountain, he was an expert at the mystic martial arts and much sought after as a teacher."

"That story has been used by legions of samurai who are trying to boost their reputations or attract pupils," Sano said. "If it's true in this Ozuno's case, why isn't he famous?"

"He's a loner who hates publicity. And he's very selective about whom he chooses to teach. He takes on one pupil at a time and trains him for years. He makes all his pupils swear not to reveal that they've studied with him or give away the techniques that he teaches them."

This aura of secrecy jibed with what Sano knew about *dim-mak* and its practitioners. Fatigued from defending himself, Sano ducked Koemon's blade; it whistled over his head. "Where can I find Ozuno?"

"When he's in town, he lives at one temple or another," Koemon said. "I hear he has friends at them who give him a place to stay. I don't know if he's still teaching. He must be ninety years old. But he still roams the country when the wanderlust takes him."

As Sano considered this promising lead, his attention drifted from the fight. Koemon's blade whacked him across his stomach. Sano doubled over, wincing from the blow, humbled by the abrupt defeat.

"My apologies," Koemon said, remorseful.

"No need," Sano said. "You won a fair victory."

They bowed to each other, hung their swords on the rack, then gulped water from a ceramic urn. Sano thanked Koemon for the information and the combat practice.

"Any time," Koemon said. "I'll put the word out that you're looking for Ozuno and send you any news I hear."

When Sano left the school, he found his detectives at a food stall, drinking tea and eating noodles. He joined them, and as he ate, he told them about the mysterious priest.

Marume, interested yet dubious, was shoveling noodles into his mouth with his chopsticks. "Even if this fellow is still in good enough shape to kill at age ninety, it doesn't sound as if he has any connection to Chief Ejima and the others."

"Or to Lord Matsudaira," said Fukida.

"Maybe one of his secret pupils does. At any rate, I think he's worth talking to." Sano finished his meal and set aside his empty bowl. "We'll go back to Edo Castle and mount a search for Ozuno. And maybe there will be some news from Hirata and Detective Tachibana."

17

Reiko paced around the room in her father's estate where she'd interviewed Yugao two days ago. When she'd arrived this morning, she'd asked Magistrate Ueda to let her speak to Yugao again, and he'd sent men to the jail to fetch her. It was almost noon by the time the door opened. Two guards brought in Yugao. Her hands were shackled; she wore the same dirty robe. She seemed surprised and displeased to see Reiko.

"It's you again," she said. "What do you want now?"

The guards shoved her to her knees in front of Reiko, then departed, closing the door behind them.

"I want to talk some more," Reiko said.

Yugao shook her head, obstinate. "I've already said everything I have to say."

She looked the worse for another night at Edo Jail. Flea bites dotted her neck, and her eyes were crusted, pink, and swollen. Reiko felt both revilement and pity toward her. "We have some new things to discuss."

Raising her bound hands to scratch her flea bites, Yugao waited in suspicious silence.

"I paid a visit to your house yesterday," Reiko said.

Yugao's swollen eyes blinked in shock. "You went to the *hinin* settlement?" She sat up straight and stared at Reiko. "Why?"

"You wouldn't tell me what happened the night your family was murdered," Reiko said, "so I decided to find out for myself. I talked with the headman and your neighbors."

Yugao shook her head in evident confusion. Her hands rubbed together, and her knees clenched spasmodically. Reiko thought that perhaps her efforts had convinced Yugao that she sincerely wanted to help. Maybe Yugao was relenting toward her and would now trust her enough to talk.

"The headman told me why your father was a *hinin*," Reiko ventured.

Now Yugao's face turned ugly with sudden rage. "You snooped into my business! You samurai people do whatever you want and you don't care about anybody else's privacy. I hate you all!"

This outburst disconcerted Reiko, who was chagrined because this conversation wasn't going the way she wanted. But she continued, "For a man to commit incest with his daughter is not only a crime but a betrayal of her love for him. Did your father do it to you that night?"

"I won't talk about my father," Yugao said with bitter indignation.

"Then let's talk about your mother and your sister. Did they do something to hurt you, too?" A new theory evolved in Reiko's mind. "Were they cruel to you because they blamed you for the fact that they had to live as outcasts?"

"I won't talk about them, either," Yugao said.

While Reiko controlled her exasperation, she saw a possible reason why Yugao had refused to talk. Maybe she was so shamed by her sordid life that she would rather die than reveal it. Maybe she blamed herself for it and wanted to be punished even if she hadn't killed her family. Because the law treated people as guilty for the transgressions of their kin and associates, it was logical for them to believe they really were.

"You should reconsider," Reiko advised Yugao. "If you stabbed your father while he was forcing himself on you, that's different from murder. If your mother and sister attacked you because you were protecting yourself, you had a right to fight back against them. Killing in self-defense isn't a crime. You won't be punished. The magistrate will set you free."

Any other accused criminal that Reiko had ever seen would have gladly seized on this explanation as a chance to save his life. But Yugao turned her face away and said in a cold, recalcitrant voice: "That's not what happened."

"Then tell me what did," Reiko said.

"I stabbed my father until he died. Then I stabbed my mother and my sister. I murdered them. I don't have to say why."

Reiko's mind flashed back to the vision she'd had of the murders at the hovel. She pictured Yugao wielding the knife, heard the screams, smelled the blood. But her imagination plus Yugao's confession didn't necessarily equal the truth.

"Listen, Yugao," she said. "My father bent the law by delaying the verdict at your trial. I've gone far out of my way for you." She'd even risked putting Sano in jeopardy. "That obligates you to tell me the truth."

Scornful contempt wrenched Yugao's lips. "I never asked you or the magistrate to save me. I'm ready to accept my punishment. So go away before I spit on you again."

Reiko prowled the room, venting her impatience. She began to appreciate the benefits of torture. A little molten copper poured on Yugao would certainly improve her manners as well as break her silence. "I'm not going away until you convince me that you're guilty," Reiko said, circling Yugao. "And if that's really what you want to do, you'll need to do better than you have, especially in light of what else I learned yesterday."

"What are you jabbering about now?" Yugao's voice was insolent, but Reiko heard a current of fear in it.

"You and your family weren't the only people in your house the night of the murders. Your sister's friend Ihei has admitted he was there, sleeping in the lean-to with her. The boy on fire-watch duty saw him running away after the murders."

Yugao sniffed, disdainful. "Ihei is a clumsy weakling. If he tried to stab anybody, he would cut himself."

"What about the warden from Edo Jail?" Reiko said. "He was at your house earlier that evening. He and your father had a fight. Nobody can call him a weakling."

"Do you really think Ihei or the warden did it?" Yugao demanded. Her gaze smoldered with animosity as it followed Reiko around the room. "Have they been arrested?" She read the answer on Reiko's face and laughed. "You don't have any more dirt on them than you've just said. If your father put the three of us on trial, he'd have to convict me before them. I was caught in the house, with the knife."

None of Reiko's experience with crime and criminals had prepared her to understand this woman who was so bent on dying for the murders. She tried a different strategy: "Let's make a bargain. I'll tell my father that you're guilty if you tell me why you killed your family."

In response to this bizarre deal, Yugao only laughed again. "I thought you had it all figured out. My father committed incest with me. My mother and sisters attacked me."

"That's only a theory," Reiko said. "I've begun to doubt that there was any incest at all. In fact, I wonder if your father was unjustly condemned to be an outcast."

Yugao scowled, leery of a trick.

"I went to the Hundred-Day Theater and met his former business partner. Did you know that Mizutani was the one who reported the incest between you and your father?" Reiko waited for Yugao to speak, but she didn't, and her expression offered no answer. "Perhaps he made the whole thing up. Perhaps he hired someone to kill your father to prevent his coming back to the carnival and claiming his share of it, and the rest of your family because they witnessed the crime."

"No," Yugao said flatly.

"No, he didn't falsely accuse your father? Do you mean your father was guilty of incest?"

Yugao said with hateful vehemence, "I mean you can take your bargain and shove it up your sweet little rear end. I've had enough of you. As far as I'm concerned, we're done talking." She plopped her hands in her lap, compressed her mouth, and stared at the wall.

In desperation, Reiko voiced the only other theory that made sense to her: "Are you taking the blame for someone else? Are you trying to protect whoever it is?"

Yugao remained obstinately speechless. Reiko waited. Time passed. The angle and brightness of the sun through the window changed; people came and went along the corridors outside the chamber. But Yugao seemed ready to wait until they both died of old age and their skeletons crumbled into dust. Finally Reiko sighed.

"You win," she said. "But I'm going to learn the truth, whether you like it or not, whether from you or someone else."

Yugao's expression disdained the words as bluffing. "Can I go back to jail now?"

"For the time being, while I look up your old friend Tama."

"Tama?" Yugao blurted the name. Apprehension echoed in her voice. Her head swiveled toward Reiko. As their gazes met, Reiko saw Yugao's defiant poise melt.

"Yes." Gratified that she'd found a vulnerable spot in the woman, Reiko pressed her advantage: "You remember Tama, don't you? What do you think she can tell me about you?"

Yugao's jailhouse complexion turned even paler as she spoke between clenched teeth: "You stay away from Tama."

"Why don't you want me to talk to her?" Reiko said.

"Just leave her alone!" Yugao shouted.

"Are you afraid of what she might say?"

"Quit pestering me!" Yugao clambered to her feet and stumbled across the room. She beat her chained hands on the door, crying, "Let me out!" Curses and shrieks spewed from her.

The door opened. At the threshold stood Magistrate Ueda, flanked by two guards. His expression was severe, disapproving. "Put me to death," Yugao begged him. "Make her leave me alone!"

Magistrate Ueda ignored her and said to the guards, "Keep watch on her while I talk to my daughter."

His eyes signaled Reiko to follow him. They went outside to a courtyard enclosed by storehouses, whose thick plaster walls and iron roofs and doors protected valuable documents from fire. Sunlight bleached the walls and pavement. Reiko could hear Yugao screaming inside the building.

"May I assume that Yugao was no more cooperative today than before?" Magistrate Ueda said.

"You may." The failure discouraged Reiko.

"Have you decided whether she's guilty?"

Reiko mulled over her entire cache of knowledge, then said, "Sometimes the most obvious answer is the correct one. I believe Yugao did murder her family."

"If you think she did it, that will suffice," Magistrate Ueda said. "I trust your judgment, and it confirms my own. Furthermore, we've made a good-faith effort to discover the truth about Yugao."

"But I still don't understand why she did it."

"Perhaps she's deranged."

Reiko shook her head. "Yugao certainly behaves as though she is, but I think she's just as sane as anyone else. I think she has logical reasons for the things she does; if only I could figure out what they are."

"The law doesn't require that a motive for a crime be determined before an accused person is convicted," Magistrate Ueda reminded her.

"I know," Reiko said, "but I may be getting closer to finding out Yugao's motive. She got very upset when I mentioned her friend Tama. I'm interested to know what Tama knows that Yugao doesn't want her to tell me. I suspect that it pertains to the murders."

"You haven't yet talked to this Tama?" When Reiko described her fruitless search for Yugao's friend, Magistrate Ueda looked concerned. "I cannot delay a verdict any longer. Three people have been brutally slain, and Yugao appears beyond rational doubt to be the killer. Until I put her to death, I'm avoiding my duty to administer justice, and I rightly deserve to be censured. I might add that it's not fair that one among thousands of criminals should have an exception made for her, especially when she appreciates it so little."

Reiko nodded; she couldn't dispute her father's point. But a sense of incompletion gnawed at her. Even if she'd made a strong case against Yugao, she didn't want to cease her inquiries. She sought to articulate why they must continue. "I believe that the reason Yugao stabbed her parents and sister to death is even more important than the fact that she's the killer. I believe that if we don't find out what it is, there will be a greater threat to law and order and the good of the public than if you let her walk free."

"On what do you base those beliefs?"

"On my intuition."

Magistrate Ueda's gaze tilted skyward. Reiko remembered many times when, during her childhood, she'd made statements that she'd insisted were true because her feelings said so. Before he could argue, as he had then, that emotions weren't facts and women were flighty, irrational creatures, she said, "My intuition has been right in the past."

"Hmm." Her father's expression showed grudging agreement.

During the murder investigation at the Black Lotus Temple, Reiko's unfounded suspicions had proved true. Now she said, "I think that whatever Yugao is hiding is too dangerous to let her take to her grave, and if she does, we'll regret it. Please give me a little more time to find Tama. Please wait at least until I hear what she has to say before you convict Yugao."

Magistrate Ueda smiled with fondness and vexation. "I've never found it easy to say no to you, Daughter. You may have one more day to investigate. At this time tomorrow, I'll reconvene Yugao's trial. Unless you can present evidence that exonerates Yugao—or justifies continuing to investigate the crime—I must send Yugao to the execution ground."

One day seemed not enough time to solve the mystery in which justice and a young woman's life hung in the balance. But Reiko knew she'd pushed her father to overstep his authority too much, and Sano would be even more displeased than when he'd first heard about her investigation.

"Thank you, Father," she said. "I'll have the answers for you by tomorrow."

18

The afternoon sun beamed down on a queue of soldiers, officials, and servants who crowded the promenade outside Edo Castle and inched up to its gate. Sentries examined each person's identification document, which consisted of a scroll bearing his name, post, and the shogun's signature seal, before letting him inside. They searched everyone's body and possessions for hidden messages or bombs. In the guardroom above the massive, ironclad portals, more sentries, armed with guns, peered out barred windows, monitoring the street traffic. In the covered corridors atop the stone walls that enclosed the castle's buildings and wound around the slopes up to the palace, guards scanned the city through spyglasses. Lord Matsudaira, goaded by his fear of attack, had increased the usual security precautions and made Edo Castle the safest place in Japan.

Sano rode with his detectives to the head of the line. The men trapped in it bowed and yielded politely to him. He heard someone calling his name, turned, and saw Hirata galloping toward him, accompanied by Inoue and Arai. Sano signaled his men to wait. Hirata and the detectives joined them.

"We've got news," Hirata said.

At the gate, the sentries recognized Sano and his companions and waved them through without inspecting their documents. They bypassed the troops who were searching people and opening trunks and saddlebags in the guardhouse and rode uphill through the passages.

"We traced the movements of all the murder victims except Treasury Minister Moriwaki," said Hirata. "His habit of sneaking off alone made it impossible. As for Court Supervisor Ono, the retainers who accompanied him outside the castle didn't see anyone touch him or any stranger behaving suspiciously around him."

Sano asked, "What about Highway Commissioner Sasamura and Chief Ejima?"

"We got lucky there," Hirata said. "Ejima went to an incense shop two days before he died. One of his bodyguards said that a wandering priest bumped into Ejima in the crowds and knocked the package of incense out of his hands. Ejima bent over to pick it up. The priest could have touched him then."

"The bodyguard didn't notice?"

"The traffic in the street blocked his view."

"Did you get a description of the priest?" Sano asked.

"He wore a saffron robe and a wicker hat and carried a begging bowl." Hirata shook his head in regret. "Just like any other priest in Japan. One moment he was there; the next, he'd disappeared."

"Did the highway commissioner also have an encounter with a priest soon before his death?"

"No, but he did with someone else, at a money-lender's shop." Although officials of Sasamura's rank earned big stipends, many overspent on lavish lifestyles and wound up in debt to merchant bankers. "A guard stationed outside the shop saw a water-seller loitering nearby while Sasamura was inside. That in itself wouldn't have been unusual—except the guard noticed that his water buckets were empty. The guard thought he was a bandit in disguise, waiting to rob people who borrowed money from the shop. He chased the water-seller away."

"Maybe the water-seller, and the priest, were the killer in disguise, stalking Ejima and Sasamura for the purpose of assassinating them," Sano said thoughtfully. "And these 'chance' encounters were deliberate."

"I think they were the points of attack," Hirata said. "Unfortunately, the guard couldn't describe the water-seller, except to say he looked like all the rest of them."

"I'd like to know where Captain Nakai was when Ejima went to the incense shop and Sasamura visited the money-lender," Sano said. "By the way, we have a new potential lead." He told Hirata about the priest Ozuno.

Rapid hoofbeats clattered on the pavement behind them. A voice called, "Honorable Chamberlain!"

Sano and his party stopped and turned to see two men on horseback approaching. One was an Edo Castle guard, the other a samurai boy in his teens, dressed in a fancy black satin kimono printed with green willow branches and silver waves, as though for a festive occasion. Both halted their mounts and bowed to Sano. The guard said, "Please excuse the interruption, but this is Daikichi, page to Colonel Ibe of the army. He has an important message for you."

The page spoke in a breathless rush: "I come on your orders to report any cases of sudden death directly to you."

"Has there been another?" Sano said, exchanging alarmed glances with Hirata.

"Yes." The page's voice shook, and tears welled in his clear young eyes. "My master has just died."

Consternation struck Sano. "Where?"

"In Yoshiwara."

Edo's notorious pleasure quarter lay on the northern outskirts of town. Many men bound for Yoshiwara, the only place in the city where prostitution was legal, traveled there by ferry up the Sumida River, but Sano, Hirata, and the detectives took the faster land route on horseback. Beyond the Dike of Japan, the long causeway upon which they rode, the flooded rice paddies spread lush and green. Peasants waded in them, pulling weeds and netting eels. Irises and lilies bloomed in the willow-edged San'ya Canal, where herons posed in waters swollen from the spring rains. Seagulls winged and jeered in a limpid turquoise sky. But Sano observed that the political strife had contaminated even this bucolic setting.

Squadrons of armed troops escorted mounted samurai officials. Merchants traveling in palanquins were protected by hired *rōnin* bodyguards. As Sano passed the teahouses that lined the approach to the Yoshiwara gate, he saw soldiers who wore the Matsudaira crest loitering around them, watching for fugitive rebels. Yoshiwara was a place of high fashion, lavish entertainment, and glamour, but Sano knew it wasn't exempt from violence. Two winters past, he'd investigated a murder there; six years ago, he'd thwarted an assassination attempt. Now it was the scene of another death by foul play.

He and his comrades left their horses at a stable by the moat that surrounded Yoshiwara and crossed the bridge. Civilian guards let them through the red, roofed gate in the high wall that kept the courtesans from escaping. Inside, they strode past the pleasure houses that lined Naka-no-cho, the main street. Laughter burst from teahouses jammed with men; samisen music spangled the air. Customers strolled, gawking at the women who sat on display inside the barred window of each brothel except for one, the Mitsuba. It was located at the farthest, least prestigious end of the street and catered to clients who wanted women for lower prices or rowdier entertainment than was offered at the better houses. Here, according to his page, Colonel Ibe had died. Bamboo blinds covered the windows. A funereal vacuum shrouded the building.

Detective Marume lifted the entrance curtain and called, "Hello! Is anyone in there?"

A samurai emerged. He was a gray-haired man with thin, precise features, his air of dignity compromised by flushed cheeks from drinking too much. He courteously greeted Sano, then said, "I'm Lieutenant Oda, Colonel Ibe's chief aide. You must have received the message I sent."

"Yes," Sano said. "Thank you for alerting me so promptly." He and his comrades entered the vestibule, where the watchman sat. Voices murmured inside the building. "Where is Colonel Ibe?"

"I'll show you."

Lieutenant Oda led the way down a corridor. On the left were two rooms. One contained a group of samurai; in the other, a flock of women, dressed in bright kimonos and made up with rouge and white rice powder, huddled with a few men and older women who looked to be the brothel's owner and servants. Sano glimpsed resignation or impatience on some faces, fright on others.

"I've detained everyone who was in the house when Colonel Ibe died and kept everyone else out," said Lieutenant Oda.

"Your cooperation is most appreciated," Sano said.

Oda slid open a door on the opposite side of the corridor. Sano entered a parlor. Its floor was littered with cushions, musical instruments, sake decanters, and cups. Lacquer trays held plates of half-eaten food that suggested a banquet interrupted. Colonel Ibe knelt alone and immobile, his upper body flopped across a tray. Sano, Hirata, and their detectives stood gazing down at the corpse. Colonel Ibe was in his fifties, his topknot streaked with gray. Sano had met him some months ago, at a meeting, but found him almost unrecognizable now. His neck was twisted sideways. His eyes were open but glazed; his moonlike face wore a surprised expression. Chewed food was visible in his open mouth. His stout body was naked except for a red-and-gold-striped dressing gown that had been tied around his waist and shrugged off his shoulders, leaving his top half bare.

"This must have been a wild party." Detective Marume picked up a man's loincloth and a woman's white under-kimono from the floor. More clothing lay strewn about.

"Which is fortunate for us," Sano said, aware of Oda listening by the door and glad that he and his men needn't improvise a way to examine the corpse without breaking the law. "Right there is the sign of *dim-mak*."

He pointed at Colonel Ibe's back. A faint bruise, shaped like a fingerprint, nestled between two vertebrae. Lieutenant Oda came over and stared at the bruise in consternation.

"Then he was killed in the same manner as the *metsuke* chief?" Oda said.

Sano said, "Unfortunately, yes."

"Then it's true. There exists someone who has the power to kill with a mere touch." Amazed, Lieutenant Oda glanced around, as though afraid for his own safety. "Who can it be?"

"That's what I must determine," Sano said. After five murders, his mission was more urgent than ever: Another man was dead because he hadn't caught the killer. Crushed by a sense of failed responsibility, Sano hid his emotions behind a stoic expression. The odor of death mingled with the smells of wine and stale food. Sano felt the presence of evil, although the killer was far removed in space and time. He walked to the exterior door and flung it open, admitting fresh air from the garden, then turned to Oda.

"I need your help."

"Of course." The lieutenant appeared shaken sober; the flush had paled from his complexion.

"Tell me everyone that had contact with Colonel Ibe, starting two days ago."

"I know some of the people, but not all—I didn't go everywhere with him," Oda said, "but his bodyguards did. They're in the room across the hall. Shall I fetch them?"

Sano assented, and Oda brought the two young samurai into the parlor. They recited a long list of family members, colleagues, and subordinates whose lives had intersected Colonel Ibe's during the critical period. When they'd finished, Sano glanced at Hirata, and they shook their heads: As far as they could recall, none of the people mentioned were the same as those who'd had contact with the four other victims.

Sano addressed the bodyguards: "Was there any time when Colonel Ibe was out of your sight?"

The men looked at each other, clearly ashamed because their vigilance had lapsed and horrified that the lapse might have resulted in their master's death. One blurted, "It was just for a moment."

"Last night, at Sanja Matsuri," said the other. "We lost him in the crowd."

Sano thanked the bodyguards and Lieutenant Oda for their information, gave them permission to take their master's body home, and told them to let the brothel resume its business. He and Hirata and their men walked down the street toward the gate.

"That festival turns Asakusa Temple into a wild mob scene," Hirata said. "It would have been a perfect place for the assassin to stalk Colonel Ibe and give him the touch of death."

"With no one the wiser until now," Sano said.

He paused at the gate, turned, and looked down Naka-no-cho. He saw the bodyguards carrying out the shrouded corpse of Colonel Ibe on a litter. As people gathered to watch, Sano heard the buzz of excited conversation and saw the crowds in the street group into clusters, spreading the news. Courtesans pressed their faces against the bars of their windows and revelers spilled from the teahouses, eager to learn the cause of the commotion.

"Do you think it was Captain Nakai?" Hirata asked.

"We need to find out where he was last night," Sano said. "And we'd better go back to Edo Castle and report this latest murder to Lord Matsudaira." Trepidation filled him as he imagined how Lord Matsudaira would react.

19

The teahouse was the fourteenth that Reiko had visited since she'd left the Court of Justice.

She'd already searched for Yugao's onetime friend in all the teahouses near the Hundred-Day Theater, but none of the customers, proprietors, or servants at them knew Tama. Extending her search into the outlying neighborhoods, Reiko stepped from her palanquin in front of this teahouse on a street lined with tenements above shops that sold preserved vegetables and fruit. It was almost identical to all the others she'd seen. A curtain hung from the eaves halfway down an open storefront. A maid leaned, downcast and bored, against a pillar at the edge of its raised plank floor. The room behind her was vacant except for the proprietor, a middle-aged man who squatted beside his sake urn, decanters, and cups. She spotted Reiko's guards, and her face brightened.

"Hello, there," she called to Lieutenant Asukai. She was past her youth, but her figure was voluptuous. Her eyes gleamed at the prospect of male company and big tips. "May I serve you and your friends a drink?"

"Thank you," Asukai said. "By the way, my mistress has some questions that you will please answer."

Curious but wary, the maid beheld Reiko. "Whatever you like."

The proprietor poured sake, and while the maid served the men,

Reiko said, "I'm looking for a woman named Tama. She works at a teahouse around here. Do you know her?"

"Oh, yes," the maid said. "We used to work together, here. Tama's father used to own this teahouse."

Reiko's spirits leapt. "Can you tell me where I can find Tama?"

But the maid shook her head. "Sorry. Haven't seen her in, oh, two years. She and her family moved out of the neighborhood. I don't know where they went. Her father sold the teahouse to him." She waved at the proprietor, who sat with Reiko's escorts, engaging them in polite chat. "Hey, what ever became of Tama?"

He shook his head in ignorance. Disappointed, Reiko pressed on. "Did you know a girl named Yugao? She was friends with Tama."

"No . . ." The maid reconsidered. "Oh, yes, there was a girl who used to come around to visit." But when Reiko asked her about Yugao's character and family, she couldn't provide any information. "Say, why all these questions? Has Tama done something wrong?"

"Not that I know of," Reiko said, "but I must find her." Tama seemed Reiko's only chance at facts that might shed light on the murders. "Where did Tama used to live?"

The maid gave directions to a house some distance away, then said, "Maybe I can find out what happened to her. I can ask around, if you like." She jingled the money in a pouch she wore on her sash, hinting for a bribe.

Reiko paid her a silver coin. "If you find Tama, send word to Lady Reiko at Magistrate Ueda's Court of Justice, and I'll pay you twice as much."

As she climbed into her palanquin, she told the bearers to take her to the house where Tama had once lived. The time until her father's deadline was slipping away, and Reiko had an urgent sense that she must discover the truth about the crimes before Yugao was executed, or there would be consequences dire beyond her imagination.

A corridor as dim and dank as an underground tunnel extended past the prison cells in Edo Jail. Down this trudged a jailer who carried a stack of wooden trays that held food. He paused to shove a tray through the slot under each locked door. Uproarious cries from the captives greeted the food's arrival.

Inside one cell, eight women pounced on their meal like starving cats. They shoved and clawed at one another and shrieked as they fought over rice, pickled vegetables, and dried fish. Yugao managed to grab a rice ball. She fled to a corner of the cell, which was only ten paces square and lit by a tiny barred window near the ceiling, to eat. The other women knelt, gobbling their food. Their hair hung shaggy around their faces; they licked their fingers and wiped them on their dirty hemp robes. Yugao gnawed the tough, gluey rice. How disgusting that a few days in jail had reduced her, as well as her fellow inmates, to wild animals! But she reminded herself that she'd chosen this fate. It was part of her plan. She must, and would, endure.

Finishing her food, Yugao reached for the water jar. But Sachiko, a thief awaiting trial, got to it first. She was a tough, homely girl in her teens who'd grown up on Edo's streets and lived with a band of gangsters before her arrest. She upended the jar and drank, then fixed a belligerent stare on Yugao.

"What's the matter?" she said. "Are you thirsty?"

"Give me that." Yugao snatched at the jar.

Sachiko held it out of her reach and grinned. "If you ask me nicely, I might give you some."

The other women watched eagerly to see what would happen. They all played up to Sachiko because they were afraid of her. Yugao scorned them for their weakness, and she hated Sachiko. She wouldn't bow to the bully.

"Don't annoy me," Yugao said in a quiet, menacing tone. "I'm a murderess. I killed three people. Give me the water, or I'll kill you, too."

Sudden trepidation erased Sachiko's grin. Yugao knew that her crime, the most serious of all, gave her a special status at the jail. The other women thought she was mad and therefore dangerous. Ever since Yugao had been imprisoned with them, Sachiko had been spoiling for a confrontation, and if she wanted to keep her place as the leader of this cell, she couldn't let Yugao intimidate her.

"You must think you're better than the rest of us," Sachiko said. "I heard the guards say the magistrate delayed the verdict at your trial and they took you out yesterday because he wanted to see you again. What for? Did he make you suck him?"

She pantomimed fellatio and laughed; the other women dutifully laughed with her. "You must not have done it good enough, or he'd have let you off instead of sending you back."

Anger burned in Yugao, but she knew that Sachiko was jealous of her, with good reason. She, unlike these other sorry creatures, had a chance to avoid punishment. She need only make up a story that someone else had killed her family. That foolish Lady Reiko would believe her and tell the magistrate to set her free. But Yugao wasn't tempted to take back her confession and bargain for her life. Whether or not they thought she was guilty, she wanted credit for the crime. It was her gift to the person who mattered most in the world to her. How she hated them for trying to trick her into saying too much and betraying him! She hated them for delaying her death sentence and prolonging her stay in this hell. Her resentment toward them enflamed her anger at Sachiko.

"Shut your ugly mouth," Yugao snapped, "or I'll shut it for you. Now give me that water."

"If you want it that bad, you can have it," Sachiko said disdainfully.

She hurled the water at Yugao. It splashed her face, drenched her robe. Murderous rage filled Yugao. She lunged at Sachiko, and the impact knocked them both to the floor. She pummeled her fists against Sachiko's face, clawed at her eyes. Sachiko beat Yugao's head, tore her hair. The other women cried, "Get her, Sachiko! Show her who's boss!"

Sachiko was bigger than Yugao, and she knew how to fight. Soon she was on top of Yugao. Pinned down, Yugao thrashed, striking out at Sachiko, whose hands grasped her throat. Yugao coughed and choked as Sachiko squeezed the breath from her. But she felt an overriding determination not to die here, in a stupid prison brawl, but to stay alive and receive her rightful death sentence at the execution ground. Her flailing hands found the heavy ceramic water jar. She seized it and bashed Sachiko across the face. Sachiko howled, let go of Yugao, and fell backward. Blood poured from her nose. Yugao flung herself on Sachiko and began beating her head with the jar.

"Stop!" Sachiko cried, sobbing in pain and terror. "That's enough. You win!"

But a savage lust for violence possessed Yugao. She mercilessly beat Sachiko.

"Get her off me!" Sachiko screamed.

Instead, the other women pounded on the door, calling, "Help! Help!"

Caught up in her madness, Yugao barely heard the iron bars on the outside of the door drop and a jailer say, "What's going on?" Suddenly the room was full of men. They dragged her off Sachiko, while she shouted and struggled. Sachiko lay moaning; the other women huddled in a corner. Guards dragged Yugao out of the cell.

"We'll teach you to behave yourself," said the jailer.

He and the guards pushed her onto her hands and knees in the passage. She fought them, but they held her. They pulled up her robe, and one man knelt behind her. She jerked as his erect organ probed between her buttocks. He plunged into her. She closed her eyes and gritted her teeth against the agony. One after another, the men took their turns. Tears streamed down her face. She told herself that this was nothing compared to the disgrace and suffering that *he* had experienced. She must endure it for his sake, until the time came to die for him.

The distant clanging of a bell impinged on her awareness. She heard one of the guards say, "That's the fire signal." The man violating her withdrew himself; the others let go of her. Yugao collapsed onto the floor, gasping. The guards rushed down the corridor. They unbarred and flung open doors, yelling, "Fire! Everybody out!"

Amid cries of fear and excitement, prisoners burst from their cells. They ran down the corridor past Yugao. She smelled smoke from a blaze somewhere nearby. A guard kicked her ribs as he followed the prisoners out of the jail.

"Get up and go unless you want to burn to death," he said.

The law ordered prisoners to be released from the jail when fire threatened it. This was one example of mercy in an otherwise cruel legal system. Yugao realized with amazement that everything had just changed. Once she'd thought that her death by execution was all she could offer *him* and they would meet again only in the paradise that lay on the other side of death. Now fate had intervened.

She scrambled joyfully to her feet. Hobbling with pain and ignoring the blood trickling down her legs, she emerged with the other prisoners into a courtyard where sunlight momentarily blinded her. Clouds of acrid smoke burgeoned above the jail's roofs in a neighborhood right outside its walls, but the air was fresher than in her cell. Yugao breathed gratefully. Prisoners swarmed from other wings of the jail. The guards hurried them out the main gate.

"Don't forget to come back as soon as the fire's out," the guards called to the departing horde.

As Yugao cleared the bridge over the canal, the city spread before her, bright and beautiful and inviting. What a miraculous stroke of good fortune! She could live, for him and with him. Dizzied with freedom and hope, she raced ahead of the other prisoners and vanished into the alleys of the slums outside Edo Jail without a backward look.

20

"I told you that a killer was stalking the newly appointed officials," Lord Matsudaira said when Sano reported the news of Colonel Ibe's death. He leveled a triumphant glance at the shogun and Yoritomo seated on the dais above him, and the two elders kneeling nearby. "Do you believe me now?"

"Yes. You were right," Ihara conceded. Displeasure wrinkled his simian features.

Kato nodded with reluctance that his mask-like face couldn't hide. Sano, seated beside Hirata on the floor near the shogun's right, observed the dismayed glance that passed between the two elders: They were worried because the latest murder had given more credence to Lord Matsudaira's theory that there was a plot against his regime.

Lord Matsudaira glared at Sano. "You were supposed to catch the killer." His eyes flicked toward the elders, hinting that Sano should have implicated them in the plot. "But instead you tell me that the killer has struck again. How dare you let me down after I put my faith in you?"

"A thousand pardons, my lord." Sano was mortified, but he accepted the censure in the stoic manner that a samurai should. "There's no excuse."

The elders looked gratified by his disgrace and glad that he, not they, had become the target of Lord Matsudaira's wrath. Hirata and Yoritomo looked worried.

"I, ahh, beg to differ," the shogun said with the same contrariness he'd previously shown toward Lord Matsudaira. "Sano-*san* certainly does have an, ahh, legitimate excuse. It was only, ahh, the day before yesterday that he began investigating the murders. You shouldn't be so impatient for results, Cousin."

Sano thought how ironic it was that the shogun, who'd always expected instant results from him, should now defend him. The shogun was clearly put out by Lord Matsudaira's control over him and seizing at opportunities to resist it. Maybe Yoritomo had been prodding him to stick up for Sano.

"His Excellency is right," Lord Matsudaira said, hiding annoyance and feigning contrition. "Forgive me, Chamberlain Sano. This latest murder isn't your fault." His dark glance at the elders proclaimed whose fault he thought it was. "Tell us what progress you've made toward catching the killer."

"I've identified a suspect," Sano said.

Lord Matsudaira leaned forward. "Who is it?"

Sano watched Kato and Ihara brace themselves for an accusation against their clique. "Captain Nakai."

Surprise showed on the faces of Lord Matsudaira, the elders, and Yoritomo. The shogun frowned as if trying to recall who Nakai was.

"But Captain Nakai . . ." Ihara began, then stopped.

Fought on Lord Matsudaira's side during the faction war. How could he be the person who is trying to undermine the new regime? The unvoiced words echoed in the room.

"Why do you suspect Captain Nakai?" said Lord Matsudaira.

Sano explained that Nakai had had contact with Chief Ejima and Treasury Minister Moriwaki during the critical period before their deaths. "And he's displeased that he hasn't been honored for his recent performance."

Lord Matsudaira narrowed his eyes and stroked his chin as he caught Sano's meaning. The elders couldn't quite hide their relief that one of his own men had been incriminated instead of them. "Let's hear what Captain Nakai has to say for himself," Lord Matsudaira said. "Where is he?"

Sano would rather question Nakai privately, but his position was weak enough already. "He should be on duty in the castle guard command post."

"Fetch him," Lord Matsudaira told an attendant.

Soon Captain Nakai strode into the audience chamber. As he knelt and bowed, he shone with pride. "Your Excellency—Lord Matsudaira—this is an honor." Sano could tell that he thought he was about to receive, at long last, the reward he craved. Then he saw Lord Matsudaira's dark expression and noticed Sano. Apprehension crept into his eyes. "May I ask what this is about?"

"Colonel Ibe has been murdered. Did you do it?" Lord Matsudaira said, eschewing formalities and cutting straight to the quick.

"What?" Captain Nakai gaped in shock that appeared genuine to Sano.

"Did you also murder *Metsuke* Chief Ejima, Treasury Minister Moriwaki, Court Supervisor Ono, and Highway Commissioner Sasamura?" demanded Lord Matsudaira.

"No!" Captain Nakai looked at Sano, and his shock turned to offense. "I told you I was innocent. I swear I am." Horrified comprehension stunned him. "You've told His Excellency and Lord Matsudaira that I'm guilty."

"Well?" Lord Matsudaira's stare challenged Sano. "Is he or isn't he the culprit?"

"There's one way to settle the question. I must ask you to wait a moment." Sano whispered to Detective Marume, "If Detective Tachibana is doing his job, he should be someplace nearby. Go find him and bring him in."

Marume went. A short interval passed, during which Lord Matsudaira and the elders waited in grim silence. Yoritomo murmured to the shogun, explaining what had happened. Captain Nakai looked from one person to another, as if for rescue. He opened his mouth to speak, then bit his lip. His muscles twitched and his hands fidgeted. All the physical strength that made him a hero on the battlefield couldn't help him now. His fear of ruination and death permeated the air like a stench. Sano felt the tension in the room building toward a point beyond tolerance. Not a moment too soon, Detectives Marume and Tachibana arrived.

"It's most likely that the killer touched Colonel Ibe yesterday, at the festival at Asakusa Temple," Sano said, then addressed Captain Nakai: "Where were you last night?"

Something like relief, combined with defiance, crossed Nakai's expression. "I was at home."

Sano turned to Detective Tachibana. "Is that true?"

"Yes, Honorable Chamberlain," Tachibana said, nervous in the presence of their superiors, but confident of his answer. "He was there all night. He never stirred from his house."

"I've had Captain Nakai under surveillance," Sano explained to the assembly. "My detective's statement confirms his alibi."

"You had your man following me around?" Nakai glared at Sano, affronted and shocked anew.

"You should be grateful to him," said Kato. "He has exonerated you."

"Indeed." Lord Matsudaira bent a speculative, disapproving look on Sano.

Yoritomo whispered to the shogun, who nodded, then said, "Captain Nakai, it, ahh, appears that you are not the murderer we seek. Go back to your post."

Flabbergasted, Nakai didn't budge. "Is that all?" he demanded of Sano. "You accuse me in front of everybody, you drag my honor through the mud, then I'm sent off as though nothing happened?" His face was red with fury. "How am I supposed to hold up my head in public?"

Sano truly regretted that he'd damaged an innocent man's reputation. He also had cause to regret that Nakai wasn't the assassin. "Please accept my apologies. I'll see that everyone knows your honor is intact and that you're compensated for any inconvenience you might suffer."

Nakai fumed, then lashed out at Lord Matsudaira: "After all I've done for you, you let me be disgraced when you should reward me?"

"I suggest you obey His Excellency's order and leave before your mouth gets you in trouble," Lord Matsudaira said coldly.

The captain rose, huffing with wounded pride. "You've never forgotten that I have connections to your enemy's clan. You've always held it against me even though it's not my fault!" He stomped out of the room. The assembly sat quiet for a moment, waiting for the poisonous atmosphere to clear. But Sano knew that more trouble was yet to come. He sensed dread akin to his own behind the stoic faces around him. Only the oblivious shogun was calm.

"I must say I'm not surprised that Captain Nakai is innocent," Lord Matsudaira said. He didn't seem displeased, either. "Nakai has been blessed by good luck. Other men aren't so fortunate." His gaze, replete with accusation, impaled the two elders.

Kato and Ihara tried to conceal their dismay that his suspicion was aimed again toward their faction. The shogun nudged Yoritomo, wanting a translation of what had just passed, but Yoritomo's luminous, frightened eyes watched Sano.

"You have a problem, too, Honorable Chamberlain," Lord Matsudaira continued in the same menacing manner. "Now that your principal suspect has been exonerated, your investigation is back where it started—with no idea who the assassin is."

Although distressed by the setback, Sano couldn't afford to let Lord Matsudaira think the situation was as hopeless as it seemed.

"There are some other leads," he began.

Lord Matsudaira cut him off with an impatient gesture. "Don't bother me about them until they prove more worthwhile than what you've turned up so far." His glance flicked to the two elders, then back to Sano, his meaning clear: Any new leads Sano developed had better point to his enemies. "Should the assassin strike again, there will be some changes in the regime's upper echelon. Don't you agree that Hachijo Island has room for more than one exiled chamberlain?"

"Yes, my lord." Sano kept his expression and tone deliberately serene. Although he'd risen so high in the *bakufu,* nothing had really changed; his rank didn't exempt him from The Way of the Warrior.

He fought anger because he must still accept abuse, no matter how undeserved.

Cruel amusement glittered in Lord Matsudaira's eyes as he perceived Sano's inner struggle. "But don't be afraid that you'll find Hachijo Island a lonely place. You'll have plenty of company." His gaze pierced Hirata, who gave an involuntary start. "As goes the master, so does his retainer."

Hirata's face acquired the look of a deer who sees a hunter pointing an arrow straight at him. Lord Matsudaira turned to the shogun. "I believe we can adjourn this meeting, Honorable Cousin."

The shogun nodded, too confused to object. As he and his men and the elders bowed and rose, Sano felt doom in the air like a thunderstorm approaching. Lord Matsudaira said, "I trust that tomorrow will be a more satisfactory day."

Outside the palace, Sano walked with Hirata across the gardens. Sunset painted a sullen crimson edge in the sky above the far western hills; clouds like a wall of smoke obscured moon and stars. Shadows bred and insects shrilled under trees that gathered night in their foliage. Flames burned in stone lanterns; torches carried by patrol guards flared in the darkening landscape.

"I regret that I wasn't able to identify the assassin," Hirata said, sounding ready to take the entire blame.

"I regret that I dragged you into this investigation." If it should cause Hirata more harm than he'd already suffered, Sano would never forgive himself. "But let's not despair yet. We're lucky that Lord Matsudaira has given us another chance. Our other leads might direct us to the assassin. And the latest murder could provide new ones."

"What are your orders for tomorrow?" Hirata said.

Sano wished yet again that he could excuse Hirata from the case. But Hirata's fate as well as his own depended on its outcome, and Sano couldn't deny Hirata a chance to save his own position and honor. "Track down the priest who bumped into Chief Ejima and the water-seller who was loitering near Highway Commissioner Sasamura."

Hirata nodded, stoically accepting the strenuous work of hunting witnesses all over town. "I'll also find out if anyone saw the killer stalking Colonel Ibe."

"One incident or another could provide the critical break we need," Sano said, although with more hope than he felt. He called Detectives Marume and Fukida to join them. "As soon as we get home, organize a hunt for the priest Ozuno. Commandeer troops from the army. I want every temple searched. If you find him, hold him someplace where he can't get away, and notify me or Hirata-*san* immediately."

They exited the gate that led from the palace grounds. After Sano and Hirata bid each other goodnight, Hirata walked with Arai and Inoue along the passage toward the administrative quarter. Sano went with Marume and Fukida to his compound. There he must sift through the information on the victims' contacts, look for new suspects, and hope to learn that they had connections with Lord Matsudaira's enemies. Fatigue overwhelmed Sano at the thought. He would probably be up all night again.

When Sano arrived at his compound, he found the lane outside deserted except for his guards loitering at the gate. The sight was so remarkable that he, Marume, and Fukida stopped in their tracks. Although Sano had cancelled his appointments, it was still early enough that there should have been officials waiting to snare him if he should appear. Inside the courtyard, his and his men's footsteps echoed in the eerie silence.

"Where is everybody?" Fukida said.

"That's a good question." Sano had an uneasy feeling that something was amiss. They met his aide hovering at the entrance to the mansion, and Sano asked him, "What's going on?"

"I don't know." Kozawa sounded as baffled as Sano was.

"Has it been like this all day?"

"No, Honorable Chamberlain. Early in the morning, there was the usual crowd. But it tapered off by midday. There have been no visitors since late afternoon—until just now."

Instinct deepened Sano's uneasy feeling. "Who is it?"

"Police Commissioner Hoshina. He and two of his commanders are waiting in the anteroom."

Sano saw a bad day suddenly turn worse.

"Do you want me to throw him out?" Marume offered.

Although tempted, Sano remembered Hirata's warning about Hoshina. He'd better find out what new scheme Hoshina was plotting against him. "No," he said, then told Kozawa, "I'll see the police commissioner in my office."

His detectives escorted Sano there. He ordered them to go keep an eye on Hoshina's men, then sat at his desk, breathing deeply and trying to shake off the tension from his meeting with Lord Matsudaira. Soon Kozawa opened the door, and in walked Hoshina.

"Greetings, Honorable Chamberlain," he said with an insolent grin. He'd removed his swords, according to the rule for visitors, but he swaggered proudly nevertheless.

"Welcome." Sano spoke in a terse tone that indicated this visit would be short. "What brings you here?"

Hoshina gave a perfunctory bow. As he knelt before Sano, he gazed around the room. Sano saw bitter nostalgia color his expression and knew that Hoshina was recalling the days when he'd been the lover and chief retainer of its former occupant. "Oh, I just thought I'd pop in and see how you're doing."

"Somehow I don't think you came for the pleasure of an idle chat," Sano said.

Hoshina smirked, ignoring Sano's hint to state his business. "It's awfully quiet around here. Isn't it amazing that a few words dropped in casual conversation can have such a dramatic effect?"

Sano's stomach took a downward fall as he perceived a connection between his deserted office and Hoshina. "What are you talking about?"

"I happened to run into a few mutual acquaintances today." Hoshina drawled the words, taking his time, enjoying Sano's discomposure. "I happened to mention to them that you're having trouble solving this murder case, and Colonel Ibe's death hasn't helped. They were very interested to hear that Lord Matsudaira is most dissatisfied with you and it's jeopardized your good standing with him." Hoshina shook his head in false sympathy. Mischief glittered in his eyes. "Rats are famous for deserting ships that are sinking."

Sano realized what had happened. Hoshina, who had spies everywhere, had been following his investigation, warning people that Sano would likely fail to solve the case and they'd better limit their contact with him or share his punishment. Should Hoshina's plot succeed as well as it seemed to be doing, Sano would lose his influence with the high Tokugawa officials and the feudal lords. His fear of becoming isolated and losing control over the government and nation assumed a new, dire reality. Sano should have foreseen that his enemy would attack him in this devious fashion, when he was most vulnerable. He glared at Hoshina, who sat grinning and waiting for his response.

"I'm not exactly surprised by your news," Sano said with disciplined calm. "Your past behavior has shown that you'll never stop trying to destroy me no matter how hard I try to make peace between us. What does surprise me is the method you've chosen this time."

"Why is that?" Hoshina said, proud of his own cleverness.

"Interfering with my business will sabotage the functioning of Lord Matsudaira's new regime," Sano said. "Your game could prove to be more dangerous to you than me. And telling me about it gives me a chance to retaliate."

Hoshina laughed. "I'll take my chances." Sano supposed Hoshina was so self-confident that he'd risked warning Sano just to see his reaction. Hoshina wasn't the smartest man in the *bakufu,* but he was certainly among the most reckless, and he would rather be dead than give up hope of clawing his way to the top. Now he ambled around the room. "I've always fancied this office," he said, appraising its generous proportions, high coffered ceiling, the walls lined with books and maps, the elaborate metal lanterns. "When you're out of it, the shogun will need a new chamberlain. And I'll be ready." He gloated at Sano. "I should mention that many officials and *daimyo* have promised to support me with Lord Matsudaira in exchange for favors when your post is mine."

Sano sensed that Hoshina had other, more personal reasons for mounting this coup against him than mere ambition. With Yanagisawa gone, Hoshina needed a target for his ire toward his onetime lover. By attacking Sano and winning the post that had belonged to Yanagisawa, he could satisfy his lust for revenge.

"Now that you've served me your notice, I'll serve you mine," Sano said. "If you expect to get away with this, you're sadly mistaken." He was gratified to see his foe's expression turn uncertain. "As for this office, it won't be yours any time soon."

He looked pointedly at the door. Hoshina took the hint and moved toward it, but he said, "Enjoy it while it's still yours," and bowed with exaggerated courtesy. He paused, and cunning sparkled in his eyes. "Oh, I forgot to tell you—I've heard some interesting news. It was about Lady Reiko."

"My wife?" Sano felt a pang of surprise that Hoshina should mention Reiko.

"None other," Hoshina said. "She's been seen gadding around the *hinin* settlement and the Ryōgoku Hirokoji entertainment district. My sources at Magistrate Ueda's court tell me she's investigating an outcast woman accused of murder. They say she's digging up evidence to acquit the woman even though she's obviously guilty. Not only is Lady Reiko interfering with justice, she's doing it on your orders because you think the law should be more lenient toward criminals."

It was all Sano could do to hide his consternation. That Reiko's exploits had come to the attention of his enemy! But he said in an even tone, "You should be careful about picking your sources. Don't believe everything you hear."

Hoshina gave him a look that scorned his words as an attempt to deny the undeniable. "Smoke is a sure sign of fire, as my new friends agreed when I mentioned Lady Reiko's dubious activities to them. They also agreed that a chamberlain who bends the law at his own whim, and sends his woman out to do his dirty business, doesn't deserve his post. This was a key factor that persuaded them to cut their ties to you."

Before Sano could think of a reply, Hoshina said, "Lady Reiko did me a favor. Please convey my thanks to her—and my best wishes to your son."

With a sardonic laugh, he swaggered from the room.

21

Sano sat motionless until he heard Hoshina speak to the men he'd brought with him and Kozawa usher them all out of the mansion. Then he leaned his elbows on his desk and dropped his head into his hands. It seemed that things couldn't get worse.

A door concealed by a painted mural slid open with a faint, surreptitious sound. Sano looked up to see Reiko standing in the passage that led to their private quarters. Her expression was solemn, her footsteps cautious as she approached Sano.

"I heard what Police Commissioner Hoshina said." As she stood before Sano, she clasped her hands in penitence. "I'm sorry I've caused you so much trouble."

Sano couldn't help regretting that he'd allowed her to investigate the crime in the *hinin* settlement, but he couldn't blame her for unwittingly playing into Hoshina's scheme. She looked so devastated that he didn't have the heart to be angry with her. Furthermore, he'd given his full consent to her investigation. "Never mind." He rose and took her hands in his. "It's not your fault."

"But you warned me that what I do could reflect badly on you," Reiko said, still upset. "I didn't believe you, and I should have. I wish I'd never heard of Yugao."

So did Sano, but he said, "Your behavior was only one factor in my problems. Without you, Hoshina would have found some other weapon to use against me."

"He mentioned Masahiro. It sounded like a threat. Would he really hurt our son?" Fright marked Reiko's face.

"Not while I'm around," Sano assured her.

He didn't say what could happen if he were ousted. The family of a defeated samurai was considered a danger to his vanquisher. Reiko would probably survive because Hoshina wouldn't consider a woman important enough to attack; but a son could grow up to avenge wrongs done to his father. Hoshina would never let Masahiro live that long. Yet death wasn't the only fate that Sano feared for Masahiro. Boys without a protector were used and mistreated, sexually and otherwise, by men in power. Yanagisawa's son Yoritomo had been lucky that he'd become the exclusive property of the shogun after he'd lost his father. Sano couldn't bear to think, let alone tell Reiko, of what suffering Hoshina would cause Masahiro. He could only do his best to come out on top and hope that she wouldn't give Hoshina any more ammunition.

"How did your investigation go today?" he asked. "Is it almost finished?"

Reiko heard in Sano's voice the hope that her investigation would end before it could do any more harm. She knew that he feared for the safety of her, Masahiro, their families, their friends, and the retainers who depended on him, not just his own. All of them would suffer if Sano were exiled, and so would the citizens of Japan if the selfish, corrupt, reckless Hoshina became the shogun's second-in-command. Reiko was still horrified by the consequences of her quest to find the truth and serve justice, and anxious to reassure Sano.

"I've learned enough to satisfy me that Yugao is guilty," Reiko said. "My father will convict and sentence her tomorrow. I'm not planning any more inquiries around town."

"I'm glad to hear that," Sano said.

He sounded so relieved that Reiko couldn't tell him that she thought discovering Yugao's motive was important enough to justify continuing her inquiries. He wouldn't trust her intuition, not at a time like this. And she wasn't certain that the danger of letting Yugao's secrets remain unknown exceeded the danger from Hoshina. She had to keep up an unimpeachable standard of behavior from now on. If she wanted to know the truth about Yugao, she must wait until Sano's troubles had blown over.

"Well," Sano said, dropping her hands, "I should get back to work."

An involuntary yawn opened his mouth so wide his jaw cracked. Reiko observed with concern that his eyes were blurred with fatigue. "Come rest awhile first."

"There's no time. In addition to starting my investigation all over, I have to figure out how to derail Hoshina's plot to unseat me."

"But you didn't sleep at all last night. You must keep up your strength. At least take a nap," Reiko urged. "You'll be able to think more clearly afterward."

She watched Sano vacillate; then he said, "Maybe you're right," and let her lead him to the bedchamber.

Sano's eyes snapped open as he awakened from sound sleep to instant alertness. He was lying on his side in bed. The room was dark except for the faint glow of moonlight through the window. In the silence of the house he heard crickets chirping and frogs singing from the garden. He could barely see Reiko sleeping under the quilt beside him. Her slow, rhythmic breaths hissed quietly. Sano realized that his nap had lasted much longer than he'd intended. The entire household had gone to bed; it must be near midnight. But in the midst of dismay that he'd wasted hours he should have spent on work, a strange, prickling sensation chilled him. His samurai instincts signaled a warning.

There was someone in the room with him and Reiko.

He lay perfectly still, feigning sleep, dreading to move. He smelled a faint, unfamiliar human scent and heard breaths that didn't come from him or Reiko. His skin felt the barely perceptible air currents in the still room. They eddied around a solid shape that loomed behind his back. Living warmth radiated from it. His mind formed a shadowy image of a man bent over him. He knew, without reason or doubt, that the intruder's intent was evil.

These thoughts and sensations occurred during a mere instant after Sano awakened. In one swift movement, he rolled onto his back, grabbed the sword that he kept by his bedside, and slashed. The intruder leapt away just in time to avoid his blade. He heard a crash as the intruder fell to the floor, then frantic scuffling sounds as the man rushed across the chamber. Reiko bolted upright beside Sano.

"What's that noise?" she exclaimed.

Sano was already flying out of bed, sword raised in his hand, his night robes tangling around his legs. "There's an intruder in the house!" he shouted. "Call the guards!"

He blocked the door. The intruder charged at the sliding partition that formed one side of the room. He hurtled straight through it. Paper tore; lattice splintered. He tumbled into the corridor outside. Sano heard Reiko calling for help. He leapt through the jagged hole the intruder had made. The exterior doors on the opposite side of the corridor had been left open to admit fresh air. Sano stumbled onto the veranda that overlooked the garden. The darkness was so thick beneath its many trees that Sano could see nothing. But swift footsteps crunched on gravel paths and bushes rustled.

Two guards, carrying lanterns, appeared beside Sano. He pointed in the direction of the sound of the fleeing intruder. "Over there!"

The guards plunged down the steps with Sano close behind them. They panned their lanterns across the garden. Beyond the boulders and flowerbeds, Sano spied movement in the darkness near a distant wing of the mansion. "There he goes!"

He and his men raced forward, but lost sight and sound of the intruder. Then Sano heard scuffling noises that climbed above ground level. He looked up as he ran, and he saw a dark lump form on the slanted eave of the building.

"He's on the roof!" Sano cried.

The lump transformed into a man-sized shape and sped out of view as Sano reached the building. The guards dropped their lanterns, climbed the veranda rail, shimmied up the pillars, and scrambled onto the roof. Sano tucked his sword under his sash and followed them. The roof spread vast before him like a sea of tiles that connected the house's many wings, its rounded ripples frozen and agleam in the moonlight. He saw the intruder skimming, fast and sure-footed, over the peaks and gables. As his men gave chase, they skidded, stumbled, and fell. Sano lumbered after them. The rough edges of the tiles gouged his bare feet. The intruder crested a rooftop far in the distance.

Ahead of Sano, a guard tower rose from the wall that surrounded the compound. Sentries leaned from the windows, holding out lanterns to see what the commotion was. Sano pointed and shouted to them, "There's an intruder on the roof! Shoot him!"

The sentries fired arrows out the windows. The night filled with the whizzing sound of arrows and the clatters as they struck the tiles. Sano frantically scanned the roofs, but he could see no sign of the intruder. The guards joined him, breathless and panting.

"He's gone," one said.

"He must have jumped onto the wall and out of the compound," said another.

"At least he didn't hurt anyone, did he?" said the first, who was the captain of Sano's night patrol.

A thought pierced Sano as he recalled awakening in the darkness with the intruder near him. Cold, pure dread trickled into his heart. "I want the intruder caught. Go to the Edo Castle defense commander. Tell him I want every guard out searching right now."

"We'll catch him," the night patrol captain assured Sano as he hurried off to obey. "He can't get out of the castle."

But a nightlong search, conducted by thousands of troops who explored every corner of Edo Castle, failed to net the intruder.

Sano, who'd waited in the guard command station, trudged home at dawn. Reiko met him at the door of the mansion. Her look of bright anticipation faded as she read Sano's face.

"He escaped?" she said.

"As if by magic." The dread that had multiplied in Sano during the long night possessed him like an evil spirit. If he spoke of it, the self-control he'd maintained in front of his men would shatter and he would break down. He hurried past Reiko into the house. "I don't know how he did it, but he could be anywhere in the city by now."

"Who do you think he is?" Reiko said, following Sano.

"I can't put a name to him," Sano said as he strode along the corridors to their private chambers, "but who else would sneak up on and attack a high official of Lord Matsudaira's new regime?"

"The assassin who killed the *metsuke* chief and those other men?" Reiko said, breathless with surprise as well as from keeping up with Sano. "Do you think he came here to kill you?"

"I know it." Even now Sano felt the assassin's deadly intent like a poison in his blood. He prayed that the memory was all the assassin had left with him.

"Does that mean he's someone within the regime?"

"Maybe. It would explain how he got into the castle."

"Why are you walking so fast?" Reiko said as they rushed past servants who hovered in the corridor.

Sano burst into their bedchamber. "Light all the lanterns," he told Reiko.

"Why? What's wrong?" she said, clearly baffled.

"For once in your life, just do what I say without arguing!" Sano shouted.

Reiko's mouth fell open in shock, but she obeyed. The lanterns filled the room with hot, smoky light. Sano flung open the cabinet, took out a mirror, and peered at his tense, haunted face. He discarded the mirror and stripped naked. He extended his arms, turning them as he inspected every minute detail of his skin from shoulders to fingertips. He examined his torso, legs, and feet.

"What are you doing?" Reiko said.

Sano turned his back to her and demanded, "Do you see a mark on me?"

"A mark?" She ran her hands over him. "No," she said, sounding even more perplexed. "What—"

But of course it was too soon for the telltale bruise to develop. As Sano faced Reiko, he saw horrified enlightenment in her eyes. Her hand clasped her throat.

"Merciful gods," she whispered. "Did he touch you?"

They stared at each other, both paralyzed by fear that he would be the sixth victim of *dim-mak*.

"I don't know," Sano said, "but I think he did. I think that's what woke me up."

"No!" Reiko clutched Sano's hands, frantic to deny it. "You must be mistaken. You don't feel anything bad happening inside, do you?"

Sano shook his head. "But I don't suppose the others did, either." In his mind he saw the intruder bending over him while he lay asleep in bed, stealthily reaching out a hand toward him. His whole body prickled with the sensation of the fatal touch. Was this imagination or reality? "They didn't know anything was wrong with them, until . . ."

Breathless and frantic, Reiko said, "I'm calling a physician!"

"It's no use. If I've been given a death-touch, the damage is done. Medical treatment can't save me."

Tears shone in Reiko's eyes. "What are we going to do?"

That fate could be altered so suddenly for the worse, in a mere instant, amazed Sano. If the killer had indeed touched him, he could be doomed even before Lord Matsudaira punished him for failing to catch the assassin or Hoshina brought him down. The thought of his life cut short, of leaving his beloved wife and son, appalled him. He had scant comfort to offer Reiko.

"There's nothing we can do now," he said, "except wait two days and see what happens."

22

A dense morning mist shrouded Edo, blurring the distinction between earth and sky. Invisible boats floated on the rivers and canals. The voices of people crossing the bridges were links in chains of sound that spanned the water.

In the slum that bordered Edo Jail, four square blocks lay in ruins. Wisps of smoke still rose from the burned timbers, blackened and fallen roof tiles, and ash heaps where once many houses had stood. Desolate residents picked through the debris, trying to salvage their possessions. But the jail loomed intact beyond the wreckage. Across the bridge and in through its gate filed the prisoners who had been released when the fire had started yesterday. They'd voluntarily returned to finish serving their sentences or awaiting their trials. Two jailers, stationed with the guards at the gate, counted heads and checked names off a list.

When the last prisoner had walked inside, one jailer said, "This is a surprise. Usually they all come back. This time we're missing one."

Reiko stared out the window of her palanquin as it carried her out of Edo Castle, but she barely noticed the sights or sounds. Fear that her husband would die inhabited her mind like a malignant presence, crowding out the world around her. The sob caught in her throat grew larger by the moment. The idea of losing Sano, of living without him, was beyond unbearable.

When he'd told her the terrible possibility that the assassin had given him the touch of death, Reiko had wanted to cling tight to him, to anchor him to her and to life. She'd been alarmed when he'd said he had to go out.

"Where?" she'd asked. "Why?"

"To continue my hunt for the assassin," he'd said.

"Now?"

Calm detachment had replaced his terror. "As soon as I've washed, dressed, and eaten." He headed toward the bath chamber.

"Must you?" Reiko said, hurrying after him. She didn't want to let him out of her sight.

"I still have a job to do," Sano said.

"But if you have only two days to live, we should spend them together," Reiko protested.

In the bath chamber, Sano poured a bucket of water over his body and scrubbed himself. "Lord Matsudaira and the shogun wouldn't accept that excuse. They've given me orders to catch the killer, and I must obey."

Reiko experienced a sudden furious hatred for Bushido, which gave his superiors the right to treat him like a slave. Never before had the samurai code of honor seemed so cruel. "If there's one time when you should disobey orders, this is it. Tell Lord Matsudaira and the shogun that you've already sacrificed your life for them, and they should go catch the killer themselves." Beside herself with desperation, Reiko pleaded, "Stay home, with me and Masahiro."

"I wish I could." Sano climbed into the sunken bathtub, rinsed his body, climbed out, and dried himself on the towel Reiko handed him. "But I have more reason than before to bring the assassin to justice." He chuckled. "Not every murder victim gets a chance to take revenge on his killer before he dies. This is a unique opportunity I have here."

"How can you laugh at a time like this?" Reiko demanded.

"Either I laugh or I cry," Sano said. "And remember, it's possible that the assassin didn't touch me. If that's the case, we'll both be laughing about this pretty soon. We'll be embarrassed that we made such a fuss."

But Reiko saw that Sano didn't believe it; nor could she. "Please don't go," she said as she followed him to the bedchamber.

He threw on his clothes. "I have only a short time to catch the assassin and prevent more deaths. And I will, if it's the last thing I do."

Neither of them voiced the fear that it might be. Sano turned to Reiko and held her close. "Besides, if I don't, I'll just worry and be miserable. That's not how you want me to spend the last two days of my life, is it?" He said gently, "I'll come back soon. I promise."

Reiko had let him go, because even though she was hurt that he wouldn't stay with her, she didn't want to deny Sano the chance to spend his precious time as he chose. She'd decided that she should go about her own business rather than fret about a fate that she was helpless to change.

Now her procession halted in the fog outside Magistrate Ueda's estate. She stepped from her palanquin and hurried in the gate, through the courtyard, which was empty at this early hour. She entered the mansion, where she found her father seated at his desk in his office. A messenger knelt before him. Magistrate Ueda was reading a scroll that the messenger had apparently just brought. He frowned, wrote a quick note, and handed it to the messenger, who bowed and left. Magistrate Ueda looked up at Reiko.

"You're here early, Daughter," he said. His frown relaxed into a smile that faded as he saw Reiko's face. "What's wrong?"

"The assassin broke into our house last night, and he—while my husband was asleep—"

She couldn't go on because the sob in her throat choked her. She saw comprehension and horror in Magistrate Ueda's look. He started to rise, his arms extended as if to gather her into them. She lifted a hand to stop him, for any sympathy would be her undoing.

"We don't know that anything happened," she said, her voice tight with self-control. "Sano feels just fine." Reiko forced a laugh. "We're probably worrying for nothing."

"I'm sure that's the case." Magistrate Ueda's expression was grave despite his reassuring tone.

"But that's not why I'm here," Reiko said, hastily changing the subject. "I've come to tell you that I'm finished with my investigation." At least Sano needn't worry that it would cause him more trouble. "You needn't put off Yugao's conviction."

Magistrate Ueda expelled his breath and shook his head. "I'm afraid I'll have to anyway."

"Why? What happened?"

"That messenger who was just here brought me some disturbing news. Yesterday there was a fire near Edo Jail. The prisoners were released. They all came back this morning, except for Yugao."

Shock hit Reiko so hard that she almost forgot her problems. "Yugao is gone?"

Magistrate Ueda nodded. "She took advantage of the fire and escaped."

Horrified, Reiko dropped to her knees. Yugao was violent and deranged, she might very well kill again. "I suppose I shouldn't be surprised that Yugao ran away. It's a miracle that all prisoners don't run when they're let out for a fire," she said.

"Perhaps not. Most of those sentenced to death are so broken in spirit that they accept their fate meekly. And they know that if they do run, they'll be hunted down and tortured. Besides, all the prisoners know they can't go back to where they came from; their neighborhood officials or police informants would turn them in. The petty criminals would rather face their punishment. Life on the run is harsh. Fugitives must resort to begging or prostitution or starve to death."

"This is my fault," said Reiko. "If I hadn't been so determined to know why Yugao killed her family—if I hadn't insisted on taking the time to find out—she would have been executed before that fire."

"Don't blame yourself," Magistrate Ueda said. "It was my decision for you to investigate the murders, and neither of us could have foreseen the fire. In hindsight, I should have accepted Yugao's confession and immediately sentenced her to death. The responsibility for her escape is mine."

Guilt sickened Reiko nonetheless. "What are we going to do?"

"I've sent orders to the police to search for her."

"But how can they find one person among the million in this city?" Reiko said, filled with despair. "Edo has so many places where a fugitive could hide. And the police are so busy hunting outlaw rebels, they won't look very hard for Yugao."

"True, but what else is to be done?"

Reiko rose. "I'm going to look for Yugao myself."

Magistrate Ueda's expression was sympathetic yet dubious. "It will be even harder for you than for the police. They at least have many officers, civilian assistants, and neighborhood officials they can set after Yugao, while you're just one woman."

"Yes," Reiko said, "but at least I'll be active instead of waiting for her to be found. And people who've seen her may be more willing to talk to me than to the police."

"If you insist on searching, then I wish you luck," Magistrate Ueda said. "I must admit that if you should find Yugao, you'll be doing me a valuable service. That a murderess is on the loose because I delayed her execution is a black mark on my record. If she's not captured, I could lose my post."

Reiko didn't want to hurt Sano—especially now, when his very life was threatened; nor did she want to hurt their marriage. Yet she couldn't let her father suffer, any more than she could let a murderess go free. Her intuition told her that learning the motive behind Yugao's crime was more important than ever. And looking for Yugao would distract her from her fear that Sano was going to die.

"I'll find her, Father," said Reiko. "I promise."

Sano's first stop was the administrative quarter of Edo Castle. He and Detectives Marume and Fukida dismounted outside Hirata's gate, where the sentries greeted them. The mist was oppressive, the streets oddly deserted except for a few servants and patrol soldiers. As they walked through the courtyard to the mansion where he'd once lived, Sano felt a pang of nostalgia so intense that it hurt.

He remembered times when he'd come home to this place exhausted, discouraged, and in fear for his life and honor. Through them all he'd been sustained by the physical strength of his body. Even when it had been injured, he'd known he would recover. He'd taken his good health for granted and never really believed he could die, even though he'd often looked death in the face. Those times seemed idyllic in retrospect. Now mortality haunted Sano. He imagined an explosion in his head as a blood vessel ruptured, and his life extinguished like a snuffed candle flame. If indeed the assassin had touched him, all his wisdom, political power, and wealth couldn't save him. Sano fought the urge to run as fast as he could in a vain attempt to escape the deadly force planted inside his own body. He must concentrate on catching the assassin. He must save other lives even if he was marked for death.

Hirata met him outside the mansion. Last night Sano had sent a message telling Hirata about the assassin's attack, and Hirata looked devastated by the news. "Sano-*san*. I—" Emotion choked off whatever he'd meant to say. He dropped to his knees before Sano and bowed his head.

Sano was moved that Hirata could grieve for him even though he'd been the cause of Hirata's terrible injury. He said in a falsely cheerful voice, "Get up, Hirata-*san*. I'm not dead yet. Save your mourning for my funeral. We have work to do."

Hirata rose, visibly braced by Sano's attitude. "Do you still want me to track down the priest and the water-seller and whoever might have been stalking Colonel Ibe?"

"Yes," Sano said. "And we'll proceed with the other plans we made yesterday."

"Marume and I have already organized the hunt for the priest Ozuno," said Fukida.

"I'll do everything in my power to catch the assassin," Hirata declared. "This is personal now."

"If you avenge your master's murder before he's dead, you'll win yourself a place in history," Sano said.

Hirata and the detectives laughed dutifully at the joke. Sano felt the strain of keeping up their spirits as well as his own. "Let's look on the bright side. Every misfortune brings unexpected benefits. What happened last night has provided new clues that I'm about to follow up on."

The Tokugawa Army's central headquarters was located within Edo Castle, in a turret that rose up from a wall high on the hill. The turret was a tall, square structure faced with white plaster. Tiled roofs protruded above each of its three stories. General Isogai, supreme commander of the military forces, had an office at the top. Sano and Detectives Marume and Fukida reached the turret via a covered corridor that ran along the wall. As they walked, they glanced through the barred windows, into the passages under them. Sano was surprised to see only the patrol guards and checkpoint sentries. The officials who usually thronged the passages were absent.

"This place is as deserted as your compound," Marume said.

"Somehow I can't believe Police Commissioner Hoshina is responsible for this, too," said Fukida.

Nor could Sano, who had an uneasy feeling about it. They entered the turret and climbed the stairs, passing soldiers who bowed to them. Sano stood at the threshold of General Isogai's office, where the general presided over a conference of army officers. Smoke from their pipes clouded the air and drifted out windows into the mist. General Isogai spied Sano, nodded in acknowledgment, and dismissed his men.

"Greetings, Honorable Chamberlain. Please come in."

Sano told Marume and Fukida to wait outside, then joined General Isogai. Swords, spears, and guns hung mounted in racks on the walls, alongside maps of Japan that showed army garrisons.

"May I be of service to you?" General Isogai said.

"You may," said Sano, "but first, please accept my condolences on the death of Colonel Ibe."

The general's jovial expression turned bleak. "Ibe was a good soldier. A good friend, too. Came up through the ranks with me. I'll miss him." General Isogai uttered a humorless laugh. "Remember our last meeting? We were pretty smug because we had things under control. Now one of my top men has been assassinated, and you're on Lord Matsudaira's bad side because you haven't managed to catch whoever did it."

He walked to the window. "Notice how empty the castle is?" When Sano nodded, he said, "Everyone's heard that the assassin got to you last night. Here, in the one place we all thought was safe. People are afraid to go out. They don't want to be next to die. They're hiding at home, surrounded by bodyguards. Whole *bakufu's* ground to a halt."

Sano imagined communication cut off between Edo and the rest of Japan, and the Tokugawa regime losing its grip on the provinces. Anarchy would spawn rebellion. Not only would the remnants of Yanagisawa's faction seize the chance to regain power, but the *daimyo* might rise up against Tokugawa rule. "This could be disastrous. Assign soldiers to escort officials on their business and protect them," Sano said.

The general frowned, dubious. "The army's stretched too thin already."

"Then borrow some troops from the *daimyo*. Bring in more from the provinces."

"As you wish," General Isogai said, although still reluctant. "By the way, have you heard that the assassin has a nickname? People are calling him 'the Ghost,' because he stalks his victims and kills them without being seen."

He gestured out the window. "Give me an enemy I can see, and I'll send all my gunners, archers, and swordsmen after him. But my army can't fight a ghost." His cunning eyes glittered with desperation as he faced Sano. "You're the detective. How do we find him and put him out of action?"

"By the same strategy that you would use to defeat any other enemy," Sano said. "We analyze the information we have on him. Then we run him to ground."

General Isogai looked skeptical. "What do we know about him except that he must be a madman?"

"His attack on me has taught me two things," Sano said. "First, his motive is to destroy Lord Matsudaira's regime by killing its key officials."

"Haven't you suspected as much since the *metsuke* chief died at the horse races?"

"Yes, but now it's a certainty. I didn't know any of the victims well; we didn't have the same friends, associates, family ties, or personal enemies. We had nothing in common except that we were all appointed to Lord Matsudaira's new regime."

General Isogai nodded. "Then the assassin must be a holdout from the opposition. But you don't think he's in league with Senior Elders Kato and Ihara and their gang, do you?" Incredulity came over his face. "They're big on playing politics, but I can't believe they have the stomach for something as risky as multiple assassination."

"Kato and Ihara aren't in the clear yet," Sano said, "but I have another theory, which I'll get to in a moment. The second thing I've learned about the assassin is that he's an expert not only at the mystic martial arts, but also at stealth."

"He had to be, to sneak inside your compound and get right next to you," General Isogai agreed.

"If he could manage that, he could get into the castle from the outside," Sano said. "He wouldn't need to be someone on the inside."

General Isogai scowled, resisting the notion that the castle's mighty defenses could be breached, but he said, "I suppose it's possible."

"So who is an expert at stealth and belongs to the opposition? I'm thinking in particular of Yanagisawa's elite squadron of troops."

Those troops had been masters of stealth and highly trained martial artists, whom Yanagisawa had employed to keep himself in power. They'd been suspected of past political assassinations of Yanagisawa's enemies, but never caught: They covered their tracks too well.

Surprise raised General Isogai's eyebrows. "I knew they were a dangerous breed, but I never heard that they could kill with a touch."

"If they could, they'd have kept it secret." A disturbing thought struck Sano. "I wonder how many deaths there have been over the years that appeared natural but were actually assassinations ordered by Yanagisawa." But Sano couldn't do much about that now. "The reason I came here is to ask you what happened to Yanagisawa's elite squadron after he was deposed."

"You've come to the right place."

General Isogai walked to a chart, mounted on the wall, that displayed a list of thirty names. Eighteen had red lines drawn through them; notations were scribbled in the margins. Sano did not recognize any of the names.

"They kept a low profile," General Isogai said. "They used aliases when they traveled around. It made their movements hard to track." He pointed at the names crossed out in red. "These men died in the battle when we raided Yanagisawa's house. My men killed half of them. The rest committed suicide rather than be taken prisoner. But the other twelve weren't on the premises at the time, and they escaped. Capturing them has been a high priority because we think they're leaders in the underground movement and responsible for attacks on the army."

Sano was glad to have new suspects, but daunted by the thought of hunting down twelve. "Have you caught any yet?"

"These five." General Isogai tapped the names. "We got a lucky break last winter. Nabbed one of their underlings. Tortured him until he told us where to find them. Staked out their hideaway, took them, and executed them."

"That narrows the field," Sano said, relieved. If he had only two days to catch the assassin before he died, he would have to work fast. "Have you had any leads on the others?"

"These last seven are the craftiest of the bunch. It's as if they really are ghosts. We move in on them, and—" General Isogai snatched at the air, then opened his empty hands. "All we've had lately are a few possible sightings, by informants who aren't too reliable."

He opened a ledger on his desk and ran his finger down a column of characters. "They were all at teahouses around town. Some were places where Yanagisawa's men used to drink before the war. I'll copy out the names and locations for you, along with the names of the seven elite troops who are still fugitives." General Isogai dipped a brush in ink and wrote on a paper, which he blotted then handed to Sano.

"Many thanks," Sano said, hoping that he now had the assassin's name and the key to his whereabouts.

"If the Ghost is one of Yanagisawa's squadron, I wish you better luck catching him than we've had," said the general.

They bowed, and as Sano turned to leave, General Isogai said, "By the way, should you and your men go up against those devils, be careful. During the raid on Yanagisawa's house, the eighteen of them killed thirty-six of my soldiers before they were defeated. They're dangerous."

Sardonic amusement glittered in General Isogai's eyes. "But maybe you already know that from personal experience."

23

It was past noon, and the sun had vaporized the mist, when Reiko left the *hinin* settlement after a search for Yugao. No one there had seen the woman since she'd been arrested. Discouraged yet determined, Reiko traveled to the Ryōgoku Hirokoji entertainment district.

Escorted by Lieutenant Asukai and her other guards, she walked down the noisy, crowded avenue. She thought of Police Commissioner Hoshina and looked over her shoulder to see if anyone was following her. As she wondered whom to ask first about Yugao, wind rattled lanterns on the stalls. Tassels ripped from armor during a fight swirled with dust along the ground. A mass of storm clouds bled across the sky like ink on wet paper. Warm rain showered upon Reiko. She and her escorts, and the hundreds of pleasure seekers, hurried beneath the roofs of the stalls. The wind swept the rain in sheets that drenched the empty avenue; puddles spread. The stall where Reiko and her guards found shelter offered cheap toys as prizes for rolling balls up a ramp through holes. One other person had found shelter here: One man—and a monkey that he held on a leash.

The monkey screeched at Reiko. It wore a miniature suit of armor, helmet, and swords. Her guards laughed. She was so surprised to see a monkey that she hardly noticed its master until he said, "Pardon my friend's bad manners."

Now Reiko saw that he was as remarkable as his companion. He was no taller than herself, with coarse, shaggy black hair that covered his head, face, arms, and legs. Beady eyes met Reiko's shocked gaze; sharp teeth grinned beneath his whiskers. To her further amazement, she recognized him.

"Are you the Rat?" she said.

"That's me. At your service, pretty lady."

"We have a mutual acquaintance," Reiko said. "His name is Hirata, and he's the shogun's *sōsakan-sama*." Hirata had told her that the Rat hailed from the northern island of Hokkaido, famous for its natives who had copious body hair. He traded in information that he picked up while traveling around Japan in search of new freaks for the show he operated in the entertainment district across the river, and he was an informant of Hirata's.

"Oh, yes," the Rat said. He spoke in a strange, gruff, rustic accent. "I heard that Hirata-*san* was cut up in a fight. How's he doing?"

"Better," said Reiko.

Her guards tried to pet the monkey. It drew its tiny sword and lashed out at them. They fell back, laughing. The Rat scrutinized Reiko with curiosity. "Who are you?" Reiko remembered that she must keep a low profile, but before she could make up a false identity the Rat pointed a hairy finger at her. "Don't tell me. You must be Lady Reiko, the chamberlain's wife."

"How did you know?" Reiko said, chagrined.

"The Rat gets around," he said with a wise look.

"Please don't tell anyone you saw me here," Reiko said.

The Rat winked and put his finger to his lips. "I don't tell tales on my friends, and any friend of Hirata-*san's* is a friend of mine. What's a fine lady like you doing here, anyway?"

Reiko's spirits lifted. "I'm looking for someone. Maybe you can help me."

"Be glad to, and for you, I'll waive my usual fee. Who is it?"

"A woman named Yugao. She escaped from Edo Jail yesterday." Reiko described Yugao. "Have you seen her?"

The Rat shook his head. "Sorry. But I'll keep an eye out." His monkey screeched, waving its sword at Reiko's guards, who had drawn their swords and were fighting a playful battle with it. "Hey, don't hurt him!" the Rat said, then asked Reiko, "What was Yugao in jail for?"

"She stabbed her family to death," Reiko said.

Interest enlivened the Rat's expression. "I'm surprised I hadn't heard about that. Where did it happen?"

"In the *hinin* settlement."

"Oh." The Rat's interest faded, as though crimes among the *hinin* were commonplace and unimportant. "Why is the chamberlain's wife looking for an escaped outcast?"

Rather than tell the whole sad story, Reiko said, "My father asked me to find Yugao. He's the magistrate who tried her for the murders."

The Rat waggled his bristly eyebrows, hinting for more explanation. Reiko kept silent. The monkey whacked Lieutenant Asukai on the leg with his sword. Lieutenant Asukai yelped in pain. His comrades howled with laughter.

"Serves you right, teasing a poor animal," the Rat huffed, then said, "The law moves in strange ways, and who am I to question it? But since I have the privilege of talking to the magistrate's daughter, maybe you can tell me whether those other murders were ever solved."

"What other murders?" Reiko said, impatient for the rain to stop so she could continue her search. Her mind drifted to Sano, and fear tightened inside her. Would the assassin's death-touch take effect before two days passed?

"The ones that happened around here, about six years ago," the Rat said. "Three men were stabbed within a few months of each other."

Reiko's attention snapped back to him. "What? Who were they?"

"Tokugawa soldiers. A lot of them come here to have fun when they're off duty."

"How did it happen?"

"The way I heard it, they got drunk in teahouses and they went out to the alleys to piss. They were found lying dead there, in pools of blood."

An eerie sensation crept through Reiko. The murders had occurred while Yugao had been living in the district, and the victims had been stabbed, as had her family. "The killer was never caught?"

"Not that I know of," the Rat said. "Last I heard, the police had decided that a roving bandit killed those soldiers. Their money pouches were missing from their bodies."

It must be a coincidence that had placed Yugao and the stabbings in the same area during the same time period. Bandits did often kill and rob people. Furthermore, how could a woman murder strong, armed samurai? Yet Reiko didn't trust coincidences.

The storm abated. The rain diminished to a sprinkle, although the sky remained overcast. People poured out of the stalls, onto the wet avenue.

"It was nice talking to you," the Rat said. "If I hear any news about your escaped prisoner, I'll send a message." He jerked his monkey's leash and told Reiko's guards, "Fun's over."

Reiko spent an hour questioning people in the entertainment district, but no one had seen Yugao. She was apparently too smart to run to a place where the police were likely to look for her. But still she might have gravitated toward her home territory because she didn't know where else to go. Reiko broadened her search into the neighborhoods near Ryōgoku Hirokoji and eventually found herself in a familiar street of tenements and shops. She saw a teahouse she recognized. The maid she'd talked to yesterday was lounging against the same pillar.

"Well, look who's back," the maid said and held out her hand, palm up, to Reiko. "You owe me. I've found out where that girl Tama is."

Reiko's bearers set down her palanquin in an enclave in the Nihonbashi merchant district. Rain drizzled on mansions that rose two stories high; pines and red maples grew from spacious gardens hidden behind bamboo fences. The streets were quiet and unpopulated, remote from the bustle of commerce a few blocks away.

"A customer from the old days happened to stop by. He said Tama's father drank himself to death, and Tama was left without a single copper to live on," the teahouse maid had told Reiko. "She went to work as a servant in the house of a rich moneylender."

The directions given by the maid had brought Reiko here. Maybe Tama could help her trace Yugao as well as shed light on the murders. Reiko watched through the window of her palanquin as Lieutenant Asukai dismounted, walked to the largest mansion on the street, and knocked on the gate. It was opened by a manservant.

"I want to see Tama," Lieutenant Asukai said. "Send her out."

Soon a woman emerged. Tama was so small that she looked like a child, although Reiko knew she must be near the same age as Yugao, in her twenties. Tama wore a plain indigo kimono; a white cloth bound her hair. She had a face as plump-cheeked and smooth as a doll's. As she beheld Lieutenant Asukai and the other guards, fear widened her innocent eyes. He led her to Reiko's palanquin.

Reiko said, "Hello, Tama-*san*. My name is Reiko. I'm the daughter of Magistrate Ueda, and I'd like to talk to you." She opened the door. "Come inside so you don't get wet." She felt an instinctive urge to protect Tama, who seemed too sweet and defenseless to survive in the world.

Tama meekly obeyed. Inside the palanquin, she looked around as if it were some alien place. Reiko thought she'd probably never been in one before: Servants didn't ride; they walked. She knelt as far from Reiko as possible and tucked her hands in her sleeves.

"Don't be afraid," Reiko said. "I won't hurt you."

Bashful, Tama avoided Reiko's gaze. Reiko said, "I need to ask you some questions about your friend Yugao."

Tama stiffened. She eyed the door, as if she wanted to jump out but didn't dare. "I—I don't know any Yugao," she said in a whisper so soft that Reiko almost couldn't hear it. Her face, honest and transparent, gave the lie to her words.

"I know that you and Yugao were friends," Reiko said gently. "Have you seen her?"

Tama shook her head. Her eyes begged Reiko to leave her alone. She whispered, "No. Not since three years ago, when she . . ."

"Moved to the *hinin* settlement?" When Tama nodded, Reiko wondered if Tama was lying again. The girl's nervousness made it hard to tell whether that was the case, or if she was just shy with strangers or afraid that her connection with a murderess would get her in trouble. "Don't worry, nothing bad will happen to you," Reiko assured Tama. "I just need to find Yugao. She escaped from jail yesterday, and she's dangerous. Do you have any idea where she might have gone?"

"Jail?" Tama gasped the word. Shock and dismay filled her eyes. "Yugao was in jail?"

"Yes," Reiko said. "She murdered her parents and sister. Didn't you know?"

Tama sat staring in open-mouthed horror: It was obvious she hadn't known. Reiko supposed that crimes in the *hinin* settlement weren't publicized. Tama buried her face in her hands and began to sob. "Oh no, oh no, oh no!"

Reiko took hold of Tama's hands and gently pulled them down. Tama's eyes were streaming and her face blotched with tears. She gazed helplessly at Reiko.

"I don't know where Yugao is," she cried. "Please believe me!"

"Have you any idea where Yugao could have gone? Are there any places that you and she went when you were children?"

"No!" Tama snatched her hands out of Reiko's grasp. She wiped her tears on her sleeve.

"Try to think," Reiko urged. "Yugao might hurt someone else unless she's caught." Tama only wept and shook her head. Reiko grabbed the girl by the shoulders. "If you know anything at all that might help me find Yugao, you must tell me."

"I don't," Tama whimpered. "Let me go. You're hurting me."

Ashamed of bullying this innocent, helpless girl, Reiko let go of Tama. "All right. I'm sorry," Reiko said. But even if she couldn't find out where Yugao was, perhaps she could still make her hunt for Tama worthwhile.

"Tama," she said, "there's something else I need to ask you. Why would Yugao kill her family?"

The girl cringed in the corner of the palanquin, still and silent as a baby bird that hopes the cat will get bored and go away if it waits long enough.

"Tell me," Reiko said, gentle yet firm.

Tama's will crumbled under Reiko's. At last she whispered, "I think . . . I think he drove her to it."

"Who did? Do you mean her father?"

Tama nodded. "He . . . when we were children . . . he used to come into her bed at night."

Reiko felt a flash of vindication at this evidence for her theory about Yugao's motive for the murders. "Is that what Yugao told you?"

"No," Tama said. "She didn't have to. I saw."

"How? What happened?"

With much prodding from Reiko, Tama explained, "I spent a night at Yugao's house. We were ten years old. After we went to bed, her father came over to us and crawled in next to her."

Reiko pictured the mother, father, sister, Yugao, and Tama lying on mattresses in the same room, as families did who lived in close quarters. She saw the man rise and tiptoe through the darkness to Yugao. She was shocked that he would commit incest with her in the presence of her friend and his whole family. The man deserved to be an outcast and hadn't been wrongly accused by his business partner.

"He thought I was asleep," Tama continued. "I shut my eyes and lay still. But I could feel them moving in the bed near me and the floor shaking while he lay on top of her. And I could hear her crying when he . . ."

Tama couldn't be mistaken. Children of her class must often see their parents coupling, and she would have recognized that Yugao's father had been doing with his daughter what he should have done only with his wife.

"Yugao must have hated her father for hurting her," Reiko said to herself. "She must have hated him all these years."

"But she didn't. The next morning, I told Yugao that I knew what her father had done. I said I was sorry for her. But she said she didn't mind." Tama's eyes reflected the surprised disbelief that Reiko felt. "She said that if he wanted her, it was all right because she loved him and it was her duty to make him happy. And she did seem to love him. She followed him around. She would climb on his lap and hug him."

As if they were lovers instead of father and daughter, Reiko thought with a shudder of revulsion.

"And he loved her," Tama said. "He gave her lots of presents— dolls, sweets, pretty clothes."

With them he'd paid for Yugao's cooperation, suffering, and silence.

"If there was anyone Yugao hated, it was her mother," Tama said.

"Why?"

"She complained about how her mother was always scolding her. She didn't like anything Yugao did. Once I saw her hit Yugao so hard that her nose started bleeding. I don't know why she was so mean."

Reiko deduced that the mother had been jealous of her daughter for stealing her husband's affections. And since she couldn't punish the man she depended on for a living, she'd taken out her anger on Yugao. "How long did this go on?"

"Until we were fifteen," Tama said. "Then I think her father stopped."

That would have been three years before the family moved to the *hinin* settlement. Reiko wondered if Yugao had held a grudge for so long. "How do you know? Did she say?"

Tama shook her head. "One day I went to visit Yugao. She was crying. I asked what was wrong. She wouldn't tell me. But I noticed that her little sister Umeko had a new doll. And Umeko sat on her father's lap and hugged him the way Yugao used to. He ignored Yugao."

Amazement stunned Reiko. The man had committed incest with both his daughters, not just one. It seemed he'd grown tired of Yugao, and Umeko had replaced her as his favored pet and victim of his lust.

"Yugao changed," Tama said. "She hardly ever talked. She was mad all the time. She wasn't fun anymore."

Even though her father had stopped violating her, she must have been crushed and angered by his desertion. Reiko asked, "What happened after that?"

"She was at my house all the time. When I worked in my father's teahouse, she would help me."

Reiko imagined Yugao had wanted to avoid her own home, where she would see the father who'd rejected her, the mother who'd unjustly punished her, and the sister who must have caused her terrible jealousy. Tama had been her refuge. But when Yugao and her family had moved to the *hinin* settlement, they'd been cooped up together, and she'd lost her friend; she'd had nowhere to go. The tensions inside the family must have reached a crisis point and exploded into murder.

"The customers at the teahouse liked her." Tama sighed. "She would go outside with them, and . . ."

Her pause conjured up visions of Yugao coupling with men in a dark alley. Reiko suspected that Yugao had been seeking love from them that she couldn't get from her father.

"Some of them fell in love with her," Tama said. "They wanted to marry her. But she was mean to them. She called them idiots and told them to leave her alone. She would go outside with other men right in front of them."

Perhaps she'd also craved revenge on her father, which she'd satisfied by hurting her suitors, thought Reiko.

"But later there was one man. A samurai . . ." Tama sucked her breath through her teeth.

"What's the matter?" Reiko said.

"He was scary."

"In what way?"

Puckering her forehead, Tama searched her memory. "It was his eyes. They were so black and—and unfriendly. When he looked at me, I felt like he was thinking about killing me. And his voice. He didn't talk much, but when he did, he sounded like a cat hissing."

Tama shivered. Then bewilderment crossed her face. "I don't know why Yugao wanted anything to do with him. We knew he was dangerous. Once, another customer bumped into him. He threw the man on the floor and held his sword to his neck. I never saw anyone move so fast." Awe and fright dazed her eyes. "The man begged for mercy, and he let him go. But he could have killed him just like that."

"Maybe Yugao wanted another man who would hurt her," Reiko mused.

"He acted almost as if she wasn't there," Tama said. "He would sit and drink, and she would sit beside him and talk, and he never answered—he just stared into space. But she fell in love with him. She stood in front of the teahouse every day, watching for him to come. When he left, she would run after him. Sometimes I wouldn't see her for days, because she was off with him."

Reiko understood that Yugao had transferred her unrequited love for her father to the mysterious samurai. She speculated that Yugao had stayed in contact with him after she'd moved to the *hinin* settlement. If so, she might have gone to him after she'd escaped from jail.

A thrill of hope tingled inside Reiko as she said, "Who is this man?"

"He called himself Jin," Tama said. "That's all I knew."

Without a clan name, it would be difficult to trace him. "Who is his master?"

"I don't know."

Reiko fought disappointment. The mysterious samurai was her only clue to Yugao's whereabouts. "What did he look like?"

Tama frowned in an effort to recall. "He was handsome, I guess."

After many attempts to coax a better description from Tama, Reiko gave up. "Do you know where he and Yugao went when they left the teahouse?"

The girl shook her head, then stopped as a thought occurred to her. "I used to work at an inn, before I came here. Sometimes, when there was an empty room, I would let them inside so they could be together."

If Yugao and her lover had met up, maybe they'd gone back to the place that was familiar to them. "What's the name of this inn? Where is it?"

Tama gave directions. "It's called the Jade Pavilion." She edged toward the door. "Can I go now?" she said timidly. "If I stay away too long, my mistress will be angry."

Reiko hesitated, then nodded, said, "Thank you for your help," and let Tama go. As she watched Tama scurry through the gate of her employer's house, she wondered if she'd heard everything Tama knew about Yugao. She had a feeling that the meek, gentle Tama had managed to hide something from her.

Lieutenant Asukai put his head through the window of the palanquin. "I heard what the girl told you," he said. "Shall we go to the Jade Pavilion and look for Yugao?"

That had been Reiko's first thought, but if Yugao was with her mysterious samurai, and he was as dangerous as Tama said, then Reiko should be prepared for trouble. Her guards were good enough fighters to protect her from bandits and the stray rebel soldier, but she didn't want to pit them against a murderess and an unknown quantity.

"First we'll fetch reinforcements," she said.

24

On a dingy street in the Honjo lumber district, Sano and Detectives Marume and Fukida mounted their horses outside a teahouse. Red lanterns hung on its eaves glowed in the misty twilight; their reflections in the puddles left by the rain looked like spilled blood. Sano watched his guards march the elderly proprietor, two maids, and three drunken customers out of the teahouse. They all looked frightened and confused because he'd interrogated and arrested them, which he'd already done with everyone he'd found at five other places on the list that General Isogai had given him.

"I can't believe any of those people is the Ghost," said Detective Marume.

"Neither can I," said Fukida. "They're not the sort that would know the secrets of *dim-mak,* or that you'd expect to find on Yanagisawa's elite squadron."

Sano had to agree. Frustration gnawed at him because he'd spent an entire day on this hunt, and the people he'd netted during the other raids appeared just as unlikely to be the assassin. But he said, "We figure that the Ghost travels in disguise. I'm not taking any chances that I'll catch him and he'll trick me into letting him go." He told the guards, "Put them in Edo Jail with the people we arrested earlier."

"Shall we try the next place on the list?" Fukida said.

Sano glanced at the overcast sky, which was rapidly darkening. At this rate, he would never catch the assassin by tomorrow night. He might die before he could stop the Ghost's reign of terror and fulfill his duty. His nerves jittered with a constant, obsessive impulse to check his body for the fingerprint-shaped bruise, the harbinger of death. He couldn't afford to waste a moment. Yet if he had little more than a day to live, he didn't want to spend it chasing a phantom through wet, desolate streets when he couldn't even be certain that the Ghost was one of Yanagisawa's seven fugitive elite troops. Sano experienced an overwhelming need to see Reiko and Masahiro. The time until tomorrow might be the last he had with them.

"We'll stop at home first," he said.

When they arrived at Edo Castle, night had immersed the city. Torches outside the gate flared and smoked in the mist. Smoke from a fire somewhere drifted over the deserted promenade. Sano and his men rode through passages deserted except for the checkpoint sentries. The castle was a fortification under siege by an invisible enemy, where most everyone in it cowered behind locked doors and legions of bodyguards. At his compound, Sano left his detectives at their barracks and went straight to his private chambers.

Masahiro came running toward him down the corridor, arms outstretched, calling, "Papa! Papa!"

Sano picked up his son and held him close. He rested his face against Masahiro's soft hair and breathed his fresh, sweet scent. Would this be the last time? Sano's heart ached as he said, "Where's Mama?"

"Mama go out," Masahiro said.

"She did?" Sano was disturbed that Reiko was out after dark in these troubled times, and surprised that after the attack on him last night, she would go about her business as though nothing had happened. Shouldn't she be here waiting for him?

He heard quick, light footsteps coming along the passage, and Reiko appeared. She wore a drab cloak over plain garments. Her face looked tired and unhappy, but it brightened when she saw him and Masahiro.

"I'm so glad you're home," she said. Masahiro reached for her, and she took him from Sano. "I was afraid you wouldn't come back."

"Where have you been?" Sano demanded.

Reiko's smile faded at his sharp tone. "I went to tell my father that I'd finished my investigation."

Sano was amazed, and hurt, that she'd thought this errand was so important she'd left the house; he might have missed seeing her before he had to resume his hunt for the assassin. She could have sent a messenger. "You waited until this late at night?"

"Well, no." Reiko hesitated, then said carefully, "I went this morning. But then my father told me that there had been a fire at the jail, and Yugao had escaped. I thought I'd better try to find her. That's what I've been doing all day."

"Wait. Do you mean that you got further involved in this business of the outcast criminal? After you told me you were finished with her?"

"I know that's what I told you. But I had to look for her," Reiko said, defensive. "It's my fault that she ran away. I couldn't just sit and do nothing."

Even though her explanation was reasonable, Sano's hurt flared into anger because she'd disregarded his wishes. "You know what a difficult position I'm in," he shouted. "I can't believe you're so selfish and obstinate!"

Anger sparked in Reiko's eyes. "Don't shout at me. You're the one who's selfish and obstinate. You'd rather have me let a murderess go free than try my best to catch her, just because you're afraid of Police Commissioner Hoshina. Where's your samurai courage? I'm beginning to think you lost it when you became chamberlain!"

Her words had enough merit to stab Sano to the heart. "How dare you insult me?" he said, his voice rising louder with his fury. "For four years, you've given me problems and more problems. I wish I'd never married you!"

Reiko stared at him, speechless and blank-faced with shock, as if he'd hit her. Then her face crumpled. Tears spilled down her cheeks. She hugged Masahiro, who wailed, upset by the quarrel. Sano's rage dissolved into horror that he'd spoken so cruelly to Reiko.

"I'm sorry," he said, his voice low with shame. He realized that the constant activity, little sleep, fear, and desperation had made him explode at Reiko. "I didn't mean it."

She bounced Masahiro, trying to comfort him, while she awkwardly wiped her tears on her sleeve. "Neither did I," she said in a broken whisper. "Please forgive me."

Sano put his arms around her, and she leaned against him. He felt her body quake as she wept. "I'll forgive you if you forgive me."

"I shouldn't have said such a terrible thing to you," she said between sobs. "I'm so frightened and upset and worried, but that's no excuse."

"I've spent all day running from one place to another, trying to catch the assassin and failing, but that's no excuse either," Sano said. "Let's call ourselves even."

If he had only one more day to live, he didn't want them to waste it on ripping each other to shreds. Reiko nodded; her eyes brimmed with love, remorse, and apprehension. Together they put Masahiro to bed, then went to their chamber. Sano collapsed on the bed that the servants had laid out. His body and mind ached with fatigue. He tried not to think about the long night's work ahead of him, nor to imagine how it would feel if death struck him down tomorrow and what would happen to his family.

Reiko knelt beside him. "I'll stop looking for Yugao. That will be one fewer problem for you to worry about."

"No." Sano couldn't accept her peace offering. "I've changed my mind. I think you should keep looking." She needed something to distract her from their worries. "It's the right thing to do." There was a bright side to every dark situation, Sano realized. If he died tomorrow, Hoshina's scheming couldn't hurt him.

"Are you sure?"

He heard hope in Reiko's voice and saw disbelief in her eyes. "Yes." Although he had his hands too full with his own investigation to care much about hers, Sano wanted to make amends to Reiko. "How did your search go today?" he said, pretending interest.

She smiled, thankful. "I found Yugao's childhood friend Tama." As Reiko related what Tama had said about the family history that she believed had led Yugao to murder, Sano tried to listen, but his fatigue overwhelmed him; he dozed. "Tama told me of a place where Yugao might have gone. It's an inn called the Jade Pavilion."

A faint chord chimed in Sano's memory. He snapped awake. Why did that name seem familiar?

"I came home to see if I could borrow some of your troops to go there with me and help me capture Yugao, if she's there," Reiko continued.

Sano bolted upright because he knew where he'd seen the Jade Pavilion mentioned. He fumbled under his sash and brought out the list that General Isogai had given him.

"Is something wrong?" Reiko said, puzzled. "What are you doing?"

Excitement coursed through Sano as he ran his finger down the characters on the paper. "I think the killer is one of Yanagisawa's elite troops. Seven of them are still at large." The words "Jade Pavilion" leapt out at him. "This is a list of places they've been known to frequent in the past. Here's the inn where you think Yugao is."

He and Reiko stared at the list, then at each other, in amazement that their separate investigations had suddenly meshed. Reiko's expression sharpened. "Yugao had a lover. He was a samurai. They used to meet at the inn. Do you think . . . ?"

"No. He can't be the Ghost," Sano said even as his heart began to race. That Reiko had stumbled onto a link to the assassin was too much to hope for.

"Why not?" Eagerness lit Reiko's eyes. "Tama described him as a dangerous man. She saw him almost kill somebody who bumped into him by accident. Doesn't that sound like the kind of person who could be your assassin?"

Sano cautioned himself against wishful thinking. "That description could fit hundreds of samurai. There's no reason to believe he and Yugao are connected. How would a *hinin* woman and an officer from

Yanagisawa's elite squadron have become lovers? How would they have even met?"

"Yugao wasn't always an outcast. She met her man at a teahouse near Ryōgoku Hirokoji, where her father once owned a carnival." Reiko studied the list. "The teahouse isn't named here, but the army doesn't know everything. It still could have been a place frequented by Yanagisawa's troops."

"It could," Sano said, letting Reiko persuade him despite the lack of evidence. "What else did you find out about this mystery man? His name, I hope?"

"He called himself 'Jin.' He talked in a whisper. It sounded like a cat hissing." Reiko added, "Yugao had relations with many men. The Ghost could have been the one that Tama says she fell in love with."

"At any rate, the Jade Pavilion is worth checking." Sano rose from the bed. "It might as well be the next place I look for the Ghost."

Reiko accompanied Sano to the door. "I just knew there was a reason I had to keep on with my investigation," she said, sparkling with excitement. "If it leads you to the Ghost, I hope that will make up for the trouble it's caused you."

"If I capture him at the Jade Pavilion," Sano said, "I'll never stand in the way of anything you want to do ever again."

He half expected Reiko to ask to go with him, but she didn't. She must know that if the Ghost was there, he would say it was too dangerous for her and she would be in the way; and she didn't want another argument even though she'd turned up what seemed to be the vital clue. She only said, "I can't wait to know what happens!"

"You'll be the first to know."

They embraced in ardent farewell. Reiko said, "If Yugao is there—"

"We'll capture her for you," Sano said as he strode outside toward the barracks to fetch Detectives Marume, Fukida, and a small army of troops. He felt energized by hope; his fatigue evaporated into the mist. He could even believe that he might live beyond tomorrow.

25

A wavering flame burned in a lamp inside a room whose shutters were closed tight against the world. Thunder rumbled; rain spattered on the roof outside. On a mattress spread on the floor, Yugao and her lover lay naked together. He was on his back, his lean, muscular body straight and rigid. She embraced him, her breasts pressed against his side, her leg flung over his, her hair fanned over them. Their bare flesh shone golden in the lamplight. Yugao tenderly caressed his face. Adoration welled in her heart as her fingers trailed over the knife-edged bones of his brow, cheeks, and jaw. Her touch worshipped his mouth, so firm and stern. He was the most beautiful man she'd ever seen, her samurai hero.

During her days in jail, and the years in the *hinin* settlement, she'd prayed that she would see him again. The memory of him had sustained her through all her hardships. Now she gazed yearningly into his eyes. Their darkness and depth made her dizzy, as though she were falling into them. But they looked through her, beyond her. She felt distant from him even while touching him, for he kept his spirit hidden in some faraway place. He hardly seemed to notice she was here.

A familiar loneliness saddened Yugao. Anxious to provoke some response from him, some sign that he cared for her, she pressed her mouth to the scars that etched his chest, souvenirs of countless swordfights. She teased his nipples with her tongue and felt them harden. As she moved her mouth downward, he stirred. She fondled his manhood, which swelled and curved upward; he breathed a sigh of pleasure. Desire for him quickened in Yugao, flushing her skin, tingling in her breasts, flooding her loins with heat. But when she took him into her mouth, he roughly pushed her away. He sat up and grabbed the short sword he kept by the bed. He held the blade upright in front of her face.

"Make love to it," he ordered.

His voice was a hiss that reminded Yugao of ice sizzling on fire, of a snake readying to strike. His throat had been injured in combat and that was why he couldn't talk except in a whisper. Yugao had heard the story from his comrades, in the teahouse where they'd met; he never told her anything personal about himself. Now his stare commanded her to do his bidding. The steel blade flickered with reflections of the lamp's flame, as though it were alive. Yugao knew this ritual, which they'd enacted many times. He didn't like her to touch him, and he avoided touching her as much as possible. Always he preferred that she pay her attentions to his weapon rather than his body during sex. She was afraid to ask why because he might get angry, but she must obey him, as she always had.

She knelt and ran her fingers up and down the cold, smooth blade. Her face, pitiful with her need for his approval, was mirrored in the shiny steel. Arousal smoldered in his eyes while he watched. His chest heaved as his breathing grew fast and shallow. Her own desire raged like flames inside her. She leaned over, extended her tongue, and slowly licked the blade from bottom to top, along its flat side. Then she licked down the razor-sharp edge. Yugao trembled with fear of cutting herself, but she saw his manhood rise erect. His enjoyment was hers. She moaned with the thrill of it.

Thunder cracked outside, shaking the floor, startling Yugao off balance. Her tongue slipped. She gasped as the blade sliced a tiny cut on her tongue; she tasted salty blood. She reared back on her heels. Her hand flew to her mouth. The sight of her wounded and in pain excited him to a frenzy. He shoved her down on the bed. Holding the sword across her throat, he thrust himself between her legs.

Yugao cried out with pleasure and terror as he moved inside her and the blade pressed against her skin. He knew he didn't have to force her; she would let him do anything to her that he wanted. But he needed violence to be satisfied. He would cut her if he chose. He had in the past. Even as she clutched him to her and heaved up to meet his thrusts, she screamed and cringed away from the sword. His face strained and contorted while he moved faster and harder. His gaze locked onto hers.

She whirled into the black vortex of his eyes. Flashes of memory illuminated the darkness. She was a young girl in her family home. Her father lay atop her; he clamped his hand over her mouth to stifle her cries as they coupled. In the morning there was blood on her bed. Her mother cursed and beat her.

But those days, and those people who had hurt her, were gone. She clung tight to her lover. He flung back his head, shouted, and thrust deep into her as he released. Her own release shuddered through her in paroxysms of rapture. Wild, incoherent cries burst from Yugao as she felt her spirit touch his at last.

Too soon, even before her sensations faded, he rose from her. He knelt on the floor across the room, his back to Yugao, while she lay drenched with their sweat and shivering in the sudden chill of his absence. She crept over to him and laid a tentative hand on his shoulder. He gazed into space, ignoring her.

"What are you thinking?" she said.

A long moment passed before he said, "Coming here was a mistake."

The reproachful tone in his whisper stung Yugao. "Why? It's quiet and comfortable and private. We have everything we need." She gestured at the bedding, the soft floor cushions, the brazier filled with coal, the bundle of food, the jars of water and wine.

"It's not safe here. And I'd be better off without you." He shrugged her hand off him.

Yugao had a sudden memory of her father fondling her sister Umeko on his lap while she watched, jealous and deserted. "But we're meant to be together," Yugao said, wounded by his attitude. "Fate has reunited us."

He laughed, a sound like metal rasping against metal. "This kind of fate will get us both killed. You're a wanted criminal. The police will be looking for you. You'll lead my enemies straight to me."

"No, I won't!" Yugao was distressed because he thought her such a liability while she loved him more than anything else in the world. "I've been careful. They'll never find us here. I would never put you in danger. I love you. I'll do anything to protect you."

She would hide him, feed him, and give herself to him no matter how he treated her. She was his slave despite everything she knew about him.

When she'd met him at the teahouse, she'd set her heart on winning his love. He was different from the other men there. Most of them had nicer manners than he did, but she cared nothing for them. She could lure them with one smile, one seductive glance. The weak, stupid fools! But he ignored her efforts to attract him. This made Yugao want him in a way that she'd never wanted any man. For the first time in her life she felt physical desire. She grew determined to have him. Whenever he came to the teahouse, she flirted with him for all she was worth. Sometimes she would take another man out to the alley, hoping to make him jealous. Nothing worked.

He usually traveled on foot instead of riding a horse as most samurai of his rank did, and once, when he left the teahouse, she ran after him. He'd stopped, turned on her, and said, "Get lost. Leave me alone."

But that had only whetted Yugao's desire. The next time she followed him, she took care that he wouldn't notice her among the crowds in the streets. She spent days trailing him all over Edo. From a safe distance she watched him meet and talk furtively with strange men. She was curious to know what he did, and one night she found out.

It was a cold, wet autumn evening. Yugao followed him through the mist that hung over the city, along roads almost deserted, to a neighborhood near the river. He'd stopped down the block from a brightly lit teahouse and taken cover in the doorway of a shop closed for the night. She'd hidden herself around the corner. Shivering in the chill dampness, she watched him watch the teahouse. Customers came and went. Hours passed; then two samurai emerged from the teahouse and walked down the street past Yugao.

He slipped out of the doorway and stole after them.

Yugao's heart beat fast because she knew something exciting was about to happen. The mist was so thick she could hardly see to follow him and the two samurai. They were shadows that dissolved even though they were but twenty paces ahead. Their voices drifted back to Yugao. She couldn't make out what they were saying, but their tones sounded urgent, frightened. Their steps quickened to a run. Yugao hurried forward, but soon she lost them. Then she heard a muffled cry, which she followed to an alley between two warehouses. She peered inside.

A breeze blowing through the alley from the river dispelled the mist. A body lay crumpled on the ground. Farther down the alley, two figures grappled and flailed in a violent embrace. Yugao heard a scream of agony. One figure fell with a thud. The other stood motionless. Yugao gaped in shock. He'd been stalking those samurai, and he'd just killed them both!

Now he saw her. "What are you doing here?" he demanded.

Yugao realized that he meant to kill her so she could never tell anyone what he'd done. But she didn't run away. His strength and daring awed her. Her desire for him burgeoned into a rampant hunger. Almost without conscious thought, Yugao moved toward him and opened her robes, baring her body to him.

He let the sword drop. He seized her and took her, against the wall of the warehouse, while his victims lay dead nearby. The brutality of the killings, and the danger that they would be caught, roused them both to a savage passion. For the first time Yugao experienced pleasure with a man. She didn't care that he was a murderer. As they reached their climax, she screamed in triumph because she'd finally won him.

The next day, she asked him why he'd killed those men.

"They were the enemy," was all he would say.

Later she heard about the murders from gossip at the teahouse. The two samurai had been retainers of Lord Matsudaira. He had issued an order that anyone with information about the murders should come forward. Yugao didn't mind that her lover was wanted for such an important crime. She admired him all the more because he was taking on such a powerful enemy as Lord Matsudaira. She didn't care why. She liked that he fought the people who'd wronged him. She gloried in having a man so brave.

But it soon became clear that she didn't have him. After that night, they met often, always at cheap inns around Edo, and he'd taught her sex rituals he liked, but outside the bedchamber he ignored her the same as before. He never showed any affection to her. Desperate for his love, Yugao had taken extreme action.

What she'd done had infuriated him rather than pleased him. He'd dropped her and vanished like smoke. Yugao was devastated. Then more calamity struck. Her father was demoted to *hinin*. The family had moved to the settlement. She'd often gone looking for him, but he was nowhere to be found.

The war had turned her luck.

A month after the battle had ended, Yugao awakened in the middle of the night to hear a voice outside the window, hissing her name. It was the voice she'd longed to hear. She jumped out of bed and ran outside. She found him lying on the ground, bleeding from serious wounds, half dead. Yugao never knew what had happened to him or how he'd found her; he never said. What mattered was that he'd returned to her. She took him in and put him to bed in the lean-to where her sister Umeko entertained men. Umeko wasn't pleased.

"That's my room," she said. "Get that sick, filthy hoodlum out of it!"

Their father took Umeko's side; he always did. "If we're caught sheltering a fugitive, we'll get in trouble," he told Yugao. "I'm going to report him to the police."

"If you do, I'll tell them you haven't stopped committing incest," Yugao retorted. "They'll make your sentence longer."

Her threat kept him and Umeko silent. That whole winter, she'd hidden her lover and nursed him back to health. When he was well, he began going out at night. He never said why, but Yugao knew he must be continuing his war against Lord Matsudaira. Sometimes he returned the next morning; sometimes he stayed away for days. Yugao waited in fear that he wouldn't come back. She was terrified that he'd been killed. The last time, after he'd been gone a month, she went looking for him, in the places they used to meet. Finally she found him, but he was angry rather than glad to see her. Although she'd wept at his coldness, he'd spurned her: "I have work to do. You'll be in my way. If I ever need you again, I'll come to you."

"Please let me stay with you," she'd begged, "at least for a little while."

She'd undressed and tried to seduce him. He'd drawn his sword and sliced off her left nipple. As she screamed in horror at the bloody wound, he'd shouted, "Go away, and don't come back, or I'll kill you next time!"

He'd finally instilled true fear of himself into Yugao. Heartbroken, she'd obeyed, thinking their relationship was over for good. She'd returned to the hovel, where her family had given her no sympathy. "Good riddance to him," her father said. "You're too ugly to keep a man," Umeko said spitefully. Her mother had laughed at her grief. "Serves you right!"

"Someday you'll pay for the way you treat me!" Yugao had cried in a furious rage.

Now they couldn't hurt her anymore. Now the fire that had set her free had given her new hope of spending her life with him. But now, after she'd managed to track him down, he was slipping away from her again. He put his clothes on and said, "I shouldn't have let you bring me here. The police will search the places and question the people that have connections with you. I can't risk that they'll find you and catch me by accident."

As he peeked through the cracks in the window shutters to see if his enemies were stealing up outside, panic rose in Yugao. "If you don't like it here, we'll go somewhere else," she said even though she hated to leave this sanctuary. She began flinging on her own clothes, a cheap undergarment and kimono she'd stolen from a shop.

The contempt in his glance cut her like a knife. "We're not going together. I don't want to lug around a piece of dangerous dead weight. It's time we split up."

"No!" Aghast, Yugao clung to him. "I won't let you leave me!" He wrenched away from her with a sound of exasperation and turned his back on her, but she pressed herself against him. "Not after what I've done for you!"

He whirled to face her. The atmosphere between them vibrated with the history of the other things she'd done to win his love, besides nursing him and sheltering him. Yugao could almost smell blood in the air, pungent and metallic.

"I never asked you to do it." Rage blazed in his eyes.

"But aren't you glad I did? They were the enemy."

"You were careless. You could have been caught. People knew about your connection to me. If the police had figured out what you'd done, they would have arrested us both for conspiracy even though you acted on your own."

"But they didn't. Fate is on our side. It protected us."

He shook his head, and an incredulous laugh hissed from him. "Merciful gods, you're insane! The sooner I'm rid of you, the better!"

He fastened his swords at his waist and stuffed a knapsack with his extra clothes and few other possessions.

"Wait!" Yugao said, frantic. Since her love and his obligation to her wouldn't stop him, maybe practical reasons would. "You said the chamberlain and his troops are looking for you. You heard they've already raided places you've been hiding. If you leave, where will you go?"

"That's my business. Not yours." But his hands faltered as he tied the knot on the bundle.

Yugao pressed her advantage: "You should lie low for a while. The chamberlain will think you've left town. He'll give up hunting you in Edo. Until then, this is the safest place for you."

A scowl darkened his features. Yugao sensed him fighting logic, resisting her. She said, "Maybe you can find some cave to hide in, but who will bring you food? Your comrades are dead or scattered all over the country. Who else do you have to help you but me?"

With a sudden burst of temper, he flung his bundle across the room. It hit the wall, then plopped onto the floor. His expression was murderous as he dropped to his knees. Yugao didn't care that he hated depending on her for survival. Kneeling behind him, she hugged him and laid her cheek against his, although he sat rigid in her embrace.

"Everything will be all right," she said. "Together we'll destroy our enemies. Then we'll be happy together as we were meant to be. Trust me."

26

The Jade Pavilion didn't deserve its elegant name. It was a ramshackle inn, crouched on the embankment above the Nihonbashi River, that catered to travelers of limited means and laborers who worked on the barges. The inn had four wings built of planks, roofed with shaggy thatch, and attached by covered corridors. Stone steps led down the embankment to the river, which rippled oily and black in the darkness. Houseboats were anchored along the waterfront. As midnight drew near, the mist thinned, revealing the moon caught like a crystal float in a torn fishing net.

Sano, Hirata, Detectives Marume, Fukida, Inoue, and Arai, and six guards walked up to the Jade Pavilion's entrance, which was situated on a narrow street lined with food stalls and nautical supply shops, all dark and deserted. Twenty troops that Sano had brought surrounded the inn. A lantern burned above the entrance, but the door was closed. Sano knocked. A pudgy, bald innkeeper poked his head out of the building.

"If you're looking for rooms, I must apologize, masters," he said. "Mine are all occupied."

"We're looking for a fugitive," Sano said. "Let us in. And be quiet."

He and his men strode in the door, along a passage to a garden of wet, overgrown grass and bushes. The smell of privies, fish, and garbage tainted the air. Verandas fronted the buildings that housed the guests. Sano and his men drew their swords, hastened onto the verandas. They flung open doors, shouting, "This is a raid! Everybody out!"

Cries and scuffles sounded inside the rooms. Out stumbled men dressed in night robes or stark naked, blinking with sleep and fear. Hirata and the detectives lined them up on the verandas. The other troops bustled into the garden, towing guests who'd tried to flee out the windows.

"State your names," Hirata and the detectives ordered. The guests obeyed, their voices mingling in a cacophony of panic.

Nobody emerged from one room. There Sano looked into darkness that appeared to be vacant. The innkeeper hovered in the garden, holding a lamp. Sano called to him, "I thought you said all the rooms were occupied."

"They were, master," said the innkeeper.

Sano took possession of the lamp and entered the room. His nostrils twitched at its stench of sickness and decay. On the floor lay a mattress covered with a dirty, crumpled quilt. Flies buzzed around a full chamber pot and a tray that held a meal of rice, tea, and soup; cold and stale. Sano bent and touched the mattress.

Hirata appeared in the doorway. "The men we caught are crew from the river barges. If the Ghost is here, this room must be his." Hirata looked around the empty room, and his face mirrored the disappointment on Sano's. "He's gone?"

"He was here a moment ago. The bed is still warm." Sano felt intense, crushing frustration because he'd gotten so close yet his quarry had vanished.

"But how could he have gotten away?" Hirata inspected the room. "There's only one door, and if he'd come out it, we'd have seen him. And the window shutters are locked from the inside. He couldn't have—"

Sano raised his hand, interrupting Hirata, as a faint noise caught his attention. "What's that sound?"

They both stood motionless and silent, listening. Sano again heard the sound, a wheeze that ended in a moan. He looked at Hirata, who nodded then mouthed, *Where did it come from?* They waited. The commotion outside died down, and Marume and Fukida came to the door. Sano put his finger to his lips, cautioning them. Again came the wheeze and moan. This time Sano pointed to the cabinet built into the wall. Marume and Fukida tiptoed across the room. They stood on either side of the cabinet, swords drawn. Sano could almost hear his companions' heartbeats quickening in rhythm with his, feel them holding their breath. Fukida slid open the cabinet door.

The cabinet was empty except for shelves that held candles, spare bedding, folded garments, and other innocuous items. Even as the letdown relaxed Sano and his men, they heard the wheeze and moan, louder now. Sano inspected the cabinet's floor. One of the boards was crooked. Marume lifted it and flung it aside. Underneath was a hole perhaps five paces square and four deep. As Sano, Hirata, and the detectives bent over the hole, they gagged at the fetid smell of urine, sweat, and rot that billowed up from it. Sano shone the lamp inside.

A gaunt face stared back at them with fearful eyes. It belonged to a man who lay curled on his side, clothed in dark-hued garments. He inhaled wheezes and exhaled moans. His trembling hand clutched a sword, which he brandished at his captors.

"Drop your weapon," Sano said. He and his men aimed their own swords at the prisoner. "Come out of there."

A convulsion seized the prisoner. His body shuddered; his limbs jerked. He squeezed his eyes shut, clenched his teeth, and uttered a screech of agony.

"What's the matter with you?" Fukida asked.

The prisoner didn't answer. His spasms passed, his body went limp, and the sword fell from his hand. He lay gasping.

"He must be ill," Sano said. "I don't think he's any danger to us. Bring him out."

Marume and Fukida cautiously reached into the hole. As they grasped the prisoner and lifted him, he shrieked, "No! Don't touch me! It hurts!" He was emaciated, all bones and shriveled flesh. White cotton bandages swathed his right leg from toes to knee. They were stained with blood and pus from a wound that Sano identified as the source of the foul, rotten odor as well as the prisoner's agony. The detectives dumped the prisoner on the bed, where he lay helpless and sobbing.

"Is that the Ghost?" Hirata said in a dubious tone.

Sano couldn't believe that this invalid was the assassin who'd terrorized the regime. Crouching by the bed and setting down the lamp, Sano inspected his prisoner more closely. The man's dirty, uncombed hair was long at the back and sides, but short stubble covered his crown, which had once been shaved: He was a samurai. Fukida held up the sword he'd retrieved from the hole. It was expensively crafted, the hilt bound with black silk cord and decorated with gold inlays, a mark of high status.

"Who are you?" Sano asked the prisoner.

His hollow eyes, underscored by dark shadows and wet with tears of pain, blazed with hostility toward Sano. "I know who you are," he whispered between gasps and moans. "You're Chamberlain Sano, running dog for Lord Matsudaira. Go ahead and kill me. I'll tell you nothing."

At least he'd identified himself as a member of the opposition, Sano thought. Then another convulsion gripped the prisoner. He cried, "Help me! Make it stop! Please!"

Hirata crouched beside Sano. He showed the prisoner a black lacquer vial. "This is opium. It will take away the pain. Answer Chamberlain Sano's questions, and I'll give it to you."

The prisoner eyed the vial with fierce, hungry longing. Perspiration drenched his pale skin as the spasms faded. He nodded weakly.

"Who are you?" Sano repeated.

"Iwakura Sanjuro."

That name had appeared on General Isogai's list. "He's from Yanagisawa's elite squadron," Sano told his men, then asked Iwakura, "How were you injured?"

"Shot," he gasped out. "During our last attack on Lord Matsudaira's troops."

The wound had festered, spreading poison through his blood, Sano deduced; he now suffered from the fever that brought convulsions, wasting, and death. "When did this happen?"

"In the third month of this year."

One month ago. "How long have you been sick?"

"I don't recall." Iwakura winced and groaned. "Seems like forever."

Sano looked at Hirata and said, "He's not the Ghost."

"He'd have been too weak to stalk and kill Chief Ejima or Colonel Ibe," Hirata agreed. "And he certainly couldn't have invaded your compound and escaped last night."

Yet although discouragement filled Sano, his captive wasn't necessarily a dead end. He asked Iwakura the whereabouts of Yanagisawa's other fugitive troops, naming each. Iwakura revealed that one was dead; four others had gone to ground in the provinces last winter, and he hadn't seen them since.

"What about Kobori Banzan?" Sano said.

Iwakura groaned; his throat contracted. "Here."

"Here?" Sano frowned in surprise. "At the Jade Pavilion?" He and Hirata and the detectives exchanged glances, wondering if one of the other men they'd caught was the last of the missing seven—and the Ghost.

"Not now," Iwakura said. "We were hiding out in this room. But he left."

"When?" Sano demanded.

"Yesterday. Or the day before." Delirium clouded Iwakura's eyes. "I don't remember."

Sano desperately wanted Kobori to be the Ghost, for if he wasn't, Sano didn't know who else was or where to look for the assassin. "Does Kobori know the technique of *dim-mak*?"

Moments passed while Iwakura squeezed his eyes shut and fought a silent battle with pain. Sano told Hirata, "Give him some opium."

Hirata opened the vial and poured a few drops of the potion into Iwakura's mouth. Soon Iwakura relaxed as the pain eased. Sano repeated his question. Iwakura nodded. "I never knew before. He kept it secret. But yesterday . . . or whenever it was . . ." His gaze blurred while his mind wandered. "Before he left, I asked him to kill me. I'm dying, I'm no good for anything. I wanted him to cut my throat and put me out of my misery. He said he couldn't—it would make trouble."

Such a death would have appeared to be murder, which would have focused police attention on the occupants of this room. Kobori the fugitive wouldn't have wanted that.

"But he said he would help me. He touched my head. He said I would die soon. It would look natural."

Sano held the lamp close to Iwakura's head. There, on the thin, waxy skin near the temple, he could just make out a fingerprint-shaped bruise. Sano inwardly cursed his bad luck. That he'd just missed the assassin!

"Where did Kobori go?" he asked.

"I don't know. A woman came to see him. He went off with her."

Shock flashed across Sano's nerves. "Who was she?"

Iwakura quaked and grunted in another convulsion. "I think he called her Yugao."

And here was confirmation that Yugao and the Ghost were together, just as Reiko had suggested. Sano whistled out his breath in a rush, marveling that her investigation had brought him a break in his. Yet when he pressed Iwakura to remember if the couple had said anything to indicate where they meant to go, the man gritted his teeth and said, "I've already told you everything I know. Give me the opium!"

Sano nodded to Hirata, but Iwakura suddenly convulsed again. His body stiffened, his eyes closed, and the life deserted him. The touch of death had taken effect. As Sano beheld the corpse, he thought, *That could be me soon.*

"If only we could have arrived earlier," Hirata lamented.

"But at least we know who the Ghost is," Sano said, his spirits buoyed despite his disappointment. "That's a big advantage. And we know that he and Yugao are together. A couple should be easier to find than a man alone."

27

Noon had come and gone before Sano and Hirata returned to Edo Castle. As they rode through the passages with their detectives, the sun shone but clouds massed beyond the distant hills. The swampy, fetid scent of the river saturated the cool wind. The castle wasn't as deserted as yesterday; soldiers escorted officials about their business. But their manners were subdued as they bowed to Sano in passing: Fear of the death-touch still pervaded the castle. Sano spotted Captain Nakai loitering near a checkpoint. Their gazes met, and Nakai seemed about to speak, but Sano turned away from his original prime suspect, an embarrassing reminder of the wrong turn his investigation had taken at the start. When Sano and his men arrived in his compound, Reiko came hurrying out of the mansion to meet him.

"What happened?" Her face was filled with gladness at seeing Sano alive. "Did you find them?"

Sano watched her air of expectancy fade at the discouragement on their faces. "You were right about Yugao and the Ghost. But we were too late." He told her what had happened at the Jade Pavilion.

"Have you spent all night looking for him and Yugao?"

"Yes," Sano said. "We questioned the other guests at the inn, but Kobori kept to himself while he was living there, and they couldn't tell us where he and Yugao might have gone."

"The sentries at three neighborhood gates near the Jade Pavilion saw a couple that fit their description pass by yesterday," Hirata said. "But we couldn't find any other witnesses who remember them."

"They must have realized they were conspicuous and traveled separately," Sano said. "My troops are out searching every neighborhood, starting near the Jade Pavilion, warning every headman and gate sentry to be on the lookout for Kobori and Yugao." Exhaustion washed over Sano and his spirits fell. This massive search was like hunting for two bad grains of rice in a thousand bales. "We came home to put more men on the streets."

"Well," Reiko said, "it's a good thing you came home, because there have been some urgent messages for you. Lord Matsudaira has sent his envoys here three times this morning. He wants to see you, and he's getting impatient."

Sano's spirits plummeted lower. He could just imagine how Lord Matsudaira would react when he heard about last night's episode. "Anything else?"

"One of your detectives came by, Hirata-*san*," said Reiko. "He's found that priest you were looking for."

Sano was so tired that he had to think for a moment before he remembered what priest. "Ozuno," he said. "The wandering holy man who might know the secret martial art of *dim-mak*."

"Where is he?" Hirata asked Reiko.

"At Chion Temple in Inaricho district."

Two days ago, when Sano had first heard of the priest, Ozuno had seemed crucial to the investigation, but he'd lost importance. "Now that we know who the Ghost is, we don't need Ozuno to tell us."

"He might still be useful," Hirata said. "Two martial artists who share the secret of *dim-mak,* both in Edo, must know each other. Maybe the priest can help us find the Ghost."

"You're right. Go to Chion Temple and talk to Ozuno. I'll expand the search for Yugao and Kobori, then deal with Lord Matsudaira." Sano braced himself for an explosion. Maybe he would drop dead before Lord Matsudaira could punish him.

"I still think Yugao's friend Tama knows more than she told me yesterday," Reiko said. "I'll pay her another visit."

The sector known as Inaricho bordered on the edge of the Asakusa Temple district. Hirata and his detectives rode through streets crowded with religious pilgrims. Shops displayed Buddhist altars, rosaries, candleholders, statues, vases of gilt metal lotus flowers, and name tablets for funerals. Gongs rang in the small, modest temples that had proliferated in Inaricho. The rustic speech of pilgrims, the cries of roving peddlers, and smoke from crematoriums flavored the bright afternoon.

"Chion Temple is somewhere around here," Hirata said.

They were passing one of the district's many cemeteries when an unusual sight caught Hirata's eye. Toward him along the road walked an old man, limping on a lame right leg, leaning on a wooden staff. He had long, unkempt gray hair and a stern face deeply lined and sun-tanned. He wore a round black skullcap, a short, tattered kimono, loose breeches printed with arcane symbols, and cloth leggings. A short sword dangled at his waist. Frayed straw sandals shod his bare feet. On his back he carried a wooden chest hung from a shoulder harness decorated with orange bobbles.

"It's a *yamabushi*," Hirata said, recognizing the old man as a priest of the small, exclusive Shugendo sect that practiced an arcane blend of Buddhist and Shinto religion laced with Chinese sorcery. He and the detectives paused to watch the priest.

"Doesn't his sect have temples in the Yoshino Mountains? I wonder what he's doing so far from there," said Detective Arai.

"He must be on a pilgrimage," Detective Inoue said. The *yamabushi* were known for making long, arduous trips to ancient holy sites, where they performed strange rituals that involved sitting under ice-cold waterfalls in an attempt to achieve divine enlightenment. Rumors said that they were spies for secret anti-Tokugawa conspirators, or goblins in human disguise.

"Is it true that *yamabushi* have mystical powers?" Arai said as the priest limped nearer. "Can they really cast out demons, talk with animals, and put out fires by sheer mental concentration?"

Hirata laughed. "That's probably just an old legend." The *yamabushi* was a just a cripple like himself, he thought glumly.

Five samurai ambled out from a teahouse opposite the cemetery. They wore the crests of different *daimyo* clans, and Hirata recognized them as the kind of young, dissolute men who sneaked away from their duties to rove in gangs about town and look for trouble. He'd arrested many such as them for brawling in the streets during his days as a police officer. Now the gang spied the *yamabushi*. They wove through the passing crowds and eddied around him.

"Hey, old man," said one of the samurai.

Another blocked the priest's path. "Where do you think you're going?"

The *yamabushi* stopped, his expression unperturbed. "Let me pass," he said in a gruff, strangely resonant voice.

"Don't you tell us what to do," the first samurai said.

He and his gang began shoving and mocking the priest. They yanked off his shoulder harness. His wooden chest fell on the ground. The samurai picked it up and heaved it into the cemetery. The *yamabushi* stood passive, leaning on his staff.

"Go away," he said calmly. "Leave me alone."

His apparent lack of fear enraged the gang. They brandished their swords. Hirata decided that their fun had gone far enough. Once he would have rescued the priest and sent the hoodlums on their way himself, but now he said to the detectives, "Break it up."

Arai and Inoue jumped off their horses, but before they reached the gang, a hoodlum swung his sword at the priest. Hirata winced, anticipating the sound of steel cutting flesh and bone, the gush of blood. But the hoodlum's sword hit the wooden staff, which the priest raised in such a swift motion that Hirata didn't even see it. The hoodlum yelped in surprise. The blow to his sword knocked him reeling backward. He fell, obstructing the way of Detectives Inoue and Arai, who were rushing to the priest's aid. Hirata gaped.

"Kill him!" the other hoodlums shouted.

Furious, they assaulted the *yamabushi* with their swords. His staff parried their every strike with a precision that Hirata had seldom seen even among the best samurai fighters. A typhoon of flailing bodies and lashing weapons surrounded the priest as the hoodlums tried to fell him. He revolved in the middle, his arm and staff a blur of motion, his stern features alert yet placid. His opponents seemed to fling themselves against his staff. One dropped unconscious from a blow to the head. Another hurtled into the cemetery, where he crashed against a gravestone and lay moaning. The three others decided that they'd taken on more than they could handle. They ran off in terror, bruised and bloody.

Hirata, Inoue, and Arai stared in astonishment. Murmurs of awe sounded from spectators who'd gathered to watch the fight. The *yamabushi* hobbled into the cemetery to retrieve his belongings. Hirata clambered off his mount.

"Take those injured samurai to the nearest neighborhood gate. Order the sentry to call the police and have them arrested," he told his detectives. Then he hurried up to the priest. "How did you do that?"

"Do what?" the priest said as he donned the harness and hoisted the chest onto his back. He wasn't even winded from the fight. He seemed more annoyed by Hirata's intrusion than by the attack on him.

"How did you manage to defeat five able-bodied samurai?" Hirata said.

"I didn't defeat them." The priest flashed Hirata a glance that appeared to take his measure, commit him to memory, then dismiss him. "They defeated themselves."

Hirata didn't understand this cryptic answer, but he realized he'd just witnessed proof that this *yamabushi* did have the mystical powers that he'd laughed off only moments ago. He also realized with a start that the priest must be the man he'd come to see. "Are you Ozuno?"

The priest barely nodded. "And you are?"

"I'm the shogun's *sōsakan-sama*," Hirata said, and gave his name. "I've been looking for you."

Ozuno didn't look surprised, or interested. He appeared to be like others of his kind—solitary and standoffish. "If you're just going to hang about and gape at me, I'll be on my way."

"I'm investigating a crime," Hirata said. "Your name came up as someone who might be able to help. Do you know Kobori Banzan?"

Emotion stirred behind Ozuno's steady gaze. "Not anymore."

"But you once did?"

"He was my pupil," Ozuno said.

"You trained him in the art of *dim-mak*?"

Ozuno sneered in disdain. "I taught him sword-fighting. *Dim-mak* is just a myth."

"That's what I once believed. But five men were recently murdered by the touch of death." Six, if Sano was the next victim, Hirata thought. "I've seen proof. Your secret is out."

The disdain melted from the priest's face, which took on the expression of a samurai wounded in battle and keeping a calm manner by act of sheer will. "You think Kobori is the killer?"

"I know he is."

Ozuno sank to his knees beside a gravestone. For the first time he appeared as frail as most old men. Yet although clearly shaken, he seemed unsurprised, as if a prediction had come true.

"I have to catch Kobori," Hirata said. "Do you know where he is?"

"I haven't seen him in eleven years."

"You've had no contact at all since then?" Hirata was disappointed, but he thought that finding Ozuno was a lucky break, even if not for the murder investigation.

"None," Ozuno said. "I disowned Kobori."

The bond between teacher and pupil was almost sacred, and Hirata knew that disownment was an extreme act of censure by the teacher and a terrible disgrace to the pupil. "Why?"

Ozuno rose and gazed into the distance. "There are many misconceptions about *dim-mak*. One is that it's a single technique. But it belongs to a wide spectrum of mystic martial arts that include fighting with weapons and casting spells." His shock at the news that his former pupil was a wanted criminal had broken his reticence. Hirata understood that Ozuno was telling him things that few mortals ever heard. "Another misconception is that *dim-mak* is an evil magic, invented for use by assassins. But that was not the intention of the ancients who developed it. They meant for the touch of death to be used honorably, in self-defense and in battle."

"They must have known it could be used to kill for dishonorable purposes," Hirata said.

"Indeed. That's why their heirs have guarded the knowledge so closely. We comprise a secret society whose aim is to preserve it and pass it on to the next generation. We take a vow of silence that forbids us to use it except in cases of extreme emergency or reveal it to anyone except our carefully chosen disciples."

"How do you choose them?" Hirata said, intrigued.

"We scout the young samurai among the Tokugawa vassals, the *daimyos'* retinues, and the *rōnin*. They must have sound characters as well as natural fighting ability."

"But sometimes mistakes are made?" Hirata deduced.

Ozuno nodded regretfully. "I found Kobori in a martial arts school in Mino Province. He was the son of a respectable but impoverished clan. He had superior skill in the martial arts, and a determination that is rare. Our training is extremely rigorous, but Kobori took to it as though he'd been reincarnated from an ancient master."

"What went wrong?"

"I wasn't the only person who noticed his fighting skills. They came to the attention of Chamberlain Yanagisawa, who also scouted the samurai class for good warriors. While Kobori was training under me, he was offered a post in Yanagisawa's squadron of elite troops. Soon afterward came the incident that led to the break between us."

Painful remembrance crossed Ozuno's features. "It's well known that those elite troops were assassins who kept Yanagisawa in power. You have heard of his rivals who were conveniently attacked and killed by highway bandits?"

"That was always the official story," Hirata said, "but everyone knows those deaths were murders ordered by Yanagisawa. His elite troops were too clever to be caught and never left any evidence that would incriminate them, or him."

"Kobori was clever, too, and expert at the art of stealth. One day I heard that an enemy of Yanagisawa's had dropped dead, for no apparent reason. He was presumed to have died from a sudden fit. But I had other suspicions.

"I asked Kobori if he'd given the man the touch of death. He didn't deny that he'd used our secret art to commit cold-blooded murder. In fact, he was proud of it." Ozuno's expression darkened with disapproval. "He said he'd put his knowledge to good, practical use. I told him that his duty was to learn the techniques and someday teach them to a disciple. But he said that was pointless. The truth was, he'd been seduced by the excitement of killing and the prestige that working for Yanagisawa brought him. I told him that he couldn't go on studying with me and serve Yanagisawa at the same time."

"And he chose Yanagisawa?"

Ozuno nodded. "He said he had no more use for our society, or for me. That day I disowned him and cast him out of our society."

"And that's the last you saw of him?" Hirata asked.

"No. I saw him one more time," Ozuno said. "Our society has a procedure for handling rogues. In order to prevent one from misusing our secret knowledge, or giving it away, we eliminate him."

"You mean kill him?"

"A dead man can't commit evil or tell secrets," Ozuno explained. "When Kobori broke his vow, he marked himself for death. I sent out word to everyone in our society. We were all responsible for getting rid of Kobori, but the primary responsibility was mine because he had been my pupil."

"Then how come he's still alive?"

Ozuno looked chagrined. "I taught him too well. When I went after him, we fought. He wounded me and escaped." With a glance at his lame leg, Ozuno said, "Other members of our society have never managed to get close enough to kill him." His chagrin deepened to mortification. "Now I am responsible for these new murders that he's committed. He is a sin that will haunt me through a thousand lifetimes."

"Maybe you can make up for it in this lifetime." Hirata began to see a solution to his own problems, which now dovetailed with his hunt for the assassin. "Can you tell me how to go about capturing Kobori when we find him?"

"Your best strategy is to bring as many armed troops with you as you can," Ozuno said. "Then be prepared for many of them to die while he's resisting arrest."

This obvious solution didn't satisfy Hirata. "What about fighting him in a duel?"

"Everyone has a sensitive spot. I was never able to find Kobori's, but it's your only hope of defeating him in one-to-one combat. I suggest you don't try."

"Would you teach me some of your secret techniques to use against him?"

Ozuno beheld him with grave offense. "I cannot. My vow forbids me."

"More lives will be lost unless you give me the ammunition to protect myself and my troops." Hirata felt a passionate need to learn the secrets that enabled a lame, frail man to defeat five able-bodied samurai.

"All right," Ozuno said reluctantly. "I'll show you some vulnerable places to strike Kobori if you get close enough."

He took hold of Hirata's hand and touched two points on his wrist bone. "Apply hard pressure here to draw breath from his lungs and weaken him." He pushed up Hirata's sleeve and lightly squeezed his upper arm in an indentation between two muscles. "Grab him here, and you'll block his energy flow. That will take him down. Then you can deliver the killing blow."

Ozuno touched Hirata on the right side of his throat, just under the chin. "A hard jab here will stop the flow of blood." Placing his finger on one spot, then another, on Hirata's chest, he said, "Strike him here and stop his heart." Then he opened Hirata's robes and pointed out a hollow in his stomach muscles near the navel. "A big kick to the core of his spirit will kill him instantaneously."

Fascinated, Hirata paid close attention. But he remembered the outlaw attack on the way to Edo Morgue, and the countless sword battles he'd fought. Hand-to-hand combat techniques wouldn't help in similar situations.

"Can you teach me some sword-fighting moves, like the ones you used against those men who ganged up on you?" he asked.

"Oh, of course. In a few moments I'll pass on to you the skills that take years to master," Ozuno said, reverting to his former surly attitude. His keen gaze impaled Hirata. "I suspect that your eagerness to learn my secrets arises from some purpose that goes beyond your search for Kobori."

"You're right," Hirata said, sheepish because Ozuno had seen through him so easily. He dropped to his knees among the graves and bowed. "Ozuno-*san,* I would very much like to study martial arts with you. Will you please accept me as a pupil?"

Ozuno made a derisive sound. "We don't accept just anybody who happens to ask. I've already told you about our system for choosing pupils."

Unwilling to take no for an answer, Hirata argued, "Your system broke down when you picked Kobori. I'm a better choice."

"So you say," Ozuno retorted. "You're a total stranger. I know nothing of you except what I see, and I see that you are rash and impertinent."

"My character is good," Hirata said, anxious to convince. "The chamberlain and the shogun will vouch for me."

"That you brag about yourself is a sign of a conceited nature," Ozuno said scornfully. "Besides, you're too old. Your personality is set. We always choose boys, whom we can mold to our way of life."

"But I have combat skills and experience that boys don't have. I have a head start on them."

"More likely you've learned so many mistakes that it would take years to retrain you."

Hirata was frantic not to let this opportunity slip away. "Please," he said, struggling to his feet and grabbing Ozuno's arm, "I need you to teach me. You're my only hope that I'll ever be able to fight again. Unless I learn your secrets, I'll always be helpless, a target for attacks, the object of everyone's scorn." He flung his arms wide, the better for Ozuno to see the crippled wreckage of his body. On the verge of tears, ashamed to beg, he said, "I'll fail in my duty to my master and my lord. Unless you help me, I'll lose my honor as well as my livelihood!"

Ozuno regarded him with merciless contempt. "You want knowledge for the wrong reasons. You want to learn a few techniques, win fights, satisfy your pride, and gain material rewards, rather than honor and preserve our ancient traditions. Your needs are no concern of mine. They certainly don't qualify you to enter our society." He waved his hand impatiently. "But this discussion is pointless. Even if you were the ideal candidate, I could not train you. I swore off teaching when Kobori went bad. Never again will I risk creating another amoral killer."

Although the priest's tone said his decision was final, Hirata was too desperate to give up. "But fate brought me to you," he cried. "You're meant to be my teacher. It's our destiny!"

"Destiny, eh?" Ozuno laughed with sardonic ill humor. "Well, if it is, I suppose I can't escape it. I'll make you a deal: If we should meet again, we'll begin your lessons."

"Fine," Hirata said. Edo was small enough that he was sure to see the priest again.

Ozuno sneered as he read Hirata's thoughts. He said, "Not if I see you first," then limped out of the cemetery. In the road, he merged with a flock of pilgrims and vanished.

28

Reiko knocked on the gate outside the mansion where Yugao's friend Tama worked. A woman with gray hair and a cross face opened it and said, "Yes?"

"I want to see Tama," Reiko said, so urgently that her voice trembled.

"You mean the kitchen maid?" Curiosity sharpened the woman's gaze. "Who are you?" After Reiko introduced herself, the woman said, "Tama isn't here."

Reiko almost wept with disappointment. If Sano was doomed to die soon, finding Yugao might be the last thing she could do for him. "Where is Tama?"

"The cook sent her to the fish market. I'm the housekeeper. Can I help you?"

"I don't think so. When will Tama be back?" As she realized that she would never be able to find the girl in the huge, crowded fish market, Reiko tried to stay calm. Falling apart wouldn't help Sano.

"Oh, she'll probably be gone for hours," the housekeeper said, studying Reiko with avid interest. "Why are you so eager to see her? What's she done?"

"Maybe nothing," Reiko said. Her hunch that Tama had withheld important information from her yesterday might be mere wishful thinking. Yet Reiko couldn't give up; Tama was her only lead to Yugao. "On second thought, maybe you can help me. Have you noticed anything strange about Tama recently?"

The housekeeper frowned in thought, then said, "As a matter of fact I have. The day before yesterday, she left the house without permission. The mistress scolded her and beat her. That's not like Tama. Usually she's such a meek, obedient little thing, never breaks any rules."

Reiko cautioned herself against hoping too much. "Why did Tama leave?"

"It was because of that girl who came to see her."

"What girl?" Reiko held her breath as her hope ran wild and her heart began to race.

"She said her name was Yugao."

Such glad relief overwhelmed Reiko that the breath rushed out of her; she clutched the gatepost for support. "Tell me everything that happened when Yugao came! It's very important!"

"Well, she showed up at the back gate," the housekeeper said, clearly enjoying Reiko's attention and wanting to draw out her story. "She asked for Tama. When I asked who she was, she wouldn't tell me anything except her name and that she was an old friend of Tama's. The servants aren't supposed to have visitors, but I feel sorry for Tama because she's alone in the world, and I thought it wouldn't hurt to let her see a friend just once. So I fetched Tama.

"At first she was so happy to see Yugao. She hugged her and cried and said how much she'd missed her. But then they started talking. Tama started to look worried."

"What did they say?" Reiko clenched her fingernails into her palms.

"I don't know what Yugao said. She was whispering. Tama said, 'No. I can't. I'll get in trouble.' "

Now Reiko understood why Tama had acted so upset when Reiko had told her that her childhood friend was a murderess and fugitive. Yugao must have invented some other story to explain why she'd turned up needing help from Tama.

"But Yugao kept talking," the housekeeper said, "and she wore Tama down. Finally Tama said, 'All right. Come with me.' They ran off together."

"Was there a man with them?" Reiko asked eagerly.

"Not that I saw."

Yet Reiko felt certain that the Ghost had been lurking somewhere in their vicinity. When he and Yugao had left the Jade Pavilion, they'd needed another place to hide. She must have thought of Tama, the one person who might be persuaded to do her a favor. And Reiko was just as certain that Yugao wouldn't have abandoned the man she'd loved so obsessively.

The housekeeper leaned close to Reiko and whispered, "I didn't tell the mistress that Tama stole a basket of food from the pantry before they left."

"Where did they go?" Reiko demanded.

"I don't know. When Tama got home, I asked her, but she wouldn't tell me."

"How long was she gone?"

"Let me think." The housekeeper tapped her finger against her withered cheek. "It was near dark when she left. She barely made it back before the neighborhood gates closed."

Reiko's hopes plunged; Tama could have covered a considerable distance, even on foot and weighed down with provisions, between early evening and late night. That left an appallingly wide area to search for the place where Tama had hidden Yugao and the Ghost.

"Thank you for your help," Reiko said, turning to leave.

"Shall I tell Tama you were here?" the housekeeper said. "Shall I tell her you'll come back?"

Need begot inspiration. Reiko thought of the food Tama had stolen, and a new strategy kindled her hopes. "No," she called as she hurried toward her palanquin and guards, "please don't tell Tama."

But she would be back. And then she would discover exactly where Yugao and the Ghost were hiding.

Sano stopped at *metsuke* headquarters for the dossier on Kobori; it included his approximate height and weight and a poorly drawn sketch of his face. After visiting General Isogai, from whom he commandeered army troops to serve as search teams, Sano rushed to the palace.

The instant he walked into the audience chamber, he knew he was in even more trouble than he'd expected. Lord Matsudaira, seated in his customary place, wore such a fierce scowl that he resembled a carved demon in a temple. Above him on the dais, the shogun cowered, frightened and baffled. Yoritomo, who sat beside the shogun, aimed a warning glance at Sano. The guards stationed along the walls stood perfectly still, gazing straight ahead, as though afraid to move. The elders were absent. In their place on the raised floor sat Police Commissioner Hoshina, who regarded Sano with cool, half-smiling composure.

Sano's steps faltered at the sight of his enemy. As he knelt below the dais at the shogun's left and bowed, Lord Matsudaira demanded, "What in hell took you so long?"

"I had urgent business to attend to," Sano said even though he knew that no excuse was good enough for Lord Matsudaira. What had happened in less than two days to sink him in Lord Matsudaira's esteem and raise Hoshina? Sano doubted that it was only because Lord Matsudaira had heard about his failed attempt to capture the Ghost last night; after all, Hoshina hadn't done any better. "A thousand apologies."

"It'll take more than a thousand to excuse you," Lord Matsudaira said, his fury mounting. "Do I understand correctly that you assigned hundreds of army troops to escort duty?"

"Yes," Sano admitted. Out of the corner of his eye he saw Hoshina enjoying his discomfiture. "With an assassin at large and the officials afraid to leave home, it seemed the only way to keep the government running."

The shogun nodded in timid agreement, but Lord Matsudaira ignored him and said, "Well, it's obvious that you didn't stop to think that security would be drastically reduced after you pulled those men from their regular posts. While they were playing nursemaid to a bunch of cowards, who was supposed to keep order in the city?" His complexion was so livid with rage that he looked ready to burst a blood vessel. "Do you think we have an unlimited supply of troops?"

"I've sent for more from the provinces," Sano said in a futile attempt to defend himself. Yoritomo wrung his hands. "I've ordered the *daimyo* to lend their retainers to patrol the streets."

"Oh, you did, did you? And do you know what's happened in the meantime?" Lord Matsudaira surged to his feet, unable to contain his temper. "While I was riding through town this morning, I was ambushed by a band of rebel outlaws. My bodyguards were outnumbered. There wasn't a soldier in sight."

Sano stared, speechless with alarm that he'd inadvertently endangered Lord Matsudaira.

"Fortunately, Police Commissioner Hoshina and his men happened to come along, and they fought off the rebels," Lord Matsudaira said. "If they hadn't, I would be dead now."

Sano turned his astonished gaze on Hoshina, who flashed him a grin of triumph.

"How convenient for you," Sano said. He wouldn't be surprised if Hoshina himself had arranged the attack, with the aim of rescuing Lord Matsudaira and making him so grateful that he was willing to forgive Hoshina any errors.

"Yes, it was convenient." Hoshina's eyes sparkled with malicious amusement. "All the outlaws were killed in the fight, in case you were wondering."

Which meant that they couldn't reveal whether Hoshina had hired them, Sano realized. Hoshina was safe. He'd taken advantage of all the misfortune that Sano had suffered during this investigation.

"I heard that this morning you commandeered more troops, Chamberlain Sano," Lord Matsudaira said, ignoring the exchange between Sano and Hoshina. "What in hell do you need them for? Why would you worsen your stupid, dangerous mistake?"

"I need them to search for the assassin you ordered me to capture." Growing angry at Lord Matsudaira's insulting treatment, Sano heard the edge in his own voice. How else could he have protected the officials? "I know who he is now. His name is Kobori. He belonged to my

240

predecessor's elite squadron. To run him to ground, I need more manpower besides my own personal troops."

The news that Sano had identified the Ghost startled Lord Matsudaira into silence and wiped the scowl off his face. Yoritomo gave Sano a relieved, delighted smile.

"So you've, ahh, solved the mystery." The shogun beamed at Sano. He cast a smug glance at Lord Matsudaira, clearly gratified that Sano had scored a point against his cousin, even if he didn't understand what was going on. "My congratulations to you."

"Don't believe him, Your Excellency," Hoshina said quickly. "It may not be true that this man Kobori is the assassin. Remember that Chamberlain Sano thought it was Captain Nakai, who proved to be innocent. He could be wrong again." Hoshina appealed to Lord Matsudaira. "I think he's so desperate to please you that he's trying to pin the murders on someone who's probably dead."

"Kobori's alive," Sano countered. "I can place him in Edo as recently as two days ago. Last night I raided the inn where he's been hiding. I only just missed him. He'd skipped out the day before."

"What proof do you have that he's the assassin?" Lord Matsudaira looked torn between skepticism and his wish to believe that the capture of the Ghost was imminent.

Sano described the events at the Jade Pavilion.

"Well, even if Kobori is the assassin, you let him get away," Hoshina said, anxious to discredit Sano. "He could have left Edo by now. Honorable Lord Matsudaira, why send troops to search the stable after the horse is already out? We need them to maintain security and hunt down rebel outlaws."

"We can't assume that Kobori is gone just because you want to believe it," Sano said. "And he's a more important target than the other rebel outlaws."

Hoshina laughed in scorn. "They've killed a lot more people than he has."

"But he's aiming at the regime's top echelon," Sano said. "Let me remind you that he's already assassinated five high-ranking officials. Unless we concentrate on catching him, he'll chip away at us until morale is so weak that the regime falls. We need to catch him before he kills again."

He felt the mark of death upon himself. Involuntary flinches twitched his body, as if telltale bruises were cropping up all over his skin. His head ached, and he wondered if his brain had started bleeding. The uncertainty and waiting were so difficult to bear, he almost wished he knew for sure that Kobori had touched him. But if he should die tomorrow, who would protect the regime from men like Hoshina, so driven by their own ambitions that they would let a deadly force like Kobori run free?

"Someone in this room could be his next victim." Sano appealed to Lord Matsudaira's and the shogun's self-interest. "Let me borrow the troops for two more days. That should be enough time to catch Kobori."

"I think that sounds like a, ahh, good compromise," the shogun said, eager to end the quarreling.

Lord Matsudaira weighed the arguments for only an instant before saying, "Chamberlain Sano is absolutely correct that catching the Ghost should have high priority." Hoshina's face fell. "But Police Commissioner Hoshina is also correct that we can't let security lapse in order to chase one of many criminals," Lord Matsudaira continued. "Take the troops off the search and send them back to their regular duties, Chamberlain Sano. Do the best you can without them. And remember that I'm counting on you."

Hoshina grinned, recognizing that this decision promised failure for Sano and more advantage for himself. Sano saw that there was no use arguing further with Lord Matsudaira. Only one person could override him now.

"Your Excellency," Sano said, "this issue is so important that perhaps you would like to settle it instead of leaving it to us. You said you thought it was a good idea to have the troops search for the Ghost. If that's your opinion, you can make it an order, and it will be done."

The shogun looked alarmed to be put on the spot, yet gratified by the thought of his own power. Lord Matsudaira and Hoshina glared at Sano. Yoritomo leaned close to the shogun to whisper in his ear.

"A certain person had better keep out of this," Lord Matsudaira announced in a quiet tone replete with menace. "Or else there may be a fatal accident to a certain other person on a certain distant island."

Yoritomo sat back and bowed his head at the threat to his exiled father.

"Well? What do you say?" Lord Matsudaira asked the shogun. "Will you follow Chamberlain Sano's advice or mine?"

Bereft of the support he needed to stand by his opinion, the shogun wilted. "Yours, Cousin," he murmured, avoiding Sano's gaze.

Sano accepted defeat with a frustration he could barely conceal. Hoshina relaxed. Lord Matsudaira said, "Before you leave, Honorable Chamberlain, I have one other problem to discuss with you. I hear that you've been absent from your office these past few days. Quite a few officials have mentioned that you're never available to meet with them, you don't answer your correspondence, and you're letting your staff handle business they're not qualified to handle."

Sano turned on Hoshina. The police commissioner must have put his new friends up to informing Lord Matsudaira. Hoshina shrugged and smirked.

"You seem to think that the duties of second-in-command over the nation are beneath you," Lord Matsudaira told Sano. "Unless you change your attitude, His Excellency may be forced to replace you, as quite a few of his officials have recommended. Is that understood?"

Stifling his anger, Sano said, "Yes, Lord Matsudaira." He shot a venomous look at Hoshina, who sat gloating and eager to inherit his post. If he lived, Sano resolved, he would find a way to rid himself of this enemy, no matter how little he liked political warfare.

"It's time to adjourn this meeting," Lord Matsudaira told the shogun.

"This meeting is adjourned," the shogun said.

"What do we do now?" Marume asked Sano as they walked through the palace garden.

"We mobilize the army and go out and hunt down the Ghost," Sano said.

No matter that Lord Matsudaira had forbidden him to use the troops for the search; Sano reasoned that he was damned no matter what he did. If he neglected his job, disobeyed orders, or failed to catch the Ghost, the result would be the same: He would lose his post, whether to Hoshina or somebody else. He would be banished or executed, leaving Reiko and Masahiro in dire peril. He might as well finish the investigation.

Especially since it could be his last.

Sano and the detectives headed down the passage to fetch their horses at his compound. If he was going to die tomorrow, at least he would spend today doing the work he was meant to do, serving honor in the best way he could. He would deliver Kobori to justice and have his revenge if it was the last thing he did.

"Honorable Chamberlain Sano!"

Sano turned, and saw Captain Nakai hurrying toward him. He groaned inwardly. Although the last person he wanted to see now was Nakai, he resolved to be gracious after what Nakai had suffered on his account.

"Greetings," Nakai said as he joined Sano and they walked together. His metal helmet and armor tunic gleamed in the sunlight; he looked the picture of a perfect samurai. "I hope all is well with you?"

"Quite. And you?" Sano said courteously.

"Not bad," Nakai replied with determined cheerfulness.

It occurred to Sano that when a man expected to die soon, he should make amends to people he'd hurt. He quickened his pace, leading Nakai ahead of the detectives, so they could talk privately. He said, "Captain Nakai, I want to apologize for suspecting you of the murders. I'm sorry you were accused and humiliated in front of the shogun and Lord Matsudaira. Please forgive me."

"Oh, that's all right," Nakai said. "It's water under the bridge. No hard feelings." He smiled and clapped Sano on the shoulder. "Besides,

I've begun to think it was a blessing in disguise. After all, it gave me the privilege of making your acquaintance."

Sano saw that Captain Nakai now viewed him as a person who could help further his ambitions. "My acquaintance may not be as much of a blessing as you wish," Sano said. He might not be around long enough to hand out any promotions, even if he was still alive tomorrow.

Nakai laughed as though Sano had made a joke. "You're too modest, Honorable Chamberlain." He obviously didn't know about Sano's precarious position. "By the way, how is your investigation going? Have you found out who the Ghost is?"

"Yes," Sano said, tolerating this chat, but walking faster to end it soon. "His name is Kobori. He was once employed by the former chamberlain. There's a citywide manhunt going on for him as we speak."

"Kobori?" Captain Nakai stopped in his tracks. A stupefied look came over his face. "That's who it was," he muttered to himself. His strong features had gone slack with amazement.

"What's the matter?" Sano was so puzzled by this odd reaction that he also halted.

"You said that Kobori is the Ghost? And you're trying to find him?" Nakai's tone was breathless; he seemed frantic to verify what he'd heard. When Sano nodded, Nakai whispered, "Merciful gods. I saw him."

"You did?" It was Sano's turn to be amazed. He stared at Nakai; so did Detectives Marume and Fukida, who'd caught up with them. "When? Where?"

"This morning," Nakai said. "On the street, in town."

Sano thought to wonder if Nakai was making up a story in order to curry favor. Yet his words had the ring of honesty. "How did you recognize Kobori?" Sano demanded even as wild hope surged within his heart.

"I used to know him," Nakai said. "Remember I told you that I have family connections with Yanagisawa? My cousin was his weapons master. He was killed in the battle. I used to visit him at Yanagisawa's compound. I thought he might help my career, seeing as he was close to the chamberlain. Sometimes he introduced me to people who happened to be around. One of them was Kobori."

Captain Nakai smiled with the air of a man who has just solved a mystery that had been puzzling him. "When I saw Kobori today, I couldn't remember who he was or where I'd seen him before. We'd only met once, years ago. But when you said his name, I suddenly knew."

This sounded not unreasonable, but Sano had a hard time believing that Kobori, subject of a massive search, was just walking about town, where a passing acquaintance had stumbled onto him. "How did you happen to spot Kobori?"

"I was just riding along, minding my own business," Nakai said. "I'd heard that Lord Matsudaira planned to go into town this morning, and I thought it would be a good opportunity to talk to him. You see, I knew I'd made a bad impression on him at the meeting the other day, and I wanted to show myself in a better light. So I followed him and his entourage."

Sano pictured Nakai tagging after Lord Matsudaira, still desperate for a promotion and more foolhardy than ever. Momentary gloom clouded Nakai's face. "Well, his bodyguards told me to get lost or they'd beat me up. So I turned around to ride back to the castle, and that's when I saw Kobori. He was standing beside the road, in a crowd of people who were waiting for Lord Matsudaira to pass."

Shock emptied the breath from Sano as he realized that the Ghost had been stalking Lord Matsudaira while Sano had been combing the streets around the Jade Pavilion in search of him. "Where exactly did you see Kobori?"

"On the main avenue."

"Did you speak to him?"

"No. I waved to him, but he didn't see me. He walked away."

"I don't suppose you know where he went," Sano said. One sighting put him no closer to catching the Ghost. Kobori could have gone anywhere in the city during the half a day since Nakai had seen him.

Captain Nakai raised his finger and beamed. "Oh, but I do. I wanted to figure out who he was, and I thought that another, closer look might jog my memory. Besides, there was nothing better to occupy my time. So I rode after Kobori. He went to a house. A girl let him in."

Sano experienced a second, even more profound shock as he comprehended what Nakai had seen: the Ghost going to ground in his lair, which he shared with a girl who had to be Yugao. A malcontent's aimless rambling about town had produced better results than many a focused, diligent inquiry. Sano shook his head in wonder at the mysterious permutations of fate. That his original prime suspect should turn up with the clue that would lead him to the murderer!

"Where is this house?" Sano said, gripped by excitement at the thought that he was on the brink of capturing Kobori.

Nakai started to answer, then abruptly closed his mouth. His eyes gleamed with cunning as he realized that he had knowledge crucial to Sano. "If I tell you where the house is, you have to give me something in return. I want a promotion to the rank of colonel and a stipend twice as large as I'm getting now." He swelled with rash, greedy exuberance. "And I want a post in your retinue."

Incredulous, scornful laughter burst from Marume and Fukida. "You have a lot of nerve," Marume told Nakai.

"You should be ashamed of trying to extort favors from the chamberlain," Fukida said.

Sano was offended by Nakai's crassness, but he desperately needed the information, and he owed Nakai a favor. Even though Nakai had his character flaws, Sano wouldn't begrudge him a place in his retinue. He could do much worse than a man capable of single-handedly killing forty-eight enemy troops in battle.

"Very well," Sano said. "I'll get you your official promotion and increase your stipend when I have time. But as of this very moment, you're mine to command, and I order you to tell me where that house is."

"Thank you, Honorable Chamberlain!" Breathless and ecstatic, Nakai bowed. He didn't notice the dark looks that Marume and Fukida gave him. He gazed at Sano with a combination of possessiveness, reverence, and eagerness to please. "I can do better than tell you where the Ghost is hiding. I'll lead you there myself."

29

An old woman, dressed in a torn, dirty cotton kimono and a battered wicker hat, swept the back alley that ran between two rows of mansions in the Nihonbashi merchant district. With her body hunched as if from decades of spine-breaking work, she crept along. Her broom gathered up vegetable peelings spilled from waste containers and debris blown in by the wind. Her feet in straw sandals shuffled through puddles of water that dripped from laundry hung on lines stretched across balconies and leaked from night soil bins. Servants came and went through the mansions' back gates, but they paid no attention to her. Street-cleaners were virtually invisible to citizens higher on the social scale.

Reiko peered out from under the hat that hid her face, watching for Tama. She'd been cleaning this alley for two hours, moving back and forth, sweeping the same debris into her dustpan then scattering it, but Tama had yet to return from the fish market. The sky faded and shadows immersed the alley as twilight approached.

When she'd left the mansion earlier, Reiko had been certain not only that Tama was hiding the couple, but that the girl must eventually take them more food. Reiko believed that Yugao hadn't wanted her to talk to Tama because Tama would tell her about Yugao's relationship with Kobori. She'd stationed some of her guards near the mansion, then outfitted herself as a street-cleaner and returned to the alley on foot, her remaining escorts trailing her at a distance. The guards who'd stayed to wait for her had pretended not to know her, but had covertly shaken their heads to indicate that Tama still hadn't shown up.

Now Reiko's back ached from stooping. She was tired of foul odors, and she'd memorized every radish peel and crumb she'd collected. A stray dog wandered into the alley, sniffed the garbage containers, then squatted and defecated. Reiko wrinkled her nose at the foul dung as she hobbled past it and hoped Tama would soon appear. The alley resounded with the noise of maids preparing dinner and chattering among themselves. Smoke infused with the savory odors of garlic and soy sauce wafted over Reiko. Her stomach growled with hunger. She'd reached one end of the alley and turned to begin another monotonous sweep, when she saw Tama walking toward her from the opposite end, followed by a porter laden with a covered wooden bucket. Reiko's spirits soared as high as the moon that shone in the sky over the alley. As Tama and the porter entered the gate, Reiko kept her head down, sweeping industriously, warning herself that she might have a long wait for Tama to lead her to the fugitives.

But soon the gate opened and Tama slipped out. She wore a cloak and carried a bundle tied at the corners. She scurried down the alley, casting a furtive look toward the house she'd just left. She passed Reiko without noticing her.

Reiko shouldered her broom, picked up her dustpan, and followed Tama. Outside the alley, the district was filled with townspeople hurrying to get home before dark. Merchants hauled sliding doors closed across their storefronts. Soldiers on night patrol populated the streets. Reiko darted through the crowds, straining not to lose sight of Tama's small, quick figure. She glanced around for her escorts.

"We're right behind you," Lieutenant Asukai murmured.

They trailed Tama through a marketplace. Vendors were haggling with a few last customers or packing up unsold vegetables. As Reiko hastened past the stalls, she heard a man's voice call, "Hey, you! Street-cleaner!" A hand grabbed her arm. It belonged to a large, hulking vendor.

250

"Sweep up that mess," he ordered, pointing to some wilted cabbage leaves strewn on the ground.

"Let me go!" Reiko swung her broom at him.

The vendor ducked, released her, and cursed. "What do you think you're doing?"

He lunged at her. Lieutenant Asukai seized him and flung him against a stall that held jars of pickled radishes. The vendor fell; jars crashed around him. Reiko dropped her broom and dustpan and ran. Lieutenant Asukai caught up with her.

"Where did she go?" Reiko cried in panic.

Across the marketplace, one of her other guards waved and pointed. Reiko saw Tama hurrying down an aisle of stalls. She and her escorts resumed the pursuit. It led them out of Nihonbashi, to the northern outskirts of town. Here the houses were farther apart, interspersed with trees and small farms. Dusk tinged with gold settled softly upon the tranquil landscape. Road traffic consisted of a few patrolling soldiers amid peasants carrying firewood or pushing barrows. Reiko lagged farther behind Tama, afraid that the girl would see her and her escorts.

Yet Tama never turned around; she seemed more intent on reaching her destination than wary of being pursued. She hurried along the road, which followed the gradual upward slope of the land. Farms gave way to hillside forest. Birds shrilled loudly in the trees that arched their boughs over the road, creating deep pools of darkness that the fading sunlight couldn't penetrate. Tama's figure was as indistinct as a shadow moving swiftly ahead of Reiko. The road was deserted except for their procession. The air grew chilly with the rising altitude and the approach of night. Reiko felt the warmth of exertion seep away from her body; she shivered in her thin garments. She could hear Tama puffing and scrambling uphill, and she stifled the noise of her own labored breaths, her own trudging footsteps. She heard an occasional twig snap or leaf crackle as her escorts followed, although when she looked over her shoulder, they were barely visible in the darkness. Above the road, amid the forest, houses spaced far apart jutted from the hillside, but Reiko neither heard nor saw any signs of human life. A gong boomed in a shrine in the city below. Dogs or wolves howled somewhere too near Reiko.

Suddenly Tama vanished from sight. Reiko hurried forward, anxious because she thought she'd lost the girl. Then she saw a trail that led off the road, cut through the forest, and snaked uphill. She heard Tama panting and stumbling in the distance. Lieutenant Asukai and her four other guards stole with her up the trail. It grew steeper, and although its surface had been smoothed by human labor, fallen branches hindered them. The darkness was almost complete here, and they walked cautiously, but Tama made so much noise that Reiko doubted she would hear them. They emerged from the forest, into open space lit by the sky's dim glow. Pausing, Reiko saw that the trail skirted a valley. Brush-covered slopes fell sharply away to its bottom, where a stream burbled over rocks. Reiko and her guards watched Tama hurry along the trail, which followed the arc that the valley carved through the terrain. Now Reiko spied Tama's destination.

It was a mansion built on three levels, upon land cleared of trees. The first level had a veranda that extended across the front and jutted over the valley and stream. Thatched roofs rose in multiple, jagged peaks. The mansion wasn't huge, but it must have been difficult and expensive to build. In daytime it would have a marvelous view of Edo from the balconies on the back, higher levels. Light shone through a window and spilled onto the veranda. Tama toiled up a staircase that climbed the slope toward the mansion. The sound of her footsteps on wooden planks rang loud across the valley.

"What shall we do?" Lieutenant Asukai whispered to Reiko.

"Let's get closer. We have to find out if Yugao and the Ghost are there." Reiko must make sure before she told Sano.

She and her guards hastened after Tama, staying close to the trees that bordered the trail. They hid themselves in shrubbery at the foot of the staircase. Tama sped across the veranda, dropped her bundle, and beat her fists on the door. It creaked open. From her vantage point Reiko could see along the veranda, and she had a good view of Tama, but since the front of the house was parallel to her line of sight, she couldn't see the figure at the threshold.

"It's about time you got here," said Yugao's voice. "I'm starved. What did you bring me to eat?"

Jubilation filled Reiko. She gave a silent prayer of thanks.

Yugao stepped out the door. Tama backed away from her. The light from the house clearly illuminated both women. "Is he here?" Tama asked in a tone breathless from exhaustion and trembling with nerves.

"Who?" Yugao crouched and started untying the bundle.

"That samurai. Jin."

Yugao went perfectly still, her profile sharp as a blade. A moment passed before she rose, faced Tama, and said, "Yes. He's here. So what?"

Reiko stifled a breath of elation. She'd found the Ghost.

"Why didn't you tell me he was with you?" Tama cried, sounding hurt and betrayed.

"I didn't think it was important," Yugao said, but a note of caution crept into her voice. "Why does it matter?"

"You know I'm not supposed to let anybody in this house. I told you that if my master and mistress find out I did, I'll be beaten. You talked me into letting you stay here. That's dangerous enough. But for you to sneak that awful man in—" A sob interrupted Tama's words. "I'll lose my job. I'll be thrown out on the street with nowhere to go!"

"Don't worry," Yugao said. "No one will ever know. You said your master and mistress never come to this house until summer. We'll be gone before then. I need you to help us for just a little while longer."

She reached out her hand to Tama in a supplicating gesture, but Tama recoiled. "He's not the only thing you've kept secret from me. You said you ran away from home and you need a place to live. You didn't tell me you'd escaped from jail!"

Yugao's hand froze in midair. She carefully lowered it. "I thought it was better not to tell you. That way, if the police caught me with you, they wouldn't blame you for helping a runaway prisoner because you didn't know that's what I am."

She was lying, Reiko felt certain, despite her reasonable tone. To protect herself and her lover Yugao had deliberately, shamelessly taken advantage of Tama and lied to her.

"Oh?" Tama was weeping, near hysterics; Reiko could see that she didn't believe Yugao either. "Is that why you didn't tell me that you murdered your parents and your sister?"

"I didn't murder them," Yugao said, quick, defensive, and firm. "I was wrongly accused."

A dizzying sense of revelation coursed through Reiko. Again she knew Yugao was lying. She was finally certain that Yugao had indeed committed the crime.

Tama regarded Yugao in tearful bewilderment. "But you were arrested. And if you didn't kill them, then who did?"

"It was the warden from the jail," Yugao said. "He broke into our house while we were asleep. He stabbed my father, then my mother and Umeko. I saw him. He had to run away before he got caught, or he would have killed me, too."

Reiko was amazed at the way Yugao's falsehoods showed the truth more clearly than her confession had. Reiko might never learn the reason behind the crimes, but she knew Yugao was the murderess she'd claimed to be all along.

"I was arrested because I was there and I was alive," Yugao continued. "The police didn't bother investigating the murders because I'm a *hinin*. It was convenient to pin the murders on me. But I'm innocent." Now her voice took on a pleading tone; she laid her hand over her heart, then reached it out to Tama. "You've known me since we were children. You know I would never do such a thing. I couldn't tell you before because I was too upset. You're my best friend. Don't you believe me?"

Even as Reiko silently scoffed at the act that Yugao was putting on, Tama flung her arms around Yugao and wept. "Of course I do. Oh, Yugao, I'm so sorry for what you've been through!" They hugged each other. Tama's back was toward Reiko. The girl couldn't see Yugao's face, but Reiko had a good view of her sly, smug expression.

"I'm sorry I was so distrustful," Tama babbled. "I should have known you could never hurt your parents or your sister no matter how they treated you. When the magistrate's daughter said you killed them, I shouldn't have believed her."

"The magistrate's daughter?" Yugao asked in surprise and consternation. She withdrew from Tama. "It was Lady Reiko who told you about the murders?"

"Yes. She came to see me yesterday," Tama said. "She asked if I knew where you are."

"Did you tell her you'd seen me?" Yugao demanded.

"No." Frightened and nervous now, Tama said, "I told her we hadn't seen each other in years."

Yugao stepped closer to Tama, who faltered backward against the veranda railing. "What else did you tell Lady Reiko?"

"Nothing."

But Tama's voice quavered; she looked everywhere except at Yugao. She was a terrible liar. Yugao clamped her hands around Tama's upper arms, gazed down into the valley, and Reiko perceived her thoughts as easily as if she'd spoken them. Tama was too weak and guileless to stand up to more questions about Yugao. Therefore, she was a danger to Yugao, and Kobori, no matter that they needed Tama to feed and shelter them. One quick heave over the railing, and Tama could never lead their enemies to them.

Get out of there! Reiko wanted to shout at Tama. *She's going to kill you!* Yet for Reiko to warn Tama would make Yugao aware of her presence. She couldn't let Yugao know she'd found her hiding place and give her and Kobori a chance to escape.

Yugao hesitated, then let go of Tama. Once again Reiko knew what she was thinking: The fall might not kill Tama; the bushes on the slope might save her. Knowing that Yugao had tried to murder her, Tama would run away; she might even report Yugao to the police. And then where would Yugao and Kobori go? Reiko sighed in relief.

"You'd better come inside," Yugao told Tama.

A gasp of fresh alarm sucked the sigh back into Reiko's lungs. Tama said, "I can't. I have to go home."

"Just for a little while," Yugao said.

A little while would give Yugao time to keep Tama quiet forever. *Run!* Reiko silently exhorted Tama. *If you go in there, you won't come out alive!*

"If my mistress finds out I left the house without permission, she'll punish me," Tama said, backing toward the stairs. Reiko sensed that she was afraid of Yugao's lover, and perhaps of Yugao as well.

Yugao hurried after Tama and caught her hand. "Please stay. I want you to keep me company. At least sit down and rest before you walk back to town."

"All right," Tama said reluctantly.

She let Yugao lead her to the door. Yugao picked up the bundle of food, then she and Tama disappeared inside the house. Reiko heard the door scrape shut.

The valley was silent except for the diminishing chorus of birdsong and the wind rustling in the forest. The sky had turned a dark cobalt hue now, glinting with stars, adorned by a moon like a scarred pearl. Reiko felt sick at having placed the sweet, gullible Tama in danger. She turned to her escorts.

"We must hurry back to town," she said. Five inexperienced fighters and herself weren't enough to capture Yugao and the Ghost. "We have to bring my husband and his troops."

They stole quickly down the trail along the valley, then groped downhill through the forest that was now so dark that they couldn't see each other or the hazardous ground underfoot. But as they emerged onto the road, Reiko saw lights glimmering along its slope below them. She heard stealthy footsteps.

"Someone's coming," she whispered.

 30

Human shapes erupted out of the darkness and surrounded Reiko, Lieutenant Asukai, and their companions. Reiko felt herself seized by strong hands, her arms pinned behind her with cruel force. She writhed and cried out and kicked. Violent, noisy thrashing exploded around her as her escorts were caught.

"I've got him!" shouted a man's excited voice.

The man who held Reiko said, "This one's female. Looks like we've captured Kobori and his lady love."

To her surprise, Reiko recognized his voice, although she couldn't place it. Another familiar voice called, "If you've got Kobori, then who's this I've caught?"

A chorus of confusion arose. Lights flared, momentarily blinding Reiko. They came from flames burning inside metal lanterns held by soldiers. There looked to be hundreds of them, a small army crowding the road, encircling Reiko. Some were armed with bows and arrows as well as swords. On the ground near her, Detective Fukida sat atop Lieutenant Asukai. Soldiers wrestled with Reiko's other guards. Reiko twisted around and saw that the man who'd caught her was Detective Marume. They beheld each other in mutual amazed recognition.

"Sorry," Marume said, embarrassed and gruff. He released her, then told his comrades, "It's Chamberlain Sano's wife and her escorts. Let them go."

Fukida and the soldiers desisted; Lieutenant Asukai and the other guards stood up and dusted themselves off. Reiko saw Sano striding toward her through the troops who parted to let him pass. Hirata came limping after him. Both men wore helmets and armor, as if in preparation for a battle. Their faces showed the same shock that Reiko felt.

She and Sano spoke simultaneously: "What are you doing here?"

"I followed Yugao's friend Tama," Reiko said. "She led me to a house up that way." As she pointed toward the trail, she rejoiced that Sano had come. He was still alive. He'd not only found her but brought the troops necessary to capture the fugitives. She would have flung herself into his arms, if not for the men watching them. "Yugao and Kobori are there."

"I know," Sano said. "We've come to get them."

She and Sano gazed at each other in shock that their separate inquiries had led them to the same destination. "But how do you know?" Reiko asked, astounded by his miraculous arrival.

"Captain Nakai told me." Sano gestured toward a big, handsome samurai who stood near him.

"Captain Nakai?" Puzzled, Reiko said, "Wasn't he your first suspect?"

"He was. Now he's my newest retainer. But I'll explain later. Right now, we have to invade that house."

Sano spoke orders to his troops. They started up the trail, led by Captain Nakai, moving almost without a sound. Only their lanterns, flickering through the trees, marked their presence.

"Wait," Reiko cried in alarm. "Yugao and the Ghost aren't alone. Tama is with them."

Concern rearranged Sano's expression. "Are you sure?"

"Yes. I saw her go in the house." Tense with urgency, Reiko said, "I think Yugao means to kill Tama. We have to save her!"

"I'll try," Sano said. "But I can't promise. My mission is to capture the Ghost."

Reiko was stricken by dread, but she nodded. Sano's orders from the shogun and Lord Matsudaira took precedence over all else, including the safety of civilians. If Tama should become another victim of Yugao, or a casualty of the raid, Reiko must accept fate. Yet she wished there were something she could do to save Tama, who wouldn't be in danger if not for her!

"I want you to go home now," Sano told her, then turned to Lieutenant Asukai. "See that she gets there safely."

"Please let me stay," Reiko exclaimed. "I want to see what happens. And I can't leave you!"

"All right," Sano conceded, partly because he didn't want to waste time arguing, but also because he didn't want them to be apart any more than Reiko did. This night might be their last together, even if he spent it hunting down an assassin while she watched from a distance. "But you have to promise me that you won't interfere."

"I promise," she said with immediate, ardent sincerity.

Memories of their past gave Sano serious doubts. He only hoped she would keep her promise this time and not go anywhere near the Ghost. The last thing he needed was to worry about her safety. "Then come on."

They followed the army up the trail. The soldiers extinguished their lanterns before they reached the forest's edge. The moon lit their way as they filed silently around the valley. Sano sensed pulses of excitement beating through himself and his men, as though they shared one heart set on battle. He remembered what the priest Ozuno had told Hirata about the Ghost.

Your best strategy is to bring as many armed troops with you as you can. Then be prepared for many of them to die while he's resisting arrest.

Yet Sano felt confidence in his army and himself; one man couldn't possibly defeat them all. Sano might already be doomed, but he would win this battle tonight. He felt Reiko's hand graze his as they walked, and he stifled the thought that this might be their last journey. Now he saw the house, and the light shining in its window, but no other sign of occupation. He joined the army in the woods, some fifty paces from the staircase. He and Hirata and the detectives gazed up at the three levels of the house.

"That's a complicated building," Hirata said quietly.

"It gives the Ghost too many places to hide," Fukida said. "How are we going to find him in there?"

"We could holler at him to come out, and when he does, we'll arrest him, no problem," Marume joked.

"There must be just as many ways he can sneak out of it," Hirata said, studying the numerous windows and balconies.

"That works in our favor as well as his. We'll use those ways to sneak in on him." Sano divided his forces into teams of three. "First we surround the property so that even if Kobori escapes from the house, he can't leave the grounds. Then we go in." He assigned teams to various positions and duties. "Remember that Kobori is more dangerous than any fighter you've ever met. Stick together in your teams. Don't tackle him alone."

While one team kept watch on the front of the house, the others started up the hill and merged into the darkness. Sano said, "Marume-*san* and Fukida-*san,* you're on my team. Hirata-*san,* you stay here."

"No—I'm going with you," Hirata said, clearly dismayed by the prospect of being left behind.

Sano recognized how hard Hirata had struggled to keep up with the investigation and how much he hated to miss the final action. But they both knew he was unfit to clamber over rough terrain in the dark, let alone confront a lethal assassin. If he went, he would slow down their team or endanger the other men. Sano grasped at the only excuse that might save Hirata's pride.

"I'm counting on you to supervise this team and guard my wife," Sano said.

Humiliation shone in Hirata's eyes even as he nodded. It was clear that he knew the team could supervise itself and Reiko's guards could protect her better than he could. "Do you remember the old priest's techniques that I showed you for fighting Kobori?" he asked Sano, Marume, and Fukida.

They nodded. Hirata had given a quick lesson to them and all the troops before they'd left Edo. Sano had doubts about how much good it would do, but at least Hirata could feel that he'd contributed something to the mission.

"Well, then, good luck," Hirata said.

Marume clapped a hand on Hirata's shoulder. "When this is done, we'll all go out for a drink."

He and Fukida moved to the edge of the forest. Sano turned to Reiko. The moonlight silvered her features. His gaze traced them, committing them to memory even though her image was already etched in his spirit. She gave him a tremulous smile.

"Be careful," she said.

Her beauty, and his fear that they would soon be parted forever, shot pain through Sano. "I love you," he whispered.

"No," she said, her voice fractured and barely audible.

He knew she didn't mean she rejected his love. She knew he'd spoken it in case he didn't survive this mission or didn't have time enough afterward to tell her. The words were akin to saying good-bye, which she didn't want to hear. Sano touched her cheek. They exchanged one heartfelt look to sustain them until he came back—or until they were reunited in death. Then Sano turned and set off into the night with Marume and Fukida to have his revenge on the man he believed had murdered him.

Reiko sat beside Hirata in the forest; her guards and the team of soldiers crouched nearby. No one spoke. Everyone was too intent on peering through the trees at the mansion and listening for noises that would tell them what was happening. Reiko projected her mind across the distance toward Sano. They had a unique spiritual connection that enabled them to sense each other's presence, thoughts, and feelings even when separated. Surely she would know if he was in danger, hurt—or dead. But tonight she felt nothing except her own mounting fear for him. A chasm of loneliness opened in her heart. She closed her eyes, the better to listen.

The night wove a fabric of sounds that muffled those of Sano and his army. Wolves howled; the wind moaned through the trees; Reiko heard the screech of predatory birds, and the stream gurgling in the valley. Temple bells signaled midnight. When she opened her eyes, she saw the mansion, still as ever. The light behind the window flickered as if the lantern inside was burning low on oil. The moon ascended to its zenith; the stars revolved on the wheel of heaven while Reiko wondered what Sano was doing. The air turned wintry, but she didn't notice she was trembling with cold until Hirata put his cloak over her shoulders. Time passed, slow as water eroding stone. They waited in tense anticipation.

Suddenly a thin, faraway voice yelled, "Who's out there?"

Reiko stiffened. She felt her heartbeat skitter. Hirata, her guards, and the soldiers stirred alert.

"Answer me!" ordered the voice.

It was shrill with panic, and it came from the house. "That's Yugao," Reiko said apprehensively. "What's going on?"

"She must have heard our troops coming," Hirata said in dismay. "She and the Ghost know they're under siege."

"Go away!" Yugao shouted, her voice sounding closer and louder. "Leave us alone!"

Now Reiko heard the familiar sound of the door opening. Yugao burst out onto the veranda. Her back was hunched, her hands curled like talons. She resembled a wild, cornered beast. She prowled behind the railing and cried, "Listen to me, whoever you are!"

Even from a distance, in the dim light, Reiko could see that terror and hatred twisted Yugao's features. Her gaze frantically explored the darkness, seeking her foes. "We won't let you take us. Get out of here or you'll be sorry!"

"Our orders from Chamberlain Sano are to bring in the fugitives alive or dead," Hirata said. "Here's our chance at one of them." The soldiers had already drawn their bows; they pointed their arrows at Yugao. "Fire as soon as you've got a good shot."

Even though Reiko knew Yugao was a murderess who deserved to die, she winced at the prospect of the spilling of a young woman's blood. And if Yugao died, she would take her secrets to the grave.

Yugao paused. Three bows twanged. Three arrows hissed across the darkness. They thumped against the veranda railing and the wooden wall of the mansion. Yugao shrieked. She flung up her arms to protect her head, ducking and turning from side to side, trying to see who was firing at her. The archers shot more arrows. She howled, fell flat, and Reiko thought she'd been hit. But then Yugao was scuttling fast on hands and knees toward the door. She crawled into the mansion, and the door shut behind her, pelted by another volley of arrows.

The archers lowered their bows and muttered curses. Hirata shook his head. Reiko was torn between disappointment that Yugao had escaped and relief that another life had not ended in violence.

Yugao shouted through the door, "You can't kill me! If you even try—" She stepped outside, holding Tama in front of her, pressed against her body like a shield. "—I'll kill her!"

Tama stood rigid, her round doll's face a mask of terror. Her hands clutched the arm that Yugao held locked across her chest. Horror seized Reiko as Yugao waved a knife whose blade gleamed in the lantern light. The soldiers took aim again.

"No!" Reiko whispered. Panic launched her to her feet.

The soldiers looked to Hirata for orders. One said, "If we shoot at Yugao, we'll hit the other girl instead."

A heartbeat passed, then Hirata said, "Hold your fire. I'll talk to her."

As Reiko exhaled in relief, Hirata stepped out from the woods. He limped along the trail toward the mansion. "Yugao!" he called.

She whirled in the direction of his voice, turning Tama with her. Her hostile gaze searched the darkness and she shouted, "Who are you?"

"I'm the shogun's *sōsakan-sama*," Hirata said.

"Stop right where you are. Or she dies!"

Yugao jerked the blade to Tama's neck. Tama screamed. Reiko

gasped; her hand flew to her own throat. Hirata froze on the trail halfway to the stairs.

"All right," he said in a falsely calm tone. "I'll stay here—if you let Tama go and come with me peacefully."

"No!" Yugao's voice shrilled higher with alarm. "Go away, or I'll cut her throat, I swear!"

"Killing her won't do you any good," Hirata said. "The house is surrounded by soldiers."

"Call them off!" Yugao ordered.

"I can't," Hirata said. "Surrendering is your only chance to live."

"I'll never surrender! Never!"

"Then just let Tama go," Hirata said. Reiko could hear that his patience was running out. "If you do, we won't hurt you. I promise."

"Liar! I don't believe you!" Yugao shrieked.

Anxious to help, Reiko spoke softly to Hirata: "Tell her that Tama is her friend. Tama doesn't deserve to die."

Hirata called out the words to Yugao. She shouted back, "Tama's not my friend anymore. She told the police where I was." Her voice was bitter with anger and resentment. "She's the reason you're here."

"I didn't," Tama cried, sobbing as she strained away from the knife. "You must believe me!"

"Yes, you did." Yugao held tight to Tama. Cruelty twisted her face. "You're a traitor. You should be punished!"

Reiko lost all hope that Hirata could talk sense into Yugao or save Tama. Yugao was beyond reason. Even though she'd promised Sano she wouldn't interfere, Reiko couldn't stand by and do nothing. She ran out of the woods, up the trail, in front of Hirata.

"Yugao!" she called even as she regretted breaking her word to Sano.

"What are you doing?" Hirata said in dismay. "Go back!"

He tugged at her arm. She shook him off. "Please let me try." Her gaze met Yugao's across the darkness.

"Well, if it isn't Lady Reiko," Yugao said. "Did you come to watch the fun? Haven't you anything better to do?"

"Tama didn't bring the army to you," Reiko said. "Don't blame her. It was me. I followed her here."

"*You.*" The word gushed, like a sac of venom bursting, from Yugao. "I should have known. All the while you were pretending you wanted to help me, you were plotting to bring me down."

"I did want to help you," Reiko said. She spoke in her most earnest, persuasive manner. Yugao had never trusted her, but Tama's life depended on her winning the woman's trust now. "I still do."

Yugao shook her head in contemptuous disbelief. "Then prove it. Get those soldiers out of here."

"All right," Reiko said, even though she could do no such thing. "But first you have to let Tama go." She paced forward until she reached the foot of the stairs. Hirata and her guards followed. She extended a hand to Yugao.

"Stop!" Yugao clamped her arm tighter around Tama, who squealed and wept. She said, "You must think I'm really stupid." She puffed air out her mouth in disgust. "Well, I know that the moment I let Tama go, they'll rush up here and kill me. She's my only protection."

Reiko knew Yugao was right, but she said, "They won't kill you. Not if you cooperate. Let Tama go."

"Shut up! Get lost, or I'll cut her right now!"

Yugao drew the blade across Tama's throat. A thin line of blood welled. Tama squealed louder, her eyes shut tight, her hands clawing at Yugao's arm. Despair sickened Reiko. Hirata said, "It's no use. She's not going to give up. And I can't let her force us to back off. I'm sending the team after her."

"Wait," Reiko pleaded, although she knew Hirata's decision was justified. Tama was a mere female commoner whose death might be a small price to pay for the capture of a murderess and an assassin; yet Reiko couldn't forsake the sweet, innocent girl. Information from Tama had led Sano to the Ghost's identity. Reiko owed her better than to sacrifice her to the hunt for Kobori. "Give me one more chance."

"Just one more," Hirata reluctantly agreed.

Reiko called to Yugao, "I don't think you're stupid. I know you're smart enough to understand that holding Tama hostage won't protect your lover. My husband is out here, and he's determined to catch Kobori. He'll gladly sacrifice Tama to get to him. So let her go." She drew a deep breath and spoke the only words that might save Tama: "Take me in her place."

"What?" Hirata exclaimed. He stared at Reiko.

Suspicion drew Yugao's eyebrows together in a frown. "Why would I want you?"

"Because if you have me, the soldiers won't touch you," Reiko said. "I'm their master's wife. If they should kill me while trying to arrest you or your lover, they'll be in big trouble."

Yugao considered the proposal for a mere instant, then said, "All right." She apparently believed Reiko's logic even though she didn't trust Reiko. "You come up here. Then I'll let Tama go."

As Reiko stepped forward, Hirata said in a furious whisper, "You can't do this!"

"I must." Reiko paused and turned to him. Keeping her voice low so that Yugao wouldn't hear, she said, "Yugao is my responsibility to capture. If she kills again, the blood will be on my hands."

"It'll be your own blood!" Hirata gazed at her as if she'd gone mad. "She'll kill you!"

"No, she won't," Reiko said. "I can handle her." She'd faced down crazed murderers in the past and survived. Confidence braced Reiko against the dread that flowed, cold and daunting, through her veins. The dagger strapped to her arm gave her courage as she put her foot on the stairs.

"Stop," Yugao said. "Lift your skirts. Put your arms up. I want to make sure you're not carrying any weapons. Turn around."

Reiko had underestimated Yugao's intelligence. After a moment's hesitation, she obeyed while clutching the hems of her sleeves, trying to conceal the dagger.

"Open your hands," Yugao ordered. "Push down your sleeves." After Reiko did, Yugao said, "Throw away that knife."

As Reiko reluctantly unstrapped her weapon, Hirata said, "Chamberlain Sano ordered me to guard you. I won't let you do it." Reiko flung down the dagger. He seized her arm. "I'll stop you by force if I must. It's my duty."

But his pleading gaze told Reiko that he was bluffing; he could never bring himself to use force on her. She gently disengaged herself. "If I refuse to be guarded, my husband won't blame you. Don't worry."

"You can come up now," Yugao said.

"What about your duty to your husband? Don't you think you should honor his wishes?" Hirata demanded. Reiko knew that under any other circumstances he would never dare address her in such a brazen manner, let alone contradict her. But he was desperate now. "Stay out of this!"

"It's my duty to help my husband, and I can help him better by going than staying." Reiko believed it even though she knew Sano would disagree. "If I can keep Yugao occupied, that will be one less problem for him."

"What about your son? If anything bad happens to you, who will raise him?"

An image of Masahiro rose in Reiko's mind, so physical she could almost feel his soft, fragrant skin and hear his laugh. Her determination wavered, but only for a moment. Parenthood didn't excuse a warrior from battle or Reiko from delivering Yugao to justice. Any expectation that she might fail would only handicap her.

"Nothing bad will happen to me," Reiko said. "Be ready to send in your troops if I should call."

"Why are you taking so long?" Yugao called. "If you don't hurry, I might change my mind."

Reiko turned her back on Hirata. As she started up the stairs, she felt him tug at the back of her sash. At first she thought he was trying to restrain her; then she felt the short, hard, narrow shape of a knife he'd tucked under her sash against her spine where Yugao couldn't see it.

"May the gods protect you," he whispered. "May Sano-*san* not kill me for letting you go off on this crazy mission!"

With every step she climbed, Reiko's heart pounded faster in anticipation. Yugao and Tama silently watched her. Yugao's steady, menacing gaze drew her upward. Tama's eyes brimmed with tears and hope of salvation as Reiko reached the veranda. Reiko advanced until she was within touching distance of Yugao. Suddenly Yugao grinned. With no other warning, she slashed Tama's throat.

"No!" Reiko screamed.

Tama uttered a terrible, gurgling wail. Blood spewed in a hot red fountain, drenching Reiko. She exclaimed in horrified disbelief. Yugao flung Tama at her. Tama crumpled onto the veranda floor, where she twitched, moaned, and died in front of Reiko. Her blood pooled around them. Reiko heard Hirata and her guards shouting and running up the stairs.

"Stop!" Yugao ordered them. She seized Reiko by the arm and held the blade against her neck. "One more move, and she's dead, too!"

Reiko felt cold steel against her skin. She saw the men standing immobile and helpless on the stairs. Breathless, on the brink of fainting from shock, and dripping blood, she had barely enough self-possession to twist her body and hide the knife from Yugao.

Yugao marched Reiko past Tama's corpse and through the door. She spoke in a tone of vindictive satisfaction: "Now you'll pay for all the trouble you've caused me."

31

"I think we've passed the house," Detective Marume said as he and Fukida and Sano toiled up the forested slope through the night. "I feel as if we're halfway to the sky."

Sano stumbled over a rock and caught himself. "We must have strayed off course." He heard furtive rustling sounds from their army far off to his right. "Let's go that way."

They cut a zigzagging path across the hillside, groping past branches that snagged their armor. Soon the trees thinned. Pale moonlight filled a cleared space. Sano and his men halted at its edge, the boundary of the mansion's grounds. Gardens descended in three terraces toward the house; ponds shimmered in the moonlight amid ornamental trees, flowerbeds, shrubs, and small, decorative buildings. Insects chirped and shrilled. Mist hovered in a thin, whitish vapor above the tall grass. Below the gardens spread the roof of the top level of the mansion. Sano heard stealthy movement in the gardens' dense, verdant darkness and glimpsed flashes of light—the moon reflecting off the helmets and swords of his army.

Beckoning his men, Sano started down the top terrace. Shadows under the trees gave them cover. Cold dew on the grass drenched his sandals and socks. He spied the hunched, indistinct figures of his troops advancing to the next terrace. The night was peaceful except for the wind, the insects' songs, the wolves' howls, the whisper of grass and foliage, and crackles of twigs and dry leaves underfoot. But as Sano, Marume, and Fukida skirted a raised pavilion covered with a roof on posts, a hoarse scream shattered the quiet.

They instinctively crouched beside the pavilion. "What was that?" Marume whispered.

A second scream vibrated with a horrendous agony that rattled Sano's nerves. Another cry, and another, followed in rapid succession. Chaos broke out down on the grounds. Men charged in all directions, no longer cautious, exposed to view. Countless more screams alarmed Sano. He and Fukida and Marume skidded down the slope to the lower terrace, where scuffles erupted under the foliage and the cries continued. Near a pond, a man lay inert and moaning. Sano crouched beside him and peered at the face below the helmet.

It was Captain Nakai. His eyes and mouth were open, round with terror. His complexion looked ghastly white.

"What happened?" Sano said.

"He sneaked up on me and grabbed me," Nakai said between gasps. "I think he broke my back."

Horror flooded Sano as he turned to Marume and Fukida, who crouched near him. "We've flushed out Kobori. He's stalking and attacking our troops." Sano heard new cries that were quickly silenced as though cut in the middle, and he knew that unlike Nakai, several of his other men hadn't survived their encounters with the Ghost.

Nakai wagged his head feebly, but the rest of him lay still. "I can't move my body!" he cried. "I'm paralyzed!"

Sano felt a heartbreaking pity for Nakai, the warrior who'd slain forty-eight men during his last battle, felled just moments into this one. Sano forgave Nakai his rudeness and over-ambition. Nakai had already served him better than most samurai ever served their masters. Nakai had led him to the Ghost and sacrificed himself to their cause.

Around them, soldiers yelled, "He's over there!" "Get him!" They raced back and forth. Swords clanged. Bodies collided. The screams resounded with awful, increasing frequency. Sano realized that although he had the Ghost within striking distance at last, his mission was in serious trouble. He tore himself away from Nakai, stood, and shouted, "Stop running wild! Get back into your teams!"

He knew what Kobori was doing: scattering the men, then luring them singly into the shadows and picking them off. "Surround the place!" Sano yelled. "Trap Kobori!"

The room was bare, the furniture and *tatami* mats stored away until summer. Dust filmed the plank floor. In the empty alcove hung a spider web adorned with dead insects. Reiko knelt in a corner, trembling and sickened from Tama's death. Tama's blood, now cold and sticky, had seeped through her clothes and stained her skin. With every breath she inhaled its raw, metallic odor; she fought the urge to vomit. Bitter self-recrimination tortured her.

Yugao stood over Reiko, holding the knife extended, its sharp point almost touching Reiko's lips. The knife, her hands, and her robes were blood-smeared, her eyes crazed. The light from the lantern flickered across her features, animating them as if with constant nervous tics.

Fear gathered inside Reiko like a pool of acid corroding her spirit. Yugao had already killed four times and wouldn't hesitate to kill again. Completely at Yugao's mercy, Reiko took no comfort from the knife that Hirata had given her. She sensed murderous thoughts moving in Yugao's mind, saw the hint of an evil smile curve her mouth, felt how fast were her reflexes. If Reiko reached behind her and pulled her own weapon out from under her sash, Yugao would attack her before she could defend herself.

"You don't have to do this," Reiko said. "We can just walk out of here." Her survival depended on manipulating Yugao. "You'll be safe."

"Don't talk such nonsense," Yugao retorted. "You'll turn me over to your father. And he'll have me executed."

It didn't seem the time for Reiko to point out that Yugao had previously demanded that Magistrate Ueda execute her. Yugao had changed her mind and didn't appear willing to change it back again. "That won't happen. I've told my father that I think you're innocent;

you didn't murder your family. He believed it. If you hadn't run away, you'd have been acquitted," Reiko lied.

Yugao sneered. "You never told him any such thing. You thought I was guilty from the start."

"No, I didn't. I've been trying to help you all along." The knife was so close to Reiko's face that she could smell the iron; her skin tingled as she imagined the slash, the pain, her blood spilling. "Let me help you now."

"Oh, I'm sure that when your father hears that I killed Tama, he'll set me free!"

"I'll tell him that you didn't mean to kill her; it was an accident," Reiko improvised. "The only things you've done wrong are escaping from jail and associating with a criminal. Just come with me back to Edo."

"Why would I want to do that?" Yugao asked in disdain. "There's nothing there for me."

"My father will pardon you. You can start a new life. You won't be an outcast anymore." Reiko cautiously held out her hand. "Just give me the knife."

Sudden rage flared in Yugao's eyes. "Do you want the knife that badly? Well, I'll give it to you!"

She slashed at Reiko's hand. Reiko cried out as the blade cut her palm. Blood oozed from the deep gash.

"That should teach you to try to fool me," Yugao said with malicious satisfaction. "Now keep your mouth shut while I decide what to do."

Sano shouted at his men, ordering them to band together and close off Kobori's escape route. But anarchy reigned, as if the Ghost had cast a spell that drove the troops mad. Sano felt his army's hysteria growing with each cry that signaled another death at Kobori's hands. He fought his own desire to run wild. Corpses lay strewn among trees and bushes. Now three soldiers fled the gardens and disappeared into the forest. A mass stampede followed them.

"The cowards are deserting," Marume said, alarmed as well as disgusted. "Hey!" he shouted. "Come back here!" He charged after the deserters.

"No! Don't!" Sano said, but too late to stop Marume.

A slender figure clad in black emerged from behind a clump of bushes on the terrace above. It stood alert but relaxed, like a tiger after a successful hunt, watching the army flee. Then he turned and looked straight down at Sano and Fukida. His eyes gleamed; his teeth flashed in a curved white line as he smiled. Sano's heart lurched.

The man was Kobori.

"There he is!" Fukida exclaimed.

Sword drawn, he lunged up the slope, compelled by the madness that had seized the army. Sano vaulted after him, calling, "We have to stick together!" They must not make the same error their troops had. As a team they had a chance against Kobori. Alone, they risked their comrades' fate.

The few remaining troops rallied to the chase, converging on Kobori from all directions. Kobori waited until Fukida had breasted the terrace and his pursuers were within some ten paces of him. Then he faded into the bushes. As Sano reached these, his men rushed about in confusion, calling, "Where did he go?" Someone crashed into him. A sword whistled through the air too close to his face.

"Watch out!" he cried.

"He ran into the woods!" said Fukida's excited voice.

Bushes crackled and foliage snapped as the horde bounded off after the Ghost. Sano cursed in frustration. They would never find Kobori in there. He was as good as gone. While the noise of his men thrashing through the woods receded into the distance, Sano sheathed his sword and bent over, resting his hands on his knees, overcome by weariness and despair.

"Chamberlain Sano," a voice whispered. It was soft, yet had a latent power that made it audible above the other noises.

Like a cat hissing, as Tama had described it to Reiko.

Sano felt his skin ripple. The Ghost was here. He must have eluded the troops, then come back.

A visceral, primitive terror froze Sano. Only his eyes moved, trying to locate Kobori in the shadows around him. His heart drummed an accelerating rhythm of dread. But although he could sense Kobori's presence like malignant decay breeding in the gardens, he couldn't see the Ghost.

"Your men are busy chasing one another in the woods," Kobori said. "The ones I haven't killed or scared away, that is." His tone was amused yet vicious, conversational yet threatening. "It's just you and me."

Reiko sat in her corner, her injured hand wrapped in her sleeve and still oozing blood. Yugao still stood before her, holding the knife. They listened to the shouts and the running footsteps outside the mansion. Yugao's gaze skittered, as if she wanted to see what was happening but dared not leave Reiko. Her hand trembled and the knife wavered with the strain that Reiko sensed building inside her. The lantern burned dimmer, a dying sun that emitted sickly ochre light and rancid smoke. The atmosphere was dense with the odors of blood and Yugao's feverish perspiration. Reiko knew that sooner or later Yugao would snap. Either she must risk her life trying to talk Yugao into surrendering, or keep quiet and die anyway.

"Do you hear that commotion?" Reiko said. "Do you want to know what it is?"

"Be quiet," Yugao ordered, "or I'll cut you again."

"My husband and his troops have invaded the grounds," Reiko said. "Pretty soon they'll be inside the house."

"No, they won't." Goaded into conversation, Yugao spoke with utter confidence. "They'll never get past him."

Reiko understood that Yugao was referring to Kobori, the Ghost. "He's only one man. There are hundreds of them. He can't fight them all."

"Is that what you think?" Yugao's expression turned sly, disdainful. "Well, you don't know him."

There came a shriek so loud that it seemed to pierce the walls of the house and so filled with agony that Reiko gasped.

"Did *you* hear *that?*" Yugao said. "Do you want to know what it is?"

Her tone teased Reiko. "He's killing your husband's men. Just listen!" More shrieks arose. "You can count them as they die. He's the best fighter there ever was!"

She brimmed with admiration for Kobori, and an excitement that was almost sexual. Reiko suddenly found herself afraid that the Ghost's wondrous martial arts skills really could defeat an entire army. She realized that she'd been counting on Sano to save her, but maybe he was already dead. She thought of Hirata, waiting outside. If she called him, Yugao would kill her before he could reach her. She had to get out of this predicament on her own.

"No matter how good Kobori is, he can't hold out against so many troops," Reiko said. "They'll kill him eventually. And you'll be left to take the blame for what he's done."

Yugao laughed. "I can tell you're not too sure of what you're saying. Why should I believe it?"

"It's true," Reiko said, trying to sound confident. "You'd do better to cut loose from Kobori. It's him that my husband is really after, not you. It's not too late to save yourself, if we go now." She rose carefully, sliding her back up the corner, watching Yugao.

"Sit down!" Yugao jabbed the knife at Reiko, who hastily dropped to her knees again. "I'll never leave him! And I won't listen to you any longer!"

Reiko ventured a different tactic: "Suppose that Kobori does win. He'll be a fugitive forever. Lord Matsudaira will never stop chasing him. What kind of life do you think you'll have with Kobori?"

"At least we'll be together," Yugao said. "I love him. Nothing else matters."

"Here's something that should," Reiko said. "Kobori has murdered at least five Tokugawa officials. But maybe you didn't know that."

"Of course I did. I know all about him. I even saw him do it once. But maybe you didn't know that," Yugao mocked. "And I don't care what everybody else thinks of what he's done. I think he's wonderful." Her face was radiant with adoration for Kobori. "He's the biggest hero who ever lived!"

Reiko thought how Yugao's past had shaped her character. Her beloved father had forced her to commit incest with him. After he'd rejected her, she'd transferred her devotion to another tyrant, Kobori.

"His hands have the blood of innocent victims all over them," Reiko said. "How can you bear for him to touch you?"

"That's part of the thrill of making love with him." Yugao licked her lips and ran her hand down her bosom. The memory of Kobori's caresses engorged her with lascivious pleasure. "Besides, those men weren't innocent. They were his enemies. They deserved to die."

Vicarious revenge was another pleasure that she derived from her lover, Reiko saw. Because Yugao must have wanted to strike back at the parents and sister who'd hurt her, how she must have reveled in knowing of Kobori's exploits. "He's not a hero," Reiko said. "You're harboring a criminal."

"I've done more than that for him," Yugao said proudly.

An ominous tingle crept along Reiko's nerves. "What are you talking about?"

"When I lived in the Ryōgoku Hirokoji entertainment district, Lord Matsudaira's soldiers would come there to drink and pick up women. It was easy to lure them into the alleys. They had no idea that I meant them any harm."

"It was you who killed those soldiers." Reiko recalled the Rat's tale of the three murders and the bloody corpses found in the alleys behind teahouses. Her suspicions had proven true.

Yugao preened, like a street magician who has just pulled a live bird out of her sleeve. "I stuck my knife into them. They never saw it coming."

Reiko's horror increased as she understood why Yugao didn't care whether Reiko knew about her crimes against Lord Matsudaira. Yugao didn't intend for Reiko to live long enough to report them to him.

"I've helped him destroy his enemies before," Yugao went on. "And tonight I'll destroy the one who led the army to us."

With an abrupt, jerky motion, she turned the knife sideways against Reiko's throat.

. . .

"Here I am, Chamberlain Sano."

Kobori's whisper seemed to issue from nowhere and everywhere. Sano realized he had the ability to project his voice, like the great martial artists of legend who'd dispersed armies by instilling fear in them and addling their wits. The Ghost exuded a spiritual force more vast, more dreadful, than Sano had ever felt before.

Sano drew his sword. Turning in a circle, he strained his eyes after the Ghost.

"Over here," Kobori whispered.

Sano pivoted. He slashed at a shape that loomed in the darkness where he'd heard Kobori. His blade hacked a bush.

"Sorry, you missed."

Again Sano struck. His blade cleaved empty shadow.

Kobori laughed, a sound like hot, molten metal sizzling through water. "Can't you see me? I can see you. I'm right behind you."

His voice hissed warm breath into Sano's ear. Sano let out a yell, spun, and slashed. But Kobori wasn't there. Either he'd approached and fled with superhuman speed, or his presence had been an illusion he'd conjured. His laughter drifted up from the terrace closest to the mansion.

"Down here, Honorable Chamberlain," he whispered.

Fear burgeoned like a monstrous growth inside Sano because he knew Kobori could have killed him at any time during the past few moments. He felt an overwhelming urge to run as his army had. But he was furious at Kobori for toying with him. And he was the only one left to destroy the Ghost. Abandoning caution, gripping his sword, he scrambled down the slope.

The bottom terrace was landscaped with pine trees that gave off a pungent scent, and a pond whose waters reflected a bridge that arched across it. Sano halted beside the pond. He raised his sword in challenge. "I dare you to come out and face me."

"Oh, but that would spoil the game."

Each word Kobori spoke seemed to originate from a different

point. His voice ricocheted from trees to pond to the sky. Sano's head swiveled and tilted in a vain attempt to track it. Cold sweat drenched his skin under his armor.

"I'm in here," Kobori whispered.

Now his voice drew Sano's attention to the house. Its veranda was empty beneath the overhanging eaves. Shutters sealed the windows. But the door was open, a rectangle of black space that beckoned Sano. From it issued Kobori's voice: "Come in and get me if you can."

Sano stood motionless while contradictory impulses vied within him. Rational thought warned him against setting foot inside that house. Kobori meant to corner him, torment him, then move in for the kill. No matter how harshly Lord Matsudaira would punish him for giving up his mission, at this moment it was preferable to stepping into a fatal trap. The animal instinct for self-preservation held Sano back.

But an honorable samurai didn't shy away from a duel no matter how stupid or insane it might seem. If Sano did so, he would never be able to hold up his head in public, even if no one else learned about his cowardice. He thought of Reiko, of Masahiro. If he lost this duel, he would never see them again. If he refused it, his disgrace would be so terrible that he would never be able to face them.

Ieyasu, the first Tokugawa shogun, had said there were only two ways to come back from a battle—with the head of your enemy, or without your own.

In addition, more than Sano's samurai pride was at issue. This might be the best chance anyone would have at the Ghost, who would kill, escape, and kill again many more times. And if the Ghost had already given him the touch of death, Sano might as well take Kobori on. To die tonight instead of tomorrow would scarcely matter. At least he would end his life with his honor intact.

Sano strode, filled with the recklessness of the damned, up the path to the house. He mounted the steps to the veranda, then paused at the doorway, concentrating on the darkness beyond. His sight couldn't pierce it; his ears detected no sounds of anyone in the house. But his extra sense perceived Kobori's presence, waiting and ready.

The chorus of insects rose to a shrill cacophony.

Wolves bayed.

A chill wind rippled the pond.

Sano stepped through the door.

32

"You can't kill me," Reiko said even as she recoiled from the blade against her neck and saw the destructive intent in Yugao's eyes. "You need me to protect you." Although she realized that Yugao was mad enough to kill her anyway, Reiko tried to dissuade her: "Troops will be here any moment. Without me alive, you're dead."

Yugao laughed, reckless and exhilarated. "I don't hear them coming, do you? He's winning. We don't need you."

Reiko heard men running away from the house: The army was deserting. And what of Sano? Even if he wasn't dead, even if Hirata told him she was in here, could he fight his way past the Ghost and rescue her? Despair overwhelmed Reiko. She said, "You'll need me to get out of Edo. There's a big hunt going on for you both. If I'm with you, my husband and my father will want to save me. You can bargain with them: Your freedom in exchange for my life."

Yugao shook her head. "He can move like the wind. When we're together it's as if we're invisible." Her gaze darted as she tried to follow the action outside. Nervous tremors from her body jittered the knife against Reiko's skin. "We'll slip right through the army's fingers. You would only slow us down."

Reiko saw her own death fast approaching. Her neck muscles convulsed under the knife. But at least maybe she could tie up a loose end in her investigation. "If I'm to die, then answer one question for me first. Why did you kill your family?"

She saw admiration mixed with scorn in Yugao's eyes. "You never give up, do you?"

"After all the work I've done on your behalf, the least you can do in return is satisfy my curiosity." And the longer they talked, the more chance Reiko had to save herself.

Yugao considered, then shrugged. "All right." Reiko sensed that she wanted the satisfaction of showing how wrong Reiko had been about her reasons. "I don't suppose it would hurt to tell you now."

The moonlight penetrated the interior of the house barely enough to show Sano a passage that extended into a black void. He pressed his back to a wall, his left hand groping along it, his right hand clutching his sword. As the darkness swallowed him up, his eyesight deserted him, but his other senses grew more acute. He heard each tiny creak of the floor under his weight; his feet felt the thin gaps between its boards. His fingers traced the pattern of a lattice partition. He smelled a tinge of male human sweat in the musty odor of closed, unaired space.

Kobori had passed this way during the last few moments. He'd left his spoor.

Sano projected his mind outward, searching for his foe as he inched along. He sensed empty rooms behind the partition and across the passage, felt the Ghost waiting for him not far away. If he could smell Kobori, then Kobori could smell him. His heart pounded so loudly that Kobori must hear it. And Kobori had probably memorized every part of the house so well he could navigate it in pitch-darkness. Sano's muscles flinched in anticipation of a strike coming out of nowhere. It wasn't too late to turn back. But valor overrode common sense. Sano kept moving.

He glanced backward at the faint, blurry shape of the doorway lit from outside. It seemed a world away even though he'd walked only thirty paces. When he slid his foot forward, the floor dropped off beneath it. He probed with his toe, which touched the riser and next step of a staircase leading to the lower level of the house. He clung to a railing as he slowly, carefully descended the stairs. At the bottom he forged ahead, down another passage. Its absolute darkness was like a living tissue that breathed mildew and dust into his lungs. He had the eerie feeling that the boundary between himself and the space around him was dissolving. He had an urge to touch his body and make sure he still existed.

"Keep going, Honorable Chamberlain," whispered the Ghost. "You're almost here."

The wall under Sano's groping hand ended: He'd reached a corner. Sano edged around it. Several paces farther, he encountered a doorway, beyond which yawned a room. The corridor led him past more rooms, around more corners. Sano pictured himself wandering through a maze while Kobori stood at the center, ready to pounce. His heightened perception verged on the supernatural. The smell of the Ghost's spoor was so strong he could taste it. He sensed weight shifting somewhere on the floor: Kobori was on the same level of the house with him.

The floor creaked once, then twice more.

Sano hadn't made those sounds. He stood paralyzed, listening to the Ghost's footfalls steal up on him, trying to sense from which direction.

"Here I come," whispered Kobori.

Sano turned toward the voice. He held his sword raised in both hands. As he waited, he felt at once invisible and exposed, terrified of the confrontation yet ravenous for it.

Footsteps approached from all directions, as if the Ghost had multiplied himself into an army. Had Kobori created this illusion, or had Sano's own mind? Sano had never felt so alone, confused, or vulnerable. His high rank and his legions of subordinates couldn't protect him. That he had power over virtually every citizen in Japan didn't matter here. The Ghost had reduced him to the masterless samurai, struggling to survive by his own devices, that he'd once been. His wife, his son, and his accomplishments seemed as remote from him as if he'd dreamed them. All Sano had now, as then, were his swords.

Even though he knew that his enemy intended him to feel this way in order to break his confidence, Sano's sense of vulnerability and isolation intensified against his will. The Ghost's footsteps quickened and closed in on him. In blind haste Sano stumbled through a door. Abruptly the footsteps ceased. Sano felt a warm current of air behind him.

It was the Ghost's body heat.

Panic jolted Sano. Before he could react, he felt a tap on his back, below his right shoulder. Fierce pain sped down his arm. His muscles stiffened in a spasm. His fingers let go his sword, which dropped to the floor. As he doubled over, his teeth clenched in agony, he was seized from behind. Hands groped over his body. He struck out with his uninjured left hand, but it swished through empty air. His right arm dangled useless and aching. He felt a yank at his waist, then heard rapid, retreating footfalls.

Kobori had come and gone.

Alone in the darkness, Sano fell to his knees, shaken and panting from the sudden, violent attack. The pain in his arm ebbed into heavy numbness, as if the blood circulation had been cut off. Sano moved his fingers, but he couldn't feel them. Kobori had struck some vital point that had disabled his arm. He felt around on the floor, desperately trying to find his sword before Kobori attacked again. But his hand swept vacant floor. He felt for his short sword at his waist, but it too was gone. Kobori had taken both his weapons. He heard Kobori's laughter, which crackled like flames.

"Let's see how well you can fight me without your swords," Kobori whispered.

"My father was an executioner," Yugao said.

She eased the knife's pressure against Reiko's throat. Reiko cautiously let out her breath and relaxed her muscles.

"He would come home and talk about how many people he'd killed and what they'd done to get in trouble," Yugao went on. "He told us how they acted when they were brought to the execution ground. He talked about how it felt to cut their heads off."

Reiko focused her gaze on Yugao's face, in the hope of keeping Yugao's attention on hers instead of on her hands.

"After the war, there were many samurai from the Yanagisawa army who were executed. They were *his* comrades." Fury on her lover's account kindled in Yugao's eyes. "My father killed lots of them. He bragged about it because they'd been important men and he was a *hinin,* but they were dead and he was alive. Every time he killed one, he cut a notch on the wall."

Reiko remembered seeing the notches in the hovel. She inched her right hand to her side, toward the knife behind her.

"I couldn't let him keep killing them," Yugao said. "That night I couldn't stand to listen to him bragging anymore. So I stabbed him. It was the most I could do for my beloved."

Finally Reiko understood why Yugao had kept her motive secret—to avoid mentioning Kobori and exposing his crimes. But Reiko also sensed that past and present grievances had combined to push Yugao over the edge. Yugao had long been nursing a bitter hatred toward her father for violating and then rejecting her. She might have endured it forever, or stabbed him at any other time, but his offenses against Kobori's comrades had finally tipped her unstable mind into killing her father.

"Why did you kill you mother and sister?" Reiko asked.

A contemptuous smile twisted Yugao's lips. "While I was stabbing him, they just huddled in the corner and cried." Her manner turned argumentative. "They could have stopped me. If they'd cared about him, they would have. The miserable cowards deserved to die."

Perhaps Yugao had wanted them to stop her, Reiko speculated. Perhaps she'd still loved her father despite everything. If so, then she'd punished them for their failure to save him from her as well as for past injustices toward her. Now there remained only one more issue to resolve.

"Why did you confess?" Reiko asked.

"I did it for *him*," Yugao said. "And I wanted him to know. I didn't expect to ever see him again, but he would hear what I'd done. He would understand why. He would know I'd died for him and be grateful."

The magnitude of her delusion astounded Reiko. "Then why did you run away from jail instead?" Reiko had her arm bent behind her, fingers on the hilt of the knife.

"The fire was an omen. It said I was meant to reunite with him instead of die for him." Yugao frowned in sudden suspicion at Reiko. "What are you doing?"

"Just scratching my back," Reiko lied.

"Put your hands where I can see them."

As Reiko obeyed, she gave up hope of striking at Yugao before Yugao could strike her. She thought up a new tactic. "You killed for Kobori. You were ready to sacrifice your life for him. What did he ever do for you?"

Yugao looked at Reiko as if she was stupid to ask. "He loves me."

"Did he say so?"

"He doesn't have to. I know."

"How do you know?"

"He makes love to me," Yugao said.

"You mean he takes his pleasure from you," Reiko said. "That doesn't mean he cares anything for you except physically."

"He came to me after the war. It didn't matter to him that I was a *hinin*." For the first time Yugao sounded eager to prove that she meant as much to Kobori as he did to her. "He wanted to be with me."

Reiko thought of the beating taken by Yanagisawa's faction during the war, and she spoke on a hunch: "Was he injured?"

"Yes. What of it?"

"So he was hurt and he didn't have anywhere else to go. And I bet that as soon as he was well, he left. Didn't he?"

The distress on Yugao's face told Reiko she'd guessed right. "He had to go. He had important things to do."

"More important than you," Reiko said. "Tell me, when you escaped from jail, was he glad to see you?"

Yugao snapped, "He has problems on his mind."

"And you became one of them," Reiko deduced. "He knew you could be his downfall. And he was right. You brought the law to him. He'll dump you as soon as he can."

"I don't care," Yugao said, but her eyes glistened with tears and misery; her voice shook as her bravado deserted her. "He's all I have."

At last Reiko saw through Yugao, to the spirit inside her hard shell. Loss and deprivation had charted the path of Yugao's life. Yugao had lost her innocence, as well as her mother's love, because of her father's depravity. She'd lost her home, her affluent life as a merchant's daughter, and her place in society. She'd lost her father's affection to her sister. After she'd murdered her family, she'd lost her kin and her freedom. Now she clung desperately to the one thing she hadn't yet lost.

"I won't let you take me away from him!" she cried.

Even as Reiko pitied her, Yugao blinked away her tears. The familiar shield of hostility hardened her gaze. "I'm sick of listening to you." Her voice was raw but tough. Her eyes blazed with hatred that had worsened because Reiko had forced her to expose herself. "It's time to shut you up for good."

Disarmed, blind, and helpless, Sano realized that if things continued like this, he didn't have a chance. He must gain control over the situation. The first thing was to get himself out of the Ghost's trap. Sano crawled along the floor until he found a wall made of wooden panels. He groped across and up it until his hand met a groove. He inserted his fingers and pulled. The panel slid.

"What are you doing?" Kobori's tone said that he knew Sano was changing the rules of the game and he didn't like it.

Behind the panel was another, made of paper framed by mullions. Light glowed in streaks through it, just bright enough that when Sano glanced around he could see that he was alone in an unfurnished room. He slid open the panel. On the other side were rough planks, fastened over a doorway. The moonlight shone through the cracks be-

tween them: The house had been boarded up to keep thieves out. Sano
pried at the planks with his left hand; his right hand and whole arm
were still numb and useless. When the planks didn't yield, he
thumped on them.

"You can't escape me," Kobori whispered.

His voice moved closer, accompanied by legions of footsteps that
echoed through the house. As Sano looked around in desperation, he
saw a flimsy staircase built of wooden slats and poles rising from a corner. He lunged up it.

"Where are you going?" Kobori's voice sharpened.

Sano reached the top of the staircase, which ended at a platform
near the ceiling. He pushed up on the ceiling, and a trapdoor lifted.
Either Kobori had forgotten to seal this exit or had thought Sano
wouldn't find it. Sano thrust his head through the opening, into moonlight and fresh, pure wind.

"Stop!" Kobori ordered, his whisper rising to a harsh volume.
"Come back!"

With an awkward, muscle-wrenching effort, Sano pulled himself
onto the roof. He stood on its rough, slanted thatch surface, massag-
ing his right arm and hand back to life. The roof spread some two
hundred paces long and half as wide, with humps over its gables.
Above Sano loomed the top level of the house, its balcony, and the
high, forested slope. Below him lay the roof of the bottom level, the
valley, and the hills that fell away toward the dim, few lights of Edo.
The moon rode low on its arc through the stars, but still shone bright.
It wasn't the best battlefield in the world, but at least here he could
see the Ghost coming.

"You wanted me badly enough to break into my house," Sano
called down through the trapdoor to Kobori. "If you still want me,
you'll have to come up here."

"If you want me, you'll have to come back inside," Kobori retorted.

A stalemate slowed time to a virtual halt. Sano flexed his arm and
hand. They tingled as the numbness faded. He realized a fundamental
truth about why the Ghost killed on the sly. It wasn't just because he
was good at *dim-mak*.

"What's the matter, are you afraid to face me?" Sano called.

No samurai could stand to have his courage called into question. Kobori said, "I fear nothing, and certainly not you. It's you who are afraid of me." His voice issued through the trapdoor like poisonous smoke. "You hide behind your castle walls and your troops. Without them, you cower like a woman terrified of a mouse."

"You hide in the darkness because you're terrified to show yourself," Sano said. "You sneak up on your victims so they can't fight back and hurt you. You're a coward!"

There was silence; yet Sano could almost feel the thatch under his feet grow hot, as if burning from the fire of Kobori's anger. No samurai could tolerate such an insult. Kobori must come out and defend his courage and honor. But Sano knew better than to think the Ghost would pop up through the trapdoor for him to nab. He scanned the roof around him, eyeing the gables, expecting a sneak attack. He glanced at the roof below him. His instinct for survival told him to run while he had another chance. But his own courage and honor were at stake.

As he turned to look upward, a shadow detached from the balcony overhead and lunged down at him. He didn't have time to dodge. Kobori landed on him. Sano's knees crumpled under the impact. He and Kobori fell together with a crash. Kobori wasn't a large man, but he felt heavy and hard as steel, all bone and sinew. He locked onto Sano in a crushing grip. They rolled down the roof. Sano saw Kobori's face, teeth bared in a savage grin, eyes glinting, close to his as they rolled. He tried to dig his heels into the thatch and prevent himself from falling off the sloped surface, but he couldn't halt his momentum. He and Kobori tumbled from the roof.

They plummeted through empty space. A roof over a balcony interrupted their fall. They bounced off it with a force that jarred Sano's spine, then fell again, toward the roof of the mansion's lowest level.

Grasping her knife in both hands, Yugao inhaled a huge whoop of breath. She swung the knife sideways above Reiko. Her features contorted into a fierce scowl. Terror entwined with despair inside Reiko. She cringed and flung up her arms to protect herself.

There came a loud, heavy thud on the roof over their heads. The room shook. Reiko and Yugao both jumped. Dust and bits of plaster showered down on them. Yugao hesitated, the knife still upraised in her hands, her scowl frozen on her face. More thuds, accompanied by scuffling noises, jarred the house. Yugao turned her gaze away from Reiko, up toward the ceiling, distracted by what must be a fight taking place on the roof.

Reiko thrust her hands against Yugao's thighs and shoved.

Yugao went stumbling backward. Surprise changed her expression. She tripped on her hem, lost her balance, and fell on her side. "You sneaky little whore!"

Reiko leapt from her corner as she whipped the knife from behind her. Yugao scrambled to her feet. Howling in rage, she lunged for Reiko. Reiko gave up hope of capturing Yugao. It would be enough if she got herself out of the house alive. She ran for the door, but Yugao sprang into her path and slashed furiously at her. Reiko dodged, jumping sideways, ducking her head, as the knife carved wild swathes through the air and cut her robes. The fabric swished in tatters as she wielded her own knife, parrying Yugao's slashes. Yugao moved so fast that there seemed to be a hundred blades whizzing around Reiko.

"You could have stopped him!" Yugao screamed. She struck with such ferocious power that every collision of their blades almost knocked Reiko's out of her hand. "But you pretended not to see. You let him do it. You treated me as if it was my fault!"

She sliced through Reiko's sleeve. Reiko felt pain sear her upper arm. She faltered. Yugao was a tornado of waving arms, flying hair, and foul curses. Her knife whistled past Reiko's ear. Reiko felt warm, wet blood trickle down her neck.

"He was mine!" Yugao shrieked. "You took him away from me!"

Insane with fury, she chased Reiko around the room. In her mind Reiko saw the bloody footprints in the hovel. Yugao was reliving the night of the murders. She thought Reiko was her mother and sister.

"You let me kill him. Now you're going to die!"

33

On the lower roof of the house, Sano thrashed and heaved, trying to throw Kobori off him. Kobori hung on. His hands struck, his fingers jabbed, his knees and elbows gouged Sano in sensitive places where nerves intersected. His energy shot like fireworks exploding along Sano's muscles. Sano yelled in agony as they jerked and seized. He managed to raise his knee between himself and Kobori. He pushed with all his strength.

Dislodged, Kobori flew backward. He fell, somersaulted toes over head, then sprang upright. Sano staggered to his feet. Every part of him ached. He swayed like a scarecrow in the wind, while Kobori stood poised to attack again.

"So you think you can take me? What are you waiting for?" Kobori taunted him.

Every breath tore the membranes of Sano's lungs. Unarmed combat had never been his forte, and six months of sitting at a desk hadn't helped. He recalled how rusty he'd been when he sparred with Koemon, and his friend hadn't been trying to kill him. Fighting panic, Sano sought to distract Kobori and prevent him from concentrating his body's and mind's energy into a death-touch.

"I'm waiting for you to realize that your crusade is pointless," Sano said. Maybe he could also demoralize and weaken Kobori. "The war is over."

"It's not over as long as I'm alive," Kobori said. "You'll be my biggest conquest."

They advanced on each other, Sano's gait hobbled by pain, Kobori's surefooted and deliberate. Sano raised his hands, preparing to strike or defend as best he could. Kobori curved his back. He moved with his elbows bent, one arm raised, the other hanging loose. His eyes took on a strange sheen. Energy radiated from him like a vibrant, frenetic hum just beyond the range of hearing. Sano could see his face and hands in sharp detail, as if they gave off their own light, in contrast to his black clothes. Only a few paces separated Sano and Kobori, when Kobori leaped into the air. His legs flew at Sano. One foot tapped Sano's chin just under his bottom lip.

Sano felt his teeth slam together, his head snap back. He reeled and fell to his knees. His vision swam as if the light but powerful blow had loosened his eyes. Kobori was standing in the same spot as before he'd struck. He'd attacked and retreated so fast that it seemed he hadn't moved at all and he'd projected his image, and his force, at Sano. His energy hummed; his grin flashed narrow and bright.

"Your turn," he said. "Or are you giving up?"

No matter how hopeless his situation was, Sano refused to yield. He struck out at Kobori. But Kobori slid away from the blow. Sano tried again, and again. Kobori seemed to know what Sano was going to do before Sano did. He was never where he'd been when Sano struck at him. He disappeared, then reappeared elsewhere, as though flashing in and out of existence. Frantic, Sano threw his fist at Kobori's ribs. Kobori blocked the blow. His knuckles slammed Sano's wrist.

The breath whooshed out of Sano. His chest caved in. He slumped over, gasping like a fish on dry land, amazed that the blow should affect his body so far from the point of impact. Kobori must have channeled his energy along his nerves from his wrist to his lungs. As he fought for air, Kobori raked his fingers across the skin beside Sano's right eye. Sano felt momentarily dazed, as if he'd just woken up in a strange place with no idea where he was or how he'd gotten there.

Kobori had struck nerves that impaired his mind.

Terror bit deep and hard into Sano. Every attack he launched came back at him. The only time he made contact with Kobori was when Kobori parried one of his blows and simultaneously dealt him another. Sano staggered while Kobori kicked his legs, jabbed his back and shoulders. With each strike Kobori uttered an explosive breath, like the *whup* of burning tinder dashed with kerosene. Nausea and vertigo accompanied the pain that flared throughout Sano's body. He took a swipe at Kobori and knocked himself off balance. As he careened down the roof, Kobori snatched his wrist. He whipped Sano around, and hit him below his navel.

Sano's heartbeat accelerated to a fast, frenetic drumming. Pressure swelled inside his head, as though it would burst. He shouted above the roar of blood in his ears.

Yugao slashed her blade at Reiko. Reiko whirled, darted, and lashed back, but although she'd won many other battles, she'd never fought anyone like Yugao. Compared to her past opponents, Yugao was an amateur, no match for Reiko's training or experience. But what she lacked in combat skill, she compensated for with recklessness and determination. Reiko cut Yugao's arms and face, but Yugao seemed impervious to pain, unaware of her blood spattering the floor as they fought.

Thumps and crashes against the roof punctuated their cries. Reiko was drenched with sweat, panting from exhaustion while she ducked and slashed, pivoted and swung. As Yugao attacked her with undiminished, maniacal strength, Reiko stepped on a loop of cloth that hung from her torn sleeve. It caught her foot. She tripped and sprawled on her back. Yugao came flying at her, the knife raised in her hands. Her face shone with ferocious, unholy triumph. She threw herself toward Reiko. As the knife slashed a downward arc aimed at her face, Reiko grasped her own weapon tight in her fists and lunged up to meet Yugao.

Yugao ran straight into Reiko's blade. Reiko felt it slice through flesh. Yugao uttered a terrible, piercing, agonized scream. Her eyes popped wide; her hands released her knife and waved frantically. Then she fell on Reiko.

Her weight knocked Reiko flat. The blade sank up to its hilt inside Yugao. Reiko exclaimed as she felt her hands pressed against Yugao's body, the awful sensation of internal organs cut, and the wet warmth of blood.

Yugao flung out her arms, which broke her fall. For a moment her face was close to Reiko's. Yugao stared at Reiko, her expression marked by shock, pain, and fury. She pushed herself off Reiko and sat, legs outstretched. Reiko clambered to her feet, her heart thudding, ready to run or fight again if need be. She snatched up the knife that Yugao had dropped.

At first Yugao didn't move. She gazed open-mouthed at the knife embedded in her abdomen and the blood on her robe. She grabbed the hilt. Her hands trembled, and her breath rasped quick and shallow. With a hoarse groan, she pulled out the knife. A fresh gout of blood spilled. Yugao raised her head and met Reiko's gaze. Her complexion had gone dead white, and blood drooled from her lips, but she glared with unforgotten rage. Clutching the knife, she dragged herself along the floor toward Reiko. Gasping and weak from pain, she collapsed. She feebly hurled the knife at Reiko. It landed far short of her. Yugao lay curled around her wound.

"Kobori-*san*!" she cried. Sobs wracked her body.

More thuds quaked the roof. Reiko shook her head, too over-whelmed to know exactly what she felt or thought. Under her relief churned a lava of emotions. Footsteps racketed along the passage to-ward her. Detectives Marume and Fukida burst into the room, ac-companied by Lieutenant Asukai and her other guards. Hirata trailed in after them.

Marume exclaimed, "Lady Reiko!" He and the other men gaped in surprise at Yugao, who lay weeping on the floor, calling for her lover. They stared at Reiko, who realized she was dressed in rags and covered with blood from Yugao, Tama, and her own countless minor but painful cuts.

"Are you all right?" Fukida said anxiously.

"Yes," Reiko said.

"Where's Chamberlain Sano?" Hirata demanded.

"He's on the roof, fighting Kobori." The words slipped unbidden from Reiko. As soon as she spoke them, she knew they were true. Every instinct told her that the noise she heard was her husband and the Ghost embroiled in combat, and that Sano was in mortal danger. She cried, "We have to help him!"

The men rushed from the room. She followed their stampede down the corridor.

Dizzy from pain, Sano flung wild, desperate punches at Kobori. Kobori smote his ribcage. A fit of shaking seized him. He fell, his body twitching uncontrollably as Kobori stood over him.

"I've heard that you're a great fighter. I'm disappointed in you," Kobori said.

Terror compressed Sano's vision and shrank the world. All Sano could see was Kobori, his face radiant, eyes afire with dark light. Sano's physical strength was all but gone. Struggling to collect his wits, he dimly remembered what the priest Ozuno had said to Hirata: *Everyone has a sensitive spot. I was never able to find Kobori's, but it's your only real hope of defeating him in a duel.*

"I've heard about you, too," Sano said, barely able to think, speaking on instinct. He swallowed blood and mucus; he pushed himself upright. "From a priest named Ozuno. I understand he was your teacher."

A beat passed. "What did he say?" Kobori's tone was indifferent, but Sano could tell he was only pretending he didn't care what Ozuno thought of him.

"He said he disowned you," Sano said.

"Never!" Kobori spoke with such haste and fervor that Sano knew Ozuno's rejection of him still hurt. "We had a difference in philosophy. We went our separate ways."

Sano praised the cosmos for blessing him: He'd found Kobori's sensitive spot. It was Ozuno himself. "You joined Yanagisawa's elite squadron," Sano said. "You used your skills to commit political assassinations."

"That's better than what Ozuno and his brotherhood of old geezers did," Kobori said. "They were content to preserve the knowledge for posterity. What a waste!"

Sano was glad to feel Kobori's energy diverted from himself. His strength revived, and although he was still dizzy, he managed to regain his feet. "I understand. You wanted more than you could get from the brotherhood."

"Why not? I didn't want to be a provincial samurai and spend my life guarding the local *daimyo's* lands, keeping bandits away and the peasants in line. Nor did I want to dedicate myself to Ozuno's obsolete traditions. I deserved more."

"So you sold yourself to Yanagisawa."

"Yes!" Kobori hastened to justify himself: "Yanagisawa gave me a chance to be somebody. To move in bigger, higher circles. To have a purpose in life."

Sano comprehended that Kobori's motives went beyond the usual Bushido code of obeying a superior. They were personal, and so must be his reasons for his crusade against Lord Matsudaira. "Well, now that Yanagisawa is gone, so is your purpose. Without him, you're nothing again."

"He's not gone forever. I'm creating such a panic in Lord Matsudaira's regime that it will soon fall. My master will return to power."

And then, Kobori believed, he would regain his own status. Sano saw that Kobori was only waging war for Yanagisawa because their interests coincided. Kobori's personal pride, not the honor that bound a samurai to his master, was at issue. As a fighter he was invincible, but his pride was his weakness. It had suffered a huge blow when Ozuno disowned him, and another when Yanagisawa had fallen and taken him down, too. Now it needed one more, decisive blow.

"Do you want to know what else Ozuno said about you?" Sano said.

"What do I care?" Kobori said, annoyed as well as clearly eager to know. "Save your breath and maybe you'll live a little longer."

Sano thought that the longer he kept Kobori talking, the better his chances of survival. "Ozuno said you never completely mastered the art of *dim-mak* because you didn't finish your training."

Indignation tinged Kobori's expression. "I quit when I'd learned everything I could from him. I surpassed him. Did he mention that he tried to kill me and I beat him up?"

"He said you'll never fulfill your potential," Sano said, putting more words in Ozuno's mouth. "You could have been the greatest martial artist in history. But you've wasted your training and your talent and your life. You're nothing but one of a thousand *rōnin* outlaws."

"I am the greatest martial artist! I've proved it tonight. Tomorrow he'll know he was wrong about me. He'll smell the smoke from the funeral pyres of all the men I've killed here." Goaded into a rage, Kobori shouted, "And he'll breathe your ashes along with theirs!"

He lunged at Sano, multiplying himself into an army that struck Sano repeatedly from all directions. But even as Sano jerked, spun, and cried out in pain, he perceived that Kobori had lost self-control. The insults to his pride, and his fear that his crusade would indeed fail, had gotten the better of him. He struck without caring whether he hit lethal points, venting his anger at Ozuno on Sano. His breaths now sounded more like sobs than like flames igniting. Sano sensed that Kobori wanted to torture him more than kill him. He forced himself to endure and suffer, biding his time.

Kobori slowed his movements, confident now of his victory over Sano, if not his future. Sano deliberately fell onto a gable that jutted from the roof. Kobori reached down to grab him. Sano's eyes were so awash in blood and sweat that he could barely see. Guided by blind instinct, he shot out his hand and locked it around Kobori's wrist. His fingers found two indentations on the bone. He squeezed with all his might.

Kobori exhaled in surprise. For just an instant, his muscles went slack as Sano's grip drained the energy from him. Sano yanked Kobori down. He stiffened his other hand and jabbed the fingers under Kobori's chin. Kobori uttered a cry of pained alarm. He reared back from Sano. His free arm swung up to strike a death-blow at Sano's face. At the same time Sano thrust himself forward in a last, desperate effort. His forehead slammed Kobori high on the right breast.

The shock of the collision reverberated through Sano's skull.

White lights exploded across his vision as if the stars in heaven were splintering.

Before Sano knew whether Kobori's blow landed on him, the universe went black and silent.

Reiko, Hirata, the guards, and detectives tore through the dark, labyrinthine house. "There must be stairs to the roof," Fukida said. Ahead of him, Lieutenant Asukai called, "Here!"

They rampaged up the staircase. Marume pushed open a trapdoor. The men clambered through it onto the roof. Lieutenant Asukai pulled Reiko up. Wind buffeted her. The thatched roof was a wide, slanted gray landscape in the moonlight. She heard no sound, no movement on it: The fighting had stopped. Then she saw two human forms lying side by side on the slope of a gable, as though tossed by the wind, their bodies broken.

"Over there!" she cried, pointing. Dread tightened around her heart.

One of the figures moved, then rose unsteadily to his feet. He stood over the other, prone figure. Reiko's dread turned to sickening horror. Two men had fought. One had conquered and survived. She thought she knew which.

"No!" Reiko screamed.

Her voice echoed across the hills. The victor slowly turned to her.

As the moonlight revealed him, Reiko braced herself to see the face of Kobori, the assassin who'd slain her husband. But instead the light illuminated Sano's face. It was so battered, bloody, and swollen that Reiko barely recognized him. But it was Sano, alive and victorious. Such relief overwhelmed Reiko that she almost fainted. She moaned and would have run to Sano, but he held up his hand.

"Don't come any closer," he said. "Kobori's alive."

The prone figure stirred. Marume and Fukida rushed across the roof. They seized Kobori and bound his wrists and ankles with his sash. Reiko hurried to Sano. He held her in his arms as she wept with joy.

"I thought you were dead!" she cried. "I thought the Ghost killed you!"

Sano gave a chuckle that turned into a coughing fit. "You should have a little more faith in me."

They looked down at Kobori, trussed like game from a hunt. His face was unmarked but deathly pale, bathed with sweat. His breath wheezed through gritted teeth. The consciousness in his dark eyes was fading like the glow of embers quenched by water. But he looked up at Sano; malicious humor animated his features.

"You think you've won," he whispered. "But I defeated you before our fight began. Do you remember the night I came to your house?" His chest heaved in a soundless laugh. "While you were sleeping, I touched you." As Sano and Reiko gazed at him, too shocked and horrified to speak, he closed his eyes. His last breath sighed from him.

34

The sun floated up through the gray dawn sky like a drop of blood swimming in an ocean of quicksilver. Temple bells rang, echoing across the hills, awakening Edo. Over the Nihonbashi Bridge streamed townspeople bound for work and travelers laden with bundles and armed with walking sticks. Along the banks of the canal, fishermen off-loaded their catch from boats. Gulls screeched and flocked. Through the crowds entering the fish market wandered a news-seller.

"The Ghost and his lady have been defeated!" he cried. "Read the whole thrilling story here!"

Customers eagerly snatched the broadsheets from him; coins exchanged hands. Near the foot of the bridge, a curious mob gathered at the place where executed criminals were displayed as a warning to the citizens. Today there were two severed heads mounted on a gibbet. One belonged to a woman; her long black hair blew in the cool, moist breeze. The other had the shaved crown and topknot of a samurai. Their faces were withered, pecked by birds, and rotting after four days of exposure to the elements. Their mouths and empty eye sockets gaped. Flies buzzed around them; maggots teemed in foul red holes. Bare bone showed on noses, cheeks, and brows. Dried gore blotched the ground under them. Only the tags affixed to the gibbet identified the criminals.

The woman's read, YUGAO, MURDERESS; WOUNDED WHILE RESIST-
ING ARREST; SURVIVED LONG ENOUGH TO BE EXECUTED. The man's
read, KOBORI, ASSASSIN; KILLED IN A FIERCE BATTLE.

Little boys swarmed around the heads, laughing and making fun of
them. One hurled a stone that bounced off the man's. They scam-
pered away.

At Edo Castle, officials walked, trotted on horseback, or rode in
palanquins out the main gate. They fanned into the Hibiya administrative district, going about their business, secure in the knowledge that
the Ghost no longer stalked the city and they were in no more danger
than usual. The wind that swept the streets carried ashes from funeral
pyres, a reminder of the men who'd perished in the battle against Kobori. Black drapery on the castle gate honored their valor.

Inside the chamberlain's compound, Masahiro stood in the garden.
The boy wore a white jacket and trousers; his bare toes peeked
through the grass. A little wooden sword hung in a scabbard tied to his
sash. His face was solemn with concentration. Suddenly he contorted
his features in a fierce scowl. He drew the sword, emitted a loud roar,
then lunged and slashed at an invisible foe.

"That was very good," Sano said as Masahiro looked eagerly to him
for approval. "Now try this."

Clad in his own white garments, he drew his own wooden practice
sword and demonstrated a series of moves. Masahiro imitated them
with more exuberance than grace, but Sano took pride in his son's
first baby steps toward mastering the martial arts. He took pleasure
from the vivid purple irises blooming around the pond, the sweet fragrance of jasmine, the coolness of the morning, and the sound of
Reiko's voice speaking to the servants nearby in the house.

He relished the fact that he was alive.

Four days had passed since he'd defeated Kobori, and six since Kobori had stolen into his bedchamber. Every night when Sano had gone
to sleep, he'd feared he wouldn't see another dawn. Every waking
moment he'd waited for an internal explosion of energy that would
stop his heart, extinguish his consciousness. He'd watched Reiko

watch him anxiously, expecting him to drop dead. Yet he had not, even though he'd suffered grievous injuries at the Ghost's hands.

By the time he'd gotten home after the battle, he'd been in such pain he'd fainted at the gate. By the next morning he was covered with bruises and so stiff and sore he couldn't move. His urine came out crimson with blood. Reiko fed him broth out of a spoon because chewing hurt. So did breathing. A physician treated him with medicinal potions and massages; a priest chanted prayers over him. Urgent summonses from Lord Matsudaira and the shogun went unanswered. Sano had abandoned the government to run itself while he lay on what he thought was his deathbed . . .

. . . until he'd begun to recover. Yesterday he'd felt well enough to get out of bed and eat solid food. Today he could move without extreme pain. The bruises were fading. There had been no single, revelatory moment when Sano knew that the Ghost hadn't given him the touch of death; rather, a gradual belief had sunken in that Kobori's last words had been a mere false threat meant to terrify him, a vain attempt at revenge. Now he celebrated each moment as a rare, fragile gift. As he gave Masahiro his first lesson in swordsmanship, he silently thanked the gods that the bond between father and son was unbroken. He rejoiced that he would live to guide his little boy along the path to manhood, to protect him, to see him grow into an honorable samurai, make a name for himself, and father his own children.

But this moment of perfect peace and happiness couldn't last. Sano had duties of grave importance.

"That's all for today, Masahiro," he said.

They sheathed their swords. "We swordfight again tomorrow?" Masahiro said.

"Yes," Sano promised, "tomorrow."

A crowd gathered outside a small shrine wedged in a road of basketry shops in Ginza. Out the *torii* gate marched Detectives Arai and Inoue, hauling two samurai rebel outlaws who'd been hiding in the shrine. Hirata followed on horseback with more detectives who carried out guns, ammunition, and firebombs that the rebels had stockpiled for attacks on Lord Matsudaira's regime. As he passed the gawking spectators, Hirata reflected on what a dramatic difference a few days could make.

Business was back to normal now that Kobori had been slain. Sano's position was secure, and so was Hirata's own. Yet not much else had changed for Hirata. He was still a prisoner of his ailing body. He still sat on the sidelines while other men acted, as he had during the battle against Kobori. His memory of that night was clouded with the shame of his helplessness. His life seemed destined to continue this way, for he hadn't seen Ozuno again, even though he'd spent every spare moment looking for the priest. Ozuno was an opportunity that fate had tantalized him with, then taken away.

But Hirata closed the door on self-pity and regret. He had his position, his family, and his good name. He still had his dreams in which he could fight and always triumph, as well as his memories of battles won. Hirata counted himself as lucky.

As he rode off with his men and their captives, he saw a familiar figure limping toward him. It was Ozuno.

Hirata felt his face brighten with joyful amazement. He scrambled off his horse and rushed to meet the priest. "Hello!" he called.

"What? Oh, it's you," Ozuno said.

The chagrin on his face struck Hirata as comical. Hirata laughed, so glad to see Ozuno that he didn't mind that Ozuno wasn't glad to see him. "I've been looking all over for you. I thought you'd left town. Isn't it astonishing that we should happen to run into each other?"

"Sometimes we find what we want when we're not looking for it." Ozuno added snidely, "And sometimes we stumble upon what we don't want no matter how hard we've tried to avoid it."

Hirata was too happy to care that Ozuno had been hiding from him. "Some of us are just luckier than others."

Ozuno nodded grudgingly. "I hear that Chamberlain Sano has captured my renegade pupil. I owe him a great debt for taking Kobori out of the world."

"He owes you a great debt for your advice," Hirata said. "It helped him defeat Kobori."

"I'm glad to have been of service." Ozuno's chronic bad temper relented, although not by much.

"Do you remember what you said last time we met?" Hirata asked. "That if we met again, you would be my teacher?"

Ozuno grimaced. "Yes, I did say that. After living eighty years, I should know enough to keep my mouth shut."

"Well, here we are," Hirata said, opening his arms wide as if to embrace the priest, their surroundings, and this blessed day. "This is the sign that we're destined for you to teach me the mystic martial arts."

"And who am I to ignore a sign from fate?" Ozuno rolled his eyes heavenward. "The gods must be playing a joke on me."

Now that Hirata's dreams were within reach, hope invigorated him. He glimpsed a vast reservoir of power that would soon be his to tap. "When do we begin my lessons?"

"We can't know how much time we have left on this earth," Ozuno said. "All we have for certain is this moment. We should begin your lessons at once."

Now that Hirata had his heart's desire, he felt less haste to claim it. "In a few days would be better for me. I have work to finish. When I'm done, you can move into my estate at Edo Castle, and—"

Ozuno slashed his hand through Hirata's words. "You are now my pupil. I am your master. I decide when I'll train you and where. Now come along, before I change my mind." His stare skewered Hirata. "Or have you changed yours?"

Hirata experienced an internal shift, as though cosmic forces were realigning his life. His allegiances to Sano and the shogun still ruled him, but he'd put himself under Ozuno's command. Until this instant he hadn't thought of what conflicts of interest or what physical and spiritual challenges might come with becoming one of the secret, chosen society. Yet he could not refuse his fate any more than Ozuno could.

Hirata called to the detectives who'd paused to wait for him: "Go ahead without me." He turned to Ozuno, who regarded him with scant approval as though he'd passed the first test, but just barely. "I'm ready. Let's go."

Inside Edo Castle, a procession of samurai marched slowly down an avenue lined with cedar trees. All wore elaborate, ceremonial armor. Each carried a large box wrapped in white paper on his upturned hands. The shogun led the procession. Lord Matsudaira walked on his right, Sano on his left. Ahead of them filed ten Shinto priests clad in white robes and black hats. Some bore lit torches; others held drums and bells. They entered a large space newly cleared in the castle's forest preserve and spread with white gravel. Clouds drifted in the overcast sky; the morning was as dim and cool as twilight. Faint earth tremors shook the ground. The procession moved down a flagstone path toward the new shrine that the shogun had ordered to be built.

During his convalescence Sano had heard axes ringing day and night as many woodcutters removed the trees. Now he beheld the shrine that honored the memory of the men who'd died in the battle against Kobori. It was a wooden building whose curved roof overhung the steps that led up to it from a raised stone platform. A grille covered the entrance to the chamber that the spirits of the dead could inhabit when summoned. Beside the shrine were stone lanterns; in front of it, a low table that held a tray of incense cones adjacent to a metal vat. The building wasn't large, but its ornate carved brackets and trim indicated that no expense or labor had been spared. Many craftsmen must have worked nonstop to finish the shrine by today, which the court astrologers had deemed an auspicious time for this memorial ceremony.

The priests lit the stone lanterns, then the incense in the vat. Fragrant smoke rose into the air. They chanted prayers, beat the drums in slow, sonorous rhythm, and rang the bells while the shogun approached the shrine. He halted at the table, where he laid his box that contained forty-nine cakes made of wheaten flour filled with sweetened red bean paste—offerings to the dead, symbolic of the number of bones in the body of one slain soldier. He bowed his head over his clasped hands a moment, then dropped an incense cone into the vat. Lord Matsudaira stepped forward and repeated the ritual. Then Sano took his turn. As he paid his wordless respects to his fallen army, emotions flooded him.

Shame tinged his gratitude that he was alive. It didn't seem fair that one man should have survived while so many perished, that he was here in the flesh and his troops only in spirit. Sorrow pained him because their destruction had preceded his victory. He joined the shogun and Lord Matsudaira beside the shrine and watched the other men in the procession perform the ceremony. There were seventy-four, each representing a soldier that the Ghost had killed. They included the Council of Elders, other important officials, and male kin of the deceased. But the thirty men seriously wounded and crippled—including Captain Nakai, still paralyzed despite treatment from the best physicians—weren't represented. Blame settled upon Sano, more distressing than the agony from the beating he'd taken from Kobori.

The ceremony drew to a slow, solemn end. The music ceased; the priests departed. Members of the procession lingered around the shrine, clustering in small groups, conversing in low voices. General Isogai approached Sano and said, "Congratulations on your victory."

"Many thanks," Sano said.

"I must apologize for the disgraceful behavior of my troops." Mortification subdued General Isogai's jovial manner. "As soon as I round up the deserters, they'll be forced to commit *seppuku*."

"Perhaps that's too severe a punishment, especially under the unusual circumstances," Sano said. "They were good, brave soldiers. The Ghost drove them out of their minds." He'd forgiven Marume and Fukida for leaving him. He'd also forbidden them to commit ritual suicide even though they'd pleaded to atone for their disgrace. "I don't want more lives lost on his account. And we need those men."

General Isogai looked unconvinced, stubborn. "I have to uphold discipline. *Seppuku* is the standard punishment for desertion. Making exceptions will weaken the moral character of the army. Can't have that. But if you order me to spare the deserters . . . ?"

Sano entertained the idea for a mere moment before he reluctantly said, "No." Although he had the power to command whatever he wished, he was as bound by the samurai code of honor as General Isogai. Bending the code would not only violate his principles but leave him open to attack. "Do as we must." Yet the impending deaths of the deserters sat as badly in his mind as the deaths of the troops slain by Kobori.

As General Isogai moved away, Yoritomo hurried up to Sano. "Please allow me to express how thrilled I am that you defeated the Ghost." Yoritomo's eyes shone with admiration.

The shogun joined them. "Ahh, Sano-*san*. You've saved us all from the Ghost. I feel much better now." He sighed and fanned himself. Then his eyes widened in horror as he took a closer look at Sano. "My, but you look awful. Those bruises all over your face! The sight of them makes me ill. I order you to, ahh, wear makeup to cover them."

Sano had thought that nothing the shogun said could surprise him anymore. "Yes, Your Excellency."

"Come along, Yoritomo." The shogun bustled away as if he thought Sano's injuries were contagious. Yoritomo gave Sano a look of apology.

Lord Matsudaira strode up to Sano. "Honorable Chamberlain. It's good to see you on your feet."

"It's good to see you." *Still on yours,* Sano added silently. During the four days Sano had been absent from court, Lord Matsudaira appeared to have consolidated his position.

Lord Matsudaira raised his eyebrows and nodded in satisfaction as he read Sano's thoughts. He looked calmer, more secure, now that his new regime was no longer threatened by an assassin. "Certain problems are much less trouble than they were a few days ago." He glanced at Elders Kato and Ihara, who stood with a few of their cronies. They eyed him with resentment. "If certain people wish to attack me, they'll have to do it themselves instead of relying on Kobori. Besides,

I've won a few new allies, while they've lost a lot of ground, because you eliminated him. Good work, Sano-*san*."

Sano bowed, acknowledging the praise yet finding it distasteful. Seventy-four men were dead, and he'd almost sacrificed his own life, but all Lord Matsudaira cared about was that the destruction of the Ghost had shored up his regime.

"But don't get too complacent," Lord Matsudaira warned him. "There are still many opportunities for you to take a wrong step. And there are just as many men who are eager to take your place if you do."

Before he slipped away, his gaze directed Sano's attention across the shrine precinct. Police Commissioner Hoshina loitered on the fringe of a crowd around the shogun. Ire enflamed his features as he started toward Sano. Before Hoshina reached him, Sano was surrounded by officials who greeted him, inquired about his health, and welcomed him back to court. Some of them were men Hoshina had enlisted in his bid for power. Sano could tell how eager they were to make up for shunning him when his position was in jeopardy, how worried that he would hold their disloyalty against them. Obviously, Hoshina's campaign against him had fizzled.

Hoshina elbowed his way through the crowd. He paused beside Sano long enough to murmur, "You win this time. But you haven't seen the end of me." Then he stalked away.

Sano felt the world settle into its familiar, precarious balance. Earth tremors vibrated his feet. He pictured cracks branching underground, toward his home, where he'd noticed that Reiko seemed troubled and distant. She hadn't confided in him, and he'd sensed she hadn't wanted to burden him with problems during his convalescence, but he knew she was upset about the way her investigation had turned out. Sano felt a sudden, pressing need to talk to her, before his whirlwind of business reclaimed him.

"Excuse me," he said to the officials.

He signaled Detectives Marume and Fukida, who cleared his path toward the gate.

．　．　．

Storm clouds massed above the pines that shaded a cemetery in the Zōjō Temple district. Rows of stone pillars marked graves
adorned with portraits of the deceased and offerings of flowers and
food. The cemetery was deserted except for a small party gathered
around a bare plot of land.

Reiko, Lieutenant Asukai, and her other guards watched a laborer
dig a new grave. His shovel upturned soil dark and damp from the
rainy season that had come early this year. The fresh scents of earth
and pine did nothing to soothe the grief that consumed Reiko.

Thunder rumbled in the distance. The gravedigger finished his
work. Reiko stooped and hefted a lidded black ceramic urn sitting beside the grave, which contained Tama's ashes. She gently lowered the
urn into the hole. She knelt, bowed her head, and murmured a prayer
for the girl's spirit. "May you be reborn into a better life than the one
you left."

Her escorts waited silent and somber. Reiko whispered into the
grave, "I'm sorry. Please forgive me."

She rose, and the gravedigger filled the hole, tamped down the dirt,
and left. Lieutenant Asukai positioned the stone grave-marker that
bore Tama's name. Reiko laid before it the rice cake, the sake decanter,
and the bouquet of flowers she'd brought. Rain pelted the cemetery.
Lieutenant Asukai opened an umbrella over Reiko's head and gave it to
her. Reiko lingered, reluctant to depart. She'd never expected to
mourn so keenly for someone she'd known such a short time. How
strange that the death of a virtual stranger could alter one's life.

She heard hoofbeats outside the cemetery. Looking up, she saw
Sano enter the gate, followed by Detectives Marume and Fukida. Sano
came to stand beside her at the grave while the detectives joined her
escorts under the pines. The rain gushed down, drenching the grave
and offerings. Reiko took meager comfort from Sano, pressed close
against her, in the scant dry haven under her umbrella.

"The servants told me I'd find you here." Sano regarded her with
concern. "What's going on?"

"I just buried Tama's ashes. There wasn't anyone else to do it."
Reiko explained, "I went to the house where she worked to ask if she
had any relatives. Her employers said she didn't. And they weren't interested in what happened to her body. So I held a funeral for her the
day after she died. No one came except my father." Reiko felt sad for
Tama, who'd been so alone in the world, and Magistrate Ueda, who
had his own regrets about how Yugao's murder case had turned out.
"And there was no one to give Tama a proper grave except me."

Sano nodded in approval. "That was good of you."

"It's nowhere near enough to do for her." Guilt plagued Reiko.
"You tried to warn me that power is dangerous. You said that things we
do with it might seem good at the time, but they can have bad consequences. Well, you were right. I abused my power and I did terrible
harm to an innocent girl."

"It was Tama herself who gave away the fact that she knew too
much for Yugao's good," Sano pointed out. "If she'd kept quiet, Yugao
would have let her go back to town, before I brought the army."

"Tama couldn't have been expected to know what or what not to
say," Reiko said. "She was just a simple peasant—whereas I should
have anticipated all the risks."

"You couldn't have known what would happen. The fire that got
Yugao out of jail was an unforeseeable circumstance."

Reiko was grateful to him because he didn't heap more recrimina-
tions on her for disregarding his advice, but she couldn't absolve herself. "You warned me that something I didn't expect could happen. I
didn't listen."

"Plenty of good came out of your investigation as well," Sano reminded her. "If you hadn't delayed Yugao's execution—and she
hadn't escaped from jail—I might still be searching for Kobori. He
might still be assassinating people."

"Maybe. But how can we know? All I'm certain of is that if I hadn't
kept Yugao alive, she couldn't have killed Tama."

"You did the best you could to save her. You risked your own life."

"I failed. I'm alive. Tama is dead." Now Reiko acknowledged the
problem that bothered her the most. "And I didn't take on the investi-

gation just because I wanted to discover the truth or serve justice. I was hankering for adventure. I found it. Tama paid the price."

Sano's expression grew troubled; Reiko saw that her words had touched a nerve in him. "You're not the only one who's ever had selfish personal motives. When Lord Matsudaira ordered me to catch the assassin, I was glad to get out of my boring duties. I wanted adventure as much as you did."

"But you had orders," Reiko said, able to justify his behavior although not her own. "You wanted to save lives and punish a murderer."

"True, but I also wanted to save my own position, which I would have lost if I'd failed. My own honor was at stake. And you're not the only one whose investigation went wrong." Pain etched Sano's bruised face. "I led an army on what turned out to be a suicide mission."

"That's a different situation," Reiko protested. "Those troops were samurai. Fighting that battle was their duty."

"They're just as dead as Tama is," Sano said. "And I'm alive."

They stood joined together by the sobering fact that they had survived while those who'd served them had not, that their lives were a burden as much as a blessing from the gods. The rain streamed down, obscuring the graves; water puddled the cemetery.

"What are we going to do now?" Reiko asked.

"We can make up for what happened."

Atonement seemed impossible, yet the idea of striving for it had a certain desolate appeal for Reiko. "I'll quit investigating crimes," she vowed. "I'll put myself under house arrest so I can't ever bring harm to anyone again." But her spirit died even as she spoke. That she should bury all her skill, experience, and ardor along with Tama's ashes! She told herself that it was a small price to pay.

"I don't have the luxury of withdrawing from the world," Sano said ruefully. "I've still got my duties to fulfill. I can't stop using my power. I can't stop making judgments even though they might prove to be faulty." He paused, deep in thought. "And I still want a chance at doing good, at using my power and position to serve honor." Determination and hope strengthened his voice. "That much hasn't changed."

That hadn't changed for Reiko, either. "But if we do act, how can we be sure that things won't go wrong again?"

"We can't. Power doesn't exempt us from bad luck and mistakes, obviously. All we can know is that our power makes the consequences of our actions most extreme."

Sano sounded tentative, as though he was working out the issues himself. "But too much caution is as bad as not enough, and inaction can be worse than action. If I hadn't gone after Kobori, he might have gone on killing, Lord Matsudaira's regime might have weakened, and Japan might have been torn apart by civil war. If you hadn't gotten involved with Yugao, I might never have caught him. Events are connected in mysterious ways. I can't help thinking that these were meant to happen the way they did, that we were meant to do as we did and not otherwise. I can't help believing that we survived for a purpose."

Reiko was skeptical, but she yearned to believe it, too. "What purpose?"

"I don't know. Maybe if we rise to the challenges that come our way in the future, they'll lead us to our destiny."

Reiko smiled with wistful amusement. "I always imagined that my destiny would be revealed to me by celestial apparitions or weird visions."

Sano chuckled. "I doubt that we get to choose how our destiny is revealed any more than we get to choose what it is. The gods might not think we're worth putting on such a spectacular drama."

Their shared humor warmed Reiko. She began to believe that her life had been spared for a purpose and she would have an opportunity to do better the next time. She hoped that when the challenges came, she and Sano would be ready to meet them.

He gazed around the wet, forlorn cemetery. "Somehow I don't think we'll find our destiny here. We should be getting back to Edo Castle."

She nodded. Together they left Tama's grave. The rain continued pouring down, and they were both drenched, their umbrella inadequate protection. Yet a faint luminescence shone in the distant sky even while the thunder boomed and the earth trembled.